ALS

Break the Rules

USA TODAY BESTSELLING AUTHOR
ROXIE NOIR

Cover: Najla Qamber Designs
Editor: Sennah Tate

CHAPTER ONE

JUNE

There's a crash behind me, and I jump, duck, and look over my shoulder without stopping.

The forest is pristine, still, and silent. There's no sign of whatever made that noise. Bears? Mountain lions? A bear and a mountain lion doing battle for the honor of being the first to get at a tasty human snack, i.e. me?

I turn back around straight into a mouthful of twigs.

"Augh!" I shout, hands flailing in front of myself.

"Almost there!" Silas calls over his shoulder, twenty feet ahead of me, utterly unfazed by the wildlife battle that's clearly threatening our very lives.

"What *was* that?" I shout, grabbing one sleeve of my t-shirt.

"Squirrel or something," he calls as I push my feet to a jog again, rubbing my t-shirt sleeve on my tongue in an attempt to wipe the tree taste off. "Could be a black bear, I see 'em in trees sometimes."

"Oh," I call, too out of breath and exhausted to say anything else, because now, in addition to watching every step I take on this narrow hillside trail, I need to watch the trees for bears.

I love nature. I love the outdoors. I love trees and rocks and dirt and… nature stuff. It's just so peaceful and calm and nice and definitely not full of murderous animals with large teeth and poison ivy, which is why I like it so very much.

"We're almost there!" Silas shouts. "C'mon, pick it up, Bug."

He stops in the middle of the trail, jogging in place, and glances over his shoulder at me as I slog up to him, careful not to trip over rocks or tree roots.

I'm sweaty. I'm sticky. Dirt is plastered to my lower legs from this trail run, and I'm fairly sure there's tree in my hair. I don't need to look in a mirror to know that I'm currently fire-engine red, my SPF 50,000 sunscreen dripping down my face and neck in long white streaks.

Okay, fine. I don't actually love nature yet, but I'm trying my hardest, and that's why I let my dumb older brother talk me into going on this trail run with him. Because I am not only the sort of person who enjoys going outside and being on trails, I enjoy running on them.

Really. I do. For real. This is great and I'm having a great time.

"Race you?" Silas says, grinning and jogging in place as I finally get closer.

He's not bright red or streaked with sunscreen. He's sweaty, sure—it's eighty degrees, even in the late afternoon, and at least 90% humidity—but he looks like a normal human right now. I guess he got the good workout genes.

"I'll kill you," I gasp under my breath, and Silas just laughs. Then he starts running again.

I can tell he's going slow for me, and I try to be grateful that he's not just sprinting off and leaving me in the middle of the forest, because even though I've declared myself a nature-loving person who loves nature, I'm not quite ready to get that up close and personal with it.

Up until recently, I've been a solid run-on-a-treadmill-and-watch-CSI kind of person.

"Watch out!" Silas calls back, still running ahead of me.

"Why?" I pant, my head swiveling side-to-side for the danger. "What's—AIEEEE!"

I leap backward mid-step, flailing my arms and going off-balance. My foot hits a root and half a second later my ass is on the ground and I've tumbled into the trailside foliage.

Across the trail, the tail of the enormous black snake slides into the dense greenery and disappears.

"June!" Silas shouts, already sprinting back to me. "You okay?"

He offers me his hand, and I take it, lifted instantly to my feet. I brush dirt off my butt and step into the middle of the trail, nervously inspecting the spot where I landed.

I just want to make sure there are no more snakes, because those sneaky bastards could be hiding just about anywhere, and I want no part of it.

"Sorry," he says. "I thought you saw it."

I shake my head, still gasping for air, one hand to my chest. My heart is thumping like a two-year-old banging on pots and pans, wild and arrhythmic.

"They're specifically designed to match the dirt, Silas," I manage to pant. "*No*, I didn't see it, they're practically invisible—"

"We've got another hundred yards before the parking lot," he says.

"—they look like sticks or logs and then it turns out they're *alive*—"

Silas pats my arm mock-comfortingly.

"C'mon," he says, then turns around and starts running again.

I follow him, because I've got no real choice.

"—they move wrong," I call. "Things shouldn't move that way. It's not right."

"Sorry," he calls back, clearly not sorry.

I continue cataloging what's wrong with snakes—poison teeth, swallow things whole, too smooth—but for once Silas wasn't lying to me, and after about thirty seconds we're back at the parking lot.

"—and they strangle their prey," I'm saying as we step out of the forest and into the small gravel parking area at the Raccoon Hollow trailhead, where I suppress the urge to hug my car. "That's fucked up, Silas. Any self-respecting animal would just bite their prey to death, but no. Snakes had to get weird about it."

Silas is resting both his hands on top of his head, taking long, deep breaths.

"Not most snakes," he says. "Most snakes just swallow their prey whole."

"Which is also horrible," I point out.

"Did you see that news article about a snake that swallowed—"

"No," I say, holding out both hands and waving them. "No no no, no, no. I do not want to hear about this, and you *know* that."

Silas gives me his best *what, innocent old me?* grin, which means that he knows he's getting to me and he's pleased with himself about it.

"I forgot how much you hated snakes," he says, semi-apologetically as we walk to our cars. "I didn't realize that seeing a few inches of one as it departed would bother you so much."

"I almost stepped on it," I say, leaning against my

bumper. "And plenty of people hate snakes. You know who else hates snakes? Indiana Jones, and he punched a whole bunch of Nazis, so I'm in perfectly good company here."

Silas opens his car, ignoring my snake rant, and pulls two big water bottles out, tossing me one. I catch it. It's still ice-cold.

We chug water, both leaning against our cars, facing each other in silence, a nice breeze sifting through the trees, the sun on its way down, this side of the mountain in shadow.

I take a deep breath, close my eyes for a moment, and feel the cool air against my sweaty, sweaty skin.

It's actually pretty nice. See? I love nature.

"I think it's gonna storm," Silas says, and I open my eyes again.

Just barely peeking over the leafy green ridge of the mountains behind us is a line of dark gray storm clouds, looking ominous.

"Looks like it," I agree.

It's late summer in the South, and that means thunderstorms. This week it's been pretty much every day; it'll be sunny until late afternoon, then storm like hell, then clear up right before nightfall. I kind of like it, to be honest, though I'm also glad that I'll be safely in my car before the downpour starts.

"You heading back to town?" he asks.

"Eventually," I say, pulling my phone out the running armband I had it in and turning it on. It's close to six p.m., and I have no service.

I sigh.

"Does the ranger station down there still have Wi-Fi you can access from the parking lot?" I ask, opening my phone and hoping that while we were running, we ran through a patch of reception long enough to get email.

We didn't.

"The ranger station has Wi-Fi?" Silas asks.

"Useless," I tease him.

"I saved you from a snake. You're *welcome*."

"You're the reason I nearly got killed by one in the first place," I counter, shutting my phone off and drinking more water.

"I don't think a king snake has ever killed a person before," he says, grinning his I'm-bugging-my-little-sister-and-I-know-it grin. "They're totally harmless."

"There's a first time for everything," I point out.

"You need Wi-Fi for a gig?" he asks, pulling his keys out of his pocket and tossing them in the air

"Yeah, I just want to make sure my editor doesn't need anything before she leaves for the day, and it's forty-five minutes back home," I say, and Silas just nods.

I don't mention that "my editor" is actually just Madison, a twenty-two-year-old who's in charge of the OMG section of hypefeed.com, and my gig is actually a list titled *Ten Celebrity Dogs So Cute You'll Hurl.*

It paid. It was something to do, and frankly, at this point in my unemployment I'll take just about any journalism-adjacent freelance work I can find, hurling or no.

"Cool," he says, and opens his car door again, tossing the now-empty water bottle onto his passenger seat. "Same time again tomorrow?"

I don't respond immediately.

"Call it aversion therapy," he says.

"I'm not averse to nature," I protest, still leaning against my car. "I'm just not used to it."

"We'll have you going on week-long backpacking trips in no time," he says. "You're gonna poop in the woods like a champ. Face down a black bear with nothing but a pocketknife and your wits."

"Well, now I'm averse to it," I say, and Silas just laughs.

Then he rubs his hand on my head, pulling my baseball cap askew.

"Dammit," I mutter.

"See you tomorrow, Bug," he says, and gets into his car. I pull my car key out of the tiny pocket I stashed it in and follow suit, dropping into my driver's seat like a ton of bricks.

"I should've gotten really into wine or something," I say out loud to myself, leaning my head back against the driver's seat. "Next reinvention, wine. And cheese. "

Five minutes later, I'm driving the wrong direction along the Appalachian Parkway, listening to an episode of This American Life about an artisanal maple syrup farm in New Hampshire that also takes in retired police dogs, because I'm going to the ranger station in the hopes that their parking lot still gets enough Wi-Fi signal from inside the building for me to check my email.

I don't think Madison, the twenty-two-year-old who runs the "OMG" section of hypefeed.com, needs me to check in with her. I'm pretty sure that if she wants changes made to *Ten Celebrity Dogs So Cute You'll Hurl*, she'll just make them.

But I need to check in. I can't help it. I like doing things correctly, so if something needs tweaking in my celebrity dogs article, I want to know.

I pull into the parking lot of the ranger station. The station is closed, because it's a little past six in the evening, but when I was visiting my family a couple years ago and they took me hiking way out here, the Wi-Fi worked all night long. That time I was also checking for emails from my editor, only *then* it actually mattered because I'd just turned in a piece about vandalism and police brutality in Raleigh.

That piece, I was proud of. It examined the internal biases of the policing system. It talked about how teens of color in Raleigh were five times more likely to be charged for the same acts of vandalism as white teens, and twice as likely to face brutality.

It spoke truth to power. It shined a light on an ugly truth. It did the things that journalism and newspapers are supposed to do.

Ten Celebrity Dogs So Cute You'll Hurl does none of these things. *TCDSCYH* does nothing but attract eyes to a webpage so that those eyes will also look at advertising and earn hypefeed.com some money.

Anyway, there's still free Wi-Fi in the parking lot.

It's not fast, but it's fast enough to check my email, and sure enough, there's one from Madison.

It says: *Cool, thanks.*

I guess she doesn't have any notes for me then, and I should probably leave this parking lot and make the drive back to my parents' house, where I'm living while unemployed, but instead I go through some emails, learning that several positions I've applied for have been filled.

Great. Nice. If I'm remembering correctly, I'm closing in on a hundred rejections. I don't even know how many I've just never gotten a response from. It's not the best feeling.

I check Twitter to distract myself from my problems. I check Instagram. Facebook. Reddit.

Suddenly, rain smacks against my windshield in big, fat drops, and I look up. I've somehow been looking at nonsense on my phone for almost twenty minutes, and the sky's so dark it looks like twilight.

Oops.

I twist the key, turn the radio back on, and pull out of the ranger station parking lot, heading back the way I came on the parkway, toward town, hoping that I can beat the storm and get home before it gets *really* bad.

Ten minutes later, it's clear that I miscalculated and am driving directly into the storm, something I probably should have checked first.

It's raining so hard that I feel like I'm under a waterfall, my wipers completely ineffective against the onslaught.

Every thirty seconds the sky strobes with lightning, the thunder instant and deafening, so loud and close it vibrates my car. The thick forest on either side of the road is waving and dancing in the wind, enormous trees bending and swaying so much they look like they might break.

"Shit," I whisper to myself, the steering wheel in a death grip, both palms sweating. Every muscle in my body is rigid, and I'm driving so slowly that it doesn't even register on my speedometer. I'd stop, but there's nowhere to pull over, and if I keep going maybe there will be soon.

I *have* to be almost back to the trailhead, right?

Lightning strikes again, so close I swear I can feel the crackle in the air, and I tense even harder, sitting bolt upright in the driver's seat. Thunder shakes the earth, the road, my car, or maybe that's me shaking.

"What Juan didn't expect," Ira Glass is saying, "was that the girl he'd spent all those months—"

I smack the radio button, and his voice shuts off because I can't deal with it right now. I take deep breath after deep breath, wishing that I'd stayed in the parking lot or just gone home after the run, because *Cool, thanks* is incredibly not worth getting struck by lightning over.

You won't get struck by lightning, I remind myself. *All these trees are way taller than you, and hardly anyone—*

There's another flash and the world goes pink-white, buzzing, pulsing, and for a split second I think I got hit, but as the thunder rattles through everything, chattering my teeth, I slam on the brakes and realize that I can do that, and at the exact same time I realize that it was the enormous tree twenty feet away, the crack so loud that it sounds like it's rending the heavens.

I watch, motionless, as it falls.

"No," I whisper out loud, powerless. "No, please, come on…"

The tree falls right across the road, ten feet in front of my car.

As it falls the slow-motion scene is illuminated by another crack of lightning, capturing the whole scene mid-action, so bright that I'm temporarily blind when I hear the cracking *thump* of the tree hitting the ground, something long and black draping itself over my windshield.

It's the snake, I think wildly, shaking, suddenly freezing. *It's the snake I nearly stepped on, it's found me and now it's going to*—

It's the power lines. The tree must have fallen into them, and now they're draped across my car, probably still live.

As if to confirm it, something sparks in the twilight in front of me, the pinprick of light barely visible through the driving rain. Lightning flashes. Thunder booms. I take a deep breath. I try to make my hands stop shaking. I turn the car off.

And then I stare out the windshield at the downed power lines and the fallen tree and try to remember what, exactly, you're supposed to do in this situation.

I almost got struck by lightning and then that tree nearly fell on me, oh my God if I'd been ten feet further down the road I'd be a pancake—

I take another deep breath, my knuckles white on the steering wheel, and make myself stop thinking about things that almost happened so I can focus on the situation at hand.

There's no service. I can't Google it. All I can do is try to remember the electrical safety talk we got in school when I was in third grade.

Another lightning crack, the sky pink-white, thunder that sounds like the world being torn apart. Everything vibrates. In the darkness after, the only thing I can see is the sparking power lines on the road ahead of me.

I let out a shaky breath and think: there's nothing I can do. More specifically, I don't think I'm *supposed* to do anything.

I don't think I'm supposed to get out of the car. I don't think I'm supposed to drive anywhere, and even if I can, the hell with driving right now.

I can't call 911, so I'm going to sit here, and I'm going to wait until someone else comes along, and then eventually I'm going to be rescued and I'm going to go home and shower and put on my pajamas and I'm going to make hot chocolate and *hell yes* I'm going to doctor it with rum.

So I sit. And I wait. I shut my eyes against the lightning and breathe through the thunder and after a little while, I stop shaking.

After a little while longer, the storm starts to move off. The lightning and thunder grow further apart, the flashes more and more infrequent, the trees on the road not swaying as violently. It could be minutes. It could be hours. I lose track completely.

And yet, no one comes down the road. Not a single solitary soul, and the wires are still right there on my car, sparking away, soaking wet exactly like powerlines shouldn't be.

I wonder if I could just drive away. I wonder if I should somehow leap from the car, since I'm wearing rubber-soled tennis shoes. I wonder if maybe I can put my car into neutral and just sort of roll back down this hill, but as I'm wondering that last thing, a truck pulls up behind me.

"Thank you," I whisper out loud to no one. I take a deep breath and look at it in my rear-view mirror, a green truck with something written across the front.

US FOREST SERVICE.

My heart beats a little bit faster, even as I remind myself that I'm literally in the middle of a national forest, that forest rangers are thick on the ground out here, that there's a billion of them and the chances of this being one particular ranger are very, very slim.

The truck door opens.

A bearded man gets out.

Not this, I silently beg the universe. *Not today. Please?*

I unbuckle and turn around in the driver's seat, leaning through the gap between the front two seats so I can see him better, but before I can be really, truly, 100% sure, he opens the rear door of the truck and leans in.

This lasts for several minutes, me leaning so far through my seats that I'm practically in the back seat of my car, the bearded forest ranger rummaging through his back seat, stomping around and doing *something* that I can't quite see.

Finally, he closes the door. He's now wearing thigh-high rubber boots over his work pants and shoulder-length thick rubber gloves over a white undershirt, his unruly hair knotted at the back of his head.

It's him.

It's definitely, one hundred percent, not-a-smidge-of-doubt-in-my-mind *him*.

The shirt is soaked through from the rain, clinging to every muscle and ripple on his tall, broad frame. My mouth goes dry and adrenaline shoots through my veins, because he looks *very* good right now and I look *very* not-good, oh, and also, I'm trapped inside a car during a rainstorm and it's not my favorite way to spend an afternoon.

Levi Loveless, Silas's best friend and my nearly lifelong crush, has come to rescue me.

I know I shouldn't complain about being rescued, but I'd much rather run into him while, I don't know, effortlessly doing an impressive yoga pose while reciting Ralph Waldo Emerson and being presented with a Pulitzer prize, my hair shiny and bouncy and my face not streaked with sunscreen and sweat.

Levi stops about six feet from my window. He stands there, assessing the situation. It's still raining. He's still getting wet. I'm still half goggling at the free wet t-shirt show I'm getting and half trying not to perv on this nice man who is, presumably, about to get me out of this car.

So I wave.

He waves back.

Cool, I think to myself. *What a super cool situation I'm in right now.*

Levi walks around the back of my car. I swivel my head as I watch him, because what else am I going to do?

"Can you hear me?" he calls from the other side of the car.

"Yes!" I call out, scrambling over the center console and into the passenger seat.

"Open the door."

I glance down at the door handle, nervous again. It's plastic, which *should* be fine, right?

I grit my teeth and pull it, pushing the door open as fast and hard as I can. Instantly I get a face full of rain, but I don't die of electrocution.

"Hi," I tell Levi, pointlessly wiping water out of my face.

"Hello," he says, still standing about five feet away,

looking incredibly unperturbed by all the weather happening around him.

Still in the wet t-shirt, which is still clinging to his shoulders and biceps and the dark line of chest hair and happy trail and okay, okay, that's enough.

"How are you?" I ask, because he makes me nervous and I need to say something.

"I'm well," he says, raising one eyebrow. "And yourself?"

I wipe water from my face again and look quickly around my car.

"I've been better," I tell him honestly.

Levi just nods.

"The wires are live and touching the metal frame of your car," he says, getting back to the point, nodding at the thick black lines draped across the hood of my car. "Which makes you getting out a little bit tricky."

"I jump, right?" I ask, because I'm pretty sure I remember that from third grade, and I'm eager to be part of the solution, not just part of the problem.

I can accept that everyone needs to be rescued sometimes, but I'm not terribly excited to play the part of the hapless princess.

"I think it's better if I lift you," he says, taking a step closer. "More control."

Oh, come on, I think, but I take a deep breath, suck up my pride, and nod.

"Okay," I say.

"Kneel on the seat and face me," he says. "I'll pick you up in a fireman's carry."

My stomach knots, but I nod.

"Be sure to maintain control of your limbs," he goes on, taking another step closer. "Don't touch the frame."

I get into position and Levi steps in, towering above me,

his boots squeaking quietly even through the din of the rain, and I'm eye-level with his belly button and doing my absolute best not to notice that his shirt is clinging to the happy trail extending downwards.

He bends until we're eye-to-eye, his serious, thoughtful face inches from mine, his deep, golden-brown eyes searching my face like there's some sort of answer there.

Thank God for the rain so he can't hear the way my pulse is drumming against my skin.

"All right," he says, then crouches. He puts his shoulder to my midsection, pulls me from the car, and lifts while I maintain strict control of my limbs.

We clear the car. His boots squeak as he steps away, into the grass at the side of the road, and for several seconds I'm ass-up and slung over Levi's shoulder like I'm a sack of dirt or concrete or grain or whatever it is that sexy lumber-jack types like to lift.

Then he puts me down, one thickly-gloved hand on my shoulder, rain still pouring down, and he looks at me. He looks at me for a long moment, checks me over like he's inspecting me for cracks.

"You okay?" he finally says.

I swallow, then nod. My heart's still tapdancing but I clench my fingers and toes and look down at myself.

I'm soaking wet and I'm pretty embarrassed and I'm definitely wearing too-short running shorts and a bright purple sports bra that's mostly visible through my now-soaked light blue tank top, and I could really, *really* use a shower, but I'm fine.

"Yeah," I say. "I'm okay."

"Good," he says quietly, and takes my elbow in his gloved hand. "Wait in the truck while I put out the flares. It's at least dry in there."

CHAPTER TWO

JUNE

He refuses my offer to help put out the flares. He refuses it firmly but gently, guiding me into the cab of his truck while I go on about how I could help, spreading an old-but-clean towel on the seat and then offering me a hand as I climb into the cab.

I admit that I don't mind being dry and safe.

I also admit that I don't hate the continuation of the Levi Loveless Wet T-Shirt Extravaganza, even though I feel guilty that he's all alone in the rain while I could be helping.

I grab another dry towel from the back of the cab, where there are plenty, and watch Levi circle my car with the roadside flares. He does it the way he seems to do everything: methodically, purposefully, as though this is all part of some plan.

He does it this way despite the driving rain, despite the lightning and thunder that are still all around us. I still jump every time the sky lights up and the *boom* sounds like it'll split the earth in half, but Levi is completely unperturbed.

There are worse things to watch. He's still got the gloves and boots on, which aren't exactly what Chippendales fantasies are made of, but the rest?

Yes. Hi. *Hello*, wet t-shirt and big muscles and broad shoulders.

My younger, hopelessly-and-secretly-crushing-on-Levi-Loveless self is feeling *very* vindicated right now. She gets even more vindication as he walks to the edge of the forest, ducks inside, then comes out holding up a huge, long tree branch.

His body tenses. His muscles knot. I use a towel to wipe the steam from the inside of the windshield. He reaches out with the branch and nudges the passenger door of my car closed, then drops it back on the ground.

I don't know when, exactly, I first started crushing on Levi Loveless. He was always hanging around with Silas, so it's hard to pinpoint.

I just know that one day, my attitude toward Levi was *he's pretty cool* and sometime later it was *I think I want Levi to kiss me*.

I was far from alone in my Loveless crush. If you were a lady of a certain age in Sprucevale, it was pretty much a rite of passage to have a crush on a Loveless brother.

There are five of them, and even as teenagers Lord in heaven were they good looking.

The girls my age were split between Eli, the second oldest, and Daniel, the middle of the five. Eli was competitive, smart, and a total wiseass, but mostly nice. Daniel — who graduated from high school the same year as me — was the hell raiser, always in trouble, down at the Sherriff's station with some regularity.

He's got a daughter and a fiancée now. Apparently, he's straightened his act out, because last time I saw him, he gave me the stinkeye for saying *damn* in front of his kid.

Seth and Caleb were a few years younger, but *everyone's* little sister had a crush on one of them. Seth was the second-youngest, good at baseball and so charming he should have had a warning sign. Caleb was three years younger than me, and despite his rugged, free-spirit vibe, he was already taking college-level math classes and the senior girls were lining up for homework help.

Levi was the oldest. The same age as Silas, three years ahead of me, a senior when I was a freshman.

He was the odd one out, because no one but me had a crush on Levi.

To this day, I don't understand why. In a batch of five abnormally good-looking brothers, he's the hottest — in my opinion, anyway, an opinion which clearly has not changed.

Levi was nice to little sisters. He rescued baby birds who fell from nests. He chopped wood for grandmothers, a moment that may or may not have contributed to my very first (and, in retrospect, very tame) sexual fantasy.

But then again, Levi was... weird.

In a school that emptied out the first day of deer hunting season every year, he was a vegetarian. He carried a book everywhere he went, and it wasn't unusual to see him reading a paperback as he walked through the hall-ways from class to class. There was a solid six months where he wore a corduroy blazer over a t-shirt to school every single day, and I never did find out why.

I have no clue what he and my brother Silas — football star, middling student, obnoxious Big Man on Campus type — saw in each other, but they've been thicker than thieves since they were kids, and adulthood hasn't changed that.

Outside the truck, Levi surveys his work, standing perfectly still in the driving rain, his shirt sticking to him like a second skin. I'm tempted to take a picture, but I know that would be straight-up creepy, so I commit it to memory instead.

Then he nods to himself and walks around to the back of the truck, takes off the gloves and boots, flops them into the bed, and opens the driver's side door.

The water's just dripping from him: his nose, his beard, his eyebrows, even his hair, knotted behind his head. I have ten thousand dirty thoughts.

"Wait!" I say, and dive between the seats.

Levi says nothing, just waits, still in the rain. I grab two more towels and spread them on the driver's seat. Lightning flashes, a couple miles away now.

"There," I say, and he gives me an amused look as he climbs into the cab and finally closes the door after himself. I hand him another towel.

"Thanks," he says, and rubs it over his head.

"I heard this news story about this guy who was a total workout fiend and got a ton of sweat on the driver's seat of his car," I say, apologetically. "And he started having all these breathing problems, and it took his doctor a full year to figure out that it was from the mold growing on his sweaty, damp car seat."

"He didn't notice the smell?" Levi asks, pulling a band from his knotted hair, letting it flop wetly to his shoulders.

"I guess not," I say, trying to remember the details of the story. "I think it was in Russia."

"Russians can't smell?"

"Too cold?" I say. I already feel like I'm in over my head here, the familiar nervous buzz starting just behind my sternum.

You know, the way I used to feel any time Levi talked to me. Back when I was a teenager with a crush, not an adult woman with… not a crush.

"You'd think that would inhibit mold growth," he says,

rubbing the towel on his head one last time, then tossing it into the back of the cab.

"It was Russian mold," I say. "I assume it thrives on cold, vodka, and stoicism."

Levi puts the keys in the ignition, looking ahead, but I swear I see the hint of a smile flicker across his face.

"I've got two options for you," he says, his hand on the gearshift, still looking through the windshield. "I can drive you down through Breakwater Gap and back up the west side of the range and into town, or I can take you to my place. I don't mind Option A, but Option B gets us both indoors and dry a whole lot faster."

Levi Loveless just offered to take me home with him.

In the most platonic fashion possible, of course, but still.

"I like the dry option," I say, pointing the heater vent at myself.

"I do too," he says, and shifts his truck into reverse, turning to look over his shoulder. "And the dog will be thrilled."

· · · · ★ ★ ★ ★ ★ · · · ·

TEN MINUTES LATER, we turn from the two-lane Appalachian Parkway onto a narrow gravel lane, the truck bumping over the edge of the pavement.

"Silas made me go for a trail run," I explain.

"Made you?" Levi echoes.

"Well, he talked me into it," I admit as the gravel rumbles underneath, the deep forest closing around us. "And, you know, I figure that doing more outdoorsy stuff is kind of a 'when in Rome' situation, so why not? Nature is nice."

I don't mention reinvention. I don't mention the shitty

past few months I've had. I don't mention the self-help books I've read, or the mantras that I'll repeat for a few days before inevitably deciding it's stupid, or the sudden, jolting realization I had one night that in order for things to change, *I* had to change.

Three months ago, I had a very bad day. I got laid off from my job at the Raleigh Sun-Dispatch, along with about thirty other people. I texted my boyfriend, crying. He didn't text back.

When I got home to the apartment we shared, he dumped me.

He said he'd been thinking about it for a while. He said I used to be fun and cool and now I worked too much and only ever wanted to talk about boring things, like politics and global warming.

And he said he "just wasn't into it" anymore, after over a year together.

There was shouting (me) and there were tears (also me) and after a few hours, he went to stay with his parents.

That night, sitting miserably on the floor of the living room because I refused to sit on any of the furniture we'd shared, I had an epiphany: Brett sucked.

So did most of my previous boyfriends. Pretty much all of them, except maybe Peter, who I just wasn't compatible with.

There was Tyler, who only ever wanted to hang out and play video games, and who ghosted me after seven months of dating.

There was Connor, who interrupted almost every sentence I said aloud and spent all our time together for at least three weeks trying to talk me into dressing as a cheerleader for Halloween.

There was Noah, with whom I once got into a shouting match about whether women should be legally required to change their names when they get married, and who cheated on me and then acted like I was crazy when I got mad about it.

Finally there was Brett, who acted like my career was a hobby, who'd mope for a full day if I talked to another man in front of him, and who broke up with me the same day I got laid off and then, a month later, held up a boom box outside my window at my parents' house and asked me to marry him.

Unsurprisingly, he refused to take *no* for an answer. I ended up calling Silas, whose *no* is quite a bit more emphatic than mine.

Brett wasn't an outlier.

Brett was part of a shitty pattern, and I had very, very bad taste in men. Enter reinvention, and trying new things, and being open to new experiences, and generally being different from the girl who'd gotten dumped and fired and who fell for men who "didn't believe" in expiration dates on milk.

Long story short, now I love the outdoors.

"I didn't know Silas enjoyed trail running," Levi admits. "Last time he went on about his fitness regimen I believe it was CrossFit."

"Oh, God, the CrossFit," I say, laughing. "He once swore up and down that he could bench me and then got mad when I wouldn't let him try."

"I can't imagine why not," Levi says.

We round a curve in the gravel road, and I catch a glimpse of a building through the trees.

"This is your house?" I ask as the truck navigates one final curve of the long gravel driveway.

"It is," Levi confirms.

I lean forward, craning my neck for a better view, the building still partly obscured by trees. I've never been to

Levi's house, but I know two things about it: one, it's in the middle of nowhere, and two, he built it himself.

Now we're in the middle of nowhere, at least a mile down a long gravel driveway, and we're coming up on what might be the most charming cabin I've ever seen in person.

I don't know what I expected, but it wasn't this.

"Oh," I say.

Levi just glances over at me.

"You built this yourself?" I ask, just as the cabin comes fully into view.

"Not entirely," he says, the truck slowing as Levi reaches up, hits the button on his garage door opener. "I hired someone to do the plumbing and electrical work. Silas helped me hang drywall. Charlie helped with the kitchen cabinets. Caleb and I spent a weekend laying the floors."

"Oh, so only mostly," I say, still staring at the cabin.

It is, for lack of a better word, lovely. It's made of wood so rich it practically glows, even in the near-dark. It's got a wraparound porch and a small flowerbed in the front. There's a walkway with slate paving stones leading to the front steps. It's not big, but it's also not small.

It's an honest-to-God mountain man cabin, only instead of being ramshackle, crooked, and drafty-looking, it's beautiful. It looks like it should be on the cover of *Lumberjack Real Estate* or *Fancy Backwoods Vacation Homes* or some other magazine I've just made up.

I wonder if something like those magazines exists. I wonder if they'd be interested in a feature of Levi's house.

"Looks like the power's out," he says, shutting off the truck. "Not precisely a surprise, but I think we can make do."

"Mhm," I agree. "You *built* this? Mostly?"

"C'mon," he says, climbing out of the cab.

23

I follow, shutting the truck door heavily behind me, eyes still on Levi's house as I follow him in, a rucksack slung over his shoulder.

Something about this feels like learning a secret about Levi. It feels like he's invited me to his secret hideout, deep in the woods, his fortress of solitude. I know that's probably ridiculous, but it's not like Levi's known for throwing dinner parties.

I follow him onto the porch, still silent, and he puts his key into the lock, then turns to look at me.

"Watch out," he says, and pushes the door open.

"For wha—"

I don't finish my sentence, because I'm hit by a missile.

A furry missile, with a wet nose and a wetter tongue, who nearly knocks me off my feet and then prances in a circle around me as I kneel on the porch, too excited to hold still.

"The attack dog," Levi says.

"Hey girl!" I say.

She licks my face, tail thumping, and I laugh.

"You remember me? Yes, you do. Yes you DO."

The dog makes a funny little *growf* noise, like she does when she gets excited.

"Traitor," Levi says mildly, still standing next to the door as he leans inside and checks something. "Yup. Power's out."

I'm now sitting on the floor of his porch — it's covered, so at least it's pretty dry — and the dog is still circling me, snuffing and *growf*-ing and licking me, her paws prancing with glee.

"I may have given her some treats while Silas was dog sitting a few weeks ago," I admit to Levi, dodging around the dog's face to talk to him.

"Some?" he says, leaning against his doorjamb, one

24

hand in a pocket. His shirt is now just damp, not soaking wet, though I'm somewhat consternated to report that the change hasn't made him less distracting.

"It might have been more like several," I admit.

It was not several. It was a lot. She's a very good dog.

"No wonder she picked you," he says. "All I do is feed her, give her a dry place to live, and supply her with toys."

I glance quickly at Levi, ninety-five percent sure he's joking. He can be hard to read, and even though I've known him for a long time, I can't say I know him well.

But then the dog is right in front of my face again, paws on my knee, doggy smile filling my vision. I realize there's a tag hanging from her collar.

"Oh good, you named her," I say, taking it between my fingers.

LEVI LOVELESS
(276) 555-1212

"You named the dog Levi?" I ask, deadpan, as she licks my hand.

Human Levi sighs.

"I put my contact information on her in case she runs off again," he explains. "Come on, girl."

The dog looks at him, and he points her into the house. I stand and follow her.

"What's her name?" I ask as I go through the door.

"I don't know," he says, the door shutting behind us.

It's dim, but not dark. The pale gray of an afternoon thunderstorm, light coming in through the house's many windows. It's deeply quiet: nothing hums, nothing ticks, nothing creaks, no sounds except for our breathing and the quiet padding of the dog, walking across the room.

Near-total stillness.

"You should name her," I say, breaking the silence. "You can't just call her *dog* forever."

Levi takes his boots off and puts them on a rubber tray, so I follow suit with my sneakers.

"I put more flyers up in Eli's neighborhood last weekend," he says.

"Did anyone answer them?"

"Not yet."

The dog gives the back of my thigh one more lick — okay, thanks — then trots off through the living room and up a flight of stairs, disappearing into a room off a landing.

"They're not going to," I tell him. "Someone dumped her."

"You don't know that."

"Yes, I do."

"No, you don't," Levi says, walking into his living room and pulling his shirt off, over his head, and tossing it onto the back of a chair.

I avert my eyes, heart suddenly thumping.

"She's house trained," he says, opening a closet. "Aside from her paw, she was well-cared-for. She's friendly. She's clearly got owners, June, and I've got no right to take their dog and re-name her."

He pulls a drying rack from the closet, opens it on the floor, and neatly arranges his shirt over it.

When he looks back at me, I pretend I was averting my eyes the whole time.

"She'll remember her old name if they ever come back, which they won't," I say. "Just give her a name. You can't call her *dog* forever."

As if summoned by this, the dog comes barreling back down the stairs, a toy held in her mouth, and she trots over and presents it to me so I grab both ends of it and tug, grateful for something to do besides pretend I'm not ogling the shirtless man whose house I'm in.

She tugs back, tail wagging like mad. Levi went camping with some of his brothers a few weeks ago and Silas dog sat, so I got to hang out with her. Turns out she loves doggy tug-of-war.

He sighs, then pulls his hair back with his hands, ties it into a knot again.

"If I name her, I'll just get attached, only for her rightful owners to return and take her away from me," he says, walking away from me, across the living room. "Better to just call her *dog* until that happens. I'll be right back."

With that he heads up the stairs, across the landing, and into a room, leaving me and the dog alone in his quiet gray living room, still tugging on opposite ends of this toy.

"Maybe I should name you myself," I tell her after a minute. She *growfs* and wags her tail. "Princess. Cupcake. Muffin. Fluffy. Tell me if any of these appeal to you."

She just wags her tail and tugs on the toy. I tug back, trying to think of more names.

"Bella. Angel. Pumpkin. Queenie. Anything?"

Growf.

"Yeah, I don't think you're a Pumpkin," I say, now sitting on the floor, still pulling back. "Maybe something more dignified, like Peaches, or Buttercup——"

"You cannot name my dog Buttercup," Levi's voice says from the loft above me.

"So she's your dog when I'm trying to give her the dignity of a name to call her own," I call back.

He pads down the stairs barefoot, wearing navy blue sweatpants and dark green t-shirt with a small Forest Service logo on one side of the chest.

Update: still hot.

"I'd hardly call Buttercup a dignified name."

"She's a dog."

"Even beasts need dignity," he says, padding off the stairs and through the living room.

"It was good enough for *The Princess Bride*," I point out.

Levi stops in front of me. He's got a small stack of clothes in one hand, and he's holding them out toward me.

"That's a movie?" he asks, eyes narrowed.

I narrow my eyes back at him in jest, though I have no idea whether Levi realizes it's a joke or not.

He can be... inscrutable.

"Technically, it's also a book," I say. "About a woman. Who's a princess. And also a bride, thus the catchy name."

"Girl, are you a princess?" he asks the dog.

The dog sits, looking up at Levi, wagging her tail and grinning a doggy grin.

"No? What about a bride?"

Same reaction from the dog, and Levi looks back at me. I'm about sixty percent sure he's smiling, but I can't quite tell.

Levi makes me feel off-balance and helter skelter, like everything I say is either too much or not enough, like I'm an object of some scientific interest. I am, generally speaking, good with people. I'm good at gauging their reactions to me, good at understanding how to speak and act to make others comfortable, good at saying the appropriate thing for a situation.

It's why I'm a good journalist. Or at least, it's why I *was* a good journalist. I'm good at getting people to talk to me.

Not Levi.

Levi is a mystery wrapped in an enigma stuffed into a crate labeled *puzzle*, and I don't think he likes me.

Let me clarify. I don't think he *dislikes* me. I just get the feeling that, to Levi, the vast majority of people fall into the *neutral feelings* category, and he feels as strongly about us as he does rocks or dirt or the sky above.

"These are the smallest things I could find," he says, and even though he's holding out a stack of clothes it still takes me a second to figure out what he's talking about, because he throws me so off-balance.

"Thanks," I say, pushing myself off the floor.

He offers me his other hand. I take it. It's big and rough and strong, qualities which certainly do not give me a dangerous, deep-down thrill.

"I'd offer you use of my shower but I'm afraid the well pump runs on electricity," he says, pushing his hands back into his pockets. "But I've got several buckets of emergency water outside, and if you'd like I can bring some in for your use."

His eyes.

I'd almost forgotten about his eyes: light brown, the color of deep amber. I'd forgotten the way they always seem lit from within, like candles behind a stained glass window.

"That's okay," I hear myself saying. "I'm fine, really, as long as you don't mind these clothes getting a little gross—"

"It's no trouble."

"Carrying buckets of water inside is trouble."

"Certainly not more trouble than I'm used to."

"How much trouble are you used to?" I ask, raising one eyebrow.

Levi half-frowns, half-smiles, like he's amused and consternated all at once.

"More than you might think," he says, and turns away from me, heads for his back door. "I'll be right back with the water and there's nothing you can do about it, June."

CHAPTER THREE

LEVI

June is now nude in my bathroom.

Presumably. It's a reasonable assumption to make, that several minutes after carrying in two large buckets of water, setting them in the shower despite her protests, and pointing out the soap and shampoo, she has disrobed and is currently bathing.

Silas's little sister. Naked. Right now. On the other side of that wall.

It's a thought I shouldn't be thinking at all, but it's impossibly distracting. I turn away, toward the dim interior of the house, averting my eyes as if that will help.

It doesn't help.

June makes me feel like I suddenly no longer understand the world I thought I inhabited. She makes me feel as though I'm walking through brand-new territory without a map or a compass.

She makes me feel as though, without warning, the solid wall that I built with my own two hands might suddenly turn into panes of clear glass. That the world is topsy-turvy and unpredictable and that there are entire dimensions to reality that I'd never even considered before, waiting for me to discover them.

And yet every time I talk to her, there's that iron fist in my gut, the squeezing heaviness that whispers *you traitor, he trusts you*. Even though I've done nothing.

Besides bring her home. Besides invite her to get naked in your bathroom while you think about the way water would run over her—

"Don't," I growl out loud to myself, standing in my kitchen, facing away from the bathroom door.

The dog gives me a look.

"Not you," I say, and she yawns.

Finally, in the absence of June, she comes over and presents the sock monkey to me. After a few minutes of wrestling, she lets me check her paw, which is almost completely healed, nothing more than a pink line in a patch of shaved fur.

A few weeks ago, my younger brother Eli was hosting a barbecue at his house when the dog wandered up. She was dirty, skinny, and limping, but she was friendly, and I've got a soft spot for animals.

June was there, along with her brother Silas, who's become something of an honorary Loveless brother. She helped me bandage up the ugly gash in the dog's paw, and next thing I knew, I was taking her home — the dog, not June — and letting her sleep at the foot of my bed.

I took her to the vet, got her paw properly looked at. No microchip. I hung flyers all over Sprucevale, posted on all the relevant internet forums. No one was missing a black and white medium-sized female mutt who might be part lab, part shepherd, and part something else.

The fact remains, however, that she was indisputably once someone's dog. Even though she was dirty and hungry, she had clearly been well-cared-for at one point. She's friendly, familiar with people.

Most telling of all, she's housebroken. She sits patiently by the back door when she'd like to be let outside. She doesn't go on the couch or the bed. She's never chewed anything that wasn't a dog toy.

She's a good dog. Possibly the best dog.

And it's painfully clear that she is not *my* dog.

I put her paw back down and scratch her behind the ears, glancing one more time at the bathroom door before I go to the closet and get out the emergency candles and lanterns, set them out on the coffee table and the countertop in case the power doesn't come back on before it's full dark.

There's a splashing sound from the bathroom. I take a deep breath and concentrate on the wood grain of the wall on the far side of the living room, the dark lines graceful and flowing like water—

"Let's have hot chocolate," I tell the dog, cutting off my own train of thought and standing.

She stands as well, tongue lolling out of her mouth in pleasant agreement, and I raise my eyebrows.

"Not you," I tell her, walking into my kitchen. "You're a dog. If I gave you chocolate I'd have to take you back to the vet, and you haven't enjoyed your visits thus far."

Her enthusiasm does not wane. I quickly gather the necessary items for hot cocoa: ultra-pasteurized shelf stable milk, sugar, cocoa, salt, a saucepan, my propane camping stove, and the dog and I head onto the front porch.

It's nearly stopped raining by now, though the air is still so damp it feels like you could wring it out. I quickly set everything up on a small wooden table between two Adirondack chairs, then settle into one and wait for it to reach the right temperature.

And I do not think about June's current state of dress or undress. I don't imagine the look that would be on Silas's face if he knew what I was thinking. I don't remember the brief weight of her on my shoulder, I don't remember the way her running shorts rode up her thighs when she sat in my truck cab, and I certainly don't contemplate the fact that every time I lay eyes on her, my mind goes blank.

I get out of the chair and start pacing back and forth on the front porch instead. I watch two squirrels chase each other around a white pine. I watch some small birds flutter around an oak tree. My mom is always after me to set up some bird feeders whenever she visits, but so far I've resisted. They're wild animals. If I feed them, they'll come to need it.

"Oh good, there you are," June's voice suddenly says, and I turn.

She's standing in the doorway, her dark hair knotted on top of her head, wearing dark green sweatpants that say GO COLONIALS in green down one leg, and a blue sweatshirt that's got two crossed billiard cues on it and says *Cumberland Billiard League* in yellow. Everything is too large for her.

"Thanks for the outfit," she says.

"Sorry I didn't have anything smaller."

"Beggars can't be choosers," she says, shrugging, walking out onto the porch in bare feet. She stands atop the steps, looks out at the forest. I watch her, lost for words, even though I understand the rules of human communication and know that now it's my turn.

I should say something witty, charming, something that would make her eyes light up with a smile, maybe even a laugh.

My mind goes utterly, completely blank.

"Who's Joe?" she asks suddenly.

33

"Joe?" I echo dumbly, trying to think of a Joe. Not a single one comes to mind.

"Joe," June says again, and points at her breasts.

Impossibly, I maintain eye contact. I do not breathe.

I have the insane, wild thought that I'm being tested. Maybe June's last breakup sent Silas, always an overprotective older brother, completely around the bend and now they're somehow working together to test my loyalty to our friendship.

It is not the thought of a rational man, but it's the thought I have.

"I don't believe I know a Joe," I tell her, staring straight into her sapphire eyes.

June is now looking at me like I'm speaking a foreign language.

"Were you in the billiard league?" she asks.

It's the sweatshirt.

Of course it's the sweatshirt.

I am an idiot.

"Only briefly," I tell her, relieved. I maintain eye contact, but I don't need to look at my ancient Cumberland Billiards sweatshirt to know that, under the logo, it says *Knock 'em in good, Joe.* "Back when I had just started with the forest service a few older rangers were in, so I joined. They mostly wanted to smoke and drink beer together, so I didn't last long."

For the briefest of moments, I let my eyes flick down to the logo and text on the sweatshirt.

"Also, I'm terrible at it. And I never did find out who Joe was, or whether he knocked 'em in," I say, stepping across the porch to stir the hot cocoa.

"He probably did," June says, leaning against the porch railing, her hands by her sides. "Even I can eventually knock 'em all in, if you give me long enough."

I taste the cocoa. It still needs a few minutes. Camp stoves don't tend to be fast.

"Is that hot chocolate?" June asks.

"It is," I confirm, settling back into the Adirondack chair, crossing an ankle over a knee. "It's a power outage tradition. My father used to break out the camp stove any time the power was out for a while when we were kids, so I started doing it too."

June gets into the other Adirondack chair and sits crosslegged, pushing up the sleeves of the sweatshirt as she does.

"Did you ever do it when Silas was there?" she asks, eyes narrowed like she's calculating something.

"I'm sure," I say.

"Well, that explains that," she says.

I raise my eyebrows, wait.

"He tried this once when he was twelve or thirteen," she goes on, sighing, leaning her head back against the wooden back of the chair. "Only he was an idiot and did it in his unventilated bedroom, where he somehow managed to catch some homework on fire."

I start laughing, despite myself.

"The smoke alarm and the carbon monoxide detector went off at the exact same time, which is honestly kind of impressive in the worst possible way. My parents grounded him for like two weeks and made him write them a five-page essay on the dangers of carbon monoxide poisoning," she says.

"Can Silas write five pages?" I ask, still laughing.

"You should've seen the font size and margins on that thing," June says, turning to face me and grinning.

"He told me he was grounded for doing flips off the roof," I say.

"Oh, he did that too," June says. "He once rode his bicycle off the roof. I don't know how no one noticed him getting it there in the first place. That one's on my parents, really. It's amazing that he survived to adulthood."

We're both quiet for a moment. It's true that Silas could be monumentally stupid when we were younger. So could I, though never quite like that.

The heavy knot in my stomach tightens.

How long have you been friends? Twenty years?
More?

"Remember the time he drove my dad's truck into the creek because a football fell off the seat next to him?" June says, staring off into the forest. "How the hell did he become a lawyer?"

I lean over, take another spoonful of hot cocoa to test the temperature, glancing at June as I do.

She still doesn't know. She doesn't know what really caused that crash.

It wasn't a stray football. It was a passenger.

Jake Echols, to be exact. June's then-boyfriend, to be even more exact. He was eighteen and had just graduated. She was fifteen, about to start her sophomore year.

I don't know the inner workings of the relationship, but I know he gave her a promise ring and swore to make a long-distance relationship work after he left the next fall for West Virginia University. I heard about the promise ring constantly from Silas.

And I also know that he bragged to his friends about getting a blowjob from some college chick.

Silas gave him a ride somewhere. They fought in the car. It got physical. Silas crashed into the creek by accident, and Jake, unhurt, hopped out of the car and ran, leaving Silas to concoct a story about a football.

A week later, Jake up and joined the Air Force, and I don't think June ever learned why.

There are reasons besides loyalty and friendship that

June is a bad idea for me. Reasons like *Silas has extensive combat training* and *Silas is not a reasonable human being when it comes to his little sister.*

"It's ready," I say, turning off the stove. "Mugs are inside. Shall we?"

CHAPTER FOUR

JUNE

"You see, these celebrity dogs are *very* cute," I say, leaning my elbows on the kitchen island. "That's what made this particular piece an important work of journalism. I'm pretty sure I'll be hearing from the Pulitzer committee any day."

Stop talking.

I stop talking. Levi and his silences make me nervous. He makes me feel like silence isn't silence, like it's something I can't hear, something I'm not paying attention to. Like if I just listen hard enough, suddenly I'll hear.

"One question," he finally says reflectively, taking another sip of hot chocolate, standing on the other side of the kitchen island. "Do the dogs belong to celebrities, or are the dogs themselves celebrities?"

"The former," I tell him. "But thank you for my next pitch."

"You could do a whole series on celebrity pets," he says. "Cats. Dogs. Birds. Hamsters."

"I could write about weird celebrity pets," I say, swirling

the last third of my cocoa in the mug. "I could write a think piece about the meaning of pets, and what exactly constitutes a pet. Is an outdoor cat truly a pet? Can a lizard love you back? If you feed the birds, do they become your pets?"

On the floor, the dog sighs dramatically and puts her head on her paws.

"Do animals have to have names to be considered pets?" I muse.

"She has a name, I just don't know it," Levi.

"You poor thing," I tell the dog.

Her tail thumps on the floor twice.

"Alice. Brenda," I guess at her. No reaction. "Chanel. Denise. Florentina."

"Georgette," says Levi. "We're going in alphabetical order, right? Harriet."

The dog doesn't react in the least.

"I don't think it's Harriet," I say.

There's another silence. I shift my weight against the counter, still standing, the pot that held the hot chocolate still sitting on a trivet to my right, empty.

I take a deep breath, wait, and listen to the silence.

"I don't want to name her while I'm still actively looking for her owners," Levi finally says, his low, unhurried voice drifting through the silence. "If I give her a name, I'll feel like she's mine, and I'd hate to do that only to have to give her back."

"You could stop looking," I say, my mug between my palms. "You don't have to. You probably won't find them if you haven't already."

"I'd want someone to find me if I lost her," he says. "How could I do any differently?"

This time the silence is mine, even as *just stop trying to find them, it's that easy* is on the tip of my tongue, because I know he's right, or at least right for himself. Levi couldn't do differently.

"Print journalism is dying," I say suddenly, and take the last sip of my hot chocolate, now cold and gritty, but still good. "No one wants to pay for the news anymore. No one even wants to read the news any more, they just want to see feel-good stories about ducklings getting rescued from storm drains and kids in Thanksgiving parades, and they want to read endless lists of *The Ten Worst Bridezillas Ever* or *You Won't Believe What These Moms Are Doing On The Beach*. I never really answered your question earlier. That's how my job hunt is going. Shitty."

He's quiet for a long moment, and then he looks up at me. I feel like a mosquito trapped in the gold-brown amber of his eyes, even as I notice other things about him: that he has a few light freckles on his cheeks, that he's steadily, slowly, rubbing one thumb along the outside of the mug as he cups it in his big, rough hand.

"I'm sorry," he finally says. "Looking for a job is shit."

"I think I have to do something else and I don't know what," I admit.

"Do you want to do something else?" he asks.

"I want to have a job and get out of here again," I say. "I want to not live in my childhood bedroom and hear my mom singing in the shower or my dad belching in the kitchen anymore. I want my stupid brother to stop acting like my ex-boyfriend is the leader of a terrorist cell instead of just some dickhead."

I shut my mouth, but it's too late because I just mentioned Brett to Levi and I didn't mean to. I'm sure he knows, because Silas has never kept anything to himself in his entire life, but I didn't want to talk about Brett in front of him.

"Anyway," I say, trying to steer this conversation back away from my bad boyfriend choices, "I think I have to figure out something else to do with my life and I don't know what that is, and to be honest I don't really want to find another career because I liked this one. Mostly."

"You'll figure it out," he says, softly. "If nothing else, through sheer tenacity."

"Tenacity," I repeat, both hands around my empty mug. "I like that. Usually it gets called pig-headedness."

Levi just smiles. He holds out one hand, across the counter, and suddenly my heart hitches. My insides get gooey. My heart beats faster and instantly, I feel like I'm six again and he's nine, climbing onto the counter to rescue my stuffed bunny that Silas put up there.

I hold my breath, then put my hand in his. He's warm and rough and even in this simple touch, I can feel his strength. My guts turn into a whirlpool.

Levi looks at our joined hands, then up at me.

"Actually, I was offering to take your mug," he says, nodding at it, in front of me on the counter.

Duh. Fucking duh, and I would like very much right to turn into goo and simply melt into the cracks of his beautiful, hand-finished wood floor because of course he wanted the mug, obviously he wanted the mug, and here I am acting like we're having some kind of *moment*.

We're not having a moment. The only moment we're having is me talking too much and him offering to take dirty dishes from his friend's kid sister, to whom he is currently being very nice because, again, *I am his best friend's kid sister*.

"Right. Sorry. Right. Here it is, be careful there's still a little bit in the bottom, thanks!" I say, already laughing nervously.

He takes the mug, turns, places them gently in his (clean, empty) sink.

"I'm gonna go there," I say, jerking my thumb over my shoulder. "Over there? I'll be there."

"I'll call the power company again," he says, and I hear the faint click of a telephone being lifted off a receiver.

I've already turned away and headed for the living room, thankful that it's dim in here and Levi can't see that I'm fire-engine red.

· · · · ★ ★ ★ ★ · · · ·

"VANDALISM, MOST LIKELY," Levi says, propping his feet on the coffee table. "Though I admit to being puzzled by the whole affair."

We're sitting in his living room, on two leather couches that are caddy-corner to one another, his slice-of-tree coffee table in the middle. Between that and the fireplace is Jedediah, his bear skin rug.

Levi had nothing to do with Jedediah's death. If I remember correctly, he was killed by poachers and Levi didn't see any point in letting something perfectly good go to waste.

I lean over the coffee table, a small camping lantern in my hand, scrutinizing the map of the Cumberland National Forest in front of me. There's a dark green area shaped kind of like an eggplant labeled **Otter Mountain Wilderness**, and near the middle of it, two hand-drawn X's.

"In a wilderness area?" I ask. "That seems pretty involved for something not many people are likely to see."

"It's the best explanation I've found," Levi says. "Some people just want to watch the world burn. This all landed on my desk a week ago and I've not made heads nor tails of it."

"Because you're in charge of trees?" I ask, still looking at the map with the lantern.

Levi laughs.

"Madam, trees take charge of themselves," he says.

I shoot him a puzzled look, then reach for another map. More wilderness area — Hickory Trap Wilderness — more X's.

"I have yet to induce a tree to listen to my advice," Levi admits. "At best, I'm a caretaker of trees. Though a middling one, judging by all this."

"You're sure it was the same person?" I ask, looking from Otter Mountain to Hickory Trap and back. "How many are there?"

"No, and three," he says.

"Three trees?"

"Three incidents, five trees," he says, and then pauses.

He leans forward, elbows on his knees, his face lit by lantern and candle and I get that nervous rush again. I feel fourteen and new to crushes, or at least crushes who noticed me back.

"Can you keep a secret?" he asks, voice low.

"Sure," I say.

He rubs his hands together, studying me for a moment.

"I'm not Silas," I say, half-smiling.

"One of the trees they cut down in Hickory Trap was Girthy Glenda," he says.

Then he pauses, as if he's waiting for the news to shock me. He's almost right, but I'm mostly shocked that there's a tree named *Girthy Glenda*.

Girthy. *Girthy*.

"She was named in the 1920s," he says, as if that

explains anything. "And she's the largest Northern Red Oak in the United States."

Then he sighs.

"Was," he corrects himself.

"Who's the second largest?"

"That I don't know."

"Well, one, I can't believe you don't know that and call yourself an arborist, and two, that tree is your number one suspect," I say. "Big Ol' Bertha just wants to be the number one red oak in the U.S."

"Northern Red Oak," Levi corrects me, sitting back on the couch.

"Glenda wasn't even the biggest overall red oak?" I tease, looking back at the maps.

"I'd prefer that no one find out she was a victim," he says. "Honestly, I'd rather no one find out about this whole fiasco."

"I think our nation deserves to mourn Glenda," I say.

There's a silence. I listen, and after a moment, I look up at Levi.

"When we visited the site we found out she was two hundred and sixty-seven years old," he says quietly, his eyes on the maps. "She was alive when the Declaration of Independence was written. She was alive during the Civil War. She survived at least three forest fires and who knows how many droughts and blizzards and thunderstorms, just for someone to cut her down for no damn reason at all."

My eyes drop to the X on the map, and I feel like a dick.

"I'd rather this not become public yet because I'm afraid of copycats," he says. "I'll never understand it, but any time we publicize vandalism on public lands, there's a rash of copycats."

We're both quiet for a long moment, and I breathe, listen, and discover that I'm already getting used to it.

"You said they were cut down by axes?" I ask, looking at the maps again.

"The trees in Slickrock Draft were," he says, leaning forward and handing me a third map. "The trunks were thinner."

"You mean less girthy?"

I don't know why I said that. Girthy. Girthy. Girthy. Send help.

"Yes," he says, matter-of-factly. "In Otter Mountain, they seem to have used a combination of an axe and a manual saw. And in Hickory Trap it was a chainsaw."

"Are you sure?" I ask, grabbing the map of Hickory Trap again. I've used a chainsaw before. Those things are heavy, and from the looks of it, Girthy Glenda was quite a hike from the nearest road.

"Pretty sure," he says. "I have a passing familiarity with what a felled tree looks like."

Point taken.

"So someone hauled a chainsaw all the way into a wilderness area to commit some vandalism?" I ask, trying to put the pieces together, because this just doesn't fit.

Levi sighs.

"I don't have another explanation," he says. "They don't seem to have taken anything. They don't seem to have left anything, they just cut down some old-growth trees."

There's a long pause. The candles flicker, and I look at the X's on the map.

"June, I'm at a loss," he says. "I want to catch whoever did this. I want to stop them from doing it again. I don't even know that they haven't. They could have cut down innumerable trees in deep wilderness, and we may not ever know."

"I'm sorry," I say. "I wish I could help."

"Thanks," he says simply, then rises from the couch. "I'm going to call the power company again."

As he walks away, I pull out my phone and check the time.

Holy cow, it's nine-thirty. I could have sworn I'd been here for thirty minutes, *maybe* an hour, but I guess I was wrong.

"All right, thank you very much," Levi says in the kitchen, and then I hear the click of a phone returned to the cradle, footsteps coming back. They pause.

"It looks as if you may be spending the night here," Levi says. "They haven't gotten this far out yet. Sounds as if there was some major damage closer to town and they're still working on that."

I am spending the night with Levi Loveless.

"Oh," I say, and the buzz in my chest becomes a full-scale rattle. "Is that okay?"

My thoughts are whirring, crashing into each other, frantic.

Maybe he's only got one bedroom, I think. *And only one bed, and for some reason only one blanket and you know it gets very cold at night, so you'll have to snuggle together for warmth, his arms around you, warm and solid...*

Ridiculous. Levi obviously has more than one blanket.

"Of course," he says.

"I don't want to impose," I go on. "If you'd rather just drive me back to my car, that's fine, or..."

I stop, because I'm not really sure where I'm going with that sentence, and I can tell from the look on Levi's face that there's no point in finishing it.

"You're not sincerely suggesting that I'm going to take you back to your electrified car so you can spend the night in it rather than here," he says.

46

"Not when you put it that way," I admit.

"Good," he says. "You can take my bedroom, I'll set up a cot in the office."

A wave of sudden anxiety washes over me. I can't sleep in his bed, in his bedroom. I *cannot*.

"I'll take the cot, it's your bed," I say.

He says nothing, just smiles and walks past me, toward the stairs.

"Levi," I call after him. "No. Come on. I can't just sleep in your bed while you——"

And he's gone.

· · · · · ★ ★ ★ ★ · · · · ·

WHEN HE COMES BACK DOWN, I argue some more, but I get nowhere. Levi just smiles behind his beard and asks if I'd like to call my parents so they don't worry.

I do. They're very relieved to learn that I'm in good hands.

We have peanut butter sandwiches for candlelight dinner. Afterward, he hands me a brand-new, still-in-the-package toothbrush, and I thank him.

I don't want to compare Levi to my exes. Frankly, it's unfair, and double-frankly, I'm tired of thinking about them.

But suffice it to say that none of them were adult enough to have extra toothbrushes. I'm fairly sure that more than one used the same toothbrush for years on end.

I protest the sleeping arrangements again. I tell Levi how much I love sleeping on camping cots, but in the end, Levi steps into his study, calls the dog, says goodnight, and shuts the door.

The man is frustratingly good at winning arguments.

Standing on the landing of the loft, I look down at the

first floor of his cabin and for a moment, I consider sleeping on the couch just to prove a point. That seems rude, though. It's one thing to protest hospitality and another entirely to reject it.

I step into his bedroom, a small lantern in my hand. I feel like I'm trespassing, like I'm still that incredibly nosy ten-year-old who went through her parents' closet once when they were out.

I regret that, by the way. I regret it a *lot*.

His bed is made. His sheets are nice. The room is simple but neat, rustic furniture, a small bookshelf, one flannel shirt tossed over the back of a chair. There are windows along two walls, simple white curtains over them. On one wall is a framed print, and I hold the lantern up to it.

It's the cover of *East of Eden*, enlarged. I study it for a long moment, trying to remember what it's about, but I finally step back because it feels like none of my business.

I look around the room quickly, a small part of me tempted to see what's in his drawers, in his closet, under his bed. For most of my life Levi has been kind but aloof, nice but quiet, present but remote and this feels like a chance to peek under the hood, so to speak.

I resist the urge. I already I feel as if I've come into this quiet, peaceful space like a wrecking ball and Levi is going to regret ever being nice to little sisters.

Finally, I sit on the bed. I take off the clothes that Levi loaned me, fold them, put them on the floor next to the bed.

I slide between his sheets, put my face into his pillow, and inhale, wondering what he smells like, but the only scent is laundry soap. He changed the sheets for me.

I lie there, thinking. I think of him soaking in the rain, wearing rubber gloves and rubber boots. I think of him lifting me effortlessly, putting me down gently. Lending me clothes, making hot cocoa.

The way he paused a moment when I took his hand, just long enough, before telling me he just wanted the mug, and even alone in the dark, I put my hands over my face.

It takes me a long time to fall asleep.

CHAPTER FIVE

LEVI

I wake up to the sound of shattering glass.

The dog scrambles up instantly and I sit up on one elbow, blinking into the dark. I was in the middle of a dream that Caleb and I were in an airport, only to find our gate, we had to put together a 500-piece puzzle of a castle.

Then the dog barks and just like that I remember where I am and instantly, I'm off the cot, onto the landing, opening the door to my bedroom.

"June?" I ask the dark, heart thumping.

"I'm here," comes the answer. "What — did something fall?"

I let out the breath I didn't know I was holding. The dog pads up next to me, and there's the sound of rustling bedsheets, June's dark form moving, more my imagination than anything I can actually see.

"Are you all right?"

"I'm fine," she says, her voice still dreamy as a light suddenly flares through the darkness and I shield my eyes.

"Oh, shit," June says.

There's a tree through one window, shattered glass on

the floor. For a long moment, both of us just stare at it. I'm trying to shove the last dregs of the dream out of my mind, trying to figure out what the best course of action is when a tree falls through your window at two o'clock in the morning.

"Is it storming again?" June asks. "Is the power back on? Is that a whole tree or just a branch? Has this ever happened before?"

Finally, I look over at her, not sure which question to answer first. She's sitting upright in my bed, lantern held aloft in one hand, the other holding the sheets up over herself.

She's not wearing a shirt.

Any answers I may have had instantly fly out of my head. All I can think of is the curve of her collarbone, thrown into sharp relief by the lantern light. The swell of her breasts under the sheet, rising as she breathes, the way the sheet falls away from her side and leaves visible a sliver of her back.

It's the dog who jolts me out of it, again. She steps forward, toward the window, sniffing, and I grab her by the collar.

"Sorry, girl," I tell her. "Careful, there's glass. Let me put her in the office and we'll clean this up."

"I'll put on clothes," June says, and I give her one last glance before guiding the dog out of my bedroom and close the door.

The dog sits, looking annoyed.

I head into the office, pull my shirt on as well. I go downstairs, put on my shoes, grab June's, then get a broom, mop, and paper bag. I'm not sure what else I'll need. I've never had a tree fall into my bedroom before.

When I go back upstairs, I stand there for a moment, collecting myself. I force myself to think about axes and saws and ladders and replacement windows, not what it would be like to get into my bed next to June.

Not about what would have happened if earlier, I'd just held her hand. Would she have pulled away? Would she have laughed? Tomorrow, would she tell Silas that I'd tried to put the moves on her in my kitchen?

I shut my eyes and knock on my bedroom door.

Half a moment later, June answers it, lantern in hand, wearing the billiards sweatshirt again, her hair still mussed from my pillow. She opens the door and steps inside silently, and I hand her her shoes.

She looks at me quizzically.

"So you don't step on glass," I tell her, and she shakes her head like she's trying to clear it.

"Right, thank you," she says. "Sorry, I'm... not quite with it yet."

"Understandable," I tell her.

I move into my room, toward the broken window on the opposite wall. A cool, humid breeze drifts past me and I shine the flashlight over the floor: glass and leaves and twigs and scattered water droplets. It's a silver maple, and an old one, judging by the size of the branch.

"What happened?" June asks, coming to stand next to me.

"Well," I start. "This tree fell through my bedroom window, and I'm glad I chose to put the bed against the other wall."

There's a moment of quiet, and I turn to find June looking at me, her eyes narrowed in the low light.

"Levi, are you being a wiseass?" she asks.

"I am," I admit. "Apologies."

"No, I like it," she says, the hint of a smile on her face. "I mean, it's — you're not usually — you know."

I don't know. I don't know and I want to ask her, but I

don't. She said she likes it and I can already tell that will keep me awake at night in the coming week, and that's enough.

"Most likely, the tree was already weak, and the storm weakened it more," I say, pointing the flashlight at the branch speared through my window. "Then finally, it fell. Silver maples only live to about a hundred and thirty. This tree could have just been old."

June bends, picks up the dustpan and broom.

"Well, it went out with a bang," she says, stepping carefully toward the window.

We clean the glass from the floor, dump it into the paper bag. June dries the water while I pull the rest of the glass from the window frame, my hand wrapped in an old towel.

Finally, it's done, excepting the tree still sticking through the window.

"What do we do about this?" June asks, reaching out and touching the bark.

"We go back to bed and wait for daylight," I tell her, watching her fingers on the branch. "I'd prefer not to use a saw when I can't see very well."

"Makes sense."

I gather the broom, the mop, the rags, the paper bag filled with glass.

"Take the cot in the office," I tell her. "I'll sleep on the couch."

"I don't mind the couch."

"June, take the cot," I repeat, already walking for the door of the bedroom.

"Levi, I don't mind the couch at all, I already took your bed—"

"I insist," I tell her from the door of my bedroom. "Good night, June. Again."

"Thank you," I hear her say as I head down the stairs.

I put the broom and mop away. I put the paper bag on the back porch so the dog can't get into it. I pull an old quilt from the closet, take off my shoes, and lay on the couch. It's slightly too short for me, but there was no way in hell I was making June sleep on the couch.

I close my eyes and try not to think. The dog comes over and lays down next to me, and I reach out, scratch her behind the ears.

I remind myself of Silas, drinking beers at my brothers' brewery, telling us how June's ex showed up at her window with a boombox, proposed, and wouldn't leave when June asked him to. I remind myself that he claimed he knew how to hide a body so well no one would ever find it, and he's probably right.

Some lines simply shouldn't be crossed. Some rules simply shouldn't be broken.

June is one of them, and I know it.

· · · ★ ★ ★ ★ ★ · · ·

I'M ALREADY AWAKE when the sun rises. I'm not sure I went back to sleep, truth be told, but sometimes it can be hard to tell.

When I flip the switch on the kitchen light, it comes on, so I pick up the phone and dial the power company, a number I've memorized by now.

It rings. I look through the window over my kitchen sink and into the back yard, bordered by forest. I wonder what happens if the road still isn't clear.

Probably, I drive her back to town the long way, up the western side of the mountain range. By the time we're there, surely the road will be clear, and I can come back home via the parkway.

But maybe she'd stay another day.

"Hello, you've reached the Blue Ridge Power Company," a bored voice says.

"Hello," I begin, standing up straight as if it'll mask how much I hate talking on the phone. "I'm calling to inquire as to whether the Appalachian Parkway has been cleared, specifically a downed tree that was near mile marker—"

"Whole thing's clear, honey," she says. "And it's a beautiful drive, so enjoy your day, all right?"

"Thank you," I say, and we hang up.

That's that, then. I pour myself a glass of water, walk to the sliding door to the back porch, and look out.

She's right. It's a beautiful day. I don't think June's awake yet, or at least, I don't hear her moving around upstairs. Her keys are on the coffee table. I write a quick note, leave it on the kitchen counter.

It's a good time for a walk.

· · · · ★ ★ ★ ★ ★ · · · ·

WHEN I COME BACK into my house, there's no sign of June. The note is where I left it. The lights are as I left them. I wonder, briefly, if she's gone, but then the ceiling over my head creaks with footsteps.

The door to the office is open, and I can see in as I come up the stairs: she's sitting on the floor, cross-legged, papers spread around her, and she's leaning over, staring at something on my laptop.

My pulse quickens, and she looks up.

"I signed in as a guest user," she says quickly, like she can read my mind.

I nod once.

"Thanks," I say. I don't think there's anything particularly salacious on my computer, but I also know that naked women have graced this screen in the past and I'd prefer June not find that.

"I got to thinking about the trees again," she says, looking up at me, pushing her hair from her face. "The vandalized ones. Well, except I don't think they were vandalized, because that doesn't make any sense because they were in the middle of nowhere and just cut down and that's not usually what people do when they vandalize something. Vandalism's for other people to see, you know? To mark territory or tell others how cool you are or make sure everyone knows that Stacy is your girl, stuff like that."

I come into the room and lean against the desk, listening.

"I did a whole series on graffiti for the Sun-Dispatch," June explains. "You know, the whole debate, is it a victimless crime, is it art, should we be prosecuting it as gang activity, does that needlessly incarcerate teens who just like writing their names on things, et cetera."

"I have a feeling this wasn't gang related," I tell her.

"You *are* a wiseass," she says, but she's smiling.

"When the situation calls for it."

"And what about this situation called for your wiseassery?" she teases, leaning back on her hands.

"Are you going to tell me what you think is going on if not vandalism?" I ask.

June's eyes drop to the papers on the floor. They're the maps from the coffee table downstairs, alongside a few atlases, a few other maps that she found in the office, and an old book on the history of the Cumberland National Forest that my mom once found at a yard sale and thought I might be interested in. I think I skimmed it once.

"It's gonna sound weird," June says.

"All right."

"You have to promise not to laugh."

"I'll promise no such thing," I tell her.

"Come on. At least don't ridicule me until I'm done?"

I shift my weight and fold my arms over myself, trying to keep from smiling. June is doing the same, but failing.

"Just tell me that you think it was aliens and get this over with," I tease, and it finally gets laughter from her.

"Okay, not *that* weird," she says. "Do you know who the Harte brothers were?"

CHAPTER SIX

JUNE

Levi goes silent and still, his gold-brown eyes staring at me, slightly narrowed. I let the silence stretch out because I'm starting to get comfortable with Levi's quietude, his thoughtfulness, and I fight the urge to fill the void with talking.

"The country band?" he finally asks.

"The outlaws," I say.

"Outlaw country?" he tries, cocking his head slightly to one side, and I grin.

"They were brigands in the early nineteenth century," I say. "I'm not sure whether they could pick a banjo or not."

"And you think they're cutting down my trees."

I raise an eyebrow at *my trees*, but I let it go.

"No, I think they've been dead for almost two hundred years and I suspect ghosts aren't very adept with chainsaws," I say. "I think someone's looking for the Harte brothers' gold."

Another long pause.

And then: "I thought that was just a myth."

"It probably is," I say. "The simplest explanation is

usually correct, you know? Either two brothers lugged a chest filled with pieces of eight a few hundred miles through the wilderness while being chased by lawmen, buried it, and then after doing all that work, drew someone at a saloon a map straight to it, or Obadiah Harte was a drunk asshole who had nothing left to lose and thought it would be funny to send people on a wild goose chase for treasure."

"But the gold doesn't have to be real for people to be looking for it," Levi says.

I point a finger-gun at him.

"Exactly," I say.

Levi pushes himself off the desk, comes to me, and sits down, his long legs stretching in front of him. His shoulder brushes mine as he does and I hold my breath for a beat, trying not to notice that it happened.

Kid sister, I think. *He just wanted your dirty mug. Kid sister.*

"You know the story, right?" I ask, pulling his computer onto my lap, tugging the ethernet cable along with it.

Yes, I said ethernet cable. He has to plug his laptop in to get on the internet. Frankly, I'm astonished that it's not dialup, though it certainly isn't fast.

"They were bank robbers?" he asks.

"They were highwaymen who held up people traveling along the Wilderness Road toward the Cumberland Gap," I say. "Mostly families who wanted to move out west, so they had everything they owned with them, and the Harte brothers would take anything they could carry. Money, jewelry, peoples' good clothes. And they seemed to have an affinity for shooting anyone who even thought about standing up to them."

"I see," Levi says.

"So, in 1825, people have had it and a federal marshal named William Gunn makes it his life's work to track these two down. They've got an advantage because they're already familiar with the area, and because believe it or not they've got a network of people willing to help them, but after a couple of years he's got them on the run, and they head north through the mountains, probably figuring that's their best chance of staying hidden."

"Was it?" Levi asks.

"It worked for a while, but eventually they had to head into a town for supplies," I say.

"This sounds familiar," he says. "One of them died, right?"

"Yup. They got into a shootout with Gunn and his men. Phineas was shot and died of infection a few days later, but Obadiah got away and rode back into the forest, where Gunn lost track of him again."

I click through the open tabs on Levi's laptop until I find the right one.

"Until two weeks later, when a dirty, skinny man walks into a roadhouse between here and Oakton, across the mountains, downs a bunch of whiskey, and starts shouting that his name is Obadiah Harte and may God strike him down if he's lying. He ends up telling a long story about being on the run and burying the gold somewhere in the forest, and he's so drunk by this point that he draws a map and gives his rapt audience directions."

I turn the computer screen toward Levi. On it is the alleged map, drawn crudely in blotchy ink on a piece of fabric, frayed at the edges.

As maps go, it's godawful: some pointy lines that are probably mountains, a shaky line, some scribbles, and a big black dot that might be the treasure or that might be a random ink stain.

"A few hours later, he stumbles back out and no one ever sees him again," I finish.

"He probably died," Levi offers, leaning in to look at the image on the screen, his chest brushing against my shoulder.

Kid sister. Kid sister. Kid sister.

"This was around 1830, so I'm fairly certain he died at some point," I say.

Levi gives me an amused sideways glance.

"And yet you keep calling me a wiseass," he says.

"He probably died of exposure somewhere in the wilderness," I say, biting back a smile. "Phineas was buried in a pauper's grave in the graveyard behind First Baptist. Every so often someone wants to dig him up for one reason or another, but it's never gone through."

"What earthly reason do they give for wanting to dig him up?"

"Mostly to confirm family lore about one of them being someone's great-great-great granddad or great uncle or something like that," I say. "Apparently people like to think that their ancestors were notorious murderers."

"They had kids?"

"They were known to visit ladies of the night."

"Ah," he says, and we go silent.

"Legend has it he also told his roadhouse audience where it was," I go on, still looking at the map. "There are conflicting accounts about it, but the general consensus is that he shoved a bag full of coins and jewelry into the hollow of an oak tree next to a big rock, within hearing distance of a waterfall, and near a stand of evergreen trees. He also claims to have planted a second oak tree at the spot, so he could find it again when he went back."

"He planted an oak tree in a forest to serve as a marker?" Levi asks. "In a forest full of oak trees?"

"Look, I didn't make the plan," I say. "No one's ever

claimed that Phineas and Obadiah were smart, just that they were vicious and greedy."

Levi reaches over me and over the maps to grab a printed picture. It's blurry and faded — clearly the printer wasn't quite up to the task — but it's good enough.

On it, there's the stump of a massive tree — R.I.P. Glenda — the trunk chopped into three-foot lengths. Next to it, two smaller trees suffered the same fate.

"Or it's aliens," I say.

"Always an option," Levi agrees, still looking at the picture. "You know, June, I think you might be onto something, but how the hell did you think of this in the first place?"

"I got really into local history when I was nine or ten," I admit. "You know, a standard ten-year-old girl interest."

"Was that the year you wore a pioneer dress for Halloween?" he asks, sliding me a glance.

Levi remembers my Halloween costume?

"Technically it was a peasant blouse from Goodwill and an old hippie skirt that my mom had, but there was a bonnet," I say.

"The bonnet's what I remember," he says. "Mainly, I remember showing up at your house because Silas and I were supposed to take you trick-or-treating, but instead your parents were furious at him for egging someone's car so I ended up going back home."

I laugh, nervousness tightening the pit of my stomach at the reminder that they used to take me trick-or-treating. If that's not a kid sister thing, I don't know what is.

"I don't know how he never dragged you down with him," I say.

"Oh, he tried," Levi says. "He tried all the time. I just never wanted any part of it."

Of course Levi was the one teenager who peer pressure never worked on.

He nods at the papers strewn across the floor.

"What next?" he asks, and I put the laptop back on the floor, then lean my elbow on my knee and my chin in my hand.

"I hadn't quite gotten that far," I admit. "I'd say we should keep track of everyone going into the forest and detain anyone with a chainsaw, but that's impossible, right?"

"I doubt that anyone going into the forest with a chainsaw is signing a trail register," he confirms.

Then he leans forward, studying a map. His knee brushes mine. I don't move a muscle.

"Logging records," he says. "If they're available, at least. They're looking for trees that were already full-grown two hundred years ago, right?"

"So we should skip anywhere that's been logged since 1830," I say.

He's silent a moment. Then he sits up, looks at me.

"You keep saying *we*," Levi says.

My heart thuds like a clumsily dropped basketball.

"Yes," I say.

He pushes himself to his feet and stands, brushing his palms together.

"This is a Forest Service problem," he says. "Strictly speaking, I shouldn't have even told you about it."

"But you already did, and I helped," I point out, still on the floor. "Listen, I can help you look up records, and go through old maps, and maybe we can take a hike and visit some of these trees—"

"No," he says, suddenly curt.

"Come on."

"June, this is *my* project, not *our* project," Levi says, his voice quiet but hard.

"Until this morning you thought this was vandalism, for Pete's sake—"

"This isn't a discussion," he says. "We're not working together."

I close my mouth and glare, angry and baffled because two minutes ago, it felt like we were working together, and now he's abruptly shutting me out of the most interesting story I've come near in months and I have no idea why.

"What the hell?" I ask, the most eloquent thing I can come up with.

Levi swallows and glances away before he answers.

"It's Forest Service business," he says, not making eye contact. "It could get dangerous. I don't know. I never should have involved you."

"In the past month the most interesting thing I've done was write a puff piece for *Aluminum Quarterly* about exciting new alloys that'll give soda drinkers a more pleasing pop top experience," I say, also getting to my feet.

We stand there for a long moment. He looks at me again, face unreadable.

"Please?" I ask.

"Sorry, June," Levi says, voice quiet but unshakeable. "Your car's in the driveway. I'm gonna go make toast and eggs. You're welcome to some if you'd like."

And with that, he leaves, walking down the stairs as I close my eyes, fighting tears of frustration.

Kid sister.

Even at twenty-nine, you're just Silas's kid sister.

"Thank you!" I force myself to call after him.

* * * * * ★ ★ ★ * * * * *

"He's always been a lovely young man," says my mom, sitting at the kitchen table, red pen in hand, reading glasses on her nose. "He used to rescue your stuffed animals from the top of the refrigerator when Silas put them there and you were too small to get them down on your own. You had quite a crush on him when you were younger."

"I never did that," Silas says, half his torso in the fridge as he hunts for something.

"It wasn't a crush," I say quickly, leaning against the kitchen counter. "He was just nice to me, that's all."

Silas pulls his head from the fridge to look at me. I ignore him.

My mom flips a paper over, skimming down it, occasionally marking something with the red pen.

"Perhaps that was it," she says diplomatically. "In any case, good thing he came along when he did. You should take him something nice in thanks. What about those cookies you used to bake?"

I imagine myself showing up at Levi's door, a plate of saran-wrapped cookies in hand. In this particular imagining I'm also wearing a poodle skirt and my hair is in victory rolls for some reason, but anxiety still swirls in my chest.

"I haven't baked for a while," I tell her.

"It's just like riding a bicycle," she says, still grading papers. "Besides, all you do is follow a recipe."

"I'll see," I say, as the microwave beeps and I pull out a bowl of leftover chili.

I'm lying. I'm not bringing Levi cookies. I'm still put out about this morning.

Are you mad about the project, or disappointed that Levi doesn't want to spend time with you?

Why not both?

"Silas, the refrigerator isn't meant for cooling the indoors," my mom says, and he sighs.

"Where'd the mashed potatoes go?" he asks.

"I ate them," she says.

"Mom!"

"I made them, I get to eat them if I want," she says, not looking up from grading papers once. Silas makes a grumpy face, but doesn't say anything.

"June, there's a bottle of your father's pizzazz sauce on the door if you'd like some for the chili," my mom says. "And I think there's still some of his butt burner if you want to go ahead and use that up."

I make a face, because *your father's pizzazz sauce* is a phrase I could happily go a lifetime without hearing, and that goes double for *your father's butt burner*. He's turned to making hot sauces in his retirement, because everyone needs a hobby, I guess.

"Thanks," I say, and Silas hands me a bottle of unmarked bright red liquid from the fridge. I'm not sure whether it's pizzazz or butt burner, but I like to live dangerously sometimes.

The floorboard just outside the dining room creaks, and a second later, I hear my father's voice.

"Let me know how that one is," he says, coming into the room. "I tweaked the recipe slightly from the last batch but I'm not sure that this round of serranos really hit their full potential. I might have had them too close to the bell peppers and I think they got cross-pollinated."

"So it's not that spicy?" I ask, tilting the bottle.

"Nah," he says. "It's too bad that my habaneros didn't take this year, I think I shouldn't have put them down in the shady corner closer to the house, they didn't get enough sunlight…"

Silas finally pulls a container from the fridge as I splash hot sauce on my chili.

"Butt burner," he murmurs, quiet enough that only I can hear.

"Stop it," I say.

"Buuuuuuutt burner."

"I have to eat this."

"Have fun eating butt burner," he grins, and I clamp my lips together so I don't laugh.

He takes meatloaf out of the container, puts it on a plate, licks one finger.

"Did you come here just so you wouldn't have to make lunch?" I ask. "Or did you also bring laundry?"

"I haven't brought laundry home in years, thank you," he says, snapping the lid back on.

Then he pauses, drums his fingers on it, and I have a feeling I know what's coming.

"You spent the night with Levi?" he asks, voice still low enough that my parents can't hear it over their conversation.

I roll my eyes at him.

"I spent the night *at Levi's house*, and if you're about to give me any of your bullshit about it—"

"It wasn't bullshit when you called me to come talk to Brett last month," he says.

I take a deep breath, because he kind of has a point.

"Brett was pointing a boombox at my window and refusing to take no for an answer," I point out. "Levi is your very own best friend who was a total gentleman about helping me out of a jam."

"A *total* gentleman?" Silas asks.

"Yes," I say.

I don't say, *even though I'm not sure I wanted him to be.*

"You don't trust your own best friend?" I point out, eating a mouthful of chili.

"I believe in trust but verify," he says. "And for the record, no, I can't imagine Levi being anything but a gentleman. I don't know that I've ever even seen him hit on someone."

I take another bite of chili, my mouth already on fire because the butt-burner is hotter than I expected.

"Does he date much?" I ask casually.

So very, very casually.

Silas just shrugs and puts his meatloaf in the microwave. On the other end of the kitchen, my parents are discussing gardening.

"He's had girlfriends before, nothing serious that I know of," he says. "Why?"

"Just curious," I say. "He seems like a catch."

That gets a frown.

"What?" I say, defensively. "He's a nice person, he's smart, he's interesting, he rescues stranded motorists—"

"Sure, he's a good catch for someone else," Silas says, still watching me.

"Yes, obviously," I say. "Objectively, Levi is a catch. Not for me, of course."

"Of course."

"That would be super weird," I say, shoving more chili into my mouth. It's way hotter than I meant for it to be, but at least I can blame my red face on the spice level, not on our discussion of Levi, who is absolutely a catch.

"June, come sit down," my mom calls. "Don't eat standing up, it's bad for your digestion."

I wave my spoon at Silas and head over to where my parents are sitting, grateful for the rescue.

CHAPTER SEVEN

LEVI

I frown, grabbing an armful of branches and tossing them into the wheelbarrow.

"Your funding is in trouble because of something you didn't say on a panel?" I ask, still trying to get this straight.

Next to me, Caleb just sighs.

"Pretty much," he admits. "We were talking about the time-evolution operator, and someone in the audience asked a question about the self-adjoint—"

I clear my throat, and Caleb half-smiles.

"—about complicated math stuff, and so I mentioned a paper I'd recently read that discussed the problem."

He unloads an armful of branches into the wheelbarrow.

"Except I only named two of the three authors, Prinszca and Yang, and of course Jean Lorien, the one I forgot to mention, is currently an adjunct in my department and has a chip on his shoulder the size of Mars," my youngest brother says.

"Who spread a rumor that your upcoming publication

wasn't entirely original work, and now it might not be published, and that puts your funding in danger," I finish.

"Yep," Caleb says grimly. "You can see why I'm not exactly stoked to spend much time on campus these days, right?"

It's Sunday afternoon and we're outside my mom's house, clearing brush that fell during Friday night's storm. Sunday dinner is a longstanding tradition for us, and we've done it for as long as I can remember.

It's also a longstanding tradition that we be put to work at some point during the gathering. Eli's inside, cooking, Seth is playing a game of Mouse Trap with our niece Rusty, and I'm sure Daniel's making himself useful somehow.

"I've been thinking of leaving academia," Caleb says. He's standing with his arms crossed, looking out at my mom's backyard, the big old farmhouse surrounded by forest. "If this is how it's gonna be, you know? I knew there would be a lot of backstabbing and bullshit, but I really thought I could keep my head down and just do the work."

"You know the joke about this, right?" I ask.

"The politics are so vicious because the stakes are so low?" he says. "I dunno. They feel pretty high to me right now."

"I didn't mean to suggest otherwise," I say.

"Oh, I know," Caleb says, pulling his hair from its knot and sticking the tie between his teeth as he rakes through it with both hands. "I just feel like I've given my life to this. It's all I've really wanted to do. I like the research. I like the teaching. Hell, I even liked the section of remedial trigonometry and algebra I got stuck with two years ago, and I was only teaching that because the temporary department head hated me."

I almost say *June's having almost the same problem* right now, but I don't because I don't want to share it with anyone. So instead, I say nothing.

"There are other jobs in the world," he says. "I don't know what they are, but I know they exist."

"Technically," Caleb admits. "I'm still good to spend next weekend at your place, right? I've got a chapter to finish."

The back door to the house slides open just then and Silas steps through, beer in hand. We haven't bothered inviting him in years, we just know he'll show up if he's in town, which he usually is.

Caleb waves. After a split second I wave as well even as a knot ties itself in my stomach.

"Your mom sent me out to help, but it looks like you're done," he calls.

"Perfect timing, then," I call back as he comes up to us. "This is the last of it."

"I don't think I've ever come here and not been given a task," he says when he reaches us. "She even asked me to clean the gutters once."

"Did you?" Caleb asks.

"Of course I did," Silas says. "I wouldn't dare refuse Clarabelle Loveless."

"I've done it," I offer. "Multiple times."

"You're her child, she'll forgive you," he points out. "I'm just some extra kid who wandered in off the street."

"You didn't wander," I say.

"Speaking of being taken in and cared for, thanks for rescuing June," he says. "Your clothes are in the trunk of my car, plus my parents sent over a veggie basket from the garden in gratitude for saving her life."

There it is. He knows.

It wasn't a secret, I remind myself. *It was perfectly chaste, above board, platonic.*

I snort and grab the handles of the wheelbarrow.

"I didn't save her life," I say. "I made her night less miserable. She'd have survived just fine in the car."

"Take the veggie basket anyway," he says.

I haven't looked at Caleb during this exchange, but I swear I can *feel* the look on his face: surprised, skeptical, amused, curious, and I want no part of it right now.

"You rescued June?" he asks as I lift the wheelbarrow and roll it back.

"During that thunderstorm Friday," Silas says. "It was very heroic, to hear her tell it. She's here too, by the way."

It was? She is?

"You can tell the story," I say, turning away from them with the wheelbarrow. "I'm gonna go put this on the wood-pile. Be right back."

"Tell me about the heroics," Caleb says as I walk away, finally breathing.

There are a million thoughts clashing through my head right now, about Silas and June and betrayal and maybe getting punched in the face, about what I'm going to say to her when I get back inside, but one is loudest.

June called me heroic?

· · · ★ ★ ★ ★ ★ · · ·

I LEAN my forearms against the railing and look out at the driveway, a glass of iced tea in my hand, and I take a deep breath.

I'm not a people person. Given the choice, I prefer solitude. I prefer quiet. Large groups make me feel claustrophobic, like there's no space in my head for my own thoughts when I'm constantly listening to everyone else's. Even when it's my own family, I feel that way after a while.

Also, I'm hiding from Rusty. I love her to death, but I need a break sometimes.

Just as I'm watching a squirrel chase another one up a tree, the front door opens. Inwardly, I brace myself.

And then June's voice says, "There you are."

I turn to look at her, wearing shorts and a t-shirt, hair pulled back in a dark knot against the hot late-August day.

Pretty. So pretty I forget how to speak for a moment.

"Close the door behind yourself, I don't want anyone else finding me," I say, and it's the wrong thing.

"Oh, sorry," she says, and steps back toward the door.

"I don't mean you," I say. "Stay."

She shuts the door, walks over to me.

"Hiding from anyone in particular?" she asks, leaning on the railing next to me.

"Rusty," I admit, and June laughs. "She wants me to play a fifth game of Parcheesi and I'm completely Parcheesi'd out."

June laughs.

"Not the answer I was expecting," she says.

"What were you expecting?"

"Well, now I don't want to say," she says. "I'll just feel like an asshole."

I glance over at her. She glances back.

"Silas," she says.

"Ah," I say, my voice perfectly neutral.

"He seems to believe that sisters should be locked inside a house until they're wed, virginity intact, to a male of their brother's choosing," she says. "Or, I don't know, sent to a convent or something."

"You're not even Catholic," I point out.

"He'd probably send me to a Satanist nunnery if it meant I could never date again," she says, annoyed, though it's clearly not with me.

We're quiet for a moment. Part of me wants to defend Silas, say he's not that bad, that he's just a protective older brother, but I doubt she wants to hear it.

"Though you'd think Satanist convents would just be nonstop gangbangs, since chastity is a virtue and all that, right?"

She looks over at me, contemplative, as if I might possibly have something to say about a Satanist convent.

"Yes?" I agree.

June laughs.

"I can't say I know much about what moral values a Satanist convent might espouse," I go on.

"Sorry," she says. "He gets on my nerves sometimes. That's not why I was looking for you, though."

My pulse skips.

"You were looking for me?"

June turns, leans her back against the railing, her elbows on either side of her, and she cocks her head slightly.

"I found logging records for most of the National Forest," she says.

"And why on earth would you do that?" I ask dryly.

"Or, at least, most of the records for the land that's now National Forest, since it wasn't established until 1936. When the Silverton Lumber Company went out of business in the 80s, they donated all their old documents to the Historical Society, who've been working on digitizing them."

She says this like it's a piece of fun trivia.

"You went through all that trouble for something that's not your problem?" I ask her, keeping my voice low.

"Give me a map and a couple of days, and I'll have a good idea of which areas haven't been logged since the 1820s," she says.

"June," I say, and the front door opens.

Silas steps out. He looks left, then right, like he's looking for someone else, and then he comes over to where June and I are standing.

I don't move, but I'd be lying if I said that knot didn't tighten in my gut.

"How many times can a child play Parcheesi?" he asks, his voice low.

"Dozens," I say. "Hundreds."

He looks over his shoulder, like he's checking that Rusty hasn't followed him out.

"She has to be cheating, right? She kicked my ass four times in a row."

"I can't be that hard," June says.

"You wanna play me? Bring it," Silas says.

"I meant cheating can't be that hard, pea brain."

"If she's cheating, I didn't catch her," I offer.

"Can you even cheat at Parcheesi?" Silas asks.

"You can cheat at anything," says June.

Silas takes a deep breath, closes his eyes, lets it out slowly, opens them again.

"What are you two doing out here?" he asks, changing the subject.

"Talking," June says, and at the exact same time I say, "Also hiding from Rusty."

We look at each other.

"Should I be defending my sister's virtue?" Silas says, with a grin that's definitely intended to annoy June.

"Silas, why on earth do you think I've got any virtue left for you to defend?" June asks, sounding faux-astonished. "Didn't I ever tell you about my orgy phase?"

"No," says Silas, pinching the bridge of his nose and closing his eyes.

"Oh, it was during college," June says brightly. "For a

while I was dating this guy who just could *not* get off unless there were at least—"

"Okay, I'm sorry," Silas says, eyes still closed.

"—seven people of any gender in the same room, and at least three of them had to be—"

"*So* sorry," he says.

"—you know, *doing it* with their hands or mouths or butts or whatever—"

June helpfully demonstrates this by making a ring with her left thumb and pointer finger, then poking her right pointer finger through repeatedly.

"Okay."

"—And since we were dating, usually I was in there *doing*, I don't know, like five people at once—"

"*Okay.*"

"—Sometimes more, it's so hard to keep track, there's just so many holes—"

"You win!" Silas says, holding up both hands. "Okay. You win, I'm sorry, I'm going to go lose at Parcheesi a million more times."

He's already walking back across the porch, and just as he opens the door, June calls out, "Orgy!" and Silas flips her off, then disappears.

"Dick," she mutters under her breath, then looks up at me. I'm still trying not to laugh. "Sorry about him," she says.

"I think you handled that perfectly," I say.

"He's always been a total pain in the ass about the guys I date but this whole Brett thing made him extra bonkers," she says, rolling her eyes. "I don't know where he gets it from. I mean, my dad is a perfectly reasonable human being about the men in my life, and then here comes Silas to get all caveman about it."

I've got an inkling, but I don't say anything. If Silas ever wants to share, that's his prerogative.

"And I've never actually been to an orgy, just for the record," she says, looking up at me.

I swear her cheeks turn faintly pink, but it could be my imagination. A trick of the light. Anything.

"Really?" I deadpan, and June grins, looks away.

"I did get invited to one once," she says. "I think it was just out of politeness, though."

That sends a hitch through my train of thought, a quick ripple. I could tell she was joking before, just to get Silas's goat, but the admission that she was invited is… different.

Different in that, for a split second, I can't help but imagine her naked, gasping, her cheeks flushed, her eyes unfocused.

One split second, I swear. Then it's gone.

"Do orgies normally extend invitations out of politeness?" I ask.

"That I don't know," June says. "I did consider going. Briefly. It would have been a good story. Anyway, logging records."

"You're changing the subject from orgies to logging records?" I say. "That's quite a switch."

"I'm pretty much scraping the bottom of the barrel of my knowledge about orgies," she says. "Unless you've got something to share."

"Can't say I do," I admit. "But we don't have to talk about logging records either, because we're not working together, the end."

"We don't have to work together," she says, raising her eyebrows. "I'm just telling you about an interesting story I'm chasing down."

I fold my arms over my chest, watch her face.

"It's a tale of lost treasure, chainsaws, and seeking justice for a murdered champion red oak tree," she goes on.

"Northern red oak," I correct.

"Well, that's the kind of detail I'd be more likely to get right if you were interested in working together," June says. "Otherwise, I might really fuck it up and call Glenda a maple."

I raise one eyebrow.

"June, is that a threat?" I ask.

"If it were, would it work?"

"No," I say, arms still folded. I glance at the door where Silas disappeared. "It's none of your business. It's a few trees, cut down in the middle of nowhere for no reason whatsoever, either vandalism or a stupid treasure hunt—"

"*Your* trees," she says.

"They're not my trees," I say. "They're everyone's trees."

"You called them your trees earlier," June points out, her voice softening.

I want to say yes. I do. Desperately. I want to give in because it means time with June, going through maps and logging records and God knows what else while we sit around and talk and drink hot cocoa and she badgers me about naming my dog.

That's what I found out Friday night, and suddenly, standing here on my mom's front porch, it hits me with a crash. I always knew she was knock-me-over-with-a-feather pretty, but I like her. I like talking to her. I like being near her and hearing her laugh and more than that, I like being the cause of it.

Besides, she might have figured out the motive behind Girthy Glenda's murder.

June is studying my face, eyes intent. She takes a step forward.

"Please?" she says, her voice low.

"You're the most persistent human I've ever encountered," I say.

June just grins. I have to look away, over the gravel driveway, and I contemplate the dumb thing I'm about to do.

"Can you keep a secret?" I finally ask.

"Of course," she says. "I swear I won't tell anyone—"

"Not anyone," I say, and hesitate for just a moment because I'm afraid that I'm about to show my entire hand, give away that I've thought of June every three-point-four seconds since she moved back to town.

"Silas," I finish.

"Ah," she says, and nods as if my reasons are perfectly clear.

I hope they're not.

"I don't see any reason for him to know that we're working on something together," I say. "I think it's better for us, and our friendship, if he just doesn't know."

"Agreed," she says, simply. "I'd prefer not to be quizzed daily on our interactions."

There it is. That simple.

Before either of us can say anything else, the front door opens.

I tense, but it's not Silas.

"DESSERT!!!" screams Rusty, as if we're half a mile away, then goes back inside before we can answer.

"We'll strategize later," I tell June. "Pie is important."

"Yes, it is," she agrees, and we head inside.

CHAPTER EIGHT

JUNE

A s usual, the moment I walk into the library I get distracted by the New Releases shelf. I'm kind of helpless against books in general, and there's just something so wonderful and shiny about *New Releases*.

Maybe a favorite author has a new book. Maybe there's someone amazing I've never even heard of before, or someone with whom I've got a passing familiarity who finally writes the book I can't resist, or someone whose name I heard once but who I've been meaning to read.

Plus, it's *free*. The library has always been one of my favorite places on earth, because not only are they filled with books, you can read *all of them*. For *free*.

I'm reading the back-cover copy of a book called *The Splintered Crown*, a dramatized historical novel about Mary, Queen of Scots, when someone comes up behind me.

"That one's okay," Charlie says, grabbing another book off the shelf and glancing at the back. "Though it had a *lot* of really detailed descriptions of Scottish weather. It's raining, it's cold, I get it, you know?"

Her curly hair is piled on top of her head, the sapphire

on her left ring finger glinting even though she's wearing coveralls right now.

"I don't even know why I'm looking at books," I say, sliding it back into place and scanning the shelves. "I've got three on my nightstand and a stack of I don't even know how many on the floor next to it, and yet I'm standing here, looking for more."

"It's not hoarding if it's books," Charlie says. "Then it's knowledge collection, and *that* makes you fancy. Hi there. That many?"

That last part isn't directed at me. It's directed at a large stack of books topped by a pair of eyes and a curly mane, about four feet off the ground. The stack totters slightly.

"Yes," the stack confirms.

"Can you carry that many?" Charlie asks. "You know the rule."

"Of course I can carry them, I already am," Rusty says, making it sound like the most obvious thing in the world.

"All the way to the car?"

"*Yes,*" Rusty says, even as the stack sways and she nearly goes with it.

Charlie gives me a look that's half exasperated, half entertained. It's a pretty frequent emotion for adults to have in Rusty's presence, particularly for Charlie, Rusty's step-mom-to-be.

"I gotta get her to her piano lesson and leave enough time to pick books up off the sidewalk," Charlie says. "See you around! Rusty, you can't even see over those."

"Yes I *can*," Rusty's voice says.

"Bye!" I call, and Charlie waves.

I adjust my backpack on my shoulders and grab another book off the shelf. According to the back, it's got elves and orcs and epic battles, and I put it back. Not my jam.

"Oh hey, Levi," Charlie's voice says.

"Hello," Levi answers.

I freeze, my hand still on the elves/orcs/battles book, because us working together hinged on no one finding out what we were doing and here, on our very first meeting, Charlie's already seen us in the same place.

I am *bad* at this.

"June's over there if you're looking for her," Rusty says, and Charlie laughs.

She laughs slightly too hard and I make a face at the book spines in front of me, still frozen in place.

Levi clears his throat.

"Oh," he says. "Is she?"

"Yes," Rusty's voice says. "Though my dad said I shouldn't bother you about her because you've got to figure it out on your—"

"Hey, okay, let's get these books to the car so you're not late to your piano lesson!" Charlie says, cutting Rusty off. "I know it's fun to see Uncle Levi but we've gotta jet, kiddo! Later, Levi."

Figure what out?

"Bye!" shouts Rusty.

"Bye," says Levi, and I finally take my hand off the book.

Figure what out on his own? Why was Daniel talking to Rusty about Levi and me?

Does literally everyone in town already know about this project somehow?

There are footsteps behind me, and then Levi's voice.

"I heard you were over here," he says.

"Ta da," I say. "It's me!"

I admit to being slightly rattled right now.

"It's good that you're here, actually," he says, stepping

up next to me and also scanning the new releases. "I realized I haven't a clue where the microfiche readers are."

He pulls a book off the shelf and peruses it thoughtfully. I take a second and sneak a peek at him, because peeking at Levi is always a good idea.

He's got on gray pants and a blue-and-green plaid shirt, the sleeves rolled up to his elbows, a messenger bag over one shoulder. The shirt fits well. The pants fit *very* well. The muscles in his forearms flex as he flips the book over and puts it back, and I quickly look back at my section of the bookshelf.

"You know where the bathroom by the reference desk is?"

"I do."

"If you go down the weird hallway to the left, past the nonfiction audiobooks, at the end there's a spiral staircase that goes into the basement," I say. "They're down there with all the local history stuff."

The library building was originally a hospital, and some of the layout is still weird.

"Ah. I'd have never found that."

"That's what reference librarians are for," I say.

I pause. I pull a random book off the shelf, pretend to look at it, and then glance over at him.

"Did I just get us busted?" I ask, still nervous.

Levi glances over his shoulder at the front door of the library, where Charlie and Rusty disappeared.

"I doubt it," he says. "Two people being at the same library is hardly gossip-worthy."

I snort. Levi frowns.

"I may have been gone for a couple years, but I do know that *everything* here is gossip-worthy," I say. "Someone's got new shoes? Gossip. Nod at someone on the street?

Gossip. God forbid you exchange words or get coffee with a friend or accept a ride from a member of the opposite sex."

"What if you sneak into the microfiche room together?" he asks.

"I'm not willing to take that risk," I say. "I'll go first. You wait five minutes and then follow. Take evasive maneuvers if necessary."

"Got it," he says, glancing at me sideways. "Godspeed, June."

He's got that half-smile on his face, the one that hitches one side of his mouth a little higher than the other.

"Thanks," I say, and turn away from the New Releases shelf. "See you in there."

· · · ★ ★ ★ ★ ★ · · ·

OUR TOP-SECRET, very sneaky plan goes off without a hitch and seven minutes later, Levi and I are in the library basement, sitting in front of the microfiche readers.

The whole library smells like books, of course, but this room *really* smells like books. Behind us are five rows of wooden library shelves, all jammed full of local history — Sprucevale, the Cumberland Valley, the Appalachians, Virginia in general — and to look at them, I'd guess that most books were printed before 1950.

Along the other wall there are narrow, high windows that let in as much daylight as they can, a few armchairs underneath them. The rest of the lighting is warm, comforting, soothing. Above all, the Sprucevale public library is cozy.

And we've got the basement all to ourselves. Old, *very* dry books about the lives of the early Sprucevale settlers aren't the most popular of reading materials.

"I have a confession," Levi says, looking over the machine.

I'm standing in front of the microfiche cabinets that line the wall, looking like a cross between a card catalog and a filing cabinet.

"You've never used a microfiche reader before and don't even know how to turn it on?" I ask.

"Is it that obvious?" he says.

I pull open the drawer marked *Sa-Sil* and pull out a stack of microfiche about an inch thick. There's more — way more — but we're not going to get to those today.

"Using a microfiche reader is a dying art," I say, and take my seat next to him, plopping the microfiche on the table between us. "Step one, the switch is on the side."

He looks around, finds it, flips it, and the big black screen glows dark blue. I slide the first sheet of fiche from its paper envelope and hold it carefully.

"See that glass plate below the screen?" I say, pointing. "Flip it up."

Levi just looks, frowning.

"Here," I say, and reach in front of him. When I do, my shoulder brushes his arm.

"Ah," he says as I flip it up, slide the fiche underneath, close it again and the logging records flash bright on the screen: row after row of notations in thick cursive.

I show him how to rotate the screen, how to zoom in and out, how to move it around, how to focus the reader.

His hands keep brushing mine. Our shoulders touch. His face is close to mine, maybe too close, and I keep my eyes locked on the microfiche screen while I show him how to use it.

Again and again, I wonder about what Rusty said. Figure what out on his own?

"That's pretty much it," I say, adjusting it one more time. "It's not hard, they're just a little fiddly."

"Why do you know all this?" he asks, eyes on the screen as he twists dials, moves the plate around. "I've never used one before."

"I worked in the library during college," I say, taking another slide from its envelope and switching on my own reader. "More and more stuff is digital, but every so often we'd get someone who needed to use one of these things, so all the student workers had to learn."

"I see," Levi says, and leans in toward the reader.

· · · ★ ★ ★ ★ ★ · · ·

WE LOOK at microfiche for two and a half hours. Most of the records are written and simply denote an area that was logged, places like Pine Deep or Boxfir Canyon or Deerlick Run. Sometimes there's a map, but they can be even more indecipherable than the written record.

It works like this: once we decipher a record, we mark that area on the map in colored pencil. There's some guess-work involved, obviously. The records are missing for some years. At one point, there was a fire, and we're missing a full decade of logging records.

But the idea is that once we're finished here, the areas that aren't shaded are the areas that haven't been logged since 1820 or so. Meaning they're the areas with trees old enough for the treasure to be hidden in.

"June, I've got a growing suspicion," Levi says. He's behind me, leaning over the scarred wooden table that our map is on.

"Go on," I say, adjusting the focus on my reader. It doesn't help the bad handwriting.

"I've got a feeling that the tree hiding the gold was

logged long ago," he says. "Some lucky lumberjack probably found himself a fortune and never told a soul."

"Now we just need to tell the vandals that and maybe they'll stop cutting down your trees," I say.

"*Our* trees," Levi corrects, and I laugh.

"They're much more yours than mine," I tell him.

I make a note, move to the next page on my microfiche. My eyes are starting to cross, but the library's only open for fifteen more minutes, so I may as well make the most of our time here.

The only problem is that I'm pretty sure the next entry is nonsense.

I lean in toward the reader, my nose practically touching the screen. I lean back. I adjust the focus, tilt my head, trying looking through just one eye, but no luck. The area logged is a word I've never seen before.

"Hey, can you read this?" I ask Levi.

He comes over and stands behind me, his hands on the back of my chair. I point at the gobbledygook on the screen.

"I think that might be a W or something," I say as he leans in.

And leans in. His knuckles touch my shoulder blades. I'm staring at the screen determinedly, but he shifts and then suddenly, he's right there, his face hovering over my shoulder. He's so close that I can feel his beard against my hair.

If I turned my head right now, I'd kiss him, I think.

I do not turn my head. I don't move. I don't even breathe. I've already learned one lesson about reading Levi's actions wrong, about thinking that we're having a moment when he's just being a gentleman.

I'm not used to gentlemen. I'm used to guys. Guys who text *hey, wanna watch a movie at my place* and think it counts as a date. Guys who think nothing of flaking on our plans at the last minute.

Levi points at the screen.

"I think it's two words," he says, his low voice close to my ear. A shiver runs through me. I swallow hard. "Is that an M?"

"It looks more like an H," I offer, still not daring to move a muscle.

"Hmm," he says.

He moves back, stands upright, pulls his chair up next to mine, his right hand never leaving the back of my chair. I breathe again, and then he sits next to me, leans in again. His forearm is against my upper back.

We're both quiet for a long moment, studying the screen. Or, at least, I think Levi is studying it. I'm staring at it, repeating *kid sister, kid sister, kid sister* to myself.

"Homestead," he suddenly says. "The second word is homestead."

I lean toward the screen.

"I think you're right," I say.

"Morgan Homestead. That's the first word. Morgan."

"Where's that?" I ask.

Of all the areas I've been noting down, this is a new one and at this point, I've gone through almost sixty years of records.

"I'm not sure," he muses. He's still close.

So, so close.

"What year are these?"

"1927," I say.

"Then probably in the northern part, near Staunton," he says, and finally he relaxes, pulls back, though his arm stays behind my back.

I finally look over at him, wait for an explanation. I'm getting used to his silences. I'm even using them myself.

"I'm afraid it's sordid," he says. "Back in 1925, there was a plan to make that part of the forest part of Shenandoah National Park instead of a national forest."

His eyes search my face. My heart hammers, so loud in the quiet library that I'm afraid he can hear it.t

"And the federal government used eminent domain laws to remove several hundred people from their homes to make way for the park," Levi says. "Some of them by force."

"They did?" I say, and Levi shrugs, glances at the screen again.

"It's not really well-known," he says. "Especially since the land never became part of the park, the forest service hasn't exactly wanted to publicize it."

"That's fucked up," I say, and then his eyes are back on my face.

"It is," he says. "Anyway, I'm betting Morgan Homestead is somewhere up there."

"Which at least removes it from our purview, it being over a hundred miles and all," I say.

"That it does."

There's a break, a pause. Silence. We're still looking at each other, his arm slung around the back of my chair, his bare forearm touching my shirt.

I listen to the silence. Instead of opening my mouth and talking over it, I pay attention: the whoosh of the air conditioning, the low hum of the microfiche readers. My own heartbeat, thundering through my body.

For once, Levi breaks the silence.

"You're thinking something," he says, voice low, quiet, perfectly library-appropriate even though we're alone in this basement.

"I'm wondering what other sordid secrets you're keeping," I say, my voice matching his.

"That wasn't a secret," he says. "It's public knowledge if you know where to look."

"Then what other public knowledge are you hiding that I don't know?" I ask.

What do you have to figure out on your own, Levi?

"If I'm hiding anything it's unintentional," he says.

For one moment, his eyes flick to my lips. My heart pumps that much harder.

"I've already learned that trying to keep information from you is a fool's errand, June."

"I'll take that as a compliment."

"Good. That's what it was," he says.

He's closer now. I don't know how it happened, but it has. My whole body is tense, strung tighter than a banjo, and I'm leaning in, toward. I didn't mean to do it, but it's happened and I am breathless with it.

Kid sister, I think. *I'm reading this wrong again. I have to be.*

"June," Levi says, his voice barely above a whisper. "I lied."

"About what?"

"That I don't have a secret," he goes on. "I'm afraid I do."

I wait. I watch him, and I listen, and my heart hammers away in my chest. My knee is warm, and I suddenly realize that Levi's hand is there, his heat soaking through the jeans I'm wearing. I don't know how long he's been touching me. I don't know how I didn't notice.

"Aren't you going to ask what it is?" he says, half-smiling.

He looks at my lips again, a split second.

I think I know the secret, and I'm also certain I must be wrong.

"What's your secret, Levi?" I ask.

"June," he says. "I've become—"

There's a clatter from the spiral stairs. A racket. A ruckus.

I nearly have a heart attack and my state doesn't improve as a pair of high heels is quickly followed by legs, then the entirety of a woman stomping down the metal staircase so loudly she must be trying to raise the dead.

She comes down just far enough to see us, bending over and peering through the balustrade.

"Library's closing in five minutes," she calls.

"Thank you," Levi calls, somehow still calm as a cucumber.

I, on the other hand, am rattled as fuck.

She stomps back upstairs and I close my eyes, willing my pulse to even out.

Levi's hand is off my knee and we look at each other, again, but whatever happened is over.

"I didn't realize it was that late," I say.

"Neither did I," he says, and stands. He puts his chair back. I take the microfiche from my reader, slide it into its envelope.

Levi holds his hand out to me. For a split second I nearly take it, and then I remember. I hand him the microfiche, and he smiles.

"I was looking to help you up," he says.

"Ah," I say, and put my hand in his.

He pulls me up. Together, we put our things away, pack our maps, leave the room. We leave the library through the back door, into the parking lot.

"When next?" he asks, walking me to my car even though it's twenty feet away.

"For this?" I ask, unnecessarily. "What are you doing tomorrow night?"

"Going through microfiche logging records," he says, smiling. "See you here, June."

With that, he smiles, nods, and walks away and I get into my own car, my mind swirling.

I can't have misread that, I tell myself. *That's impossible.*

I close my eyes, lean against the headrest.

Unless I did.

I give myself a few minutes before I finally start my car and drive back to my parents' house.

· · · · ★ ★ ★ ★ · · · ·

A WEEK GOES BY, Thursday to Thursday. Most days I meet Levi in the basement of the library and we put the puzzle together, piece by piece.

In the meantime, he puts a bulletin out, telling forest rangers to watch for anyone with a chainsaw, just in case they weren't already. He posts rangers around the wilderness areas we think the vandals might be likely to look. He puts out a call for hikers to report any freshly felled trees they might find.

And nothing else happens. There's not another hand on my knee. He doesn't offer to tell me a secret again, doesn't put his arm around me. Proof that I read it wrong, somehow, that my childhood crush has rattled my brain and muddied my thinking where Levi is concerned.

Kid. Sister.

Then, a week after our first library meeting, he calls me before I've even gotten out of bed.

"There's been another one," he says, his voice grim.

CHAPTER NINE

LEVI

"Was this one a champion?" June asks, rifling through her backpack in the passenger seat.

"She wasn't," I say, one elbow on my open window, watching the car in front of me. It's one of the last Fridays of summer before school starts again, and that means tourists on the Parkway.

Lots of tourists. Millions of tourists, driving at mediocre speeds, slamming on their brakes before every curve, slowing to look at spectacular views instead of pulling over at the viewpoints that the Forest Service has so generously provided them with.

"It was old, though," she says, then looks at me for confirmation.

"It was," I say.

"Do you know how old?" she asks, squirting sunscreen into her palm.

"I don't," I tell her, navigating another curve behind the world's slowest sedan. "It was reported by a couple of backpackers who found it looking for a good place to set up camp a few nights ago. Good thing they read national forest bulletins, I guess."

The sedan slows, so I slow as well, downshifting as I glare at the car.

"Same M.O. as the others? Trunk chopped into pieces?"

"Sounds like this time they hacked up the roots as well and dug under it a little," I say.

June pulls down the visor, and then sighs. Probably because there's no mirror.

"Sorry," I say, stealing a glance at her.

"Just tell me if I've got extra on my face," she says, already rubbing in the sunscreen.

It's been a week and a day. Or a week and twelve hours; it was nine o'clock at night when I nearly told her the secret I've been denying to myself, when I nearly kissed her, when I nearly crossed that uncrossable line.

Thank God for the librarian who came at exactly the right time.

Really. I'm glad. June is a bridge I cannot cross, a road I cannot drive down. I can't betray Silas like that.

Not when he's the most intensely loyal, brave human I've ever come across, ever since the day we met in first grade because he beat up the third grader who stole my lunch.

He didn't even know me at the time. Silas was already cool, already popular, already the king of the playground, and all he saw was a short, skinny kid get his lunch stolen.

In return, I taught him how to stay out of trouble. Please note: I didn't teach him to stop getting into fights or to obey the teachers.

I taught him not to get caught.

After a few years he'd gotten smarter and I'd finally hit a growth spurt, but we were already fast friends and somehow, it stuck through middle school, through high school, through the football team and my father's accident, through me leaving for college and Silas heading to Afghanistan.

My point is, I don't take my bond with Silas lightly.

My point is also that whatever I think of June, I'd best not act on it. She may be funny and smart, she may be relentless and curious and sharp as a tack, and she may be so pretty that it makes me lightheaded to look directly at her, but she's my best friend's little sister.

Plus, she's leaving again soon. She told me earlier this week, alone in the microfiche room, that she's applied for ninety-seven jobs since getting laid off.

Ninety-seven. There's no way she doesn't get offered at least one.

The problem isn't that I'm afraid of Silas. The problem isn't that I don't want June.

The problem is that anything between us would inevitably be over far too soon. Weeks? Months? I've got no way of knowing when June might suddenly get a better opportunity and move away, leaving me behind, broken hearted.

I'm not a quick fling guy. I'm not built that way, for brief, physical relationships. I'm not my brother Seth. I don't just want June, I want *her.*

And even if I were, I couldn't jeopardize my relationship with Silas for something over in a few months.

If June were staying, I'd do it. If I thought that we could have something real, something deep, if I thought that we could be more than ships passing in the night, I would go for it without looking back.

But that's not reality. This is reality, and I've weighed my options and chosen the only rational one.

"Am I good?" June asks, turning toward me. I wait for

the road to straighten out, and I look over at her, inspecting her face that still takes my breath away.

"There's a streak on your nose," I tell her, and she rubs it in.

"Thanks," she says. "All right, I'm officially ready to visit a tree crime scene and catch some tree murderers."

I can't help but smile.

· · · ★ ★ ★ ★ ★ · · ·

"How much further is it?" June asks, holding her water bottle to her lips.

I look at the map, considering.

"Not far," I tell her, because distances can be tricky on trails. "We're almost—"

"Do *not* tell me we're almost there, I'll have an aneurysm," June declares.

I lower the map and look over at her.

"Every time I go on a trail run with Silas, he tells me we're 'almost there' when we've still got like two miles to go and I think my lungs might explode," she says. "And now I have an allergic reaction to the phrase 'almost there.'"

I smile, look at the map again.

"I think we've got about another mile on the trail, then maybe half a mile cross-country," I tell her.

"That's a euphemism for *not on the trail*, right?" she says.

"It's not a euphemism, that's what it's called," I say. "A euphemism is a pleasant name for something unpleasant. Like calling prostitutes *ladies of the night*."

"That's your go-to euphemism?" June asks, one eyebrow lifted.

"Is there a problem with it?" I ask as she caps her water bottle.

"Just interesting that it's the first one you thought of," she teases.

"I chose to spare you the first one I thought of," I tease back.

"Well, now you have to tell me."

We're heading along the trail again, surrounded by the forest. It's a hot day but not too bad here, in the shade.

"I don't," I say.

"Come on," she says, looking over at me, thumbs hooked in the straps of her backpack. "What was more incriminating than prostitute?"

"I've never visited a prostitute, if that's what you're getting at," I say. "You could just ask, June."

"I wasn't, but thank you for the information."

We hike in silence for a minute, around a curve in the trail.

"C'mon, tell me," she says. "You said yourself it's useless to keep information from me."

I sigh, because she's right. She's right and moreover, I like it about her.

Usually.

"The first one I thought of was *pass gas* instead of *fart*," I admit, and June starts laughing.

"See?" I say.

"I'm not laughing at fart," she says. "I'm laughing at what you must think of me that I don't mind *prostitute* but you don't want to say *fart* in front of me."

"I'm thinking that the last time you were at my mother's house for dinner, you concocted a story about your participation in orgies that included the phrase 'five people doing it,'" I say, sneaking another glance over at her.

June is slightly flushed, the color rising in her cheeks though I'm sure it's the hike and not me.

I hope it's not me. I've thought about that moment in

the microfiche room incessantly since it happened. I've thought about what would have happened the librarian had left and I'd kissed June anyway, if I'd told her the secret, if I'd been reckless and careless for just one moment.

I'm aware that I'm sending mixed signals. It makes me feel like shit, but I also can't stop.

"Okay, that's fair," she admits.

· · * * ★ ★ ★ ★ * · · ·

AN HOUR LATER, we're at the crime scene. It's exactly as reported: three trees downed, creating a small clearing. Close by is Hellbender Creek, fast and cold. Not far is Burgess Falls, which isn't big or impressive enough to justify a trail to it, but which is lovely all the same.

"That *is* a big tree," June says. She's standing slightly in front of me, surveying the scene. I'm surveying her, in a tank top and running shorts, because it's nearly impossible not to.

"How old is it?" she asks.

"I'd have to count the rings to know exactly, but I'm guessing at least a hundred and fifty," I say, coming around her to stand at the stump. "Maybe closer to two hundred. They used the chainsaw again."

June sheds her backpack, rolls her shoulders, looks around. Carefully, she walks through the site, staring at the ground.

"No tire tracks," she says. "Just in case we weren't sure they hiked in."

I glance behind myself, toward the steep hill we just came down. It'll be interesting to get back up it.

"I don't see too many people getting a vehicle in here," I say.

"There are footprints," she says, crouching. "They look

like they were made by hiking boots, so that's not helpful."

"Tree's been dead a few days," I say, touching the stump with my fingertips. "The leaves on the branches are still mostly green."

"And nobody heard a chainsaw going?" June asks, still examining the ground.

"Forest absorbs noise pretty well," I say, shrugging. "If anyone did hear it, they might not remember to report it, or they might assume it's rangers clearing brush, or who knows."

We're quiet for a few minutes. I crouch next to the stump. It's slightly sticky, the sap still beading up from the roots.

A hundred and ninety-two rings. I sit on the fallen trunk and look at the stump, thinking.

This isn't a great tragedy. I'm aware that a tree isn't a person or even an animal. They're not conscious, they don't feel pain, they don't have emotions.

But all the same, this tree was alive for nearly two hundred years and someone came and killed it for no reason, then just left it here to rot.

"How old?" June asks, sitting down next to me.

"One ninety-two," I say, and she whistles.

"It's not even an oak," I say. "It's a poplar."

June gasps, horrified. I glance at her to see if she's making fun of me, but she's not.

"It's not even the right kind of tree?" she says.

"Not if they're on a wild goose chase for the outlaw gold," I say. "If they're just cutting down old trees because they're monstrous people, then it's the right kind of tree."

"I just don't get it," she says. "Why not just climb the tree to see if the treasure is up there, or why not dig below it? That can't possibly be harder than carrying a heavy-ass chainsaw through the woods."

"If that's what they're after," I say. "It could be anything. They could think that aliens are telling them to cut down old trees. They could be trying out new chainsaw blades. Maybe they just hate trees."

"Why would someone hate trees?" June says, offended by the thought. "Trees are nice."

"I agree."

We sit there for a few minutes, in silence. There's a breeze, mottled sunlight that shifts as the trees sway. It's a beautiful day, sunny and cloudless. June's here. I sit on the trunk, soak it all in because I don't know when this will happen again, if it will happen again.

"Lunch?" I finally ask, reaching for my backpack.

"Sounds lovely," June answers.

* * * * * ★ ★ ★ * * * * ·

"A HUNDRED AND THIRTY MILLION DOLLARS?" I say, repeating it because I can hardly believe my ears. "Million? With an M?"

"Give or take some inflation," she answers.

We're walking along Hellbender Creek toward the waterfall, scanning the ground for... well, for anything. So far, this hiking trip has been a bust on the *solve tree murders* front, even though I've enjoyed every moment of it.

"That's all?" I ask. "I'm not an expert on buying a state, but that sounds low."

"It was a very good deal," June says, shrugging. "Especially since there turned out to be gold and oil up there."

She stops, bends down, looks at something, then straightens again, shaking her head.

"I don't think you could buy a county for that much today," I speculate.

"Depends on which county," she says. "There's probably somewhere in Nevada that you could get for a song. And don't forget that's adjusted for inflation. At the time it was seven million, and people flipped their wigs about it."

"Why do you know how much Alaska cost?" I ask, still watching her from the corner of my eye. "Elementary school project that stuck with you?"

"No, because I'm unemployed," she says. "You start your day searching for jobs, and you see there's an editor position open in Sitka, Alaska, so you look up where *that* is, and before you know it you're googling *towns in Alaska with no roads going in or out* and you're wondering if you should watch *Northern Exposure* and sooner or later you're down a Wikipedia hole, learning all about how the Secretary of State probably bought it just because it was too good a deal to pass up."

I grin at that, even as I think *she's looking for jobs in Alaska?*

"He couldn't afford not to buy it," I say. "I'm pretty sure I once bought a ten-pound block of butter for the exact same reason."

"How'd that turn out for you?"

"There was no gold inside, but I did put most of it into the freezer for a long time," I say. "So both Seward's Folly and Levi's Folly had *being cold* in common."

June laughs, and it makes me smile.

"Tell me you named it Levi's Folly," she says. "Please."

"I don't usually name butter, but you can think that if you'd like," I offer.

"I would," June says.

We continue along the creek. June kicks a rock, glances under it.

"Did you apply for the job in Alaska?" I ask, forcing myself to sound casual, like it doesn't matter to me where she finds employment.

Because it doesn't matter. It doesn't.

"Yeah," she sighs. "I almost didn't, but then I decided to have an adventurous spirit and all that. You know, go where life takes you! Be open to all sorts of experiences! But I hope I don't get it. I hate the cold."

We're at the waterfall now, the spray just barely reaching us. It feels good on the hot day, and we both stand there for a moment, taking it in. It's not huge, it's not flashy, not particularly impressive, but it's lovely in the way that all waterfalls are lovely.

Also, we're the only ones here.

"Levi," June says. "C'mere."

She's standing on a big, flat rock on the edge of the pool, and as I walk toward her, she crouches on it and points into the water.

"There. Almost to the bottom."

I crouch next to her, trying to follow her finger, but I don't see anything through the ripples over the surface.

"There's something down there," she says. "Right there. It might just be a fish or a tadpole or something, but…"

She trails off. I lean in, closer, our shoulders touching.

Alaska. Silas.

This is a bad idea.

"I got nothing," I say.

She sighs, shifts so she's kneeling on the rock, leans in toward me microscopically. My heartbeat quickens, and I stare into the pool, pretending to look into the water and having a thousand other thoughts instead.

I don't have to tell Silas. He doesn't have to find out, I can keep a secret, June can keep a secret.

We can have this for a little while, and then she'll leave, and it'll be all right anyway.

I know I'm deluding myself.

"Okay, see that big dark gray rock over there, just below

the fallen branch?" June asks.

I settle toward her. Our knees touch. She's close enough that I'm looking over her shoulder, finding it nearly impossible to focus on the branch and the rock, anything but her nearness.

"Right," I say.

"If you look directly down from that," she says slowly, lowering her finger by degrees. "In the water there's that sort of... pink rock? And then there's that sinister-looking blob and to the left of that, there's something red."

Still nothing, even though I'm looking where she's pointing, ignoring the fact that we're touching, and her face is inches from mine, and our legs are rubbing together.

"Right... *there*," she says, and leans in further, until my beard brushes against her face, sending a shiver through me.

I want to turn, put my hand on her face, kiss her. I want to kiss her like I should have in the library. I want to kiss her like she doesn't have a brother and won't ever leave Sprucevale.

"See it?" she asks, her voice hushed, barely audible over the noise of the waterfall.

I don't. I don't, and then I do. A red blob, too bright to be a rock, too odd to be natural.

"I do," I finally say, after waiting a few more long moments. "Good eye, that's pretty far down."

"Thanks," she says.

She drops her arm to her lap, but she doesn't move otherwise, still so close to me that I can feel her body heat. All I'd have to do is turn my head, and I'd...

...what? Be face-to-face with Silas's little sister?

Be an inch from kissing a girl who's going to leave town again the moment she gets a job offer?

Be maddeningly close to betraying my best and oldest

friendship, all for something that has zero chance of working out?

"You think you can reach it?" she asks.

I lower myself to the rock, stick one arm into the water. Not even close.

"Shit," says June.

I wriggle out further, my chest off the rock.

Still no good. It's far out and down deep, probably three or four feet.

"Maybe we can try me holding your feet?" she says.

"It's not gonna work," I say, and push myself to standing in one quick movement.

"I bet I can find a branch that'll reach," she says, standing next to me and brushing her hands off. "If I rip one off a live tree do you promise not to—"

She stops talking as I pull my shirt over my head. Her mouth clamps shut.

I swear she turns slightly pink, and I don't hate it. I don't hate it at all.

"June, don't you know better than to deface trees around me?" I ask, bending and taking off my hiking boots.

"It's just minor— uh, are you going in?"

"It's much simpler than letting you dangle me," I tease, stuffing my socks into my boots and tossing them behind me.

"Oh," she says, and now she's *definitely* pink. "I'm sure it's nothing, you don't have to—"

I unbutton my pants. I shouldn't. I'm pushing this too far, but June's reaction is like a drug, flustered and blushing, the way she keeps darting a glance at me and looking away.

"You can avert your eyes if you'd like," I suggest.

"Right," she says, and turns around.

I admit to being slightly disappointed.

CHAPTER TEN

JUNE

Levi Loveless just stripped in front of me.

Levi Loveless, taciturn arborist, quiet nerd, and solitude-loving mountain man, just stripped in front of me, and he was smiling while he did it.

I'm confused.

I'm also turned on. Very, very turned on. So turned on that I'm surprised how turned on I am, and I've definitely had semi-sexual fantasies about Levi before.

This is nothing like last week in the library, with all the whispering and the almost-touches. Nope. These current thoughts are raunchy and highly inappropriate and definitely involve Levi on top of me with my legs wrapped around his—

"Got it," he calls.

I open my eyes and take a deep breath.

"What is it?" I call back, not turning around.

There's a snapping sound.

"I think it's some kinda hair thing," he says. "I'm decent, you can look."

I turn halfway, and then immediately turn back because

he is *not* decent, he's standing waist-deep in water still very definitely naked. Water that was dripping down his chest, his abs, making his shoulders and arms shine in the sun.

I exhale and stare at some trees, concentrating on them so I stop thinking dirty thoughts about Levi, my platonic friend.

Trees are kind of phallic, I think.

"You said you were decent!" I shout.

"This is decent," he says.

"No, that's still naked," I say.

"All right, I'm sorry," he says, and there's splashing. Sloshing. The sound of clothes being picked up, pants being pulled on.

"I'm wearing pants now," he says, and finally, I turn. He holds the object out to me, and I take it, ignoring the fact that he still isn't wearing a shirt.

"It's a hair clip," I confirm. "Maybe one of the murderers is a woman?"

"Or someone somewhere upstream is a woman," Levi says, finally pulling his t-shirt back on.

Thank you, Jesus.

Sort of. My feelings are complicated.

I turn the hair clip over in my hand. It's one of those claw-style ones that look like chompy animals with teeth. I'm not quite sure what they're called, my hair's too straight to use them. They just fall out.

Levi sits on the rock to put his socks and shoes on.

"Ready to head back?" he asks.

· · · * * * ★ ★ ★ * * · · ·

I LOOK UP THE TALL, steep slope.

Very tall. Very steep. Very covered in slippery pine needles.

"We didn't climb down this," I say. "Are you sure we're going the right way?"

"Yes, I'm sure," Levi says, patiently. "You don't remember scrambling down this?"

"Not *this*," I say.

"It's easier than it looks," he says. "They key is to face forward, grab onto trees, and really dig your toes in."

He points.

"Put your foot there, and grab onto that," he says.

I do it. He points to two more objects, a tree root and a rock. I grab one and put my foot on the other, and before I know it, I'm bear-climbing up this slope.

Turns out that Levi's right and it's not that bad, it just looks daunting from the bottom, but as long as I've got a good handhold, it's all right. Not easy, but all right, and we climb up the slope together, though he beats me.

"You're almost there," he says from the top.

"Anything but that," I say, grabbing a tree the same thickness as my wrist.

"Sorry, forgot," he says. "It's true, though."

I pause, looking for something to grab onto with my other hand.

Finally, I see a tree root, just a smidge out of reach. I dig my toes into the ground, hold my breath, and reach for it.

I works. I close my hand around it, use the leverage to brace my feet, look for another handhold.

Then it breaks.

"Shit!" I yelp, already sliding. I throw my hands out, grabbing at dirt and leaves and pine needles, both knees landing hard on the ground and scraping along.

I slide directly into a patch of underbrush and in trying to stop myself, I manage to grab a rock with one hand and then sort of flop half-over, grabbing at nothing with my other hand.

I've got one leg in the air, the other covered in dirt, and my backpack snagged on something and is now over my head and it took my shirt halfway with it.

"June!" calls Levi, alarmed.

"I'm fine!" I shout, kicking at the plants and twigs and leaves and vines entangling me, trying to free my arm before Levi gets down here so I can *please God please* pull my shirt back down.

I kick. I roll over, onto my stomach, and I shimmy my backpack and shirt back in place, kneeling on the angled ground.

"Are you okay?" Levi asks, sliding to a perfect stop right next to me, both feet and one hand on the ground.

"Totally fine," I say. "Just discombobulated, I promise."

I look back down the hill. It's steeper than most hills one climbs, but it's not really steep enough to justify my dramatics.

As I catch my breath, I decide to blame the pine needles. Slippery little fuckers.

"It's your shoes," he says, nodding at my feet. "Running shoes don't have as much gripping power as hiking boots. Thus the sliding."

He holds out one hand and I take it, silently thankful for the excuse.

Levi nods at a tree stump above me.

"That one'll hold," he says. "Here."

I push off his hand with my right arm, grab the stump with my left.

"You got it?" he asks.

"Got it," I say, pushing my feet under the bed of pine needles and finding the nice, solid, grippy dirt underneath.

I continue up the slope, more carefully this time, testing everything I grab before using it to hold any of my weight.

I manage to get to the top where it flattens out without anything else embarrassing happening, and Levi offers me his hand. I take it without thinking, and he pulls me up.

"That was exciting," I say.

"You'll get the hang of it," he says, adjusting his pack. "You sure you're all right?"

He gives me a long, slow look from head to toe, and I clear my throat, brush off my shirt, look away because it feels like he's doing more than checking for injuries, but I know I'm wrong.

"I'm fine," I say. "A couple of knee scrapes, but I'll live."

"I'd say we're almost back to the trail, but you hate that," he says, half-smiling like he does. "So I'll say we're less than a quarter mile away."

I laugh.

"Thank you," I tell him, and we start walking.

· · * * * ★ ★ ★ * * · ·

ABOUT A MILE after we get back on the trail, my back starts to feel weird, like my pack is rubbing me the wrong way or something.

About a mile after that, a spot right by my shoulder blade starts to itch. I stop and adjust my pack, pulling it higher on my back. That doesn't help. I release it so it sits lower, but that doesn't help either and the itch is slowly escalating.

I check my pack, to see if something is caught on it that's tickling me. I check my shirt as well as I can. Nothing.

As we hike, the itch gets bigger and bigger, spreading

out from my shoulder to my ribcage. Something tickles on my hip, just under the waistband of my running shorts, and the back of my left arm.

I deal with it. Probably bug bites from being near that pool of water in a damp area, which means they'll go away soon enough, provided I don't scratch them.

"I did once work with someone who insisted on keeping a stash of willow bark," Levi is saying as we come within sight of the trailhead parking lot. It's late in the day, so everything is in shadow. There's just his truck and one other car there, no one else present. "She insisted on chewing it to cure headaches, so sometimes you'd be talking to her and she'd just pull a piece of it from a bag and start chomping on it like crazy. Reminded me of a mad beaver."

"Did it work?" I ask, laughing, thankful that this is at least sort of keeping my mind off the itching.

"Not in the least," he says. "I kept offering her Advil, but she got real snooty and told me she didn't put pharmaceutical poisons in her body, so I let her keep chewing on tree bark."

I try to imagine a version of myself that would prefer chewing tree bark to taking an aspirin. I can't.

"Eventually, one of the rangers came across her hacking bark off of a weeping willow tree," Levi goes on. "I think he got a real kick out of letting her know that *black* willow is the one that's got the same compounds as aspirin, and she was chewing on tree bark for no reason at all."

I snort, adjusting my pack for the one millionth time. It doesn't help. Everything itches.

"I would have thought that park service employees would be better informed," I say.

"The rangers generally are," Levi says. "She was in communications and didn't leave the office a whole lot, even though we invited her along on expeditions sometimes."

"Ugh, communications people," I tease. "Always typing, using all those words."

We come out of the trail and into the small gravel parking lot, then head for his truck. He glances over at me, eyes smiling.

"I'm simply offering an explanation for why she spent months if not years chewing on the wrong kind of tree," he says. "She also once tried to smudge our offices with sage and set off the fire alarm. I wasn't happy."

We reach his truck, and Levi slings his pack from his shoulders, tosses it into the back, and I do the same.

I'm rewarded with an itch *explosion* anywhere my shirt brushes against my body, and I grit my teeth against and Do. Not. Scratch.

I really hope I didn't fall into a chigger nest or something, I think. I've never gotten chiggers, but I'm not interested in tiny insects burrowing under my skin.

"You all right?" Levi asks, as he's been asking for at least the last mile.

"Just these bug bites," I say, craning my head over my arm and trying to at least get a good look at that one. "I think I must have landed in a—"

There's no circular welt like I'm expecting.

There's a line of blisters.

"Oh, *fuck*," I say. "I got poison ivy."

Levi doesn't say anything, just comes around the back of his truck and very carefully takes my elbow in his hand, studies the back of my arm.

Then he whistles under his breath, something I've never heard him do before.

"Looks like you're very sensitive to it," he says. "You ever gotten it before?"

"Yes," I say, eyes closed, resigned to my itchy, itchy fate. "But not since I was a kid."

The memories are flooding back: huge welts up both shins, bloodied and then scabbed after a couple of days because I always, always ended up scratching them. Or the time I got it on my foot and could barely wear shoes for a few days. Or, dear God, the time Silas threw some on a bonfire and I swear it got *up my nose* from breathing the smoke in.

"If you can make it back to my place, I can fix you up," Levi says. "Try not to scratch."

He's still got one elbow in his hand, but for possibly the first time ever, his touch isn't what I'm focusing on.

"Thirty minutes," he says, and opens the passenger side door for me.

· · * * ★ ★ ★ * * · · ·

I TWIST AROUND, trying to get a good look at my back in the mirror. As always, it's hard, for the obvious reason that my eyes are on the front of my body.

It looks ugly, though. There are at least two huge raised welts that go from my right shoulder blade almost to my left hip, looking like tiny, gross, fluid-filled mountain ranges on my back, surrounded by other ugly streaks with the telltale rash and bumps. There are some on my sides, one on my belly, one on the back of my left arm.

I might lose my mind from the itching. I swear it wasn't this bad when I was a kid and got poison ivy, though this is by far the worst I think I've ever gotten it.

There's a knock on the bathroom door, and I grab a towel, hold it over my front since I'm currently topless, my shirt and bra in a paper bag that Levi provided since they're covered in poison ivy oil.

"Come in," I call, triple-checking in the mirror that I am, in fact, something like decent.

The door opens just enough for Levi's hand to enter, holding a black t-shirt. I take the shirt.

"Thanks," I say.

"At this rate you'll have gone through my whole wardrobe by Thanksgiving," his voice says from the other side of the door.

Quickly, I drop the towel and dive into the shirt, pulling it on in record time, even though the door's partly open. I think, for about the fiftieth time, about Levi stripping down in front of me at the pool of water, about the saucy look he gave me as he did.

It was something. It had to be something. If there's one thing I know about Levi Loveless, it's that he doesn't go giving out saucy looks for no reason.

"Okay," I say, stepping back.

"Okay, you're going to wear all my clothes?"

I pull the door open.

"Okay, I'm decent," I say.

"Ah," he says, and looks at my boobs.

It lasts about a quarter of a second, but it happens. It happens and even though my brain is whispering *kid sister, kid sister*, I'm starting to doubt myself because that wasn't a *kid sister* look.

In general, it hasn't been a *kid sister* day.

"Where would you like me?" I ask.

Levi nods toward the back door of his house.

"Porch," he says. "Let me grab my kit."

I step aside and he comes in, opens the bathroom closet into which, amazingly, I haven't snooped yet even though I'm a dedicated, inveterate bathroom-snooper. I'll open any closet, any medicine chest, any under-the-sink area, because I am *that* person. Luckily for everyone in my life, it's pretty much always boring. Everyone's got Advil and band-aids, and even if you've got stool softener or something, guess what, so does everyone.

I crane my neck to see around Levi and into his closet. To my non-surprise, it's very well organized. On the bottom are a few rows of neatly folded towels, then various bathroom supplies, and then the top two shelves are shoeboxes labeled with various maladies.

Levi pulls out *Poison Ivy/Sumac* from its place on the shelf between *Sunburn* and *Insect Bites*, shuts the door, and we walk out onto his back porch, the dog following close behind.

Every single step I take brushes his shirt against the welts on my back and makes it itch more. I don't even realize I'm holding my breath until I let it all out, standing on the porch, looking at Levi's back yard as the dog bounds out and a squirrel rushes up a tree, chattering.

"You all right?" he asks, setting the box on a table.

"Just itchy," I tell him very, very truthfully.

He grabs a chair, turns it around, gestures to it.

"Sit backward," he says, then clears his throat. "And pull your shirt up, please."

I sit as instructed, straddling the chair, and for one second I think: *I could just take off my shirt. He did it to me, didn't he?*

And then I'm staring into the middle-distance at the end of Levi's back porch, the forest beyond it, and I'm thinking of him standing there in the water, waist-deep, his broad body shining and wet as he smirked at me, holding up the hair clip.

He *smirked*. I didn't know he did that. Levi Loveless smirked at me while naked and I have no idea what to do with this fact, other than think about it without ceasing.

"Just enough that I can see the rash," he says behind me, and I remember that I had a task.

I don't take off, but I pull it over my head and leave it on just my arms. Technically, I'm covered, my modesty intact-ish, but my whole back is bare and I feel naked.

The silence I get in response makes me feel more than naked.

"Does that work?" I ask after a beat, my heart tapdancing.

He doesn't reply, just brushes his fingers down my back, making a noise in his throat that I can't quite decipher. It sends a shiver down my back and I remind myself that he's looking at huge, gross, raised poison ivy welts.

"That bad?" I ask.

"You're certain you didn't take a nap on a patch of it while I wasn't looking?" Levi asks, the chair behind me creaking slightly. My heartbeat hitches in my chest and I focus on the trees beyond his back porch and not on his proximity to my bare skin or the fact that one wrong move could leave me topless.

"Oops," I say, trying to sound lighthearted, and behind me there's a latex *snap*.

I glance over my shoulder. He's right behind me, knees spread wide around my hips as he pulls blue latex gloves onto his big hands.

"I've learned to be overcautious," he says, the hint of a smile on his face. The inside of one of his knees brushes my outer thigh, and it sends a buzz through me even though my entire brain feels like it's taken up by nothing but itching. "Besides, I've seen worse."

I'm unconvinced.

"Have you?" I ask, still looking over my shoulder at him.

"Sure," he says.

"You're an awful liar," I tell him. "At least give me the honor of having the craziest poison ivy you've ever seen."

"Will that make you feel better?" he asks.

He touches the back of my neck, lightly swiping a few stray hairs away. I have to hold my breath and close my eyes, and it's only partly because of the itching.

It's mostly because right now, I very, *very* badly want Levi Loveless to touch me, and I want more than a fingertip on my neck. A lot more.

I've got more than one itch that I'd like scratched.

"This is going to sting," he says, dousing a cotton ball in rubbing alcohol. "But it'll get the rest of the oil off your skin."

Anything is better than the itching, I think, and I take a deep breath.

Levi locks eyes with me.

"I'll be fast," he promises, his voice suddenly soft.

I just nod, turn away, and close my eyes.

He's right. It stings. Everything it doesn't sting it itches and I inhale sharply, my toes curling in my shoes.

"Remember to breathe," he says as the cold stinging itch makes its way along my back. "Try to distract yourself."

I think of him again. Naked. Waterfall pool. Red hair clip.

I bite my lip and imagine that I hadn't turned around and averted my eyes, that I'd just watched him as he'd gotten out of that pool.

I could take my shirt off right now, I think over the din of pain and itching. *See what he does then.*

See whether I'm still the kid sister.

It's a bad distraction, but it's a distraction nonetheless.

CHAPTER ELEVEN

LEVI

"Done," I say. "Part one is over."

"Nnngguh," June offers, taking a deep breath, her back expanding and contracting, her ribs visible under the surface of her skin for that moment. "Okay. Okay."

She shakes her head, her back arching and I grit my teeth even harder, reminding myself *first aid, first aid*.

It's a hard reminder because despite this — despite the fact that she's got welts on her back the width of my finger, and despite the fact that I know this stings and itches like the dickens — it's hypnotic. *She's* hypnotic and she's barely wearing a shirt.

Gasp. She gets goosebumps every time I touch her, and I know it's just the coldness of the rubbing alcohol, but I can't help but watch them peak and fade and think *what if*.

Namely, *what if* I went against every rational, logical argument I've made to myself regarding June? *What if* I ignored my friendship with Silas and her surely-imminent departure from Sprucevale?

I can't. I know I can't, but what if?

I cap the alcohol, take off the gloves, reach for a jar.

"This shouldn't be so bad," I say.

"What is it?" she asks.

"Aloe vera," I tell her, opening the jar and taking a big glob on one finger.

"I thought that was for sunburn," she says, and I touch it to the topmost welt, smooth it down diagonally over the ugly bumps and bright red rash.

"Works on poison ivy too," I say, grabbing another fingerful. "It's a very useful—"

She jerks suddenly, her muscles tensing, and without thinking I grab her hip on my hand, my thumb on her lower back.

"Sorry," she says. "That spot stung."

"I'll be careful," I promise, leaning in. I rub my thumb along her lower back, the skin warm and soft, the tiny hairs tickling at me. It sends a shiver down my own spine and I shouldn't be touching her like this. I should be soothing her wounds and sending her on her way, but it feels normal, natural.

Touching her like this — even in this tiny way — feels *good*.

June just breathes. She breathes and I tend to her poison ivy, quickly but certainly, feeling the way her back expands with each breath, feeling her warm skin beneath my fingers, memorizing every time she tenses or moves or arches, every small gasp she takes.

I finish. I take my hand from her hip, put the cap back on the jar, resist the urge to lean forward and plant my lips on the back of her neck.

"Done," I tell her. "Let that dry for a minute, and you should be…"

"Slightly less itchy?" she teases, her chin resting on her forearms.

"Something like that," I agree, and she turns her head,

looks at me over her shoulder. I put everything back into the box, close the lid as June watches me.

Her eyes on me feel like sunlight. A bright streak, blinding if I look directly back at her.

"I'll be right back, I'm going to put this away," I tell her, and I stand. I walk into my house, through the living room, back into the bathroom even though I'm feeling slightly dazed, slightly unsure of exactly where the floor is beneath my feet.

The way June makes me feel.

In the bathroom I open the closet, slide the box back into its place between *Sunburn* and *Insect Bites*. Then I stand there, just staring into my bathroom closet.

It's an organized closet, with built in shelves and a space for a hamper. Silas occasionally makes fun of me and calls me Martha Stewart, but he's also never failed to find fresh toilet paper or a clean towel.

I like organization. I like it when things have labels. I like knowing where I stand and what to expect, what's coming down the pike.

I close the closet, then stand there and lean my forehead against the door, because I have never felt more disorganized in my life. I've never felt so much chaos. I've never decided on one course of action despite so desperately wanting to take another.

I know what the right thing to do is. Nothing. Nothing is the right thing to do.

Actually, doing nothing is proving nearly impossible.

"Are you okay?" her voice asks, and my eyes fly open, my forehead still against the cool wood of my bathroom closet door.

"I'm fine," I say, straightening. "I was just... checking."

I turn, face her. She's got the shirt fully back on and she leans her hips carefully against the bathroom counter.

"That the closet is flush with the floor. At a right angle."

I point to where the closet meets the floor, as if that'll convince her that I was considering carpentry and not counting the reasons I shouldn't kiss her. It feels as though there are several thousand, though I suspect they're all variations on the same few.

"Is it?" June asks after a pause.

I clear my throat, so at odds with myself that I've nearly forgotten what she's asking.

"Yes," I finally say. "Yes. It's fine. I just thought for a moment that it might be… not fine."

"Thanks for fixing me up," she says. "You're good at that. And prepared."

"I've got four younger brothers, I pretty much had to be," I tell her, truthfully. "Plus Silas."

June laughs lightly, then glances away.

"And now you've fixed up a kid sister," she says.

"Kid sister?" I ask, frowning.

I take a step forward, toward her. I take two steps. I can't stop myself.

"Yeah, you know," she says, her voice still light. "Since I'm Silas's kid sister, I kind of figured I was practically yours, too."

She finally looks up at me in the half-light of the bathroom, her eyes deep pools in her face, her dark hair pulled back, her lips slightly parted.

"That's not at all how I think of you," I say before I can stop myself.

I take another step closer and now she's right in front of me, much closer than she should be, but I can't help that, either.

"How do you think of me?" she asks, her voice nearly a whisper, her blue eyes bottomless.

There's a moment where I could still lie, where I could pull back, make the right choice.

"Far too often," I tell her, the words spilling from my lips.

I reach out. I touch her, run my fingers lightly along her jaw and June tilts her head, her eyes still locked on mine.

I could still stop this. I could drop my hand and walk out of this bathroom and tell June to leave and I wouldn't cross that line that I can never uncross, but I don't.

I slide my fingers into her hair, my thumb on her cheek.

And I lean down and kiss her.

There's a moment when she doesn't kiss me back, when she's nothing but soft and yielding, and then she does. June kisses me back fervently, ardently, and she slides her hand around my neck and pulls me down and I already know I'll never be able to bring myself to regret this.

She tugs at me, pulls, opens her lips under mine and deepens the kiss. My heart thunders and echoes like a marching band in a subway tunnel but despite that, despite my wild urge, I'm careful with her.

I don't touch her back even though I want to pull her into me and push her against the counter all at once. She has one hand on my chest, and I lock my fingers around her wrist, hold it there.

The kiss ends and we stand there, centimeters apart, in perfect stillness.

"Is that the secret you were going to tell me in the library?" she asks.

"Yes," I say. "I thought better of it at the time."

She leans forward and her lips are on mine again, greedy and soft. I kiss her back, restrained, careful.

In the kitchen, my phone rings. I ignore it, keep kissing June.

It stops, then starts again, the sound tearing through the

quiet of the house and I growl softly without meaning to. June lets me go, pushes herself onto the counter and I step forward, hands on her knees.

The phone keeps ringing. I ignore it until I can't, pull away from her, both of us breathing hard.

"You should get that," she says. "It sounds important."

The phone stops ringing. We both listen to the silence.

Then it starts again.

"All right," I growl, kiss her once more. "I'll be right back."

I feel like I'm moving through quicksand as I walk through the living room, into the kitchen, the damned phone ringing away the whole time. I grab the ugly tan receiver off the wall and hold it to my ear, the coiled cord bouncing.

"What?" I demand.

Silence on the other end.

Then, just as I'm about to hang up: "Levi?"

It's Silas. It's Silas and he sounds faraway, lost, ragged, and just from that one word I know exactly why he called.

"What's wrong?" I ask.

"I've been calling you all day," he says, and I can practically see him pacing in his townhouse, walking back and forth with the blinds shut over the front window, the lights off.

"I was in the forest," I explain, closing my eyes, facing the wall, waiting.

There it is: the heavy crash of guilt into my chest at my betrayal.

"Right," he says, and I can tell he's trying to sound like himself but he's failing. I've gotten this call a dozen times before, and now I can tell that it's *this* call within a second of answering my phone.

"Do you want to come over?" I ask, just as the bathroom door opens and June steps out, holding the paper bag filled with her clothes and backpack.

"I had a bad night," he says, finally answering my very first question. "That's not true. I had a couple bad nights. I haven't really slept. I can't really sleep."

He's jagged, raw, on edge. June walks to my front door, sits on the floor, pulls her shoes on.

The weight on my chest threatens to crush me, and I shut my eyes. I feel like I'm balancing on the edge of an axe blade.

"Can you drive?" I ask, trying to sound calm, serene. As if I wasn't kissing his little sister sixty seconds ago. "I can come over there."

"Don't come over here," he says quickly, the jingle of keys in the background. I get the impression that he's been practically waiting by the door, waiting for me to answer my phone. I've got a cell phone, but it doesn't get service in the forest or at my house. "I'd rather come to your place. It's better. It's quiet. I'll be there in thirty, okay?"

"Okay," I say, because it's the only thing I can say.

Silas ends the call, and I put my phone back on its receiver. The cord bounces.

"That was Silas?" June asks, sitting cross-legged on the floor. The dog is on her back in front of her, tongue lolling out as she enjoys some belly scratches.

"It was," I confirm, mind racing.

I can't explain. I don't know how. It's not my place to explain.

"I'm sorry—" I start.

"It's okay," she says, looking up at me as I walk over to her.

There are a thousand things I want to explain, and I can't.

"It's not," I say, and offer her my hand. She takes it and

123

stands carefully, like she's trying to keep my too-large shirt from touching her back.

"Levi," she says, softly but firmly as she opens the door and I walk her to her car. "My back is a mess of itchy, oozing welts right now, and I am going to go home and sit in a bathtub full of oatmeal until I, too, am an oat."

"I'm not sure that's how it works," I tell her, opening her car door.

"It had better because I'm pretty sure oats can't itch," she says, tossing the paper bags with her clothes in them onto the passenger seat.

Then she pauses. She looks up at me.

"Don't tell Silas," she says, and I nearly laugh.

"No," I agree.

"I don't think he would take it well, and I don't know—"

She breaks off mid-sentence, looking up at me, still standing in her open car door.

I kiss her again. I don't even mean to, I just do.

"I don't know either," I tell her.

I don't. I'm fairly sure that right now I don't know a single thing, least of all what I've gotten myself into.

June smiles, cocks her head slightly.

"I gotta go before I get busted," she says. "See you around, Levi."

With that, she closes the door, reverses, then drives down my driveway and out of sight.

I give myself five minutes to sit on my porch steps and wonder what the hell just happened.

Then I get up, go inside, and methodically make sure that every trace of June is cleared out before Silas gets there.

CHAPTER TWELVE

LEVI

"It was the child bride this time," Silas says. "The night before last."

He's sitting on my couch and the dog is next to him, her head on his lap as he scratches her ears, his feet on my coffee table.

"I wish you'd come over yesterday," I tell him, leaning against my kitchen counter, looking out into the living room. Two mugs are sitting next to me, waiting for hot water.

"It's so stupid," Silas says, his head back against the couch. "I thought I could handle it by myself this time, I really did. I even called my therapist and she walked me through some stuff, but—"

The teapot on the stove just barely starts to whistle, and I snatch it off before it can get going, pour the water into the waiting mugs.

"You don't have to handle it yourself," I tell him, simply.

"The guys next door got the new *Call of Duty* game," he says. He heaves a deep breath. "I can hear it through the wall sometimes, and it's nothing, I know it's nothing, but sometimes after a bad night I hear one of those and…"

He trails off, but he doesn't have to finish the sentence because I know what comes next. Next is he's back in *the desert*, listening to the bombs drop at night. Next is he's in a tank, trying to spot IEDs. Next is they're going into a village and everyone there is eerily quiet.

"It's not nothing," I tell him, stirring the tea.

I leave out *they should turn down their fucking game*.

"It should be," Silas says. "Video games should be nothing. *Bride of Chucky* should be nothing, and fireworks should be nothing, and trucks racing past me on the interstate should be nothing. All that should be goddamn nothing, Levi."

I take the strainers from the tea, put them in the sink, walk the mugs over to the living room, put them down on coasters on the coffee table and sit next to him.

"It's okay that it's not," I say.

"Everyone keeps saying that," he tells me, eyes still closed, head still back on the couch, still absent-mindedly petting the dog. "Everyone's a fucking liar."

I'm pretty sure that *everyone* is me, his therapist, and maybe his buddies from the Marines.

Silas says he hasn't slept in three days, and he looks it. He says he called in to work sick yesterday morning and hasn't left his townhouse since, and he looks it. His eyes are red-rimmed, deeply circled. His dark hair is wild and tousled, his stubble two days deep. His clothes look as though they've been slept in, or worse, tossed-and-turned in.

"It was that movie," he says. "*Bride of Chucky*. It's not even a good movie. It's not even scary. I thought it would be fine because I've been watching movies again, and it's been okay, and then it wasn't."

He finally opens his eyes, looks around, focuses. Leans forward and grabs the tea that I made him.

"I even watched that movie *Pearl Harbor* and I was okay," he says.

I clench my jaw and then take a swallow of my own tea, because if I don't, I might ask him what the *fuck* he thinks he's doing.

"Isn't that movie supposed to be terrible?" I ask after a moment.

"It is," Silas confirms. "It's bad and boring and the whole thing is a tedious love story, and I watched every minute of it and then slept like a baby."

He takes a gulp of tea, looking into the mug.

"But fucking *Bride of Chucky* is also terrible, yet it made me dream of a pre-teen with an infant and only one hand," he says. "It's more than anyone should have to deal with, Levi."

"It is," I confirm.

I breathe, take a sip of my tea, breathe again as if that simple act can lift the crushing weight from my chest.

I betrayed Silas. Right there, in that bathroom, I kissed his sister like my life depended on it and I betrayed him. I knew I shouldn't do it, and I went ahead with it anyway.

"What's in this tea?" he asks.

"Chamomile and lavender."

"It's good," he says, looking into the mug. "I assume the recipe for it has some bullshit name like *Serenity Now* or *Peace Be Upon You* or *Flashback No More!?*"

"I don't remember the name of the recipe, but it did recommend serving it on American flag coasters," I tell him, and he snorts.

"Last week I was sitting in on this eminent domain deposition we're trying," he says, head back, staring at the ceiling. "And the lawyer on the other side — this huge

127

corporation who wants the government to kick everyone out of a trailer park and make them homeless for five grand apiece so they can put a store on the land — was wearing a flag pin on his lapel. I wanted to shove it down his throat."

I look at him steadily, and finally, he looks over at me.

For a split second, I see June in his face, and then it's gone. I swallow hard, will myself not to think about her. Not now.

"Is that what children got blown up for?" Silas asks, his voice suddenly quiet, his bravado gone. "So some bigwig could make an extra million dollars in his year-end bonus at the expense of people who have almost nothing? Is that what I was fighting for?"

"Not everything that happens is your fault," I remind him gently.

"It feels like it sometimes," he admits. "It feels like I should be able to stop these things and set them right, and..."

He trails off again, trusting me to know what he means. And I do.

From the outside, Silas and I are opposites: he's loud, gregarious, always popular; I'm quiet, bookish. He joined the military and I got a master's degree in trees. He spends his days arguing with people, and I'm usually happiest on a week-long solo hike.

But for all his bluster, all his machismo, and all his posturing, Silas is a pure soul. He loves his family. He loves his sister. He loves his country, despite its faults, and everything he does and everything he's ever done has been because he truly believes that he can make the world a little bit better.

"Levi?" he says after a beat.

"Yes?"

Silas sighs. Then he turns and looks at me.

"Can I lean on you?" he says. "Just for a minute."

"Of course," I say, even though I know it's never just for a minute.

Silas moves over on the couch, puts his head on my shoulder, and closes his eyes.

That's all. It's a simple movement, really, but it's the deepest act of friendship I've ever experienced, the simplicity of human touch. I'm here, and Silas knows it. He trusts me with his secrets, his darkness like I've trusted him with mine in the past.

He's asleep in about sixty seconds. I knew he would be. That's part of the reason he comes over when the PTSD gets bad, because he knows that he'll be able to sleep at my house.

I swallow guilt. I swallow the feeling that I've betrayed my best friend, and I try like hell to scrub June from my mind.

But I can't. Even with her brother here, sleeping on me, trusting me in a way he trusts no one else, I can't.

· · · ★ ★ ★ ★ ★ · · · ·

AN HOUR LATER, Silas wakes up, his eyes even more blood shot than before. The sun is just going down, so I make us dinner and more tea.

After dinner, he falls asleep on the couch the same way he always does when he comes over like this. I take an old quilt from the closet and put it over him, then read on the other couch until my own eyes are closing.

This is how we always do it: he comes over, we talk, he falls asleep on my shoulder. He wakes up, we eat dinner, and then he passes out on my couch for about twelve hours. I always sleep downstairs with him because sometimes he wakes up, shouting, and I have to remind him where he is.

It's our secret. Everyone knows that we're close friends, but no one knows why. They don't know what he did for me when we were sixteen and my father died. They don't know that a few times a year, he falls asleep resting his head on my shoulder.

No one ever will. I can keep a secret.

But I apparently can't keep myself from betraying him.

By one in the morning, I've decided what I'm going to do.

It's the only thing I *can* do.

* * * * ★ ★ ★ ★ * * *

"HEY, I meant to ask you this morning, but I forgot," Silas says. "It's cool if June comes to your mom's dinner, right?"

I rest the case of beer on the trunk of Seth's car, my phone sandwiched between my ear and shoulder. Seth frowns at me.

I want to say *no*. I really, really want to say *no* because I want to say what I have to say to her in private, not with my entire family and Silas and God only knows who else hanging around, making faces at me like they're the only ones who've figured out I have a crush on June.

"Of course she can," I say, staring into the blackness of Seth's trunk.

"Cool, be there in fifteen," he says, and ends the call.

I flip my phone shut, put it back in my pocket, lift the case of beer. I'm glad that Silas is back to himself after last night. Every time that happens — a few dozen times over the course of eight or so years, gradually declining in frequency — I'm always afraid that this time I won't be able to help.

And I don't always. Sometimes, like today, he's his

bright-eyed, bushy-tailed self again. Sometimes he's only a little better.

"June's coming?" Seth asks, balancing his case of beer on one leg and slamming his trunk shut.

I shoot him a look.

"How does everyone know everything around here?" I mutter.

"You say that like you're not the main perpetrator," he says, grinning at me. "You're nosier than the rest of us put together."

"There's absolutely no way that's true," I say. "I'm well-versed in minding my own business."

"Sure," Seth says, in that way that I hate. He's still smiling, even though June is coming and she's going to be *with* Silas and my heart feels wrapped around itself. "But for the record, the only person who ever calls you is Silas, and I can't imagine who else he'd be asking about since I don't think he's seeing anyone right now."

I sigh, hoisting the case onto one shoulder. Seth does the same.

"And before you ask about *that*, you know that if Silas started seeing someone there would practically be flyers all over town because half the womenfolk practically toss their panties at him every time he leaves the house," he says. "There would be skywriting. An announcement would be broadcast over the radio. Someone would—"

"Jealous much?" I ask, but Seth just laughs.

My second youngest brother, shall we say... gets around.

"I've got no reason to be," he says, bounding up the porch stairs. "Trust me."

I just sigh and open the screen door, letting him walk through.

"I'm glad June's coming, she's cute," he says.

I freeze, the door halfway open. There's a buzzing sound in my ears.

Seth starts laughing.

"Kidding," he says, and pushes the door the rest of the way open with his back. "Well, not kidding that she's cute, but I'm not dumb enough to go for her. Not with that brother."

I glare. He just grins at me over his shoulder, then carries the beer on into the house, and I follow.

Apparently, I'm that dumb.

CHAPTER THIRTEEN

JUNE

"It has to go around the stake first," Rusty informs me.

"No, it doesn't," Daniel says. "Rusty, we already went over the rules."

"It's a house rule," she says. "Once it goes through both wickets it has to go around the stake and *then* back through."

"You can't make up house rules midway through the game," Daniel chides. "Also, that's not a house rule here."

"After this game, it's a house rule," she says, like she's negotiating.

"We'll talk," Daniel says, a phrase I've noticed him using a lot. "June, please go ahead and finish your turn."

"Thanks," I say, lean down, and hit my croquet ball with the mallet. It goes through a wicket, so I hit it again, through another wicket, and it stops in the middle of our croquet course.

"Okay, now *you* have to get it around the stake before you go back through," Rusty is telling her dad.

"No, I don't," he says patiently.

"I regret telling her about house rules," Eli admits to me, *sotto voce.*

"I can't imagine why," I say, leaning on my croquet mallet.

"I tried to tell her that it was a house rule in checkers that if you get killed, you go back to the start of your board," he goes on, watching Daniel knock a ball around. "And she didn't believe me, but she *did* demand an explanation of house rules, and now I'm living in a hell of my own creation."

"Sounds like you deserve it," I say, and he just sighs.

"Maybe," he says. "Wish me luck, it's my turn."

It's Sunday afternoon, after dinner, and I'm currently part of the "keep Rusty entertained" task force. Yes, it takes three adults, and yes, the three of us are barely managing, but this kid is a force of nature.

I spot something from the corner of my eye, and I jerk my head around to glance at the house.

A squirrel runs across the roof. Not Levi. Not even *remotely* Levi, though my heart's still pounding.

I don't know what happened yesterday.

I mean, technically I know. I kissed Levi in the bathroom. I kissed him a bunch, and it was great, and I really enjoyed it, and then my brother called and reminded me that I'm inserting myself smack-dab in the middle of something I shouldn't insert myself into.

Levi and Silas have been friends for literally as long as I can remember. It amazes me that they're still as close as they are, after thirty-something years. I don't know anyone else who's managed that. I don't know anyone else who's even come close.

And the second Levi stepped out of the bathroom to answer the phone yesterday, I started wondering what the hell I was doing.

I felt *guilty*. Really guilty, even though it doesn't really make sense, not if you think about it. There's no reason why me making out with Levi has to affect his relationship with my brother, except I'm stupid and I know that it will.

Besides, I don't really trust myself right now. I have bad taste in men, and I know it, and even though I'm pretty sure Levi is different, I don't trust my own judgement.

What happened to my self-improvement project? What happened to being a brand new June, to personal reinvention and all that?

This is what I tried to talk myself into while I soaked in oatmeal for three-and-a-half hours last night, even though every thirty seconds I was back to thinking about Levi's lips on mine, his hand around my wrist, the gentle-but-firm way he pushed me against the counter—

"JUUUUUUNE."

I look down at a very annoyed Rusty, and instantly figure out that it's my turn.

"Sorry," I say, and move to the center of the field, knock my mallet into my ball. It goes through two wickets, and I try again to remember the rules of this game.

"Wooo!" Daniel says, holding his arms aloft.

I just look at him, confused.

"You just won," Eli explains. "That's the last stake. Unless you want to play with the rule that after you hit that stake, your ball becomes poison—"

"Nope!" says Daniel.

"Just kidding," Eli says, grinning. "Winner does clean up, though."

"We'll stay and help," Daniel says. "Rusty, can you grab those—"

"I don't mind," I say quickly. "Really, go have some pie, I'll be right in."

"Okay!" Rusty shouts and starts running back to the house.

"You sure?" Daniel asks.

"I got this," I tell them.

He and Eli shrug, then follow Rusty back to the house.

I'm glad for a few minutes alone, because the Loveless Sunday Dinner is nonstop cacophony most of the time, and I just need to breathe and maybe also process the looks that Levi keeps giving me.

I'd also like to decide whether our brief conversation about stoplights in town was veiled flirting, but I don't think it was. I think that Levi might truly hate the intersection of Courthouse Road and Route 39.

"June," his voice suddenly says, and I whirl around, croquet mallet in hand.

"How'd you do that?" I ask, because I heard *nothing*.

My pulse is racing so fast it could compete in NASCAR.

"I'm very stealthy," he says, bending to pluck a stake from the ground. "Also, I went through the forest. Those assholes didn't help you clean up the game?"

"You're calling Rusty an asshole?" I tease, trying to maintain my composure.

Levi just looks amused.

"She has her moments," he says. "But mostly I meant my brothers."

"I won, so I volunteered," I tell him.

We toss the rest of the croquet set into the bag, and I zip it up but before I can lift it, Levi grabs it from me and hoists it over his own shoulder.

"I'm perfectly capable of carrying that," I tease, my palms already sweaty.

I glance back at the house. I can't see inside, but I'm

absolutely certain that someone's watching us. Probably my brother. Probably Levi's brothers, too.

I want to kiss him anyway. I know I shouldn't and I know all the reasons that I shouldn't and yet the desire is burning a hole right through my middle.

"Of course you are," he says, perfectly calm. "Doesn't mean I'm going to let you as long as I've got arms."

Neither of us seems to be moving back toward the house, and I look up at Levi's serious face.

My insides feel like a washing machine.

"I came out to talk to you," Levi says, his voice serious as the grave.

The pit of my stomach suddenly drops out. I swallow hard.

"I shouldn't have kissed you yesterday," he says, his voice soft. "I'm sorry."

I'm already nodding like my head is on a string, being jerked around.

"You're right," I say. "Totally right. Yes."

Inside, I'm screaming. It's the right thing and I know it's the right thing but I'm screaming anyway.

He gives me a long, long look, his eyes searching my eyes until I finally look away, my arms folded over myself.

"I like you, June," Levi says. "I can't pretend that I don't. But to be anything more than friends would be—"

"A bad idea," I finish for him, because I feel like he's talking at a glacial pace, and I also feel like if I don't say something I might explode. "Definitely a bad idea, because it would mess up your relationship with my brother and *my* relationship with my brother and it would just be too weird all around, the whole thing."

It didn't feel weird. It felt right, not weird, and I know it and I'm nearly certain that Levi knows it, but neither of us is going to admit it right now.

"Exactly," he says. He takes a deep breath, adjusts the bag over his shoulder, lets it out. "I'm glad you think so too."

"I definitely think that," I say, then look over my shoulder at the far end of the yard, where it meets the woods. "Um, I think there's another croquet piece over there and I'm gonna go grab it, I'll just meet you back at the house, okay?"

I don't wait to hear Levi's response, I just walk for the woods. There's nothing over there, I just needed to get away from him for a moment because despite everything, I feel like shit.

I stand at the edge of the yard, staring up at the trees in full summer foliage, and breathe. I breathe deep and I breathe hard and I tell myself again and again that this is the right choice. I did the right thing. I'm applying for jobs in *Alaska*, for Pete's sake, I can't just take up with Levi for a month or two and then leave him and Silas to the fallout while I'm far away.

This is good. This is correct. I'll get over it.

I just really, really want to cry my eyes out right now.

CHAPTER FOURTEEN

JUNE

I read the plaque on the building for approximately the 1,573rd time.

Burdet House
Built 1808
Sprucevale Historical Society

The Burdet House — built 1808, now home to the Sprucevale Historical Society — is a nice house. It's brick, with a small porch off the freshly painted front door. The porch has white columns. The rest of the house has blue shutters that match the front door, the windows look original, and the whole thing looks extraordinarily well-cared-for.

Which is what I'd expect from a historical society, so that all checks out.

I check the sidewalk to the right. I check the sidewalk to the left.

No one.

I pace to the end of the block again, the brick sidewalk

slightly uneven under my feet, the houses on both sides of Charles Street all at least as old as the Burdet House, and then I pace back.

I read the plaque again and repeat the whole shebang, because after Sunday, I'm nervous as bees in a blender. I know full well that our conversation — our *mutual agreement* — didn't really have a lot to do with us and was about circumstances. I know it had nothing to do with our professional relationship or our attempt to find tree murderers.

I turn, pace, pace back.

Colleagues, I remind myself. *People are colleagues all the time and it's no big deal.*

I turn, and there he is, rounding the corner at the end of the block, and I stop in my tracks. I stand still. I wonder what people normally do with their hands when they're acting perfectly normal and natural, and as he draws closer, I settle on shoving them into my pockets.

"Hi," I say when he's ten feet away.

Levi also has his hands shoved in his pocket, his work slacks on along with a plaid button-down shirt with the sleeves rolled up. The man does have a look, and it's a very good—

Nope.

"Hey," he says.

There's a pause.

Then: "Good to see you, June."

"You too," I say, and I mean every syllable of it because it is. Even if I can't and won't have him, it's good to see Levi.

"You said you cracked our case wide open?" he says, and he's got that half-smile on his face, and I relax a little.

This will be fine, I tell myself. *You'll work through your tension issues and everything will be extremely normal.*

"I didn't say that," I say, heading onto the porch and

heaving open the heavy door. "I just said you should see something."

He takes the door from me before I can open it all the way and holds it for me. Inside is the front hall of the Historical Society, in what was once the foyer of a very nice house.

"Is that you again, June?" a voice calls.

"Yup, just me," I call back.

A woman comes around a corner, holding a manila folder. She's got gray hair in a bun, half-moon glasses on a chain, and she's wearing slacks and a blouse with slightly-too-large poofy bow at the neck.

In other words, she looks exactly like she should be running a historical society.

"Guests need to sign in," she tells Levi without preamble. "And yes, before you ask, we do require your email address *and* phone number and please don't think you'll be the exception to the rule. The sign-in book is right over here."

"Yes, ma'am," Levi says, and allows her to guide him to the sign-in sheet, where he dutifully fills everything out as instructed.

"And don't just let the pen drop when you're finished," she says as she walks away. "We just had painters in a few months ago and the ink stains very badly if you're careless!"

The moment she disappears, Levi turns and looks at me.

Then he holds the pen up, its chain fully extended, and lets it drop.

"Whoops," he says.

"I'm sorry," I tell him. "She's always like that. I've been here a thousand times and with every single visit, you'd think I came here specifically to carve my name into a historically accurate fireplace."

"Well, did you?" he asks, that half-smile on his face.

My heart skips a beat, recovers, and I look away.

"Only the once," I tell him. "Come on, it's upstairs."

· · · ★ ★ ★ ★ ★ · · ·

"Huh," Levi says, leaning over the table. "I think you might be right."

Standing off to one side, I smile to myself, then quickly bite it back.

"That's…" he says, still examining the photo, tilting his head to one side. "You're right. I think that's just a stain, not part of the map."

He looks from the enlarged photo on the right to the smaller photo on his left, both of Obadiah Harte's infamous napkin map. The enlarged photo is fifty years more recent than the smaller photo, and one of the lines running along it is definitely lighter and has definitely changed color in a way that the rest of the ink hasn't.

"Right," I say. "So if you look at it with the knowledge that that line isn't part of the map, what's it look like?"

Levi sighs. He lifts his messenger bag over his head and puts it on the floor, then leans over the table again, both hands flat on its surface, and studies the photo. Then he turns his head and studies the map I've got laid out to the right, the one with logged areas shaded in.

After a long moment, he finds a spot on the photo with one finger and the map with the other.

"This squiggle looks like the Lantern Range right here," he says, his finger running down the spine of some mountains. "That could be where Hellbender Creek

142

empties into Marsh Bottom Run, right at the foot of Bareback Peak."

I turn slightly pink at *Bareback Peak*. Obviously, it was named before the slang took off, but I can't believe no one has changed the name since then.

"And these dots on the napkin look like where we found old trees cut down," he finishes.

Finally, he looks up at me, still leaning over the table.

"How'd you figure this out?" he asks.

I shrug.

"Came to me in a dream," I say.

It didn't. I couldn't sleep Sunday night, so instead, I went on a deep dive of the Harte's Treasure legend. I stared at the stupid hand-drawn-on-a-napkin map for ages. I stared at our logging map. I went over the words Obadiah allegedly said before running off into the wilderness to almost certainly die.

Because I didn't want to think about Levi. Because for a mutually-made, mutually-beneficial decision this one feels pretty shitty even if it's the right thing, and I needed to focus my attention elsewhere.

"A dream?" he asks, one eyebrow raised.

"I have useful dreams," I say, then point to the photo he's still looking at, careful not to brush against him. "There's two more dots."

"Did he not remember where it was hidden?" Levi asked.

"No, he was an asshole who got off on the idea of people looking in all these spots for his treasure after he died," I say. "I'd bet money there's nothing in any of them, but that's not the point."

"The point is that someone thinks there is," Levi finishes for me, still looking at the map.

My heart flutters and I wonder, for the tiniest of

seconds, what he would do if I leaned across this table and kissed him right now, whether he'd kiss me back or pull away.

Then he looks up, right at me, like he can hear what I'm thinking. My mouth goes dry. I try to think of something, *anything* to say but I can't.

There's only one thought: I want to kiss him, and I can't, and I want to.

"I guess we should formulate a plan," he says, his voice suddenly low, quiet, gravel like the bottom of a river.

I let it flow over me, swallow, and try out a smile.

"I guess we should," I say.

· · · · ★ ★ ★ ★ ★ · · ·

"*EXCUSE ME*," the voice says from the doorway of the study room.

I gather my patience, then look up and force a smile onto my face.

"Yes, Marjorie?" I ask, polite as you please.

"We are *closing in ten minutes*," she says, her half-moon glasses somehow hanging onto the very end of her nose. "That means the two of you need to clear out of here because I'll need to check this room after you leave, *obviously*."

Today marks the first time I've been inside the Historical Society in years and years, but some things don't change: it still smells like brick and old paper, the floors squeak in all the same places, and Marjorie Thompson is a grade-A bitch.

"We're leaving now," I say, forcing a smile.

She glares, then leaves, and I roll my eyes so hard I might sprain them.

"Want me to steal something?" Levi asks, still looking down at our map.

"Not funny," I tell him, pulling my laptop bag onto my lap.

"Not a joke," he says, and looks up at me, his brown eyes deep, steady, as always. "Give me the word, June, and I'll take anything you want, just to piss her off."

"You wouldn't," I say.

"I would," he says, then pauses. "I heard the way she just talked to you, June. Just tell me what I should steal, and it's done."

There's a tiny smile playing around his lips, the slightest hint of a tease in his voice.

"What's she most proud of in here?" he asks, looking around. "That bust? That map?"

"She probably knows who you are, plus she has your address and phone number," I point out. "Can we please just leave before you ruin the historical society for us?"

Now Levi's grinning, a grin with a sly, dangerous edge and I don't hate it. I don't hate it at all.

"Marjorie has *an* address and phone number," he says, pushing his chair back and standing. "Not mine, though."

"*Now*," her voice says and Marjorie herself follows shortly after, turning sharply through the door. "If the two of you aren't out in one more minute, I'll have to revoke your privileges to—"

"Marjorie, we're leaving," I say, finally out of patience. "It takes a second to pack up our stuff and put things away, all right?"

"Mrs. Thompson," she snaps, her arms folded over herself. "I prefer to be addressed respectfully, as I'm sure you're well aware."

I can practically feel the anger rolling off of Levi, and I

quickly shoot him a *please shut up and don't steal anything* look. He glowers back at me.

I pack up the map, slowly. I put the two photos of the napkin map back, extra-slowly. It takes a full three minutes before we're ready to depart, and Marjorie is watching us the entire time.

She was always an unpleasant woman, but I don't remember it being quite this bad. Maybe I've just forgotten.

"Thank you," she says acidly as we finally depart the study room. "And don't clomp down the stairs like a herd of elephants!" she calls after us as we descend the two-hundred-year-old wooden staircase.

I stomp extra. So does Levi, and I also stomp extra as I cross the foyer, push the door open into the slightly-cooler-than-daytime early evening air.

A moment later, Levi appears behind me. We turn and walk down the sidewalk together without saying a word, and as soon as we're out of sight of the Burdet House, he holds one hand out.

"What?" I ask.

"I got you something," he says, and I open my hand under his.

He deposits a pen with a few inches of chain still attached to one end.

Despite myself, I start laughing.

"Did you steal the sign-in pen?" I ask, glancing over my shoulder to double-check that Marjorie isn't watching.

"I did, and I'd do it again," he says, rubbing his hands together.

Then he glances over at me, smiling and mischievous, almost devious. I've never seen him like this before, but there's nothing I can do but smile back at him, pen in hand, laughing.

"You hungry?" he asks.

CHAPTER FIFTEEN

LEVI

I hold the hot pizza box on one hand, fingers spread, like I'm a waiter holding a tray of champagne at a fancy event, only I'm holding pizza and standing next to my pickup truck.

"You seriously don't have a stash of fast food napkins in here?" June asks, her voice muffled and echoey from inside the cab.

I look away from her, toward the river, because she's half in my truck and half out of it, bent at the waist as she searches for nonexistent napkins, and it's distracting as all hell.

"I seriously don't," I answer her.

"Someone must have put some in here while you weren't looking," she says, still buried in my truck.

Despite myself, I glance over. The late-summer evening light is just starting to fade, but I can make out the curve of her backside all too clearly, the dip of her lower back, the way she arches just slightly as she reaches for something inside the cab.

As I watch, she shoves herself harder into the truck,

kicking up one foot. Her shirt rides up an inch and now I can see a pale strip of skin.

I hold my breath. I stare. I wonder if her poison ivy is better, if I should ask, if she'd show me, if I even want that.

I shouldn't. We agreed that the kiss was a mistake. We agreed that we're on the right path now, that we're friendly colleagues and nothing else, and we both know we're doing the right thing.

It's just that the wrong thing also feels pretty right.

"You really don't," she says, her voice full of wonder as she pulls her torso out of my truck. "Huh."

"I told you," I say, still holding the pizza box.

"I know, and I didn't believe you," she says, pulling her shirt down and brushing herself off. "Everyone's got fast food napkins. Maybe Starbucks if you're fancy. What do you do if you spill your coffee while you're driving?"

"I don't drink coffee in my car," I shrug. "Actually, I don't drink coffee."

June looks at me like I've sprouted another head.

"Are we discussing my caffeine needs or are we eating this pizza?" I ask, faux-sternly.

"We're finding napkins because pizza's messy and I don't want to just wipe my greasy hands on my jeans," she fires back, her eyes laughing.

"I've got a roll of paper towels in my tool box."

"And you didn't mention this while I was tearing apart your truck for McDonald's napkins?" she asks, grabbing the side of my truck and stepping one foot onto a tire.

I shift the pizza box and offer her a hand, but it's too late because she's already hopped over and is sitting in the bed of my truck, pushing her hair out of her eyes.

I didn't mention it because I was somewhat distracted, I think.

"I told you I didn't have napkins and you didn't believe me," I point out.

She takes the pizza box from my hand and I push myself up onto the side of the truck, hop over.

"Well, first, that's a ridiculous claim to make," she says, putting the box on the floor of my truck bed and flipping the lid open.

I sit opposite her, stretch my legs out, open the toolbox that lives behind the cab of my truck, and grab the paper towels. I hand her one.

"And second?" I prompt as she removes a piece of pizza from the box.

"Second," she starts, then takes a bite and chews, thinking. "Second, everyone has napkins in their car."

"Not everyone," I point out.

"You're right," she teases. "I should have known that everyone but you has napkins in their car."

"What else does everyone do that I don't?" I tease back. "I'll take a list, June."

We're now both sitting against the sides of my truck, facing each other, legs stretched out as we eat pizza and the sun goes down, the river rushing by the boat launch a few dozen feet away.

We didn't even discuss whether we should eat together in town somewhere. June's positive that Marjorie Thompson, the harridan at the Historical Society, won't tell anyone that we were together, but anything else feels too risky.

June doesn't want Silas knowing that we're spending time together like this. I don't want him knowing.

"Eat meat," she says, turning her half-eaten piece from side to side, like she's deciding the best plan of attack. "Watch football. Own a television. Eat at fast food restaurants. Have a cell phone."

I wonder if everyone else really *does* have napkins in their car and if it's really that strange that I don't.

It wouldn't be the first time I'd be the odd man out in

some small, insignificant way. It might not be the hundredth, because to be honest, I stopped counting years ago.

I don't eat meat. I read too many books. I haven't played a video game in years. I don't watch sports. I don't even own a television.

Sprucevale's my home, and I don't see myself ever leaving. There's a lot I love about this place and I can't imagine being anywhere else. I don't even feel like a square peg in a round hole.

I'm more of... an octagonal peg in a round hole. I *almost* fit.

"All right," I say. "I'll work on becoming a Big Mac-chomping football fan. Maybe I could wear some camouflage and shoot some guns while I'm at it."

June looks at me for a moment, her face unreadable, her slice of pizza hovering uneaten in front of her mouth.

"It's not a bad thing," she says. "I'm sorry, Levi, I didn't mean—"

"I'm kidding," I say softly.

"I like that you're different," she says, her voice matching mine.

My heart flares, beats faster, and there's a bright moment where this seems possible, where June and I could simply stay in this truck and eat pizza together and never deal with other people or the future.

"I have a cell phone," I tell her instead, taking another bite, and the moment's over. We are who we are, and we can't be anyone else.

"I've never seen you use it," she counters, attacking her slice from the side.

"You called me on it," I point out.

June frowns, thinking.

"I thought that was your land line."

"Why would I answer that at ten a.m. on a Tuesday?"

June chews, swallows.

"All right, fine," she says. "You've got a cell phone and that makes you extremely average and normal."

"That's a big statement," I say, reaching into my pocket. "You sure you want to go that far?"

I pull out my phone.

June starts laughing.

"I take it all back," she says. "Is that an antique? Does it work?"

"Am I still average and normal?" I tease, waving my silver flip phone.

"Definitely not," she says, tearing at the crust with her teeth. "You're an alien. The government should abduct you and study you to see how you survive in Earth's atmosphere."

"I sleep in a recharging pod in my basement every night," I tell her, putting my phone back. "Takes me half an hour every morning to put my human suit back on."

"You've got a recharging pod, but not a smartphone?" she asks, taking the last bite of her pizza.

"I'm a complicated alien," I say.

· · * * ★ ★ ★ * * · ·

"Thanks for the ride," June says as the truck pulls to a stop alongside her car. "And the pizza. And entrusting me with the truth about your otherworldly origins."

It's dark out, nearly ten at night, because after we finished eating pizza we sat in my truck for another two hours, letting darkness fall over us while we talked.

We talked about aliens. We talked about Alaska. We talked about tree murders, and Silas, and pirates, and whether anyone's ever actually found buried treasure.

June maintains that no one ever has. I maintain that someone has, just never the treasure they were hoping for.

We sat there, and we talked, and we pretended that our knees weren't touching. I pretended that I've never kissed her, that I've never wanted to kiss her, and by the time we got into the cab of the truck so I could drive her back to her car, it felt like it was working.

But now she's sitting next to me, her blue eyes still startling in the dark, and she's looking at me like she remembers, and it feels nearly impossible to pretend.

"As long as you can keep the secret," I say.

"Of course I can," June says, the hint of a smile in her voice, in her eyes. "I'll never tell a soul, Levi."

There's a pause, a heavy moment where I feel like we're strung together, like there's something between us more than words and air.

But then she looks away, unbuckles, opens the door. I shove my truck into park, turn the engine off.

"Don't you dare walk me to my car," June says, already hopping out. "It's four feet away."

I'm already pulling the keys out, unbuckling.

"I can't be——"

"No!" she shouts, laughing, as she slams my door shut and opens hers, already in her own driver's seat before I can get out of my truck.

I sigh, and she grins and waves from behind the wheel.

Then I look at her for one more moment, and I drive away.

· · · ★ ★ ★ ★ ★ · · ·

WHEN I GET HOME, my house feels empty. Even though the dog runs up and greets me, tail wagging, it feels empty.

It's never felt empty before.

I've lived here alone for years now, and it's felt quiet and still, peaceful, filled with perfect solitude, but never *empty*.

I turn on the lights, hang my messenger bag on a hook, walk to the back door, let the dog out. I stand on the back porch and watch her barely visible form as she runs through the back yard, stopping and sniffing and snuffing.

It's been nearly a month and I haven't heard a peep from anyone else about her, even though I've put up probably hundreds of flyers. I can't bring myself to believe that no one misses this very good dog.

After a while, she comes back, excited and slightly damp from the dew in the grass. I pet her, scratch her ears, and she licks my hand.

"All right, girl," I say, crouching down. "What's your name gonna be?"

CHAPTER SIXTEEN

JUNE

P *lease write a few paragraphs about your relevant work experience.*

I put my laptop down on the comforter in front of me, then reach forward over my crossed legs, stretching. I should probably stand up at some point tonight, but I think by now my butt might actually be part of my mattress, so why ruin a good thing?

I rock briefly from side to side. I take a deep breath, then yawn, my face pressed into my blankets. It's twelve-thirty in the morning and I should have gone to sleep a few hours ago, but I... didn't. At this rate I'll be fully nocturnal in a few more weeks, and then maybe I can start applying for jobs at Vampire Daily and the Goth Telegraph.

Okay, if I'm having those thoughts I definitely need to go to sleep.

After I finish this job application, to be the Metro Editor at the Bluff City Herald-Trumpet, which is a big name for a fairly small paper.

Bluff City is in South Dakota. It has a population of 25,000 and is most famous for allegedly being the last place that Wild Bill Hickok slept before he traveled on to Deadwood, South Dakota, where he was shot over a poker game several weeks later.

I open the relevant file on my computer and copy and paste the few paragraphs in. I don't know why job applications love to make you fill out all the parts of your resume before simply uploading your resume, but at this point I've done so many of the things that it's pretty much second nature.

I copy. I paste. I make sure that I didn't misspell anything. I click *next*.

But when I get to the last screen, where I'm supposed to double-check my work before submitting it, I hesitate because I'm not at all sure I want to work for the Bluff City Herald-Trumpet. I'm not sure I want to move to Bluff City, to leave Virginia again, to start over in another town where I don't know anything or anyone.

I'm not sure the job is worth it.

My finger's still hovering over the button when something hits my window with a loud *click* and I jump.

For a moment, I stare at my curtain-covered window. The only light in my room right now is my bedside lamp, and it suddenly feels kind of spooky.

It's just the tree branches hitting the glass, I tell myself, and hit *Submit* before I can worry any further about moving to South Dakota.

Then I think: *There hasn't been a tree outside this window since I was seventeen.*

There's another *clink*, and this time my pulse shoots upward. I close my laptop, push it away. The window is just beyond the foot of my (twin) bed and I stare at it.

It's a serial killer, I think, because I've read way too many true crime stories where this exact scenario happened. *Or it's robbers who think the house is empty, or it's*

155

someone trying to murder his ex-wife who's got the wrong house, or...

Another *clink*. I take a deep breath, turn my light out, and scoot toward the window even as I wonder if I should call the cops instead.

I scootch closer. Closer. I can see a sliver of window behind the curtain if I press my face against the glass, and there doesn't seem to be anyone out there.

Probably just bats smacking into the glass, I think, even though I've never heard of that happening before. *Or bugs or something. I did have the light on.*

Finally, I'm perched on the edge of my bed. I take a deep breath. I grab the curtain.

And I look out the window.

Levi Loveless is standing on the ground below, looking up at me, tossing a pebble up and down in his hand.

My pulse keeps racing for entirely different reasons, and I slide the window open.

"Are you throwing rocks at my window?" I hiss, because my parents are asleep across the hall. Just because I'm an adult doesn't mean I want to wake them up and explain the situation.

"They're small," Levi says from below.

"My parents are asleep."

"I thought you were grown," he teases.

"Is that why you're throwing rocks at my window instead of texting me like a normal person?" I whisper. "I know you've got a phone, Levi."

He's laughing as he pulls his phone from his pocket and flips it open.

I still can't believe the man has a flip phone.

Levi: Come downstairs.
Me: Who is this?

"It's me," he says, his voice hushed, still laughing. "Please?"

I bite my lip, trying not to laugh out loud as I put my phone in my pocket.

I like this side of Levi. It's a side I've only ever seen glimpses of before in the past two weeks — sweet, slightly goofy, teasing and funny, different from the serious, quiet man I thought he was. It's a strange revelation, but a good one, even if I wish I liked it less.

"One minute," I tell him, and pull back from the window.

I shut it. I pull the curtains closed.

I wonder what I'm doing and why on earth Levi has shown up beneath my bedroom window at twelve-thirty in the morning. I wish that the sight of him down there had made me feel differently, that I was indifferent and vaguely curious instead of suddenly buzzing and feeling like I'm being lifted aloft by several large birds.

I tiptoe down the stairs and through the living room, still wondering. I haven't heard from him at all since we ate pizza in the back of his truck two nights ago, and I wish that didn't bother me. I wish I thought less about him sitting there, as night fell, laughing and showing me his cell phone or telling me that he's an alien.

I wish I thought less about him, period.

When I get outside, Levi's leaning against his truck, his shoulder-length hair out of its usual knot.

I'm not sure I remember seeing him with his hair down before. He looks different. Relaxed. Like himself.

"I named the dog," he says as I walk up to him.

I don't know what I was expecting him to say, but that wasn't it.

"You do know that the last time a man came to my

window, I called my brother to get rid of him," I say. "I'm sure he told you about that."

"He certainly did," Levi said. "And if I were in my right mind it might have deterred me."

"You're in your wrong mind, then?" I ask, tilting my head slightly, keeping my voice down.

He glances at my still-lit window, then looks back at me.

"You didn't ask what I named the dog," he says.

"What did you name the dog?"

"Hedwig."

"Huh," I say slowly, considering the name. "Hedwig? Like that, with the W sound and not the V?"

"The V sounded too harsh. I know it's correct, but it doesn't sound right. Not for her."

We lock eyes. There are no streetlights here and there's not much of a moon, so it's nearly dark and I can only see the highlights of Levi: the ripples of his hair, the line of his nose, the curve of his cheekbones.

He's beautiful. It's a word that doesn't get applied very often to six-foot-something lumberjack types, but it should be because it's true. Levi's beautiful in the moonlight and it makes my heart trip over itself, the soles of my feet tingle.

"Did you come here at twelve-thirty in the morning to tell me you named your dog?" I ask.

Levi smiles, holds out one hand. I step forward and take it, his skin warm and he enfolds my fingers in his.

"No," he says. "I came here to say that I think you should come back to my place for a nightcap."

My heart twists, flutters. We're now standing toe to toe and I'm looking up at him, my hand in his.

I wonder, sincerely, if I'm dreaming. I decide that if I am, I'd prefer to stay asleep.

"At half-past twelve?"

"It's night, isn't it?"

I want to. I want to say yes. I want to let Levi take me home and kiss me again and probably do other stuff, because even though it's old-fashioned, I know what someone says when they mean *nightcap*.

Instead, I say nothing, my voice stuck in my throat.

"I know," he says after a moment. "I know, and I don't care."

"That's not true," I whisper. "You care and I know it."

There's that slight smile, the glance away before his eyes alight on mine again, his thumb rubbing slowly, steadily over the back of my hand, the friction sending hot shivers down my spine.

"You're right, June," he says. "I care. And yet I'm inviting you over for a nightcap without much regard for anything besides the fact that I want to, because I've weighed my options and I've found the alternative lacking."

"A nightcap?"

"Yes," he says. "I'd like to take you home, fix you a drink, and seduce you, and I'd like to do it without thinking even once of your brother."

"You know I'm going to say yes," I tell him. My blood feels like it's crackling through my veins, every nerve alive and jangling.

"That's the idea."

"You're sure?"

I can't help but ask. I don't want to, but it comes out of my mouth anyway, reason trying to make one last, final stand.

"I'm more than sure," Levi says, and holds out his other hand.

I take it. He pulls me in and then our bodies are touching, my hands behind my back, our fingers interlaced, my feet on either side of his.

"Say it already, June," he teases.

159

My mouth is dry, my heart fast, and I've forgotten every word I once knew.

"Say what?"

"Say *yes*."

"Yes," I say, and Levi kisses me.

It's been five days since our first kiss and I can feel every minute. I can feel every single time that I thought about this and then tried not to, every moment spent wishing or regretting or some potent combination of those two things.

Levi locks his fingers around mine. He pulls me in, harder, our hips resting together as my back arches, my arms held behind me.

There's a moment where he pulls his mouth away from mine, pauses, and I'm the one who closes the gap between our lips. He lets one hand go and I stand on my tiptoes, push my fingers through his hair, open my mouth and let him in.

I want Levi. I'd take him right in this truck if I had slightly less sense. I want him and I want more than drinking cocoa and talking about trees, more than hiking together through the forest, more than gifts of stolen pens and secret pizza. I've taken everything that he offered, and it wasn't enough for either of us.

Finally, we pull back. I'm breathing hard and my heart is beating harder. Levi's hand has somehow made it under my shirt and is tracing slow circles on my lower back, my hand on his chest, my mind racing with the things we could do without ever leaving my parents' driveway.

"You ready?" he asks, rough, quiet, so low I feel it in my bones.

"Yes," I whisper back.

CHAPTER SEVENTEEN

JUNE

The car ride back to Levi's house is strange and wonderful. I wind down my window and stick my hand out, diving it through the humid night air, the anticipation like snowflakes against my skin.

We hold hands except for when he has to shift gears. At stop signs, he leans over and kisses me, and it takes everything I've got not to unbuckle and crawl onto his lap.

And we talk. We talk about the oddness of late-night radio, about whether anyone else is awake. The world is quiet, asleep in the way that only a small town can be, in the way that makes it feel like we're existing together in a space that only the two of us can inhabit.

We leave town, turn onto the Parkway. The Milky Way is bright above us. *Africa* is on the radio, and Levi pulls off the road at a vista point, the inky blackness of country night stretching in front of us.

"What?" I ask, voice hushed.

He leans in and kisses me, fingers curling through my hair.

"Just that," he says when we part, that sneaky smile on his face as he pulls back onto the road.

I don't think I've ever been seduced before, not properly. I'm not even sure that I know how it ought to go, other than like this, with anticipation so strong I want to crawl out of my own skin.

Booty calls, yes. Boozy hookups, yes. I'm not a stranger to the act of sex but I'm a stranger to patient seduction, to letting the tension ride, to not rushing, and I didn't even know it until now.

Levi turns into his long gravel driveway, shifts gears, takes my hand again. My skin prickles when his house comes into view, the porch light on.

I'm already unbuckled when he puts his truck into park, kicks down the parking brake. He's barely gotten his own seatbelt off as I straddle him, still in the driver's seat, and I kiss him as slowly as I can stand to.

"That drive is longer than I remember," he murmurs. "But I don't think I've ever counted the minutes before."

"Twenty-four," I murmur back.

"I think that's a record," he says. His hand is under my shirt again, fingers stroking my bare skin. I push my hips against him, the movement pure mindless need.

He's hard. He's hard like iron and that discovery slows me down, takes my breath away because despite all this, despite the kisses and the promise of seduction, I'm surprised that Levi wants me.

The kid sister.

"You were probably being reckless," I say. I shift my hips gently, slowly, and Levi sucks in a breath, his fingers tightening on my skin.

It's the most gratifying sound I've ever heard.

"I was absolutely being reckless," he says, his voice buzzing against my lips. "And I don't intend to stop."

We kiss again. He lifts me out of his truck, follows. We hold hands and walk to his front door and he kisses me in front of it.

"Get ready," he tells me as he pulls his door open, and there's the dog — Hedwig — on me the moment I enter Levi's house, all paws and kisses and excited little *growf* noises.

"Hey, girl," I say, already crouching down and scratching her between the ears. "I heard your name was Hedwig now."

She wags her tail, and behind her Levi pulls off his shoes, smiles at me, then walks into his kitchen.

"Come on, Hedwig," he says over his shoulder. "You're supposed to be in bed."

She just looks at me, tilts her head, and pants.

"C'mon, girl," he calls again, and this time she follows him, and I take off my shoes and then I do, too.

"Which one of us were you calling?" I tease.

He's got his back to me, pulling something from a high cabinet.

"I like to think I know better than to call you *girl*," he says. When he turns around, he's got a bottle of whiskey in one hand, two glasses in the other. "I do know your name. Quite well, in fact."

"You're really making us drinks?" I ask as he sets the bottle and glasses on the counter. The kitchen is dimly lit, the only light coming from the fixtures on the bottoms of the cabinets.

"I said I would, didn't I?" he asks, grabbing a few more bottles. "I invited you for a nightcap and I like to be a man of my word."

I step up to the other side of the counter, let my palms drop to the cool stone surface, still not completely convinced I'm not dreaming.

"What if I said I didn't want a drink?" I ask, teasing.

"Then I'd say you've never had me make you a drink before," he teases right back.

He pulls the cork from a bottle with a *pop*, starts pouring. I just watch him, my own personal hot bartender as he mixes, swirls, pours something else. He adds ice. He puts a cherry on top.

Finally, he walks around the counter to where I'm standing and hands me a glass. We both take a sip: strong, a hint of sweetness, a hint of something odd. I take another sip.

"What is it?"

"An Old Fashioned."

He steps closer, slides one hand around my back. Levi leans in and kisses me, his lips cool on mine at first, heating quickly. I think I might be weak at the knees.

I don't think this might be a dream anymore. Levi is real as real can be, solid, grounded and right here in front of me.

"You taste like whiskey," I tell him when we part, my glass still in my hand.

"Strange," he says, taking another sip of his drink before he sets it on the counter with a clink. I sip again, too, and then he takes my glass, puts it on the counter next to his.

We kiss again. He still tastes like whiskey, the whiskey tasting like forest and rock somehow. I take his lower lip between my teeth and he makes a noise, a growl from somewhere low in his chest.

I slide a hand up his shirt, find his skin, and he lifts me onto a barstool, curls my legs around his hips, the edge of the counter cool and hard against my back.

"You like it?" he asks, voice low, his forehead resting against mine. My eyes are shut, and I can't see him but I can hear the teasing smile in his voice, that version of him that I didn't know existed until not long ago.

"I do," I say.

He pulls back slightly, reaches behind me, takes a glass off the counter and takes another sip.

"I'm glad," he says. "I made it myself."

"I didn't know we were talking about the drinks," I say, taking the glass from him, swallowing the last sip. He watches me like he's trying to memorize my movements, then reaches into the glass with two fingers, plucks the cherry out by the stem.

"Then we weren't," he says, and brings the cherry to my mouth.

I take it between my teeth. He pulls the stem back with a quick *pop* and then watches me while I eat it, sweetness and whiskey exploding between my teeth.

Then slowly, carefully, he kisses me again, runs his hands along my body, pulls me closer, deepens the kiss. He takes my hips in his hands and presses himself into me, his hardness obvious, the friction of it setting off sparks on my skin.

I feel like a thunderstorm still stuck high in the clouds, crackling with built up electricity that has nowhere to go. I need grounding. I need release but right now there's nothing I can do but wait.

We kiss and I pull at Levi's black t-shirt, push it up over his torso, but instead of taking it off he takes my wrists in his hands, pulls them away.

"Not yet," he murmurs.

"I've already seen you naked," I say.

"You didn't look."

"I tried not to," I say, biting his lip between my teeth, listening to his sharp inhale. "You can be difficult to resist."

Levi laughs softly, lets my hands go, curls his fingers around my thighs just above my knees.

"And that coming from you, of all people," he says. "June, you've wreaked utter havoc on my better judgement despite my very best efforts."

We kiss, hard, our bodies locked together and then Levi pulls back, gives me his hand, helps me down from the barstool.

"Upstairs," he says, and I go.

He follows right behind me, his hand in mine, and I enter his bedroom and he shuts the door behind us and before I can even turn around, he's pulled my shirt off over my head and tossed it to the floor, his hand in my hair, his lips on my neck.

I step back, press myself into his solid, thick form as his arms go around me.

"Is your back all right?" he asks, his lips right next to my ear.

"Almost good as new," I tell him, the first time I've thought about my poison ivy all day.

He lets me go, steps back, and I feel his fingers tracing the paths of where it was. It still itches a little and I shiver as he touches me, setting off an even deeper itch.

He kisses my neck again, my shoulder, and then before I know it he's walking me to his bed and then I'm kneeling on it and then he's pushing me down, his weight on top of me, his cock nestled between my still-clothed buttocks.

I gasp, push up, arch my back underneath him as my body turns to pure, molten heat. I want. I want and that's all. I want him here and now and just like this, I want him to tear my clothes off and fuck me from behind and make me scream into the mattress and for a few seconds, I think I might get my wish.

He kisses my shoulder so hard that his teeth scrape me.

He undoes my bra, reaches under me as I arch myself up, undoes my jeans. He pulls my bra off and my jeans off and he grinds himself against me one more time, the friction so tantalizing I nearly moan, and then he rolls me over.

I'm gasping for breath and he settles himself between my legs, my fingers in his hair. He kisses my mouth, my neck, my collarbone. I tug his shirt over his head, and he fits his teeth around one nipple, flicks his tongue across it.

I groan. I can't help myself, and then Levi's hand is drifting lower, over my panties, and his fingers skim over the thin fabric. Briefly, his thumb finds my clit and circles it and no sooner do I make another noise then he's pushed them aside and he's skin to skin with me.

His lips find my neck, my ear.

"Be as loud as you want," he says. "There's no one around but me for miles, and I'm clinging to every last syllable."

Then he kisses me and as he does, he slides his fingers inside me all the way to the knuckle and crooks them with his thumb still on my clit. I shout. I dig my nails into his back, and he inhales sharply and it doesn't matter, because he does it again and I can't stop myself.

Levi rocks against me while he strokes me, hard as an iron spike against my thigh as he brings me closer and closer to the edge until suddenly, finally, he stops and pulls his fingers out and I sit up, push him backward. I push until he's standing and I'm still sitting, his lips on mine as I unbutton his pants and push them off his hips.

I grab his cock through his boxers and Levi groans into my mouth as I stroke him from tip to root, his hips driving forward. I do it again and then get his boxers off too, and now the biggest cock I've ever seen in person is naked in front of me.

I stroke him and he moans. I do it again and I swear he

growls then pushes his lips against mine, and then somehow he lifts me and he's sitting on the edge of the bed and I'm standing, his cock still in my hand, and I pump him again as my panties come off.

"C'mere," he says, low and husky. "Closer."

I push myself against him, hand still wrapped around his shaft.

"Closer," he says again and pulls me until I'm straddling him, knees astride his hips.

"Like that?" I whisper.

"Almost," he says, that smile on his lips.

He holds my back with one hand and with the other, he reaches out and opens the drawer on his bedside table and I hear a telltale crinkle. Levi tears open the condom and puts it on, and I roll it down his cock with both hands, nearly shaking with anticipation.

"June?" he murmurs.

"Yes?"

"Closer."

He has me by the hips, lifts me, and I sink onto him with a single stroke, my hand knotting in his hair as my breath leaves me in a rush, my face pressed to his.

"Like that," he whispers into my ear, his voice ragged and rough as he rocks me back and forth. "Just like that."

"Just like that," I echo, my arms around his shoulders. He sinks deeper with every movement, each nudge and stroke and suggestion lighting up the pleasure centers inside me.

Gently, he pushes me back and without breaking rhythm, pulls my knees up, wraps my legs around him. He changes the angle and pulls me down onto him and I shift my hips and anchor my hands on his knees and Levi thrusts and I shout, "Oh, *fuck*," and he does it again and again and *holy shit*, I'm five seconds from coming.

"Levi," I breathe, the word coming out like a prayer.

"Say it again."

I gasp. I gather my wits.

"Levi, go slow," I beg. "Please."

"Like this?" he growls, pulling me in hard, sinking deep.

"You have to go slow," I whisper, sinking one hand into his hair, pulling our faces together. "Go slow, please, please—"

Levi captures my mouth with his and my words turn into whimpers and he doesn't slow down, not even a little. He kisses me and he pushes deeper, harder, and our mouths are together and I'm half kissing him and half whispering *not yet, not yet, not yet* and I'm still whispering that as I come so hard my vision goes white.

I feel like I'm being taken apart, like I'm origami being unfolded, flattened back into a sheet of paper. It feels like a force bigger than me, more powerful and when it's over I'm left gasping, flushed, shaking.

"—so fucking beautiful," Levi says as I kiss him. I kiss him and I take him as hard and deep as I can, and I do it again and again until he groans and buries his face in my neck and grabs my shoulder so hard I think it might bruise and in that moment I'm fiercely, desperately possessive of him.

Then we stay like that, our arms around each other. Levi turns his head, burrows into my neck and I hold him tighter, his hair sticking to my arms, his skin damp with sweat.

Finally, he raises his face to mine, kisses me, and then I untangle myself. He stands, excuses himself for a moment, and I flop onto his bed.

It's almost two in the morning, I just did the wrong thing, and it was immensely satisfying.

CHAPTER EIGHTEEN

LEVI

When I get back to my bedroom, June is sprawled on the bed and I sprawl next to her. It's hot and humid, even at night, so I find her hand with mine and tangle our fingers together. It'll have to do for cuddling for the moment.

"I would be extremely amenable to doing that again," I finally say, minutes later, and June just starts laughing.

"Good," she says.

"Not immediately," I admit.

"Can I tell you something?" she asks.

"Anything," I say, looking over at her. "You could tell me you're behind the tree murders and right now, I wouldn't mind."

"What if I'd orchestrated all this just to get you in bed?" June muses, still laughing.

I consider this for a moment, staring at my ceiling.

"Worth it," I finally say.

"You'd be mad tomorrow," June says.

"What were you going to tell me?"

She turns her head and now we're looking at each other

across my mattress, our hands entangled, both of us still giddy and riding a high. June bites her lips together like she's reconsidering.

"June," I say.

"I've never come that fast before," she admits quickly. "Usually it takes, like, three vibrators and a marching band."

I'm grinning like an idiot.

She narrows her eyes, watching me like she's trying not to laugh again.

"I was going to apologize but now I think I might not?" she says.

I bring our joined hands to my lips, kiss her fingers.

"Are you kidding?" I ask. "I'm getting that on a plaque."

"Please don't."

"I won't put it up somewhere embarrassing," I tease, kissing one more finger.

"No plaques. Please?"

"No plaques if you stay over," I say.

"Only if we sleep in the same bed this time," she says. "Do you still have that extra toothbrush?"

· · * * * ★ ★ * * · ·

I'M NOT USED to anyone else being in my bed. To put it mildly, it has been *a while* since I dated, so when I wake up with June's hair in my face, I have no idea where I am.

Then she turns to face me, and I remember. She opens her eyes slowly, two pools of pure, vibrant blue, and I lean in, kiss her on the forehead.

"Morning," I say.

June glares daggers.

"*What,*" she says, then rolls over and falls back asleep.

I make a mental note: *not a morning person*, and then I go back to sleep myself.

· · · * * ★ * * · · · ·

"You fixed the window," June says. She's sitting on my bed cross-legged, leaning back on her hands, looking at the window that had a tree branch through it a few weeks ago.

"Yes, I fixed a broken window," I say, pulling a shirt over my head. "Is that a surprise?"

"Not when you put it like that," she says, smiling.

"How do you feel about eggs and pancakes?" I ask, pulling my hair back into a knot.

"Positively."

"Would you like some before I take you home?" I ask, leaning over the bed.

"That sounds lovely," she says, and gives me a lingering kiss.

I practically float down the stairs on a cloud, humming some tune that I made up as I descend the final few steps into the living room.

And then I stop dead in my tracks, because Caleb is sitting on one of my couches, laptop open on his lap.

"Hey," he says, nodding without looking up.

I stand there, frozen. I think *agog* is the word.

There's no way I can tell anyone. Not yet. Especially someone who knows Silas pretty well, such as one of my brothers.

After a moment he glances up at me, then frowns.

"You okay?" he asks.

"Yeah," I say.

"I just let myself in," he says, jerking a thumb over his shoulder at the front door. "It's still cool if I crash here for the weekend, right? I don't know if I can spend five more minutes in Warwick, and I really need to work on my dissertation."

Finally, I remember, and I heave a deep breath. Right. It's the weekend, and Caleb is going to stay here because my house is quiet and peaceful and, according to him, it's the best place to think deep math thoughts.

"Yes, right," I say. "Of course. Certainly. But I just realized that I forgot something upstairs in my bedroom so I'm just going to go back up there and—"

"Is my shirt down there?" June shouts.

Caleb's eyebrows go up so fast they nearly shoot off his face, and I clear my throat.

"No," I call back.

"Never mind, found it," she says. "But did I leave my socks—"

"My brother's here," I shout up.

Silence.

Then: "Which one?"

"Caleb."

"Hello," Caleb calls, already shutting his laptop. "This seems like it's a bad time."

Then he stands and looks at me, lowers his voice.

"June?" he asks me.

I clear my throat.

"Yes," I confirm. "And I'd appreciate it if you kept this to yourself."

Caleb raises one eyebrow and looks very, very amused.

"You mean if I kept it secret from Silas," he says.

"Keeping it to yourself includes keeping it from Silas, yes," I say.

The bedroom door opens. June emerges, comes down the stairs.

"Hi, Caleb," she says, smiling just a little bit too much.

"Good morning," he says. "How are you?"

"I'm well," she says. "Yourself?"

I don't think I've ever seen Caleb look more entertained in my entire life.

"Oh, quite well," he says. "I'm doing *so* well right now, June. It's nice to see you. Also, surprising."

"Likewise," June deadpans. "Levi's given you a key and told you to drop by whenever, I presume?"

"Yes to the key, no to the whenever," he says. "In fact, Levi was fully aware that I was coming this morning to spend the weekend at his house, and it looks like he forgot."

Now they're both looking at me: June with one eyebrow raised, and Caleb grinning like he's won the lottery. Which, in Loveless terms, he kind of has.

"I'm afraid my social calendar got somewhat scrambled," I say to both of them, rubbing my knuckles on my forehead. "Caleb, would you like pancakes?"

"I would *love* pancakes," he says, and puts his laptop bag back down.

June turns to me.

"Can I call my parents from your landline so they don't think I've been murdered or kidnapped?" she asks.

I nearly ask the two of them if we should just run an ad in the local paper about June spending the night, but I bite my tongue.

"Of course," I say.

· · · ★ ★ ★ ★ ★ · · · ·

"Wait, I didn't hear about any of this," June is saying, pointing the tines of her fork at me. "They weren't actually together when they went public with their relationship, and then they were fake-together but also really together, but still pretending to be fake together and not actually together?"

"It got very complicated," I say, cutting a triangle of pancake and putting it into my mouth. "I couldn't keep track of who thought what about that relationship."

"This is what I miss by not living in Sprucevale anymore," Caleb says reflectively. "All this nonsense you people get up to."

"We kept you up to date on Daniel's ridiculous situation," I protest.

"*Seth* kept me up to date on Daniel's ridiculous situation," Caleb corrects. "And he's the only one who bothered to tell me that Eli was secretly hooking up with Violet last year—"

"You were through-hiking the Pacific Crest Trail," I point out. "I had no idea when you would have cell service, or whether you'd be checking, or whether the situation would have changed by the time you got my voicemails—"

"Seth managed," he says. "For a while I got into the habit of turning my phone on every time I got to a high point in the hopes that I'd have a block of gossip texts."

"Levi doesn't believe in texting," June says.

"I know," Caleb says. "You know about his phone, right?"

June laughs.

"I had no idea those still worked," she says.

"It's only five years old," I say, frowning because I don't approve of them ganging up on me.

"What happened with Eli and Violet?" June asks. "I thought they were just... together."

Caleb pushes his plate away and grins again. I swear that being the first to know my gossip has made my youngest brother practically giddy, and I'm very annoyed by it.

"They *hated* each other growing up," he says. "And then — Levi, jump in whenever — they wound up working at the same place about a year and a half ago, and next thing everyone knew, Eli's car was parked outside Violet's house every night while they also swore up and down they couldn't stand each other."

"They thought no one knew," I explain to June. "Eli doesn't always think things through, and apparently neither does Violet."

Caleb gives me *a look*, and I ignore it pointedly.

"But they got over themselves and now they seem quite happy," I finish.

"Why not just tell people they were dating?" June asks, her elbows leaning on the table, mystified.

"Because Eli can be the most difficult person alive when he puts his mind to it, and apparently Violet gives him a run for his money," I say.

"All of you love convoluted situations," Caleb says. "You could always meet a girl, ask for her number, and take her on a date. Perfectly simple, no need for high-level sneaking, secrecy, and skullduggery that'll inevitably get found out."

June and I look at each other.

"I think Seth takes girls on dates," I volunteer, and Caleb just gives me another look.

"That's not dating," he says, standing and holding out his hands for our plates.

"Wait, what's Seth doing?" June asks.

"Who, not what," Caleb says. "You really have been away, haven't you?"

"Apparently," June says. "Tell me everything."

· · · · · ★ ★ ★ ★ · · · ·

"Do you mind parking a couple houses away?" June asks as I turn into her neighborhood. "I told my parents I went out for a long walk so it would probably undermine my lie if I showed up in your truck."

"I could just say I found you on the side of the road, looking lost," I say.

June gives me a look.

"Or I could come up with a better lie than that," I offer.

"Could you?" she asks, laughing.

I pull to the side of the road in front of a big brick house that looks almost, but not quite, like June's parents' house.

"I could say," I tell her, thinking. "That you accidentally wandered into the forest, and I just so happened to be in the forest at that very moment and came upon—"

"Can I just stop you there?" she asks.

"You walked into town and I saw you at the Mountain Grind," I say. "And I offered you a ride home. There, how's that?"

"Now we're getting somewhere," she says. "But I'm just gonna stick with long walk for now."

We look at each other, both in the cab of my truck. It's full daylight and anyone driving past could see us, and I know that, but I can't bring myself to care.

Then we both start talking at the exact same time.

"That was really—"

"What are you doing—"

We stop. June starts laughing, and I smile, take her hand in mine, kiss the back of it.

"What are you doing later?" I ask.

"That's not the question you should be asking," she says, leaning against the headrest of my truck, relaxed and beautiful, her blue eyes on me. "The question you should be asking is, what's *Caleb* doing later?"

"He has mysteriously elected to spend the remainder of the weekend at my mom's house," I say.

"In that case, I'm free," June says. "What time should I come over?"

"Any time," I tell her.

We kiss goodbye, long and slow. I'd rather not. I'd rather have stayed in my bed all weekend without a care in the world, but she'll be back tonight and that will have to be good enough.

"See you soon," June says, then gets out of my truck and shuts the door. I watch her as she walks past two houses, then turns into her own driveway, and I can't help feeling deeply wrong at not walking her to her front door.

I watch her until she's inside, and then I turn around and go back home.

CHAPTER NINETEEN

JUNE

There's no one in the living room when I enter my parents' house, and I breathe a sigh of relief. To be honest, my mom didn't sound at all convinced when I told her that I'd decided to take a long walk by myself very early this morning, and I had visions of her and my dad, waiting just inside the door, ready to start shouting questions the moment I came in.

But instead there's no one here, just the sound of running water and dishes clinking together from the kitchen.

I might actually get away with this.

For the record, my parents are very accepting of the fact that I'm an adult who does adult things sometimes, but it's a very *don't ask, don't tell* situation. Besides, I really can't fathom telling them *hey, Levi Loveless came by at twelve-thirty last night and offered to seduce me, so I've been over there, what are your weekend plans like?*

I shut the door softly behind myself. I tread quietly across the living room, heading for the staircase. If I'm quiet enough, I think I can get upstairs without alerting my parents in the kitchen, which means I can change and get a little breathing room before I have to explain—

"How was your walk?" a voice asks.

I stop cold in my tracks. It's not one of my parents.

It's Silas, the very last person in the world I'd like to talk about my 'walk' right now.

"June?" he says, something clanking in the kitchen sink.

I give the stairs one last longing look, then turn to the kitchen doorway.

"It was great!" I say. "Finally starting to cool off a little in the morning."

"Where'd you go?" he asks, pulling out the sprayer and dousing the skillet he's just finished washing.

I clear my throat and walk into the kitchen, open the fridge door to give myself a few extra seconds.

"Just down to Fox Run," I say. "I couldn't sleep very well, so I went down there and read for a while, then headed back."

I remember I don't have a book with me.

"On my phone. I've got some books on my phone, it's very convenient," I say, and finally grab the creamer from the fridge. "Is there any coffee left?"

"Nah, but you can make some more," he says, and shuts off the water, carefully balancing the skillet atop an impressive mound of other pots and pans in the drying rack. "I'll take some if you do."

"Will you?" I deadpan. "Is that why you're still here, just so I'll make some more coffee?"

"Yeah, I decided it was easier to wash all the breakfast dishes and wait for you to get back instead of just making more coffee myself," he says, wiping his hands with a dish towel and then leaning back against the sink.

"Suspected as much," I say, and reach into the cabinet for the filters and the coffee. I put a new filter in the machine, eyeball the amount of grounds — not to brag, but I'm very good at that — and then when I go to fill the pot with water, I realize Silas is still just watching me.

"What?" I ask, defensive, unnerved. My hand tightens on the handle of the pot.

He knows, I think to myself. *I have no idea how but he does and it hasn't been a day but I'm already ruining their relationship.*

"Are you all right?" he asks, his voice suddenly gentle.

"What?" I finally answer, too surprised to say anything else.

"Look, I'm not trying to pry or anything, but you've been acting different lately," he says, arms folded over his chest as he looks away, toward the kitchen table. "I know that between the breakup and the job hunt and how much you always hated it here, you've been having a hard time. I got kind of worried when Mom said you'd gone on a walk this morning."

I swallow hard, guilt settling deep in the pit of my stomach.

"I'm fine," I say, shaking my head and shutting off the water. "I mean, yeah, things have been kind of rough lately but I'm really fine, I just wanted to go for a walk, get out of the house, go be by myself for a little while."

I'm pretty sure I'm blushing, and I definitely can't bring myself to look Silas in the eye right now, so I turn away from him and pour the water into the coffee maker.

Behind me, he takes a deep breath, clears his throat.

"You know you can always talk to me," he says.

The way he says it, he doesn't quite sound like himself. It's Silas, obviously, but it sounds… rehearsed.

My heart plummets.

"You don't even have to tell me about it. I can help you find the right person, if you want, or I can just listen if that's what you need. Therapy is amazing. Just let me know. You're not alone, June," he says.

I feel like dirt.

I feel like lying, sneaking, best-friend-screwing dirt as I finish pouring the water into the coffee maker, then hit the button.

You should be pissed, I think. *If you knew the truth, you'd be so pissed at me and oh, God, I'm the world's worst sister.*

"Thanks," I manage to say as I turn around, rubbing my palms against my shorts. "I'm okay. Really. But thank you."

He sighs, then in two steps he's across the kitchen and he wraps me in his arms, practically lifting me off the ground.

"I'm here if you need me, Bug," he says, and I squeeze him back. "Whatever it is, okay?"

Tell him.

Just tell him, and get it over with, and let him be angry instead of sweet and caring because that would be so much easier to take.

It's on the tip of my tongue, *I had sex with Levi and I'm gonna do it again,* but I bite it back because I'm not the one who'll really have to reckon with Silas.

It's not me he'll be pissed at. I mean, he'll do some hollering for sure, but I have a zero percent chance of being punched in the face.

But I want to tell him. I do. I want him to stop worrying about me and be happy, because right now I'm happier than I've been in a long time and I can't tell him.

"I know," I finally say into his shoulder. "But I'm fine. Really."

Finally, he steps back, ruffles my hair — which I hate and have always hated and he knows it — and looks at me.

"What are you up to today, Bug?" he asks, head cocked to one side.

"That depends on how many more times you call me Bug," I tell him, and that finally gets a smile. "I have an article I should write, and a couple of other job leads —"

I'm going to Levi's tonight...

"It's Saturday," he objects. "Forget work. Want to get lunch and a movie? My treat."

Guilt. *Guilt.*

"All I had to do to get you to buy me lunch was take a walk early in the morning?" I ask, trying to keep my voice light.

"I'd probably have offered if you'd gotten a sudden, drastic haircut or something," he teases.

"*Would* you notice a sudden, drastic haircut?" I tease back.

Silas hangs the dishtowel on the stove and grins at me.

"Don't stereotype," he says. "I'm very perceptive. Go shower, I'm not taking you out if you smell bad."

"You're one to talk!" I shout over my shoulder as I head upstairs.

· · * * ★ ★ ★ * * · ·

WE GET barbecue at a hole in the wall joint the next town over, and then Silas makes me see a romantic comedy about a woman who runs a pet wedding business and, by the end of the movie, finds love of her own.

I wanted to see the gritty World War II epic that's out right now, but Silas absolutely refused, and since he was paying for it, I saw the dog wedding movie.

It wasn't my thing, but it was fine.

And moreover, it works. I don't know if the movie worked — luckily the theater was nearly empty, because we whispered throughout most of it — but it's a really, really fun day. Silas is right that I didn't like Sprucevale at all when I left it over ten years ago for college, and he's also right that I'm not crazy about the place now.

But spending a day with my big brother helps remind me what I do like about it. He's here. My parents are here. On the street, I run into at least five different people I know, and they all seem happy to see me.

Finally, he drops me back off at my parents' house and makes me take all the leftovers, then leaves again with one last, big hug.

"I had fun, Bug," he says.

I sigh dramatically at the nickname.

"Thanks," I say. "Me too. Even if I can't believe you made me watch that movie."

"Arf arf means I love you," he says, and I snort.

Silas leaves. I put the leftovers in the fridge, wave to my parents, check the time.

I make myself wait, just a little while. I work on *Twelve Owl Reaction GIFs That Will Make You Say HOO BOY.* I watch the clock, and wonder how soon is too soon, or if there's such a thing as too soon. I don't want to be too eager, or too gung-ho, and scare him off. Guys don't like that, right?

At 6:30, my phone rings, and I knock it onto the floor in my eagerness to answer it.

"You're still coming, right?" Levi asks.

"Of course," I tell him.

"Well, you don't seem to be here," he says, his voice low and slow and lazy.

"You said evening."

"Half past six is evening by my measure," he says. "Sun's going down. Moon's coming up. Get over here already."

I can't help but smile at the wall of my bedroom.

"All right, I'm leaving now," I tell him, shoving my

laptop into my bag so I can work on *Twelve Owl Reaction GIFs etc.* over there tomorrow morning.

"You haven't left yet?" he says in mock-annoyance.

"I forgot we were on country time," I tease, laughing.

"We'll get you right soon enough," Levi says, that smile in his voice. "Hurry up, I'm making dinner."

"What is it?"

"You'll find out when you get here," he says, and I'm still smiling when I hang up the phone. I'm smiling as I find my largest purse and shove a change of clothes into it, then rearrange the lump until from the outside it looks like normal purse contents, not *I'm spending the night somewhere else* contents.

I skip out of my room. I float down the stairs, and on the landing, I take a deep breath and prep myself.

I don't like lying to my parents, because I don't really feel justified doing it. I'm almost thirty, and to be honest, they're pretty cool parents.

I just can't quite handle the *hey so I'm gonna go have sex* discussion, and even if I could handle some form of that, the next question would be *who with* and I think it's best to just avoid the whole thing all together.

"Hi!" I say brightly to my mom in the living room, reading, and my dad making dinner in the kitchen, both visible from the stairs even though they're on different sides of a wall.

"Hi, sweetie," they chorus back, Sprucevale's classic rock radio station drifting toward me from my dad's ancient kitchen radio.

"You're going out?"

"I'm making my special spicy eggplant," my dad says. "You're gonna miss out."

"Sorry," I tell him. "Yeah, I'm meeting Mandy Hargrove for dinner, figured we'd do some catching up and we'll probably stay out late so I'm sure you'll be in bed when I get back, and since this morning was so great I'm going to get up again and go hiking really early so I might not even be back until mid-morning or so. Don't wait breakfast on me!"

I smile. I smile hard. I might smile a bit too hard as I clamp down a giggle that threatens to rise from my throat and give me away completely.

My dad just whistles, still stirring his eggplant creation.

"Knock 'em dead, sweetheart," he says. "Have fun, see you tomorrow!"

"Thanks!" I say and walk through the living room.

"You're getting dinner with Mandy?" my mom asks from the couch, her book in her lap.

Oh no.

I stop in my tracks, and I don't even know how or why, but I know I'm busted.

"Yep!" I say brightly. "I haven't really seen or talked to her since high school but then I ran into her the other day and we decided to catch up."

In the back of my mind, I'm running through all the criteria that made Mandy Hargrove a good alibi: my parents barely know her or her parents, she's still in town, and we did hang out sometimes during high school.

"Well, that sounds fun," she says. "And tell Levi we say hello."

I stare at her for at least three very long seconds. It's moments like this that I'm convinced my mother is a psychic, or a witch, or a psychic witch or an alien with the ability to see through time and space or *something*.

Finally, I clear my throat.

"Who?" I ask.

It's a dumb response, because while I wouldn't have been shocked if she gave me some pushback on where exactly I was going, I didn't think she would know precisely what I'm up to.

She looks up again, amused this time.

"Junebug, did you forget that land lines have caller ID?" she asks.

I open my mouth, then close it. Then I clear my throat.

"Yes," I admit, feeling very, very dumb.

I'm also feeling very lucky that Silas didn't answer my parents' phone this morning, because then he'd have seen where I was calling from and I'd have fucked this up almost before it started.

Now my mom is laughing as she puts her bookmark in her book and walks over to me, one hand on my shoulder. Classic rock radio is still coming from the kitchen, and I can hear little snippets of my dad singing along.

"Levi has always been a lovely young man," she says, giving me a hug.

"You can't tell Silas," I say.

"Who do you think I am?" my mom says lightly.

I just sigh.

"Your brother is *your* problem," she says gently, patting me on the back. "But we did always like Levi. Unless you ever want me to rip his heart bodily from his chest with my bare hands. In that case, just say the word, sweetheart."

"Thanks," I say.

I guess I know where Silas got it from.

"Have fun," my mom says. "And be safe!"

I give her a suspicious look, because I'm sort of wondering where this extremely cool version of my mom came from. Granted, I haven't lived with her since I was eighteen, but she very definitely was not this cool back then.

"Is this a trap?" I ask.

She sits back on the couch and picks up her book.

"Nope," she says. "You're grown, just don't come home pregnant."

Then she looks up at me.

"Or do, I'd love grandchildren and your brother sure doesn't seem to be getting me any," she says thoughtfully.

I just point to the door, stunned, then walk to where I'm pointing. My mom laughs.

"See you tomorrow," she says, and I cannot get out of my parents' house fast enough.

CHAPTER TWENTY

LEVI

June rolls over, still breathing hard. The sheet tangles around one leg and she doesn't bother to kick it free, just flops an arm over her head and looks around.

"Did you face your house west so your bedroom would look good at sunset?" she asks, glancing at the windows behind my bed. "If you did, it worked."

"No," I say, still sprawled on my stomach where I've been for the past several minutes, unmoving. I might never move again. I don't mind. "I faced it east so that the sun could come in first thing every morning, and the other wall faced west by accident."

"You deliberately pointed windows at the sunrise?" June asks, turning her head toward me, her blue eyes slightly narrowed, skeptical.

"I'm never in here at sunset," I point out. "But I'm usually in here at sunrise."

"You're in here now," she says, raising one eyebrow. "And the sunset thing is working."

"Are you trying to get me to admit that I built my house specifically to dazzle my hundreds — nay, *thousands*

— of female conquests?" I tease, sliding my hand over her stomach, stopping somewhere in the vicinity of her ribcage.

"Gross," she says, but she's laughing.

For the record, I have not been with hundreds of women. More like a handful, none particularly worth noting. None except June, at least, and maybe it's that first wild blush of infatuation but in my mind, she gleams like a flashlight among fireflies.

I take a deep breath, gather my wits, and finally sit up in my bed, resting against the headboard. I've got one foot still caught in the sheets, but getting it untwisted seems like far too much effort right now.

"Are we still good on the lasagna?" June asks, arching her back a little to look up at me. The movement makes her breasts bob slightly, her stiff pink nipples sway.

I stare. I stare blatantly, and I don't care that she sees me staring blatantly.

"Seven more minutes," I tell her, and June just nods.

I didn't intend the lasagna timer to be a challenge, but June arrived about thirty seconds after I'd put it in the oven.

Then we were kissing, outside on the porch. Then she was straddling me in one of my Adirondack chairs, and then my shirt was somehow off, and then we were on my couch with my head between her naked thighs, and ultimately we wound up here, in my bed, while the sun goes down.

I can't say I'm unhappy with this progression of events.

June rolls onto one elbow, shoves the pillows up behind herself, then scoots to sitting next to me, her head back against the wooden board, the sheet wrapped around one thigh and hiding absolutely nothing.

"You never told me about your tattoo," she says, and

reaches her hand out to touch the left side of my chest, one finger tracing the lines.

"You never asked," I point out.

"You don't seem like the tattoo type," she says. "So either you got super drunk once and asked some guy you knew to ink some lines on you, or it means something."

"It means my brothers have far more influence on me than I'd like sometimes," I say, looking down at her finger. "We all went together. It was Caleb's eighteenth birthday, and Eli was home from wherever he was living at the time, so he and Daniel talked the rest of us into getting them."

"They all match?"

"They're all constellations."

"Which one's this?"

She traces it again with her finger, five quick lines, simple, elegant.

"*Corvus*," I tell her. "The crow."

One, two, three, four, five.

"This looks nothing like a crow."

"Take it up with Ptolemy," I say.

"I will," she says. "Tell me about it."

"There's a legend, but I can never remember it," I say. "Something about Apollo cheating on his lover and a crow lying for him about a snake. I got it because I like crows."

Her finger traces one-two-three-four-five-four-three-two-one.

"They're very smart birds," I go on, her finger on my skin mesmerizing, hypnotizing. "They use tools, solve puzzles, remember faces. If they like you enough, they'll bring you presents."

Her finger pauses, and June looks up at me.

I've never told this story to anyone.

I nearly don't tell it to her. It was years ago, but I know June knew me then and she remembers years ago. I was a weird, awkward teenager and I finally became a slightly less weird, less awkward adult and that feels hard-won.

"I made friends with the crows when I was in high school," I tell her. "After dinner every night, it was my job to take the table scraps out to the compost in the back yard, behind my mom's house. My parents' house, then, and when I was about fourteen, I realized that every night, the crows would sit in the trees above the pile and wait for me. Then, when I left, they'd descend and feast."

I clear my throat. June is dead silent, her pointer finger tapping on the first star in the constellation.

"So I started saving the best scraps for them. Stuff I thought they'd like, mostly meat. It was my dad's idea, actually. He liked animals. I'd put the compost in the compost heap and then feed the crows right next to it so they wouldn't have to dig through the trash."

I'm staring through the windows across the room from me and I draw one knee up, rest an elbow on it, and despite everything, despite being thirty-two and having a good job and a master's degree, despite owning the house that I built, despite having a beautiful woman naked in my head, I can't stop thinking *you're a weirdo, Levi, you're such a fucking weirdo.*

"And they liked you," she says, and she says it with no malice, not a hint of teasing in her voice, just pure...

...wonder. I think it might be wonder.

"They started bringing me things," I say. "My father and I would walk out there at night, and they'd be sitting in the tree, and sometimes there would be something on the ground for us. And you know, usually it was some sort of shiny trash, a piece of bicycle reflector, a strip of aluminum, screws and bolts. But one time it was a watch. Another time it was a silver dollar."

"The crows stole someone's watch for you?" June says. "Holy shit."

Finally, I look down at her, and I can't help but laugh.

"It was pretty beat up, and it was a cheap watch to begin with," I say. "But I kept it all the same. I kept everything the crows gave me. We were friends for two years. My father even tried to teach one to say *Levi* but it never really worked, they were too wild."

"I wish it had worked," June says, and *now* she's laughing but it's a good laugh, a sweet laugh. "Can you imagine hiking through the forest and a crow flies overhead and as it does, you just hear, '*Levi...*'"

"Now I'm even more glad it didn't work," I tell her.

"Why'd you stop? You went to college?"

"I stopped before that," I say, and I pause. I clear my throat. "After Dad died. I didn't mean to. I just never did it again."

"Oh," June says. She takes my hand, squeezes it between both of hers, and kisses me on the shoulder, and then she doesn't say anything else.

I'm glad. I turn and kiss her on the top of her head and I'm so intensely glad that she says nothing except *oh* because, in the years that span his accident until now, I've heard every single condolence, every trite statement, every banal saying that comes out of peoples' mouths about death. I've heard all of them and if I never hear another again, it'll be too soon.

She was there, of course, in the aftermath, at the candlelight vigils and memorial services and the funeral and the dedication when County Route 14 technically became Thomas Loveless Road, at the pancake breakfasts and luncheons. I don't remember her specifically — she would have been thirteen, and I was sixteen and lost at sea — but I know she was there.

But I remember Silas. Silas who was, somehow, always there, always over at our house or making me come back to his. Silas who was the homecoming king and football star and who had, allegedly, already had sex with a sorority girl, but who spent hours holding me while I sobbed and never told a single solitary soul.

Silas, whose kindness I've repaid by bedding his little sister.

"Anyway, nine years later I let my brothers talk me into getting a constellation tattoo and I found this one," I say. "I think it could be worse."

"I like it," June says. "It's simple. Elegant. They could have talked you into flaming dice, or a naked chick."

"I'm not sure they could have," I tell her, and she laughs.

"What do the others have?" she asks. "You can't just tell me there's a list and then not tell me the list. I *hate* that. Like when you read that 'poisonous snakes are the fourth deadliest animal in the U.S.' and then the article *doesn't tell you the first three.*"

I just look down at her.

"Dogs, then bees, then livestock is number one," she says. "I looked it up, obviously."

"Daniel got the snake. *Serpens*," I say, because I know the Latin name, of course I know the Latin name. "Because, and I quote, *snakes are badass.*"

June snorts.

"He was twenty-two," I say. "This was pre-Rusty. Eli got the dragon with the north star in its tail. Seth got Scorpio because it was his girlfriend's zodiac sign, and Caleb got the sextant because he's always been a nerd."

"Was this before or after he had senior girls fight over whose math homework he'd help with first?" June asks. "When he was a freshman."

"Caleb?" I ask, confused.

"Mhm," she confirms. "Mandy Hargrove once slapped Danica Nelson because she interrupted a tutoring session with Caleb. I was there. I saw it."

"*Caleb?*" I ask again, and then: "Is tutoring a euphemism for something else?"

"Literal tutoring," June says. "In the library. When I was a senior. A slapfight, I swear to God. You were in college by then."

I can't imagine it. My youngest brother has always been the most straightforward, the most practical. He's always been utterly determined that he can think and logic his way out of any situation, that if all involved parties simply agree to see reason, most situations will resolve themselves.

From downstairs, the oven timer dings.

"A slapfight over Caleb?" I ask, just checking one last time as I unwind my foot from the sheets.

"You know how some girls get hot for their teachers," she says, laughing, pulling herself out of the bed. "All that authoritatively explaining *sine* and *cosine.*"

"Bizarre," I mutter, pulling on my boxers and heading downstairs.

· · * * * ★ ★ ★ * * · ·

TEN MINUTES LATER, I'm still in my boxers and June is wearing nothing but panties and the shirt I had on until an hour ago. We're on the back porch in the last of the fading light, plates in our laps, Hedwig running around and chasing birds and squirrels and whatever it is dogs do.

"Oh," June says suddenly, then looks up at me. "My mom knows."

I look at her, then past her at the porch, at the small back yard, at the forest beyond it, the warm humid night air drifting over my mostly bare skin, and I can't bring myself to care.

I just shrug.

"My brother knows," I say.

"She said she wouldn't tell Silas," June goes on. "And I don't think she will. She never told him when I dated Derek Brandt after he joined the service."

That gets my attention.

"You dated Derek?"

"Briefly," June shrugs. "We broke up after like a month for some reason I don't even remember."

"Was it because he was a total creep who sold pot to fourteen-year-olds under the bleachers at football games?" I ask.

"No," June says, thinking. "Wait, I remember. *He* broke up with *me* because I stopped letting him copy my biology homework."

Next time I see Derek, I'd like to punch him, I think, and the violence and anger of the thought surprises me, deeply felt though it is.

"He wasn't my finest hour," June says. "You know, we could just tell him."

"I don't think Derek needs to know anything about us," I say, trying to sound light, like there's not a tightness in my chest at the idea of someone treating June like that.

"Ha ha," June deadpans. "But maybe we're making a mountain out of a molehill here, you know?"

In the backyard, Hedwig yips at something. The moon is just rising and if I look closely, I can see the bats coming out of their homes, darting across the pale brightness.

June is going to break my heart. I don't need tarot cards or scrying bones or the second sight to see that it'll happen, because I know. She'll leave Sprucevale and with it, she'll leave me, and then it will fall to me to gather myself and move on.

It'll be easier if Silas doesn't know. It'll be easier if I find myself in the wreckage of one relationship, not two.

Right now, I'm at the zenith of the pendulum, the top of the arc. The point when it seems like maybe, this time, it'll just hover in the air like that forever, defying gravity and the laws of physics.

It never does. This moment won't last, either, when I have both June and Silas, but I'll be damned if I don't try to make it last a little longer.

"Not yet," I say, after a moment. "When the time is right."

June just shrugs.

"Sure," she says.

· · · ★ ★ ★ ★ · · ·

THE WEEK after I drive to her house and throw rocks at her window, she spends every night at my house. The next week, six nights, and the week after that, five, and then that number holds steady.

I give her a key. She has a toothbrush, plus several small containers on my bathroom counter that she tells me are her 'skincare routine.' I don't question any of them, but she does smell nice.

She keeps coming to Sunday dinners at my mom's house with her brother, and we sneak kisses upstairs, in the backyard, in the kitchen when no one's looking.

Another huge, old tree is murdered in the forest, and we hike out to visit its remains, but there are no more clues. On the way back, we hit on the idea of installing camera traps: remote cameras triggered by motion. We usually use them for wildlife, but they'd work for this, too.

I order them, a Byzantine process since this is the Forest Service we're talking about. June keeps applying for jobs, getting rejections. She has a couple of phone interviews and one video interview, but none of them go anywhere.

Secretly, I'm relieved. I know she likes journalism and I know that she feels meaningless and adrift without her career, but I'm greedy and I'm selfish and I want her to stay.

We still don't tell Silas. We go on dates to other towns, even a weekend away in West Virginia, and neither of us tells a single soul where we're really going or who we're going with. Each of my brothers individually makes a different *that's very interesting* face when I tell them that I'm going alone to a bed and breakfast for a weekend to study a particular kind of pinecone, but I don't care.

June's mine, at least for now.

CHAPTER TWENTY-ONE

JUNE

From: editorial@herald-trumpet.com
Subject: Telephone interview, 10/2

Dear Ms. Flynn,
We recently received your application for our Metro Editor
position, and we think that you may be a good fit. Are you
available for a telephone interview this coming Tuesday,
October 2?
Regards,
Edmund Sanderson
Editor-in-Chief, Bluff City Herald-Trumpet

· · * * * ★ ★ ★ * * · ·

I blink at my inbox, mouth half-open around a straw as I
stare at my phone. In front of me, my laptop is open
and displaying about a dozen various gifs from *Parks and
Recreation*, mostly of Ron Swanson making grumpy faces.
It's for a listicle that I'm half-heartedly writing at the

Mountain Grind, Sprucevale's premier and only coffee shop.

Yes, I'm checking my email on my phone while my computer is in front of me. Habits are weird sometimes.

I wasn't expecting to ever hear from the Trumpet-Herald. According to my job application tracking spreadsheet, I applied for this position over a month ago and I'm not *quite* qualified — they wanted two years of editorial work plus five reporting, and I've only got the five reporting.

But here they are, inviting me to a phone interview for what's by far the best job I've applied for. There's a part of me that suspects Silas is behind this, somehow, just to make me feel better, but regardless of that I put my drink down, open the email on my computer, and type a response that's a more professional version of *hell yes, let's do this*.

I proofread the email twice, then hit send. I take another long pull from my iced raspberry mocha, already wondering if I should have laid off the caffeine before five p.m.

I completely, utterly, and decisively ignore the fact that this job is in South Dakota. I'll worry about that when and if it becomes an issue, because right now all I've got is a phone interview. I'm not even quite qualified for the job, so it's pretty unlikely it'll ever get past that point, and at the very least, every phone interview is good practice for the next phone interview.

Quietly, I've been applying for every position I can find at any small-town paper that's two hours or less from Sprucevale. There aren't very many, and they're either far below where my pay grade should be or they're far above it.

I'm just about to re-start my listicle, *Thirteen Times Ron*

Swanson Really Felt All Our Feels, when a prickle on the back of my neck tells me to look up.

Levi is standing in the middle of the Mountain Grind, hands in his pockets, looking up at the chalkboard menu posted over the coffee bar. My heart flips. My stomach knots. I bite the inside of my lip to keep myself from smiling too much, because this place is Gossip Central.

After a moment, he glances over and nods, that quiet smile at the corner of his eyes, and as he steps forward to order his drink, I swear I'm just as nervous as the day his truck pulled up behind mine in that thunderstorm.

I pretend to work. I don't. I scroll aimlessly through pictures while secretly watching Levi: ordering, waiting, getting a napkin, sprinkling something atop his drink and then putting the lid back on.

Then, at last, he walks over, and I try not to act like a schoolgirl.

"I didn't know I'd run into you here," he says by way of introduction.

It's true. I didn't tell him I was coming here.

"Ta da," I say. "I had to get out of my parents' house before they drove me *actually* insane."

Levi takes a long sip of his drink, watching me.

"I haven't seen you in a while," he says formally, a little bit too loudly. "How have you been?"

Ah, so this is what we're doing, I think, and try not to laugh.

Levi's a terrible liar. Maybe the worst liar I've ever met. He saw me this morning, because I was naked in his bed.

"I've been well," I say. "Still the same. Looking for a job. Bumming around town."

He clears his throat, shifts his stance slightly.

"Do you want to sit?" I ask, gesturing at my table's other chair, currently across from me.

"Thank you," Levi says, and then glances around in a

pretty unsubtle fashion before moving the chair around the corner until it's next to me, then sitting.

"Extremely un-suspicious," I tease.

"I don't know what you're talking about," Levi dead-pans, still drinking his drink.

Under the table, our knees touch. My heart pumps a little bit faster. I fight the urge to reach under the table, touch his leg, put my hand on his. I like touching him, even casually, even after four weeks — five? I can't keep track — with lots and lots of touching.

"He's meeting me here in twenty minutes," I say, pushing my laptop away, taking my own nearly empty drink in one hand. "To congratulate me on a hundred official job rejections."

"He's celebrating that?" he asks, his eyebrows dipping slightly and *very* skeptically.

"He's not being a dick, it's some motivational thing he read... I don't know, somewhere. You know how Silas is," I say. "I guess the idea is that if you try for a certain number of rejections, along the way somewhere you're bound to get an acceptance."

"Shoot for the moon, and even if you fail, you'll land among the stars," Levi says, taking another drink.

"Now you're a motivational poster too?"

"Well, it's patently untrue," he says, and there's the smile again. "The moon is tens of millions of miles closer than the closest star, so if you shoot for the moon and miss, you'll either fall back to Earth as a pile of flaming wreck-age, or you'll float forever through the vacuum of space."

"I'm so inspired right now," I deadpan, and he nods at my computer, where my email is still open.

"Interview?" he asks, and I glance at the screen, instantly wishing I'd closed it when he came over.

He's not even being nosy. It's all right there in black and

white letters, and have you ever tried to not read something that's directly in front of your face? It's impossible.

"Tuesday," I say. "Just a phone interview, it's this editorial position at a newspaper that I'm not even qualified for, they must just be reaching out to everyone who applied or something."

"Don't sell yourself short," he says, keeping his voice low. "You're good at what you do, June. Don't forget that. They'd be lucky to have you, technically qualified or not."

He glances at the screen again before I reach forward and shut it, but I'm certain it's more than long enough for him to read *Bluff City Herald-Trumpet*.

"Okay, quit snooping," I say, and I try to sound light, teasing. "Why are you drinking fancy coffee? What happened?"

"It's decaf," he says.

"It's still got whipped cream," I point out. Levi doesn't drink regular coffee ever, and only occasionally indulges in coffee-adjacent beverages like this one when he wants to feel better about something.

"There was another murder," he says. "Further north than the others. Right where we thought the next one would be."

Then he frowns.

"And we still didn't catch them," he says, tapping his thick fingers on the cup, still clearly frustrated. "One of the junior rangers we posted said that he saw two people coming out of the woods and onto the road right at dusk, and it looked like the man was carrying some kind of machinery, but of course, before he could catch them they got into a black SUV and drove off."

"Dammit," I hiss. "What he was driving, a skateboard?"

"He was on foot," Levi says, like it's obvious. "It's hard

to be quiet and sneaky when you're in a Forest Service vehicle that sounds like an angry bear every time you rev the engine."

He has a point. And he does, after all, know more about this than I do.

"It's very easy to hide from a vehicle, and vehicles are very bad at pursuing through the forest," he says. He takes another sip. He glances one more time at my closed laptop. "But I do have good news."

"They left their name, address, and a signed confession nailed to the tree stump?" I ask.

"The camera traps finally arrived," he says. "That's why I came to town, actually, because I got a phone message from FedEx that the delivery address didn't exist, so they just left them at Bob's Mailboxes and More."

"You mean the driver didn't feel like driving down to the ranger station," I say, and Levi just shrugs.

"Your present came, too," he says casually, as if I know what he's talking about.

I blink. Then I look around quickly, over my shoulder at the Bible study group, past them to the teenagers who've got their textbooks open and are clearly paying them no mind whatsoever.

"My present?"

"I got you something," he says, taking another sip of his decaf confection, that smile hiding behind his beard.

My heart just about stops, and I swear I can feel the blush rising all the way from my toes, my pulse beating faster.

"What is it?" I ask, leaning in. Something about the way he says it makes me think that Levi bought me some kinky sex toy and has chosen this venue to reveal it to me.

"Something I think you'll really like," he says, raising

one eyebrow. "Something I think we'll both get plenty of use from."

I clear my throat and look away, pressing one cold hand to my cheek, as if that'll make me stop blushing like a whore in church. Which, between the apparently-scandalous nature of this gift and the people behind me discussing the Gospel According to John, isn't too far off.

"Are you gonna tell me or make me guess?" I ask, trying to stay cool, even though Levi is now grinning. *Grinning*.

"As much as I'd love to hear you guess I'm fairly certain you'd be wildly incorrect," he says. "For starters, it's perfectly G-rated."

Oh.

I glance around again, just to double-check, but I don't think anyone heard Levi tell me that my gift is G-rated, a phrase that would definitely raise some eyebrows.

"You did that on purpose," I accuse, forcing myself not to smile.

"Guilty as charged," he says.

"Are you going to tell me what it is?"

"No," he says. "But it's in my truck, if you'd like to come see it. I hate ruining a good surprise."

· · · ★ ★ ★ ★ ★ · · ·

I'm strangely nervous as I cover my eyes, standing on the sidewalk half a block down from the Mountain Grind. It's past sunset and cool out, an autumnal breeze blowing.

I am not well-versed in gifts from boyfriends, to put it mildly. Well, that's not exactly true; most of them never gave me anything, which was fine with me, but Brett the trust fund kid liked to give me jewelry.

Jewelry I always hated. I'm not a huge fan of jewelry to begin with, but this stuff was just ugly — mixed metals, weird designs that were last popular in the 80s, and pieces that were just so *not me* it was almost laughable.

Even the ring he proposed with after I'd moved back home — you know, when he was shouting at my window — was ugly. Big, but ugly, more fit for a sixty-five-year-old oil heiress in Dallas than, you know, *me*.

I never said any of that, obviously, though I did try to get him to stop giving me things and he never did. Every single time I'd wear it for a while and feel like I owed him something vague and indefinable in return, and then I'd stop wearing it and a few months later the cycle would repeat.

Anyway, I hope it's not jewelry.

"Okay," Levi says, and I hold out my hands. He puts a box in them, too big and too heavy to be jewelry, and I'm relieved.

"Can I open my eyes?"

"Yup," he says, and I do.

I stare at the box in my hands for a second, because while it's definitely not jewelry, I'm not quite sure what a Webgear Nighthawk Z10 AR7220 is.

Then I turn and hold it up in the streetlamp, and once I see the picture on the front, I start laughing. And laughing. I turn back to Levi, who's grinning, his hands in his pockets as he leans against the door to his truck.

"You like it?" he asks.

"Are you sure about this?" I tease. "It could cause brain cancer and kill all the bees."

"I looked into it and the science suggests that those fears are unfounded," he says.

"I told you," I say, looking down at the wireless router in my hands.

It's the opposite of jewelry: intentionally ugly but very useful.

"Now you can look at gifs while sitting in my living room," he says. "We could even watch movies."

I gasp. He frowns.

"What?"

"Watch out or I might drag you kicking and screaming into the internet age," I tease.

"I'm neither kicking nor screaming at present," he says. "I'm acting perfectly reasonable about this."

I flip it over in my hands. There's still plastic on it, shiny under the glow of the streetlights, the back of the box covered in tiny text. My heart skips a beat.

"Thanks," I finally say, looking up at him. "This is…"

South Dakota, I think.

"Really sweet," I finish, and hand it back to him.

Our fingers brush as I do, and there's a second where we're both holding onto the box and neither of us is letting go, and in that second this just feels *stupid*.

Stupid that I can't kiss him right now, in public thanks. Stupid that I can't give him a hug or hold his hand without worrying that word will get back to my brother.

Then I release the box and get over myself, because I'm not the one who'll get punched.

"I know it drives you crazy that I don't have Wi-Fi," he says, tossing it onto the passenger seat of his truck.

"It doesn't drive me *crazy*," I say.

"Two nights ago you laid on my couch and told Jedediah all about how it's fat bear week, but since the internet was only upstairs he'd never know the glory of voting on the fattest bear in Alaska," Levi says. "And then you described as many of the fat bears as you could remember."

Now I'm laughing, despite myself. Jedediah is Levi's bearskin rug.

"I'm sure he'll be delighted to vote on fat bears," I say.

"I imagine you could also vote, if you had a mind to do so."

"Vote on what?" Silas's voice says.

I nearly jump out of my skin as he steps up beside us, melting in from the dark like a vampire in a black-and-white horror movie.

"Jesus!" I say. "Could you not?"

"I shouted your name like five times walking down the street," he says, annoyed.

"You did not."

"Yes, I did. I shouted your name from the cross walk, and then from next to that white car—"

"Fat bear week," Levi interrupts, and we both look at him.

He raises one eyebrow.

"We're discussing our fat bear week votes," he goes on. "It's an event run on social media by Katmai National Park in Alaska, in which—"

"I know Fat Bear Week," Silas says, in a tone of voice that suggests *everyone* knows about Fat Bear Week.

There's a pause. An awkward pause, at least to me, because I can practically hear Silas thinking *what's so funny* and *why are you out here by Levi's truck* and *Levi, were you about to abduct my little sister?*

"Well, I guess we should get going," I say, looking from Silas to Levi and back. "Uh, I think that router should work just fine for your house, Levi. It's a good one."

I think Levi's bad lying is rubbing off on me.

"Thank you for coming out and giving your opinion," Levi says. "I'm glad to know I've made the right purchase."

"You're putting Wi-Fi in your house?" Silas asks, apparently not noticing that the two of us have transformed into conversation robots. "What's next, a smart phone?"

"Haha," Levi says. "Good one. Maybe."

"Don't get your hopes up," I tell Silas, and then jam my hands into my own pockets before I can do something crazy and impulsive, like touch Levi. "Dinner?"

"Yeah, I'm starving," Silas says. "How about the Burger Lounge?"

"Sounds good," I tell him.

"Sunday?" he says to Levi.

"I'm not sure," Levi says, slowly, looking at me. "I have to be in the woods then."

Tell him. Let me just tell him.

Please.

"Next Sunday, then," Silas says. "Later, Levi!"

"Bye!" I chirp, waving.

I don't want to wave. I want to give Levi a proper girl-friend goodbye kiss, and I want to tell him that I'll see him tomorrow night and I'll set up his router and then we'll snuggle on his couch and watch a movie together, but I don't do any of that because we're still keeping this a secret from my stupid brother.

"See you," Levi calls, waving.

Then I turn and follow my brother down the street.

CHAPTER TWENTY-TWO

LEVI

"Okay, smile and wave," June says.

I wave both arms over my head, like I'm trying to get her attention, and hear a very, very faint click.

"I heard it," I say, and behind a tangle of Virginia creeper, June sighs.

"Would you have if you hadn't been listening for it?" she asks.

I don't answer for a moment, and then her head pops out of a tangle.

"How am I supposed to know the answer to that?" I say. "I *was* listening, and I heard a distinctly camera-like click."

We're standing deep inside the Cumberland National Forest, in a grove of old-growth oak trees, all of which are over two hundred years old. The stand is shaded in a semi-ravine, granite walls shooting up on both sides, and it's cool and damp down inside.

I'm next to a huge oak tree, and June is a hundred feet away, in the only sunny spot in the whole place, adjusting a camera trap in a tangle of undergrowth.

I really hope there's no poison ivy in there, I think.

"This thing is impossible," she mutters, mostly to herself. "These buttons are tiny, and there's no words, just these symbols on the world's smallest screen, and how am I supposed to know if the half-shaded circle is the shutter sound or the…"

I offer her no answers, because I have none. I am, however, grateful that she came along on this mission with me, because I'm certain she's better at wrangling the technology than me.

"Okay," she calls. "Gimme that booty shake."

I wave my arms over my head again.

"C'mon, Levi, drop it low," she says, laughing.

"What have you got in that water bottle?" I call, waving my arms one more time, just for good measure.

I don't really booty shake. I mean, if she *insists*, I can give it a try, but I doubt it's my best move.

"You didn't hear that?"

"Nope."

"Good. That means I got it working," she says, and a moment later she emerges from the tangle and comes toward me. There's a twig stuck in her ponytail, and when she gets close enough, I pull it out.

"Thanks," she says, and then looks back at where she left the camera, squinting. "Wow, you really can't see it. That's pretty good."

I just look up at the massive oak tree that I'm standing next to. I wish I didn't have to do any of this, because I wish someone wasn't cutting down my trees for no reason whatsoever.

If they were doing something with the tree, I'd feel a little bit better about it. Not much, but five percent, maybe ten. If at least these trees were becoming shelter or furniture or for the love of God, even firewood, that would be better.

But they're not, and it feels like there's almost nothing I can do about it. The forest is seven hundred thousand acres, and even though the bad guys are clearly targeting trees in a smaller area than that, it's impossible to guard every tree. We can't even guard the trees that June and I think are at risk. The best we can do is put up cameras and hope we catch the murderers in the act.

"I hope it works," she says, leaning against me.

"We'll have to wait and see," I say, sliding my arm around her, wondering what the camera's capturing. It feels a little strange to touch her where anyone else can see, even though that someone is a camera with a memory card no one but me will likely ever access.

But it feels good. I wish the way we are here, in the forest, on our own, could be the way we are in public. I want to hold her hand, give her kisses, put my arm around her sometimes. I want people to know that she's mine and I'm hers, but instead we act like virtual strangers or — when we forget ourselves — like secret friends.

You could have that, I think. *You could just tell him.*

The only thing in your way is your insistence on this secret.

It's true. I know that. I know that I'm walking along a knife's edge and any day now, I'll fall off to one side or the other. June's got a phone interview three days from now for a job in South Dakota, and I've forced myself not to think about it.

Even if she doesn't get that job — she doesn't think she will, I think she doesn't give herself enough credit — there will be more applications and more interviews and before long, she'll be gone and I'll still be here with Silas.

"We should go set up camp," I say, my lips in her hair

as I plant a kiss on top of her head. "The sun sets early these days."

"Do you know where we're going?" she asks. "Just for the record, I'm lost as hell."

"You've got a map, a compass, and your wits," I remind her. "You're not lost, you're just not sure where you are yet."

"All the same, I think you should take the lead," June says. "If it's up to me I vote we camp right here, because I'm tired."

"One more mile," I tell her, pulling away.

I grab her pack, hold it up, and she shrugs it on, thanks me.

"You're saying we're almost there?" she teases.

"I would never say that," I tell her. "I know better."

· · * * ★ ★ ★ * * · ·

THE SPOT I've got in mind is more like a mile and a quarter away, but that quarter seems like a detail best not mentioned. We've already hiked seven miles today, two of them cross-country with no trail. I'm tired, and I do this sort of thing routinely. June's exhausted, but she helps me set up our small campsite anyway.

I make her sit down while I quickly make us dinner, and we eat sitting on a space blanket, leaning against a fallen tree, a chill coming on with the dark.

After dinner, we build a fire and we sit against the log, watching it, our tent glowing in the background. June leans against me, and even though we're both wearing a couple of layers in the autumn night, her heat seeps through her clothes and onto my skin.

We stay like that for a few minutes. I listen to the fire, to the swish and hush of the trees overhead, to the sigh of the forest, to the music of the birds, to the distant burble of a creek.

"This is why you like nature, isn't it?" June asks after a while, her head nestled against my shoulder.

"Yes," I say simply. "Have you convinced yourself that you like it yet?"

She laughs softly, her body shaking against mine.

"Almost," she says. "This is nice. I kinda see why you like it."

Then she pauses. I don't say anything, because there's nothing that needs to be said.

"But on the other hand, how do you not think that there's a mountain lion hiding just beyond those trees over there, waiting to eat you?" she says. "Or a human murderer, or a bear, or, I don't know, a swarm of bees."

I glance over at the trees she's indicating.

"Maybe there is," I say, shrugging. "Probably not, though. But it's definitely quiet, and peaceful, and the air smells good and there's dirt below your feet and all you have to think about right now is when to put the fire out and go to bed."

"Is this the time to mention that I brought whiskey?" June asks.

"So you forget about the mountain lions?"

"And the bears."

"The bears are probably asleep by now, since it's dark. They're crepuscular," I remind her, and she laughs.

"Like Dave?"

I grin at the fire.

"Right, like Dave," I say. "I assume you've heard all about him?"

"For sure," June says, and heaves herself to her feet, leaving a cold spot on my side as she walks to her pack and starts rummaging through it. "I'm surprised she hasn't talked me into doing a special investigative report yet."

The *she* in that sentence is my niece Rusty, and Dave is, of course, Deepwood Dave, our very own alleged lake monster. Rusty's been on a cryptozoological kick lately, and Dave is her current object of fascination.

He is, of course, crepuscular, meaning he only comes out around twilight and dawn.

June finally finds a slim flask, comes back, sits where she was before, settles back into me.

"I owe you a new bottle," she says, unscrewing the top of the flask. "This is the last of it."

"Don't bother, I'll get another barrel from the cave next week," I say as she takes a sip, then hands me the flask.

June clears her throat slightly.

"The cave?" she asks.

"Mhm," I confirm, taking a pull from the flask. This whiskey burns a little more than the last batch, but it's still pretty good stuff.

"A whiskey cave?"

"It's just for aging it," I tell her, screwing the top onto the flask. "I make it in the still behind my mom's house."

June turns and looks at me like I'm an alien.

"You make whiskey?" she asks, like she's scandalized.

I open my mouth, then close it, trying not to laugh.

"You're not a cop, are you?" I ask.

"Okay, first, this would be the wildest undercover operation ever if I were, and two, *you make whiskey?*"

"It's been a while since I made a batch, but yes," I confirm, handing her the flask. "I figured someone ought to put great-granddaddy's still to use."

"Levi. That's *illegal*," June says, but now she's laughing.

"Only technically."

"Technically illegal is illegal," she points out.

"Guess I'm a criminal, then," I say, stretching my legs a little further toward the fire and grinning at her. "You like bad boys, June?"

She turns her face away and takes another quick bolt from the flask.

"No," she says, laughing. "I like nice men who rescue sweet dogs, grow their own tomatoes, and make their beds every morning."

"And distill illegal whiskey."

"That sounds dangerous," she says, leaning against me, the cap back on the flask.

"I'm not running whiskey, just making it," I say. "According to family legend, that's the dangerous part."

"Don't stills explode sometimes?" she asks, her cheeks slightly pink in the firelight.

"Only if you do it wrong," I say, taking the flask again. "It's not as if I'm running a meth lab. *That's* dangerous."

"If you tell me you've got a meth lab I *will* freak out," June says.

"I don't have a meth lab and I've got no intention whatsoever of starting one," I say. "That sort of thing crosses the line from technically illegal to *illegal* illegal, besides which I've got no desire at all to mess with that shit."

"What else do you secretly do that I don't know about?" she asks, her voice low, teasing.

"I thought you knew about the whiskey," I tell her, honestly. "I figured Silas would have told you by now."

"Silas thinks I'm still thirteen," she says, sighing. "He gets weird about it if I have a beer in front of him. Joke's on him, though."

"Why?"

"Because I also had a huge crush on you when I was thirteen."

I'm mid-pull, and I'm so surprised that I start coughing.

June turns, gives me a surprised look.

"What?" I ask.

"You didn't know?"

I wipe my mouth with the back of my hand, the whiskey slowly making its way into my brain. It's not much — two sips, probably not even a full shot — but it's just enough to make me a little warmer, a little bolder.

"No," I say, baffled. "You? Had a crush on me?"

June starts giggling. She's not a giggler, normally, so it must be the whiskey.

"Yeah," she says, like she can't believe I didn't know. "For years and years and years. Since I was like…"

She glances away, like she's trying to remember.

"Well, definitely by the time I was in middle school," she says.

Her blush is deepening, and I'm searching my memory banks for anything to shed light on this revelation, coming up empty.

"I had no idea," I admit.

"I think that's for the best," she says, and she's still laughing. "What good ever comes of a sixteen-year-old noticing a thirteen-year-old's crush? At best it's awkward, and at worst it's… weird."

"Well, weird was my thing in high school," I say. "Which I guess you noticed."

June goes silent for a moment.

"I didn't think you were weird," she admits, suddenly quiet. "I thought you were fascinating. I'd never met anyone like you."

I'm quiet, trying to dredge up high school memories I'd long ago pushed to the back of my mind. June is there in some of them, but only ever as Silas's kid sister.

I had *no idea* how she'd turn out.

"I've still never met anyone else like you," she says. "And I've met way more people now."

"Thanks, I think," I tease.

"It was a compliment," she says, snuggling harder against me, taking the flask. "And I'm glad that you never noticed, because believe it or not, Silas has actually chilled out about my dating life since then."

"Oh, I'm aware," I say dryly. "Brett's still alive."

She takes one more swig, shakes her head, closes the flask.

"That's actually pretty good," she says. "I'd never have guessed it was from your bathtub."

"My mother's back yard, thanks," I say. I take one more sip, then put the flask down, still half-full.

"You're not afraid of him, are you?" June asks. "There's no way he'd hurt you."

I uncross my legs at the ankles, cross them with the other one on top, the soles of my hiking boots facing the fire. It needs more wood, but I don't want to get up right now: this is heady and perfect, just June and me alone in the wilderness, a sort of perfection I'd never imagined existed up until now.

"I'm not afraid of Silas," I say, slowly. "I'm afraid of losing his friendship."

You will leave, I think, unbidden.

You'll leave and then I won't have either of you.

"I get it," she says, softly. "You guys are close."

"Did he ever tell you what happened to Jake Echols?" I ask suddenly.

June's quiet for a second, like she's trying to remember the name.

"The guy I dated in high school who disappeared one day and it turned out he'd joined the Army without telling anyone?" she asks, then looks over at me. "Something happened to him?"

"Remember the time that Silas drove his truck off the road and into a creek for no reason at all?" I ask.

June's eyes narrow, and I can see her trying to connect the dots.

"Yes?" she says.

Then her eyes go wide, and she pales.

"Is Jake dead?" she whispers. "He never joined the Army, did he, that was—"

"Whoa, whoa," I say, holding up a hand. "He's alive as far as I know. But he's the reason that Silas crashed his truck into the creek that time. Jake was in the car, and they started throwing punches because Silas found out he'd cheated on you."

June's mouth drops open. She turns to stare at the fire for a moment, then looks back at me.

"Dammit," she says. "That bastard."

"Silas never told you?"

"*No*, he never told me and now I'm going to kill him," she says. "Who the fuck does that? Why didn't he just tell *me* so I could break up with him? Did he think I wouldn't? I totally would've."

There's another pause.

"I never even spoke to him again. Technically, we never broke up," she muses, mostly to herself. "I guess we're still dating. You like being my side piece?"

"There are worse fates," I deadpan.

"Dammit, Silas," she mutters to herself.

CHAPTER TWENTY-THREE

JUNE

Levi and I spend another day and a night in the forest, alone together. For over forty-eight hours, I don't see another human being besides him.

We eat backpacking food next to a fire. We sleep in a tiny, two-person tent that's smaller than his bed, and we spend most of the days walking and talking to each other.

The second night we finish the whiskey and start kissing, and then we have sex in the tiny tent, even though it's cold out, and we're tangled and half-sandwiched between sleeping bags and the fading firelight is playing over the outside of the tent and I come within a single breath of telling Levi I love him, but then I don't.

It's as perfect a weekend as I've ever spent. By the end I'm sore in muscles I didn't know I had, my shoulders ache, I've got blisters the size of Texas and I really, really need a shower, but it's perfect.

I like this. I still don't love nature, but Levi does, and watching him here, in his element, practically bursting with his own kind of quiet joy, I know I could learn to love it.

On the last day, Monday, he hands me the map and the

compass and tells me it's my job to guide us out of there using nothing but those tools and my wits.

And I do it. I mess it up a few times, but he helps out, gives me tips, and before I know it, we're back to the trail, our wilderness jaunt over.

"See?" he says as I stuff the map into his pack. "I told you. Just your wits."

"And a compass. And a map," I point out. "And some help."

"I'm going to keep at you until you like it out here," he says, adjusting his pack on his back. "One day, June, you're going to wake up and say to yourself, *I'd really love to take a hike.*"

"I do like it," I tell him, and I think I surprise us both.

"Even though there are bears?" he asks, eyebrows lifting.

"Well, according to my boyfriend, who is the Chief Arborist of this very forest, black bears are no big deal and I shouldn't really pay them any mind," I tease.

"What's an arborist know about bears?" he asks dryly.

"A lot, I hope," I say. "Otherwise I'll probably get eaten."

We hike the last mile out on the trail, a million times easier than the cross-country trekking we'd been doing, and the whole way we talk about nothing: bears and raccoons and which animals are the funniest and whether cats have a sense of humor. We talk about his brothers and I complain about my dad's names for his hot sauce, and none of it feels like a secret, clandestine affair.

It feels like he's my boyfriend and we're just some couple taking a weekend hike. It feels like this weekend hike could turn into another one and then another, months of weekend hikes stretching in front of us that turn into years.

The thought makes my heart pound, but I ignore it like

I've learned to ignore anything that isn't today, tomorrow, maybe the end of this week.

And then, suddenly, we're finished. Almost without warning the trail ends in the trailhead parking lot where we started Saturday morning, and our adventure's over. Out of habit, I turn my phone back on as we walk toward Levi's truck, then stuff it back into my pocket as we sling our packs into the bed.

I'm buckling my seat belt when it dings.

And dings. And dings, then dings again, and my first thought is *oh no something happened to my family*, so I pull it out frantically, but it's not my parents or Silas.

Instead I have five missed calls and two voicemails from a phone number with a 605 area code. I scroll down, frowning, as Levi starts the truck, looks over at me.

"Everything good?" he asks, one arm loosely draped over the steering wheel, right hand on the gearshift.

At the bottom of the notifications, there's an email: *Urgent request to reschedule phone interview.*

"Shit," I whisper to myself, already opening my phone.

"What's wrong?" he asks.

I don't answer for a moment, waiting for this email to load. I've only got one bar of service, out here in the middle of nowhere, and it's taking its sweet time.

"June," Levi says, low and quiet and patient as ever, and suddenly I can't bring myself to look at him.

"Everything's fine," I say, shaking my head. "I just, um, got some voicemails and an email about rescheduling my phone interview that was supposed to be tomorrow."

I don't say *for the job above my pay grade in South Dakota*. I have the sinking feeling that he knows.

"Rescheduling to when?" he asks, and now he's not looking at me either, he's checking his blind spots and his mirrors and he's backing out into the gravel parking lot.

Finally, the email loads. It's short, to the point: three o'clock central time, which is four o'clock eastern.

Which is... in seventeen minutes.

"Four?" I say, still staring at my phone. I can't look at him. I can't.

Levi clears his throat, looks at the clock on the truck's dashboard for a long moment, like he's thinking.

"Service here is pretty in and out," he says quietly, thoughtfully. "Probably best if we drive closer to town so at least you get a better signal by then."

I swallow hard, and I start to wonder what I'm doing and why on earth I'm doing it, but I shove that thought back down until I can't hear it anymore. This is me. This is what I do, what I've always wanted to do and what I need to do and by God, I'm going to do it right now and worry about what it means later.

· · * * ★ ★ ★ * * · ·

"WELL, it certainly sounds like you might be an excellent fit for the Herald-Trumpet," Edmund says, his voice on the other end of the line slightly faint, like the distance between here and South Dakota matters to cell phones.

I look out over the valley, at the sun lowering in the sky, and I blink at it.

"That's wonderful to hear," I say, standing up a little straighter. "The Metro Editor position sounds like it's a fascinating opportunity."

There's a brief moment of silence. Papers shuffle on the other end. Behind me, on the Parkway, a car goes past the vista point where I'm standing. Fifty feet away, Levi's sitting in the bed of his truck, reading a paperback as if he planned on spending his time like this.

I swallow and look back at the view, because I can't look at him right now.

"June, we'd like to move you into the next round of interviews," says Adrianne, the paper's Managing Editor, also on the line. "That would mean coming to Bluff City for an in-person interview one day next week. Would you be amenable to that?"

"Yes, that sounds wonderful," I say. "I can't wait to meet the whole Herald-Trumpet team."

I shut my eyes, the words rolling out of me like rocks down a hill. By now I've parroted so much job-application-business speak that I practically dream about it.

"Perfect," she says, and I hear papers shuffling in the background again. "Does Tuesday work for you? I'm afraid that the closest airport in Salt Plains only has a few flights a day, so you may need to fly into Rapid City and rent a car. But I'm sure you'll figure it out, you seem very resourceful."

I navigated my way out of the wilderness an hour ago, I want to tell her, but I don't.

"I'll be sure to check into all my options," I say.

"Great," says Edmund. "We'll email you to confirm the details in a few minutes. It was a delight to speak with you, June."

"Likewise," I say, eyes still shut.

We exchange a few more pleasantries, and then finally, I hang up the phone.

This is what you want, I remind myself. *You've spent months feeling pointless and useless. You need a job. You need a career.*

You need to not give any of that up for bad reasons.

I should be happy. After months of trying, I've finally scored an in-person interview, and I should be over the moon about it but I'm not.

I take a deep breath. I look out over the valley one more time, the first leaves just starting to turn yellow and orange, and I think about how two weeks from now it'll be a carpet of sunset and it'll smell like Halloween and apple picking. I think about curling up on Levi's back porch with hot cocoa and a blanket, looking out over his yard and the forest beyond while Hedwig fetches sticks and runs them back to me.

Maybe I could take up knitting. I could learn to can, make jam, preserve... preserves, I guess, and I could start a blog about being a country house-girlfriend.

Except that's not me. I'm not homey and I'm not comfy and I've never preserved a preserve in my life, because I was meant to be off chasing exciting stories and fighting with editors to get the truth out and doing cool, exciting reporter things.

Like what? I think, still looking out over the valley, lost in thought, my phone by my side. *Covering Town Hall meetings about Sewage Awareness Wednesday and trying to make the local school's Fourth of July Parade sound interesting?*

You don't even care about the parade in Sprucevale, and you know half the kids in it.

Then I turn sharply and walk back toward the truck where Levi's waiting before I can think any more about this.

"Hey," he says, an easy smile on his face, like he's glad to see me even though he's been close by this whole time. "How'd it go?"

He stands, puts a bookmark into the book he's reading, hops over the side of the truck and down onto the pavement next to me.

Is it weird that I find bookmark use sexy? I kinda do.

"I think it went well," I say, and the next thing is right on the tip of my tongue: *I have to fly to South Dakota next week for the last round of interviews.*

I don't say it. I hold my breath. I glance down at the

black screen of my phone like it'll tell me what to do, but it's stubbornly silent and hint-free, and then I look back into Levi's earth-brown eyes and I can't do it. I can't say it.

Not now. Not after this weekend that was strangely perfect despite the tree murder and the lack of showers.

"That's great," Levi says, but he doesn't look at me either. He looks away, at the horizon, and he sounds oddly distant. He takes a deep breath.

"I hope it works out," he says, too fast, like he has to push to get the words out. "Are you spending the night or going home?"

"I told my parents I was visting Gina in Richmond until tomorrow," I say, naming my college roommate.

"Got it," Levi says, and opens the truck's passenger door for me. "We can Netflix and chill."

I pull the door shut and he walks around the front, my eyes tracking his form in the low light of sunset and I think for the thousandth time *how is every woman in this town not crawling all over him?*

"Do you know what that means?" I ask when he gets into the driver's seat.

Levi smiles as he turns the key and the engine protests for a moment before starting.

"Apparently not," he says.

Tell him, I think. *Just tell him now and get it over with. You'll just feel worse the longer you don't tell him.*

"I'll show you," I offer, and he pulls out of the viewing area and back onto the Parkway.

· · · ★ ★ ★ ★ ★ · · ·

THAT NIGHT, we shower, and then we eat leftovers and then watch Netflix and chill and then we *Netflix and chill* and even afterwards, when we're tangled together and he's got his head on my chest and the moon is out and everything is so, so quiet, I don't tell him.

I swallow my heavy guilt, and I hold him close, and I don't say anything.

· · · ★ ★ ★ ★ ★ · · ·

THE NEXT DAY, I'm determined to tell him. I go back to my parents' house first thing, and I tell them. My mom hugs me and my dad ruffles my hair and they both tell me they knew it was just a matter of time, and then they demand all the details so I tell them that it's an editor position, that I'd be making $41,000 a year, that I'd be overseeing a section of the paper while also pursuing some of my own stories, and with every word out of my mouth it sounds better and better.

It's a pretty good job. It is. There are very, very few *really good* jobs in print journalism these days, and they're all for people with twenty years' more experience than me, but I can settle for pretty good if it'll get me *really good* someday.

Right? I can, right?

I book my flights: Roanoke to Salt Plains, and I book a room at the Bluff City Motel 6. I print everything out and put it into a folder so that I've got it all ready, even though I don't leave for almost a week.

Silas calls me when I'm at the grocery store, buying eggplants and basil so I can make stir-fry for Levi before I tell him. More accurately, I'm holding an eggplant and then looking from it to my phone, trying to figure out why it doesn't look anything like the picture. Are there multiple varieties of eggplant?

"Heard you finally got an interview," he says, already ribbing me. "Nice job. Guess I don't have to take you out for pity dinners anymore."

I put the eggplant into my basket and make a face at the rest of the produce.

"You can still take me out for dinner," I say. "It's not a done deal, and I'm barely even qualified for the job, they're probably only interviewing me to round out the candidates or something—"

"Stop it," he says, his voice suddenly quieter. "They're interviewing you because you're smart, hardworking, and you'd be great at the job."

I pick up some basil and frown.

"Did you get hit on the head?"

"What?"

"You're being nice to me," I say.

I can practically hear him roll his eyes.

"I bought you dinner last week because you didn't have a job," he points out. "I'm nice to you *all* the time, Bug."

And I'm sleeping with your best friend.

"Fine, you're nice," I tease. "Thanks. It seems like it's a good job."

"You need a ride to the airport?" he asks, out of the blue.

I narrow my eyes at the basil.

"I'm not gonna say no," I warn him. "But I'm flying out of Roanoke at nine-fifteen, so I need to be to the airport at seven, so we've gotta leave out of here at—"

"The ass-crack of dawn, yes," he finishes the sentence for me, though not quite the way I would have. "And despite that, I'm offering you a ride."

"Okay," I say instantly.

"Cool," he says. "Are you coming to Fall Fest on Saturday at the brewery?"

"If I don't get a better offer."

Silas just laughs.

"Not in Sprucevale you won't," he says. "Drinking a

beer while watching a bunch of kids in a pumpkin-shaped bouncy house is about the best entertainment you're likely to find, Bug. See you Saturday."

"Silas," I say, and then I stop short.

I know why he's calling me and offering me a ride. He's worried. He's told me as much: I've been acting weird, and he's a little worried about me, so he's trying to give me some quality Big Brother time.

"You okay, Bug?" he asks.

I've been seeing Levi. We're together, and I can't tell you, and I feel so awful that I can't tell you.

I clear my throat.

"I'm good," I say. "See you Saturday?"

"I'm gonna kick your ass at horseshoes," he says, and we hang up.

· · ★ ★ ★ ★ ★ ★ · ·

I DON'T TELL Levi that night. I cook him dinner and then spend the night, but despite nearly telling him at least thirty times, I don't work up the courage.

I don't work it up Wednesday, either, or Thursday, and every moment I don't tell him I hate myself more for being such a coward.

It's going to happen whether I tell him or not, and I know it. It's only going to feel worse the longer I wait, and I know that, but every time I finally resolve that I'm just going to spit it out, *I'm flying to South Dakota on Monday for an interview*, the words stick in my throat and I don't say anything.

And it feels like shit.

CHAPTER TWENTY-FOUR

LEVI

"I'm just not sure I anticipate room for that kind of program in our budget," the woman's voice says. "Even if we approve these new mining contracts —"

"Do *not* approve the mining contracts," a man snipes. I think his name is Nelson, but I'm not a hundred percent sure on that. "Those contracts would spell travesty for the Forest Service and for the entire Crenenga River Basin—"

"That's an overstatement," says a third voice. "That mining would create minimal impact while funding very important work to minimize the impacts of global warming on the forest."

"Sure, while creating *more global warming*," Nelson says.

"*In either case* we're going to have to put a hold on the Trout Friends Initiative for at least another year!" says the first woman's voice, sounding extremely exasperated.

Conference calls are the thing I hate the second-most about my job, coming slightly behind in-person meetings. This one has been particularly painful because I'm not exactly sure why I'm required to be here — the mining and the programs they're talking about are all in another forest entirely, and while I don't like the mining either, I've got no say whatsoever in whether it goes forward.

Basically, my job title has "Chief" in it, so they made me call in, even though I've nothing to do with mining and even less to do with trout.

"We can't do that," someone else snaps. "I've been working on Trout Friends for—"

My cell phone buzzes in my pocket, and I stop doodling on a notepad and grab it. The tiny caller ID screen says CALEB LOV, so I hit the mute button on my work phone and flip it open.

"There's a brewery emergency," he says, sans preamble. "Seth's putting the beer signal up in the sky."

"What kind of brewery emergency?" I ask, frowning at the closed door of my office, feet still on my desk.

The Southeastern Regional Budget Meeting has been going on for a *while*.

"They need a lot of wood chopped," Caleb says dryly. "Before Fall Fest starts tomorrow."

"Is this some kind of prank?" I ask, slowly. "Chopping wood at the brewery sure sounds like a pretense to get me over there for some reason I'm not going to like."

Caleb just snorts.

"Yeah, I'd probably think that too if I insisted on keeping my girlfriend secret from everyone in my life and particularly the man who'd been my best friend since childhood," he says. "You know, instead of telling him and letting things shake out, like a normal person might do."

I sigh and rub my eyes. I've explained my reasons to Caleb, and I'm not about to do so again.

"Why do we need to chop wood?"

"Because part of the after-dark allure of Fall Fest is the several bonfires they'll have going, but the people they contracted for firewood seem to have dropped it off in the form of ten-foot tree sections," he says. "I'm heading over there now. Seth says Daniel's swearing, so it sounds pretty bad."

"Daniel swears all the time when Rusty's not around," I point out.

Then I pause.

"Wait, are you in town?"

"Yeah. I've been staying at Mom's," he says.

"You didn't tell me?"

"You seemed busy."

I look down at my feet, clad in hiking boots even though I'm in the office today. It *is* a National Forest, after all. They can't expect me to wear wingtips.

"I'm sorry if I traumatized you," I offer, even though it's now been over a month.

Caleb just laughs.

"Don't be. You didn't. You seem really happy. I've always hated being the third wheel. I just needed to get out of Marysburg for a while since I'm not teaching or anything this year," he says. "Can I tell Seth and Daniel you'll be there so maybe they'll freak out less?"

The people on the phone are still arguing about trout and mining, though it seems that someone's thrown a wrench into the proceedings in the form of asking about campground upkeep.

"Yes, of course," I say. "I'll head over after work."

"Spectacular," he says, the same dry, almost-sarcastic edge to his voice that's always there. "I'll see you there."

· · · · ★ ★ ★ ★ · · · ·

I HEAD OVER AFTER WORK, calling June on the way and explaining the situation. She expresses regret that she won't be there to watch me chop wood, but she understands and says she'll see me tomorrow.

When I pull up to the brewery, the sun's nearly at the mountains, casting gold and blue light over the whole valley. Loveless Brewing is a little ways outside town, nestled on land between two farms, backed by the forest.

It's got a huge patio in the front that leads onto a grassy area that's usually got lawn games out, dotted by fire pits surrounded by Adirondack chairs. Even though it's a brewery, it's actually a pretty popular family hangout spot on weekend afternoons.

Inside there's a taproom, with a bar along one end. Most of it's taken up by long wooden tables and benches, a few bar-height tables, and dartboards along one wall.

All they serve is their own beer, with occasional guest taps, so it's less *drinking establishment* and more *chill hangout zone.*

Then, of course, the rest of the huge building is taken up by the brewing and bottling equipment. That's Daniel's zone. I don't go unless invited.

"Oh, good," my mom's voice says the moment I open the brewery doors. "Seth and Caleb are out back. I think Seth might have kittens, you know how he is."

"That would be something," I say, and next to my mom, Rusty starts giggling.

"Fifty-four," she says, in answer to the index card my mom's holding up.

"Correct," my mom says, and puts it atop a stack on the table, then holds up another one.

I head toward the back. On the way I pass Daniel, a keg lifted on one shoulder, who just nods to me in the hallway.

"Thanks!" he calls, as we pass each other, and I push through the back door.

Outside, Seth and Caleb both have their shirts off already, a pile of logs waiting to be split in front of them, and a smaller pile of split logs to one side.

"Hey," calls Seth, slightly out of breath.

"I told you he was coming," Caleb says, also slightly out of breath. "He's got a job. Eli should be here any minute, too."

"I have a job," Seth says, pointing at the pile of wood with an axe. "This is it. Though usually it's more spreadsheets and less manual labor."

"I'm sure this is good for the soul," Caleb says.

"I'm not," Seth says, grinning.

"You roped Eli into chopping wood?" I ask, rubbing my hands together, assessing the situation.

The situation is thus: we have a shitload of wood to chop.

"Well, he agreed to it," Seth says. "He's perfectly capable. There's another axe over there."

My sleeves are already rolled up, but I push them past my elbows, lean down, grab the axe.

"Remember the time we ran out of firewood for the woodstove during that snowstorm one year?" Caleb says, like he's recalling a fond memory. "Eli had just been stacking random shit underneath a tarp to make it look like he was chopping firewood, so when we went to get more, we were out."

I heave a chunk of tree onto one of the chopping blocks they've already got set up, give it a good, long look.

"He got grounded for a month and had to miss the middle school winter formal that year," I say. "You remember him trying to negotiate his punishment with Mom?"

Seth laughs.

"Yeah, didn't he try to talk her into grounding him

from his senior prom instead, even though it was five years away?" he says. "You gotta admit, it wasn't a bad idea."

"Tell me it didn't work," Caleb adds.

I hoist the axe, swing, split the wood apart.

"Nope," I say, grabbing a chunk and tossing it onto the pile. "Not even close. You think Mom would fall for that?"

I grab another chunk, and for a few minutes, we chop wood without talking. I feel like I'm a teenager again, chopping wood for the wood stove in the family room that, *of course*, my mom replaced with central heat after Caleb graduated and left home.

Not that I blame her. Without the free labor of young men, a wood stove must be a huge pain in the ass.

Caleb and Seth were never my wood chopping comrades — that was Eli and sometimes Daniel — but it feels familiar, like home, nonetheless.

After a few minutes, I'm warm, despite the chill in the air.

After a few more, the sweat's pouring down my back. The sun is still going down, so I look around, see if anyone else is around. They're not, so I join my brothers in taking off my shirt and toss it onto a tree branch.

"Holy *shit*," Seth says the moment I turn around.

I look over my shoulder, half-expecting a bear to emerge from the forest.

"Your back," he explains.

"Yeah, I've been working out," I deadpan, because I have no idea what he's talking about.

Now he's grinning. I don't like it.

"Hip thrusts?" he asks.

I hoist, heave, split, and my heart thumps a little harder while my mind races because Seth is definitely getting at something and I don't plan on giving up any information.

"What exactly are you trying to say, Seth?" I ask, tossing the wood onto piles.

Now he's got both eyebrows raised, still smiling like he's been given an early Christmas present.

"Really?" he asks, and Caleb sighs.

"There are fingernail marks on your back, Levi," he says.

Shit.

I have a brief, one-second memory from a few nights ago, June shouting my name as she arched underneath me, a flash of pain along my shoulder blades that I forgot almost immediately.

"I ran into a tree," I tell them, backing toward my shirt, tugging it off the branch.

Caleb just sighs, but I swear Seth's about to start giggling.

"Were you running backwards?" he asks.

I don't answer.

"Were you running backwards, and then when you hit it, you kinda rubbed back and forth on it like a bear?" he asks. "And the tree just so happened to have branches shaped in perfect half-moons like fingernails?"

I clear my throat as I pull my shirt back on.

"Yes," I say.

"Levi."

I grab more wood.

"Who?"

Say nothing.

"Levi. *Who?*"

"It's nothing."

"Levi Beauford Love—"

"Who do you think?" Caleb finally says as I bring the axe down, splitting the wood.

Seth drops a piece of wood onto the block, then looks at Caleb, eyes wide.

"You're kidding," he says, voice hushed, sounding so scandalized that if he had pearls, I think he'd be clutching them.

Caleb just shrugs stoically, and I level a glare at him.

"Seriously?" says Seth, and then looks at me. "Does *he* know?"

"I don't know what you're talking about," I maintain, shooting another glare at Caleb the Traitor, just for good measure.

"All I said was *who do you think*," he says. "You're the one who showed up here looking like you'd just gotten finished at the BDSM dungeon."

"Sounds like I came at the right time," Eli's voice says.

I look up. My younger brothers turn to see Eli standing there, next to the woodpile.

Great. Another one.

"How's the dungeon?" he asks Seth, who just grins.

"I don't know, he does," Seth says, pointing at me and looking absolutely gleeful.

Eli's eyebrows just about fly off his forehead. I do my best to ignore him, splitting another hunk of wood down the middle.

"You're shitting me," he says.

"Nope," says Seth.

"I have no information whatsoever on the existence of a dungeon, kinky or otherwise," I grumble.

"Do they still make other dungeons?" Caleb asks. "Seems like there's only the one kind anymore. You never hear about a regular prison dungeon."

"Again," I say, as Eli and Seth both give him *looks*, "this is not a topic on which I am knowledgeable."

"Mind if we back up to why we think Levi was in a

dungeon, BDSM or not?" Eli asks, already taking off his shirt and then reaching for an axe.

"I ran into a tree and they're making wild assumptions," I say.

I know there's a zero percent chance of being believed, but I have to try.

"Show him your back," Seth challenges me, laughing. "See if Eli believes you, either."

"You ran into a tree with your back?" Eli asks.

"A tree with fingernails," Seth supplies.

I split another piece of wood, toss it onto the finished woodpile.

"A tree with — holy shit, no way!" he says.

I contemplate simply turning around and walking into the woods. I think I could make my way home eventually.

"Levi, you fucked a tree?" Eli asks, faux-astonished. "Congratulations, I really thought you'd never get up the nerve to approach one."

I point my axe at them, one by one.

"You're all dead to me," I tell them. "I don't have brothers anymore. Except Daniel."

"Should I go tell him you lost your tree virginity?" Eli asks. "I think he's inside. I'm sure he'd be proud. You used protection, right?"

Seth is nearly giggling, Eli's grinning like a shithead, and even Caleb is looking far more amused than I'd like.

Eli grabs a hunk of wood, tosses it onto a chopping block.

"Remember the time you delighted in harassing me about the fact that everyone knew I was sleeping with Violet?" he asks, rhetorically, bringing the axe down. "I do."

"You mean when I provided you with the service of

telling you that your secret was not, in fact, any such thing?" I counter.

"Who is it?" Eli says to Seth, ignoring my very good point.

Seth points at Caleb. Caleb sighs.

"Who do you think?" he says, for the second time.

"It's *ma'am*, right?" Eli asks. "Please don't tell me it's someone else. If I have to tell Violet that Levi's sleeping with someone and it's not June, she might kill me just for being the messenger."

I say nothing, but I take a deep breath and close my eyes for a moment. Over the summer, in what was not my best moment, I called June *ma'am* because when I saw her, my brain short-circuited completely.

Of course, I did this in front of Daniel and Eli, and have been hearing about it ever since.

"You're safe," Caleb says.

"Traitor," I tell him.

"They all suspected," he says, sounding mildly apologetic at best.

"We think it's still a secret from Silas," Seth offers, and Eli just whistles under his breath.

"Shit," he says.

"Right?" Seth agrees.

"Didn't he force some guy to join the Army because he cheated on June?" Eli asks. "That was Silas, right?"

"I'm not going to cheat on June," I say, a little louder than I meant to. Even saying that makes the skin on my back crawl unpleasantly.

"I didn't mean that you would," Eli says. "Just that I understand why you haven't told him. Did I ever tell you he helped me break into Bramblebush that time? He brought his own night-vision goggles and stole a golf cart."

Sounds like something Silas would do.

I don't answer Eli, because we're all still chopping wood and the night is getting dark. In a few more minutes we'll have to go find better lighting, because I think we might all be here for a while yet.

Besides, I don't particularly feel like giving my brothers my justification for not telling June's brother about us. I know they'll understand, but that doesn't mean I want to say the sentence *June is going to break my heart and I know it* aloud.

I'm just about to go see what I can do about lighting when someone new walks up to the woodpile.

"Shit," Violet says. "I didn't bring any singles."

Eli stands up straight, pushing his hair out of his eyes.

"If you've got a twenty, I can make it worth your while," he says, grinning.

"*No*," says Caleb.

"You sure?" Violet asks, laughing. "I'm pretty demanding."

"Stop it," says Caleb.

"Gross," agrees Seth.

"Really? From you?" says Eli. "As if you've never—"

"Have I ever made you listen to my weird foreplay? No," says Seth. "Hi, Violet, how are you doing?"

"Levi's sleeping with June and we all just found out," Eli tells her.

"Silas doesn't know," Seth adds.

"It's a secret," says Caleb.

Violet *gasps*, both hands flying to her mouth.

I say nothing.

"Yes!" she yelps. "Fuck yes!"

"Yeah, probably sounds something like that," Eli deadpans, flicking a glance in my direction.

"*Dude*," says Caleb.

"Are they for real?" Violet asks me, ignoring Caleb. "Please say yes. Please?"

I give each of my brothers a *look* in turn.

"That means yes," Seth offers.

"Ooh, unless he's sleeping with someone even more forbidden and would rather we think it's June than the real person," Eli says, thoughtfully. "Who would that be?"

The four of them just look at each other in silence, thinking.

"Is his boss female?" Seth finally asks.

"Levi," Caleb finally says. "Please? Look how happy they'd be."

I heft the axe in one hand, letting the rough wooden handle spin against my palm. I stare at it in the near-dark and accept my fate.

"I'm dating June," I finally say. "For a little over a month, and no, her brother doesn't know yet. Are there any further questions?"

"Yes," Violet says, promptly. "Tell us everything."

"Not a question," Eli points out, and Violet just flips him off without even looking while Seth and Caleb laugh and Eli grins.

"Well," I start. "June and I are dating."

All four of them look at me, waiting.

"We'll have to drag this out of him, won't we?" Violet asks.

"We could use some more light out here," I point out.

"Of course we are. Have you met Levi?" Caleb asks, rhetorically.

CHAPTER TWENTY-FIVE

JUNE

I have to tell him. I have to. I'm already a monster for not saying anything, and the longer I don't tell Levi that I've got this job interview next week, the worse it's going to get.

I should have just done it Monday, when I found out. When he asked how the call went, I should have just said, *they want me to interview in-person next week.* Nine words. Eleven syllables. Two seconds, max, of speaking.

But I didn't, and then I didn't some more, and now it's been five days and I still haven't, and I've made an enormous mountain out of a tiny molehill.

I'm afraid of his reaction. What if he's heartbroken?

What if he's not?

"You okay, Bug?" Silas asks.

I whip my head around and stick a big smile on my face. It's probably too big and too fast, but oh well.

"Fine," I say, perkily. "Why?"

"No angsting about job interviews at Fall Fest," he tells me. "It's Fall Fest, not Fall... Mess."

I just let *Fall Mess* sit there for a moment and watch

Silas silently as he drives past cow fields. Behind them, the forest is a red-gold that practically glows, the fall colors combined with the sunset.

"Fall Mess?" I finally ask. "That's what you came up with?"

"Yup," he says. "And if you don't cheer up, I'll make even worse jokes."

"I'm not sure that was a joke," I say.

"Oh, I'm sure," he says. "That was the height of hilarity and there's more where it came from."

I hide a smile and lean back in the passenger seat, watching the road disappear under his SUV as we drive toward Loveless Brewing.

Loveless Brewing, where my secret boyfriend is. You know, the one who doesn't know that I've got an interview soon for a job that's halfway across the country.

"You don't even have a girlfriend," I point out. "How are you making dad jokes already?"

"You don't need a girlfriend to be a father," Silas says. "Technically, all you need is a one-night-stand and an accident. Doesn't even need to be a whole night, you could just—"

"Ahhhhhhhhhh!" I shout, covering my face with my hands.

"—I'm just saying, could be a five-minutes-in-the-bar-bathroom stand," he says, clearly laughing at me. "Sperm is sperm."

"Never say that to me again," I tell him through my fingers.

"What? Sper—"

"*What did I just say?*"

"That you're a stick in the mud who can't handle a joke."

I look over at him. He's grinning like the total dick he is.

"Can I walk the rest of the way?" I ask.

"You could, but it's about half a mile," he says. "By the time we finish arguing about where to let you out we'll be there anyway."

He's right, because thirty seconds later we're pulling into the nearly-full gravel lot at Loveless Brewing, a big building a few miles outside town, sandwiched in the middle of farmland.

A teenager in a bright yellow reflective vest waves us into a parking spot. The vest also has blinking red lights on it, and the teenager doesn't look too excited about that part.

The evening air is crisp, autumnal, with just a whisper of the winter that's around the corner. It smells like dried leaves and dirt, with a hint of woodsmoke and apple cider donuts.

Find him and tell him, I think to myself.

You owe him that. Once you tell Levi you can have as much beer and as many donuts as you want, but you have to tell him first.

My stomach is a knot as Silas and I head for the entrance to the patio, currently festooned with jack-o'-lanterns and dried corn stalks. One of the jack-o-lanterns is a vague, round-ish shape that, upon closer inspection, I'm pretty sure is supposed to be a wombat.

I think Rusty made that one.

Beyond the is the patio, lit by lights strung back and forth overhead, and past that in the yard they've set up a pumpkin-shaped bouncy house, a huge inflatable slide, and a whole bunch of yard games. Between the yard games and the road are four or five fire pits, all with wood piled high.

We both pull out our wallets, but the guy with the

tickets waves them away. I think, but am definitely not sure, that his name is Steve.

"Levi put you on the list," he says to Silas, already putting a wristband on. "You're June, right?"

I do my best not to blush slightly, and I'm pretty sure I fail even though there's nothing here to blush about. Levi's a nice person, of course he'd put his friend's sister on the list.

"Yup," I confirm, get a band, and we walk into Fall Fest.

It's been going on since the afternoon, but I had to finish a freelance article about stop signs for the Sprucevale Lance-Star, and Silas was doing something for work, so we couldn't get here until now.

The bouncy house and inflatable slide are nearly still. The kids seem to be mostly gone, with the exception of a squadron of eight-to-ten-year-olds sprinting around and shrieking. Rusty's probably one of them. Hell, she's probably the ringleader.

The patio is pretty full though, all the cafe tables and lounge chairs in their various configurations claimed by adults drinking beers.

None of the adults seem to be Levi, at least that I can see. Also, I can *smell* apple cider donuts, but I can't see them. They've gotta be somewhere.

Truth first, I remind myself. *Donuts next.*

"You want something?" Silas asks, making the universal *drinking a beer* hand gesture.

"Sure," I say, still scanning the patio and field beyond for Levi, heartbeat ticking up.

"What do you want?"

"Whatever you get," I tell him, shrugging with a shrug that's hopefully nonchalant.

"Cool," he says, and heads toward the nearest bar area.

Levi's not on the patio. He's unsurprisingly not on the slide, and I feel like I can assume that he's not in the bouncy house. I wander further afield, trying to look like I'm just hanging out and waiting for a beer delivery, not like I'm watching everyone with a hawklike gaze, trying to find one specific person.

Finally, I spot him. He's alone, wearing what's essentially his uniform of well-fitting jeans and a plaid shirt rolled up to his elbows, walking around the corner of the building toward the back.

Alone. Good.

Maybe I should have a beer first, I think, but I shake my head at myself. Ridiculous.

I take a deep breath and start after him.

I haven't gotten five feet before I hear someone shout my name, and look over to see Charlie, Violet, and Violet's best friend Adeline.

Charlie's waving, a beer in her other hand, her hair bouncing. I hesitate, glancing after Levi, feeling like my bravery and my chance are both slipping away.

"Juuune!" Charlie hollers, so I put on a smile and head over.

Charlie is smiling. She's smiling a lot.

She's smiling… too much.

"Hi," I say, and then because I have to say something, "Great party."

There's something going on. I can tell: the looks on their faces, the sudden weird buzz in the air. Something is going on and I don't like it.

"It had better be," she laughs. "I was here until ten last night fixing the rotted-out floor on that gazebo, and Daniel made all the boys come over and chop wood for the bonfires."

"Yeah he did," says Violet, grinning.

246

"I can't believe you didn't call me," Adeline adds.

"You've told me one billion times that you have zero interest in these guys," Violet says. "You know I can get you Seth or Caleb's number. You know that."

"I'm not interested in *dating* them," Adeline says, sounding slightly exasperated. "But they're all cute and you know how I feel about men chopping wood. You *know*, Violet."

"It was very good," Charlie says.

Adeline raises an eyebrow.

"I'm engaged, not blind," Charlie grins.

"I heard there would be bonfires," I say. "Are they going up soon?"

"I think so," Violet confirms.

Then she takes a long sip of her dark beer, looking at me.

"Don't you love bonfires? They're so cozy, and warm, and romantic, and you can really snuggle up with someone and maybe get up to some stuff," she says, wiggling her eyebrows.

"Violet," admonishes Adeline. "Be nice."

"Can you?" I say, my voice about an octave higher than it should be.

Do Charlie and Violet know what we have in common? I wonder.

"Oh, you can get up to some *stuff*," Charlie confirms, her own beer nearly empty.

"So much stuff," adds Violet.

I'm pretty sure this is not their first drink of the night.

"I thought you guys were going to be cool," Adeline says dryly, looking from one to the other.

I clear my throat.

"Cool about what?" I ask, smiling what I'm pretty sure

is a weird smile and wishing Silas would hurry up with my own beer.

"You know," Charlie says, and then winks at me.

It's a big, demonstrative wink. She winks so hard that she leans a little, her curls bobbing.

She knows. I am now one hundred percent sure that they know about Levi and me.

I'm equally certain that it's not my place to confirm this to them. It's Levi's secret to keep, and even if I'm being terrible girlfriend right now, I'm going to keep his secret as well as I can.

"I don't know anything?" I say, still trying to get out of it. "What is it I know?"

Violet leans in toward the center of the group.

"We're in a club," she stage-whispers. "The three of us. Not Adeline. Though Seth and Caleb are both single, I think."

"Again, not my type, thanks," Adeline stage-whispers back.

"What club?" I whisper, determined not to give it up until I have to.

"Levi told us," Charlie whispers, also at top whisper volume.

The three of them look at each other.

"Well, sort of," Violet says. "It's slightly more accurate to say that the guys got it out of him at axe-point."

I dig in my heels, metaphorically. Also physically, a little bit.

"Got what out of him?" I ask.

Behind me, Levi clears his throat. I whirl around.

"Hello," he says, standing there casually, one hand around a beer and the other in his pocket as he slowly scans each of us, looking suspicious.

"Hi," I say, my palms suddenly sweating for several different reasons.

"No," he says, thoughtfully, coming forward to join our circle. "I don't think I like this."

"What's not to like?" Charlie asks, still smiling too much.

"*Au contraire*, it seems like there's plenty for you to like here," Violet adds.

"They've been drinking," says Adeline. "And they're both total lightweights."

"Yeah, and you're that Russian chick from the beginning of the Indiana Jones movie where the bar gets set on fire," Violet says.

"Marion Ravenwood," I say. "She wasn't Russian."

"Right, her," Violet says, pointing at me.

Tell him now before you lose your nerve, I think. *Just excuse yourselves and walk five feet away and say the words: I have a job interview in South Dakota on Wednesday.*

"Bless her heart, she's still trying to keep you two a secret," Adeline says.

Levi sighs.

"My brothers found out that we're seeing each other," he says, his voice low, quiet.

I glance at Charlie, Violet, and Adeline, all of whom look somewhere between *pleased* and *extremely pleased*.

"*Seeing*," Charlie says, making air quotes with her free hand.

"Stop it, you know Levi's delicate," Violet admonishes her.

Levi frowns.

"Not what I heard," Charlie says, and Violet snorts.

"You haven't told Silas, though," I say to Levi, trying to ignore the peanut gallery. Silas has been way too normal · today to know.

"No," he confirms.

There's a brief pause.

Then: "Not yet."

"I think you could take him," Charlie offers. "As long as you had the element of surprise on your side."

"Silas did *two* combat tours," Violet says, skeptically.

"Three," Levi corrects, then turns to me. "Can I get you anything?"

"Silas is actually bringing me a beer," I say, then lift one eyebrow. "What happened?"

"It's a long story," he says, then catches someone's eye in the crowd, nods.

From about twenty feet away, I see Silas nod back. That's a convenient thing about being six-foot-two: you can always find and be found in crowds.

As he approaches, Violet leans in and murmurs in my ear.

"He's got fingernail scratches down his back," she says, then leans away again.

My face flushes with heat. Actually, my whole body does — in the unpleasant way, not the good way — and as my brother approaches with my beer, I'm pretty certain my face is the brightest red possible, and I'm deeply grateful that it's nearly dark out.

"Hey," he says, holding up the beers and handing me one. "I just got you the amber ale, it sounded good. What's up, guys?"

If he notices the weird, sudden quiet or the intense interest with which he's now being regarded, he doesn't act like it.

"Nothing much," Adeline says casually, saving us all. "We were just talking about our favorite horror movies. Mine's *Halloween*."

"*The Shining*," says Violet.

"*Slumber Party Massacre*," offers Charlie.

"That one sounds fun," says Silas, raising one eyebrow. "How many scantily-clad pillow fights does it have?"

"Just the one, but it's a good one," Charlie says, grinning. "I like it because it's too dumb to actually be scary. What's yours?"

Silas takes a long swig, and I could be wrong, but I think a muscle in his jaw tightens.

"Does *Nightmare Before Christmas* count?" he asks. "I never did like scary movies."

"That's more of a Christmas movie," Violet says. "Maybe *There's a Big Pumpkin, Charlie Brown* is more your speed?"

"That's not its name," Adeline points out.

"And there's nothing wrong with not liking scary movies," Levi says.

"Exactly," agrees Charlie.

"Yeah, but you must have one that you've seen and kinda like," Violet says. "I mean, what about the classics, like *Psycho*, or..."

She trails off, looking past Charlie, and we all turn.

Daniel's making a beeline for us, mouth in a grim line.

"Hey," he says when he reaches our group, his hand automatically going to Charlie's lower back. "There's a Seth emergency. I need your help."

"What—"

"Delilah's here," Daniel says.

There's a brief moment of silence as I wonder who on earth Delilah is.

Levi's the first to speak.

"Shit," he whispers.

CHAPTER TWENTY-SIX

LEVI

"Where's Seth?" I ask, keeping my voice low. "Does he know?"

"Not yet," Daniel says. "Caleb's got him inside and she's out here, but we've gotta get one of them *out*."

"I know," I say, shoving my hand into a pocket and scanning the crowd, struggling to remember what Delilah looks like. All I really remember is the hair, and who wouldn't remember that?

"And we can't let him know what's going on," Daniel says, voice still tense. "You remember the incident at the Whiskey Bucket, don't you?"

"I'd rather not, truth be told," I say, still scanning. "But I take your point."

"This brewery almost didn't open," he says.

"I know, I remember," I tell him. "Can we just keep them apart for the remainder of the night?"

Next to me, Silas perks up instantly.

"We're just trying to keep two people apart?" he asks, already standing straighter. "Is that the only goal here or is there also a secondary objective?"

"I've got a secondary objective," Violet says. "*Who the fuck is Delilah* is my secondary objective."

"It sounds kinda familiar?" June says to her, but they both shrug.

In my pocket, I ball my hand into a fist, fighting the urge to touch her. I just want to put an arm around her shoulders, a hand on her back, but I don't. Not while Silas is here.

I *have* to tell him. My reasons seem less and less important by the day.

"Should be fairly simple," Silas says. "We set up a few sentries whose job it is to redirect Seth if he comes too near the target. Meanwhile, we try to create a diversion, a way to get him out here that he won't suspect. We lure the target away from his path out of the fest, and *voila*, mission accomplished."

"Delilah," I remind him. "The target's name is Delilah, and she's a person."

"Right. Like I said," Silas tells me, shrugging.

"She's over there," Daniel says, nodding vaguely forward.

I turn and look. Her back is to me, but there's a mane of curly, bright red hair, and that's all I need.

"Guys," says Violet. "Who. Is. *Delilah?*"

"Delilah is Seth's ex-girlfriend," Charlie explains. "They dated for six years. The last two of high school and all of college."

Violet looks over her shoulder at Delilah, then back at Charlie.

"Seth didn't take the breakup well," Daniel explains.

"He seems to have gotten over it," Violet points out dryly.

Daniel and I just share a glance.

"Sure," I say, as neutrally as I can.

253

"Okay," Silas says, already taking charge. "Who here knows the target?"

"Delilah," I remind him. I've got no affection for the woman, but *target* is just... unsettling.

"Who here knows Delilah?" he asks.

Daniel, Charlie, and I all raise our hands. June makes a face and half-raises hers, shrugging.

"Maybe?" she says.

"Okay," Silas says. "Levi, you're with me. Daniel, Charlie, you're with Seth. June, Violet, and Adeline, you're our sentries."

"Question," say Violet, half-raising her hand.

"Wait until the end, please," Silas says. "Daniel and Charlie, go join Caleb with Seth. June, Violet, Adeline, your job is to roam the crowd and keep a line of sight on the— on Delilah. If she seems to be moving toward the building, engage her."

"I didn't bring my sidearm," June says, sarcastically.

"In *conversation*, smartass," Silas says. "Levi and I will post at the doors, and will be the last line of defense, ready to physically block her from entry until Seth has exited the premises. And if anyone sees Eli, send him to me. Violet, what was your question?"

"You answered it," she says, taking a swig of her beer.

"You should also all keep an eye out for Caleb," I tell them. "We don't need him coming into contact with Delilah, either."

Violet gasps, dramatically.

"Is that why they broke up?" she asks in a hushed voice.

"What? No," says Daniel. "Caleb bore the brunt of the breakup, so he hates her the most. That's all."

"Ahh," says Violet, finishing off the last of her beer. "Okay, team. Let's go!"

She fist-pumps into the air and turns, already looking for Delilah. I glance down at June.

"You good?" I ask, half-smiling. She looks back up at me, face serious.

"Yep," she says, then looks away and something inside me tightens, just a twitch.

I need to tell Silas. I do. I will.

"Levi. C'mon," Silas says, and June turns away, walks after Violet. I watch her as she crosses the patio, weaving between tables, then finally catches up to Violet near the edge of the lawn, saying something into the other girl's ear.

"Coming," I answer, and we make our way to the door as Daniel and Charlie go through, giving us conspiratorial eyebrow raises as they do.

Silas stands to one side of the door, and even though he's holding a beer, he tucks his other thumb into his belt loop and stands practically at attention.

"You look like a bouncer," I tell him, crossing my legs and leaning against the building. "Relax."

"I *am* a bouncer," he says. "I don't know what happened, but I know she's not getting into this building."

"She's a hundred and forty pounds soaking wet," I tell him. "I don't think she'll be a problem if it comes down to that."

Silas sighs, then takes his thumb from his belt loop, drinks his beer, and manages to look a little less like a cop.

"Can I ask you something about June?" he says, after a moment, as he scans the crowd, watching for a mop of red hair.

I feel like I've swallowed a cold steel spike.

"Of course," I say.

"You guys seem like you've become friends," he says.

Then he pauses, looks at me. My heart is beating like a thunderstorm, my nerves crackling.

This is it, I think. *He knows.*

I don't have to tell him. He knows.

"After a fashion," I say, and he looks away.

"Has she seemed weird to you this past week?" he asks, scanning the crowd again. "I mean, I know this whole situation with the ex-boyfriend and the getting fired and moving back home has been hard on her, but she's seemed really, I don't know, *anxious* for the past week."

My heart slows, and I take a sip of my half-empty beer, partly relieved that he still doesn't know, wishing that he did so this could be over.

"Maybe a little," I say. "Though I don't see her often. Not often enough to know if she's acting strange, certainly. I don't see her nearly that often. No."

I drink more beer so I stop talking.

June *has* been acting a little weird, but I'm fairly certain it's because she's waiting to hear back after her phone interview last Monday. The one with the paper in South Dakota.

My chest constricts at the thought, and I look away, pretending to keep an eye out for red hair. Every day that passes without her hearing back, I feel a little lighter, a little more like I get to keep her a while longer.

Then, inevitably, I feel awful for feeling that way, for wishing ill on June's ambitions.

"It's probably just the job interview she's got coming up," he says. "But I don't know. She's not usually this jumpy, and I swear sometimes she looks like she's about to cry."

She hasn't said anything about another interview. My heart stalls, thumps unpleasantly, and I take a deep breath, trying to force my biological functions into compliance.

"What's the interview?" I ask, as casually as I possibly can.

Please let it be in Roanoke, in Richmond, maybe even Northern Virginia...

"It's for an editor position in South Dakota," he says, still looking out, over the crowd. "She's already had a phone interview or maybe two for it and now she's flying out to meet them in person. I don't know why she's so nervous, it seems like it's almost a done deal if they've gone through all that, you know?"

Someone's lighting the first bonfire, and that's all I look at, all I can bear: a lighted stick inside an inverted cone of wood, flickering brightly through the cracks as the tinder goes up, the bigger pieces trying to catch.

South Dakota.

She didn't tell me.

Maybe she just found out. I'm sure it's because she just found out.

"I haven't noticed a difference in her behavior, nor her demeanor," I hear myself say, my own voice sounding distant. "But, again, I don't—"

"Right, see her enough to notice," Silas finishes for me. "I swear, she's been a basket case about it all week."

All week?

I exhale, hard. I'm still staring at the fire, concentrating so hard that I can almost feel it lick against my skin, wrap around a hand, consume me.

Why wouldn't she tell me?

I thought we told each other things.

Something unpleasant starts at the base of my spine and works its way up, a black snake slithering upward, winding between my vertebrae.

"It is a good job?" I ask, and to my own ears I sound breathless, deranged, but Silas doesn't seem to notice.

"Yeah, but it's in South Dakota," he sighs. "You know, I really want her to be happy, but I kinda hope she doesn't get it. I like having her around, even though she's kind of annoying sometimes."

She didn't tell me. I think I might crack in half.

"That's far," I say, and somehow, I sound normal.

"Yeah," he says. "I volunteered to take her to the airport Monday and I kinda wish I hadn't, she's gotta be there at seven in the morning which means we gotta leave at…"

I can barely hear him over my heartbeat, thundering away in my chest: *Dakota Dakota Dakota. South Dakota. South Dakota.*

"…but whatever, she'll owe me, I guess," Silas finishes. "There are worse things than—"

The doors fly open and Caleb appears. I just stare at him, still feeling as though I'm stuck in glass, unable to think or move.

"Where is he?" Caleb says, wide-eyed. "Did he come this way?"

"Who?" I ask.

"*Seth,*" Silas and Caleb both say in unison.

"And no," Silas tells Caleb.

"He's gone," Caleb says. "He said he had to take a piss and that was ten minutes ago. He's not inside, so he must be out here—"

Caleb is already standing up tall, trying to see over the crowd. Seth shouldn't be too hard to spot right now, but none of us are managing.

June is flying to a job interview.

In South Dakota.

That she didn't tell me about.

I feel nauseous. I couldn't care less about finding Delilah right now.

"There," Caleb says suddenly. "Shit. *Shit.* They're close. Tell me he doesn't see her."

Then he's off, moving between people and tables, navigating with an odd grace peculiar to my youngest brother.

Silas and I follow. Or rather, Silas follows and I let myself be pulled along, still barely paying attention.

"No," Caleb hisses, stopping suddenly. I nearly run into him, then step to one side, follow his glance.

Delilah is talking to a couple, beer in hand, laughing.

Fifty feet away, Seth is walking straight toward her across the lawn, bouncy pumpkin dark and motionless behind them.

"Don't," Caleb mutters, mostly to himself. "I can't do this again, Seth."

Then he's off, striding across the grass, blocking Seth's way. Caleb holds up a hand, says something. Seth shrugs, gives him a look, says something else that I can't quite hear.

South Dakota.

Caleb leans in, speaks urgently, and Seth shakes his head. He takes his younger brother by the shoulder, gives him a smile and a squeeze, walks around him.

There's a moment where I think Caleb might tackle him, but he doesn't. He just turns and walks away, back toward the building.

Silas and I watch. There's no way we intercede now without making a scene and probably making it worse, so we do nothing.

Right before he gets to her, her back to him, he pauses. He takes a long sip of his beer, like he's gathering his wits or his courage.

Then he reaches out, taps her on the shoulder. Delilah turns. For a split second, she stares.

And then she smiles. It's a genuine smile, coupled with a laugh of disbelief, a slight nose scrunch.

Seth's face lights up like someone's flipped a switch at the power station.

He *laughs*, shrugs, points over his shoulder at the brewery. For a few moments, they stand there, talking like old friends.

Then she holds her arms out, still laughing, and Seth accepts the hug.

It's not a long hug. It ends a moment later, both of them still smiling. They each say one last thing, and then Seth turns around, walks back in the direction he came from until he disappears.

Silas just looks at me. I look past him, wondering where June is, whether I can get her alone and ask what's going on, whether she was ever going to tell me.

"I guess that's it," Silas says, and shrugs, firelight flickering over him.

CHAPTER TWENTY-SEVEN

JUNE

"No, you cannot throw a can of soda on the fire to see if it explodes," Daniel says. He sounds tired.

"It will," Silas confirms.

"Just one," Rusty says, as if this is still a negotiation. "I have a hypothesis about it."

Rusty recently learned that word, and I've heard her use it several times already today. Mostly, she uses it to try and convince her dad or Charlie that they should let her do something dangerous in the name of science.

It hasn't worked yet, but I think she's wearing them down.

"How am I supposed to know what happens if I don't try the experiment myself?" Rusty asks, using her most innocent voice.

It's a few hours after Seth found Delilah. Rusty is wide awake. Her dad and stepmom-to-be seem exhausted.

"It explodes and gets soda everywhere," Silas says. "Just trust me."

"That's not very scientific," Rusty says doubtfully.

"Hey Rusty," Eli pipes up. "Do you know what Sasquatch footprints look like?"

That gets the kid's attention.

"Yes," she says with complete and total certainty.

"Then there's something I need your help with," Eli says, rising from his chair and beckoning his niece after him. "Violet pointed these out to me, but I'm not quite sure…"

His voice fades as he leads Rusty off, away from the bonfire, and there's a moment of blessed quiet.

Then the quiet stops. Silas starts talking about something or other, and Charlie joins in, and then Daniel and Violet are also giving their opinions, and I feel like I can't hear myself think. I've had three beers over a few hours and my head is buzzing in a way that's not unpleasant, but that definitely makes it a little hard to think.

And I still haven't told Levi. I haven't really had the chance, but I haven't made myself the chance either, and now I've avoided something unpleasant for so long that it's become a serious issue.

From across the bonfire, I can feel him looking at me, and I swallow hard.

Just do it, you coward, I think.

I meet his eyes. His gaze is steady, unreadable, but the light is strange and Levi's not exactly an open book. I tilt my head ever-so-slighty, raise one eyebrow. He nods.

"I'll be right back," I tell no one in particular, then step away from the bonfire and toward the brewery building.

The night is cool, almost cold, and it feels good against my fire-and-alcohol-heated skin. I close my eyes, tilt my head back, breathe it in, and despite myself I think *I'm going to miss this*.

Inside the brewery is dark, all the chairs up on the tables, the bar wiped down. I didn't really have a destination in here, just wanted Levi to follow me, so I wander aimlessly: the shuffleboard table, the dartboards, behind the bar.

I pull down one tap out of idle curiosity, wondering if they're still on, then instantly push it back when a stream of beer comes out.

"I keep telling them to charge for tasters," Levi's voice says, followed by the hush of a door swinging shut.

"Of course you do," I tell him, wiping my hands together, drying the droplets of beer that landed on my shirt. "You drink for free."

He doesn't say anything, walks to the bar. He puts his hands out on the polished wood, palms down, and just looks at me.

He looks at me like I'm a riverbed and he's the river, like he's flowing over and through me, like his gaze can make its way into the tiniest of crevices, between the rocks that make up my rapids, like he can dislodge wrecks I've long forgotten.

I let him wash over me.

I let him look, and I watch him in the near-dark of the brewery, no light except the vague flicker of the bonfires outside and the pale moon trickling through the high windows.

"Why are we here, June?" he asks, unmoved.

I take a deep breath. I shake my hands, clench and release them, because they've stopped feeling like part of my body.

"I have to tell you something," I say.

My heart doesn't pound, it buzzes. It's a chainsaw, roaring and snarling, all teeth and no mercy as it plunges further into me.

"What is it?" he asks after a long, long moment.

I open my mouth, and nothing comes out. Nothing at all.

I can't say it. It should have been simple, and I've made it impossible, that one small sentence, *I have a job interview in South Dakota.* I should have told him nearly a week ago and now I still haven't told him at all and here I am, lower than the lowest form of life I can think of.

"I…"

I'm a worm. A moss. Lichen.

"I just wanted to see you alone," I finally whisper. It's true, but not the truth.

He leans forward, over the bar. It's strangely easy for me to forget how tall Levi is, how wide his shoulders are, how much muscle he has on his frame, but right now I remember every inch and every ounce, and I think he wants me to.

"Is that all you wanted?" he asks.

Tell.

Him.

I don't.

"That's not enough?" I ask, suddenly coy, my heart still buzzing, in freefall.

His eyes bore into mine, colorless in the dark. There's something in them I've never seen before, a part of him I don't know revealed, something like lust and something like need, but it's not either of those things.

"Come closer," he says, and now his voice is nearly a growl and I step forward, my hips against the bar sink.

Levi reaches out, slides his fingers through my hair, pulls me forward until our lips meet in a rough kiss.

Instantly, I open my mouth. His tongue finds mine, pushes its way into my mouth, his hand knotting in my hair. I'm on tiptoe and I go to put one hand on his face, but he catches my wrist in his other hand, brings it down to the bar top.

When he pulls away, I catch his bottom lip between my teeth. I bite harder than I mean to, but Levi just groans, my hair still wrapped in his hand.

"If you're not careful I'll give you exactly what you're asking for," he says, his voice low, raspy, his breathing hard.

It's half threat, half promise.

"I haven't asked you for anything yet," I say.

His hand shifts, lets go of my hair, slides along my jaw until his thumb is on my lower lip.

"You're right," he says. "You haven't asked me for anything. You told me."

I suck his thumb into my mouth. I can't help myself. I look him straight in the eyes and move my tongue along the rough, salty pad, let him feel my teeth against the knuckle.

I want him and I need him and I'm not telling him the truth. It makes me reckless, careless. I'm more than reckless, more than careless. I have the wild, unshakeable urge to light everything up and burn everything down, tell everyone about Levi and me in the worst way possible. I want to make it so that Silas can't look me in the eye for months.

"You're telling me right now, June," he says, his eyes on my lips like he can't tear himself away. "That you want me to come back there, bend you over the bar, and take you like an animal."

I shiver all the way to my toes.

"You're telling me that the scratches you left on my back weren't enough for you," he goes on, closer, quieter. "You're telling me that I make your knees shake and your toes curl and if I make you wait one more minute, you might leap out of your own skin."

Levi pulls his thumb from my mouth roughly. Before I

can even react, he's vaulted onto the bar and then off again and he's in front of me, unruffled, all fire and moonlight.

I've always thought that Levi was beautiful, for as long as I can remember.

But tonight, right now, I realize something that's never occurred to me before.

Levi's dangerous.

CHAPTER TWENTY-EIGHT

LEVI

June stands behind the bar in the dark brewery wide-eyed and defiant and so beautiful I can't breathe. She's always beautiful but right now there's a special kind of ache brought on by the fire and the moonlight, the way it lights her deep blue eyes.

She hasn't told me about the interview yet. She isn't going to. She's happy to let me find out when she disappears without another word, only her brother to tell me what's happened.

"Am I right?" I ask, my voice scraping the bottom of its register as I take a step forward, then another step. "About what you want and why I'm here?"

"Yes," she whispers.

I bend down and kiss her, my fingers working their way through her hair as I press myself into her, open her mouth under mine, feel her teeth against my lips.

I kiss her harder, push her backward. I have the wild urge to let her draw blood so that at least she'll hurt me in a way that I can see, a wound I can tend to properly.

June hits the wall, gasps, one hand on my shoulder.

With my free hand I take it, pin it over her head, press my body against hers until the ache dulls just a little. I'm hard as an iron spike. I know she can feel it.

I know, from experience and the way that her hips move against mine, that she wants me.

I let her wrist go, push my hands under her shirt, her skin soft, pliable. I grab her hard enough that I can feel each rib and I let my mouth leave hers, move to her earlobe, her neck.

"I should leave a mark," I growl, nipping at her skin. "It's fair, don't you think?

She swallows, the muscles moving under my lips.

"The scratches were an accident," she murmurs. "I don't even know when I made them."

I move my hands to her back, unhook her bra.

"Wednesday," I tell her, pushing the cups of her bra over her breasts, her stiff nipples between my fingers. "You shouted my name and shredded my back and now you're telling me you don't remember?"

I pinch both nipples, and she arches her back, her eyes closing, her breath leaving in a whoosh.

"I remember Wednesday," she gasps, her chest heaving in my hands. "I just don't remember hurting you."

I pinch her nipples one percent harder and she grabs my shirt, twists it in her hand like she's begging me without words.

"You didn't hurt me," I say, and I'm almost laughing, teasing her. "You think anything could hurt when I'm deep inside you and you're coming so hard you scream my name?"

Even in the dark, I can see her cheeks turn faintly pinker and I give her nipples one last, hard squeeze, take her chin in one hand.

"You did it," I murmur. "You were there, and you were

naked and willing as hell, and if I recall correctly you begged me over and over again not to stop."

I yank her jeans undone, push my other hand between her legs.

She's unbelievably wet, her lips puffy and swollen and I slide one finger between them, pull it back to circle her clit.

"You don't get to blush when you did what I'm only describing, June," I tell her. "And you particularly don't get to blush about it when you're this wet virtually in public."

"It's involuntary," she says as the palm of her hand finds my cock through my pants. "I can't help it."

"The blushing or getting wet?" I ask, one hand still on her face, the other circling her clit slowly.

"Both," she says.

I kiss her and I slide my fingers into her all at once, and she bucks and makes a noise into my mouth as I push her back against the wall, harder, her wetness soaking my hand.

I'm going to miss her, desperately, and I don't want to think about it so I kiss her harder and stroke *that* spot inside her, the heel of my hand pressed against her clit, and I feel the way her body trembles under mine and that's all I think about.

I want her. I want her *now*, here, and that's not new.

What's new is the ferocity of my desire, the angry edge to it. I want — *need* — to make her feel something, to make sure she never forgets me or this moment.

"June," I say, still stroking. "Walk to the counter and bend over it."

I pull my fingers out of her.

"That—"

"Now."

She does it and I feel a sudden rush: power, control, ownership. In this one way, at least, June is mine and that's what I think as I'm right behind her, pushing her jeans down to her knees, stroking her with one hand, bending over and murmuring into her ear.

She's mine. She's mine.

"Do you want to know what happens next?" I ask, teasing at her entrance.

"Yes," she whispers.

I could do anything.

Right now, she is mine.

"I'm going to eat you out bent over this counter," I say, speaking slowly so she can savor every word, my voice a rumble. "I don't give a damn who's outside and I don't give a damn if they come in because right now, June, you're all mine and nothing else matters."

I slide my fingers into her again, watch her as she bites her lip.

"Then," I go on. "Once you finish, we're going to walk outside and you're going to tell everyone that I'm giving you a ride home."

I find her clit with my thumb and her eyelids flutter.

"Then what?" June murmurs.

"Then we go to my house and fuck," I tell her, and I drop to my knees.

I find her clit with my tongue instantly and June gasps, shifts, rises to her toes and I tease her, drawing my tongue around that button in a slick circle, fingers still buried inside her, stroking from within.

She's musky, tangy, slightly salty and slightly sweet as lick her harder. I flatten my tongue against her clit, drag the length of it against her until she groans and sighs, the sound of her voice bouncing off stainless steel.

I can't make her admit that she's leaving. I can't — I won't — make her stay here for me. I can't make her give up her dreams to live in the middle of nowhere.

But I can make her come.

I pull my fingers out to a soft sigh, add a third, push them back in to the sound of her breath going ragged as she pushes back into me, wordlessly begging for more. I stroke her and lick slowly, up and down, dragging my tongue against the most sensitive parts of her until she's panting, groaning, her muscles trembling around my fingers.

She whispers my name, and if I wasn't already rock-hard, I am now, my cock straining against my zipper as she grabs the edge of the counter like she's bracing herself. The fingers of my other hand dig into her thigh as I lick harder, longer, sunk inside her up to the knuckle.

June gasps, holds her breath, gasps again, the sound almost like a whimper as she bucks back against me, pushing me even deeper.

I close my lips around her clit and suck.

She comes. She clenches around me and she groans and every muscle in her body tenses, then relaxes as she whispers my name again. Now her hand is on my head, her fingers trying to work through my hair, but I don't stop. I don't let go.

After all, she's mine, and she's mine all the more as she comes again and this time her knees buckle for just a moment, her channel clenching even harder around me. Now my name's out loud, not whispered, her knuckles white on the edge of the counter. I can feel the shockwave as it passes through her body, a shudder, a ripple.

I don't stop. I suck at her harder, her juices now running from my fingers and into my mouth. I suck and I lap her up and she's on her toes, hand in my hair, and I can't tell if she's trying to move away or toward me but she's saying my name and she's sure not asking me to stop, and I don't.

This time she shakes when she comes. This time I have

to hold her up, even as I think she might break my fingers. I finally let her go and she's face down on the metal counter, one arm over her head, her other hand still tangled in my hair.

This is June, undone.

I pull my fingers out of her, lick them off, stand. She turns, pulls her jeans back up and before she's done, I'm pressing her backward, against the counter again, in full view of anyone who enters but I'm so far beyond caring I can't see it in the rearview mirror.

I kiss her hard, deep, and she kisses me back. I know I taste like her and I want her to know it, to taste herself on my lips.

She does. She must. She slides her fingers underneath the waist of my jeans, pulls me in until I'm crushed against her heat, my mouth still on hers.

"Go tell them," I growl.

"Not yet," she says, and then my button is undone, the zipper down.

Her hand closes around my cock, strokes. I groan into her mouth, the thrill and the ache going all the way to my bones.

"Go," I say again, my voice harsher, rougher.

"Stop talking," she tells me and suddenly my cock is out and she's pumping me, and I can't help but to thrust against her, my fingers in her hair again, a sound I don't recognize coming from my chest.

Then June is on her knees, my hand still in her hair, and one second later her mouth is around my cock, lips sliding down my shaft.

Reality unravels. That's what it feels like, at least, at my cock hits the back of her throat, and she swallows against the head, her hand fisted around the base.

Then I'm leaning over her, one hand against the

counter, the other in her hair as her head moves up and down my shaft, the world slowly exploding in front of my eyes.

It doesn't take long. It never does. I manage to say her name, once, my voice rough, just before I come and she pushes her mouth down my shaft, swallows. She swallows again as I come, and again, and I have to hold on tight because if I don't, I think I might fall forever and never come out the other side.

And then it's done, and I can see again. June pulls back with one last lick at the head of my cock, and it makes every muscle in my body jerk. I pull her to standing, push my lips against hers while she still tastes like me.

I ravage her mouth, there in the dark. I plunder her. I want everything she has to give; I want more than she has to give and right here, right now, I'm tempted to take it.

My hand is still in her hair, and I pull her head back, drag my lips along her jaw, press them to her neck where I can feel her pulse, hammering away.

I'm tempted to tell her that I know. Right now, when we're both raw and vulnerable, I want to tell her that I know she's about to break me, but I don't. Instead I tug her hair a little harder, take her earlobe between my teeth, wait for the catch in her breathing before I speak.

"*Now* you go tell them," I whisper, my voice rough. "I'll be waiting in my truck."

CHAPTER TWENTY-NINE

JUNE

"I'm getting ready to leave," Silas says, still sitting by the fire. "I'll give you a ride back, tell Levi not to worry about it."

Everyone else is just *looking* at me. I can only look at Silas — the only one who really matters right now — but I can feel all those other eyes on me, knowing. *Knowing.*

"He already went to go get in his truck," I say, jerking one thumb over my shoulder, toward the parking lot. "Stay as late as you want, I know you've been really busy at work lately so just have a good night, hang out with these guys, I'll see you later?"

My mouth is dry, and worse, I still taste like Levi. I swallow hard but it doesn't go away and I can't help but replay that moment: his soft growl, his fist in my hair, the way he arced over as he lost control and I swallowed him, again and again.

Tonight, for the first time, I'm afraid of those moments. I'm afraid of how badly I want them, of how closely I treasure them. I'm afraid that those are the moments when people make bad decisions, when they pass up their dreams and then ten years later, they realize they're stuck.

"Is everything okay?" Silas asks, frowning. "Did something happen, June?"

I feel a mess and I'm sure I look it, so I steel myself, straighten my spine, gather my wits.

"I'm fine," I say. "Just tired, and I wanted to get a head start on some freelance work tomorrow, you know?"

"I had Levi here pretty late last night," Daniel adds, coming to my rescue. "You know how old men get tired."

"Hey," Silas protests.

"You didn't finish your story about the goat," Eli points out. "Levi's a very responsible driver, she'll be fine."

I could kiss both of them right now. Except, you know, not.

"True," Silas allows. "All right, see you tomorrow, Bug."

"Bye!" I say, and I'm off before he can re-start his story about the goat.

"Right," I hear Silas start. "So my buddy in North Carolina owns this farm…"

The night is cool, almost cold, but I'm not bothering with a jacket. I'm already too hot in my own skin, flushed and uncomfortable, practically running to get to Levi's truck where he's waiting for me and where I know I still won't tell him.

Tomorrow, I promise myself.

First thing tomorrow, I tell him.

Then I round the corner of the building and here's there, leaning against the side of his truck, arms folded himself and ankles crossed, contemplating the sky and waiting.

"They buy it?" he asks, voice low and slow.

"Silas did," I say, more breathless than I should be from the walk alone. "No one else, though."

"They don't matter," he says, and pulls me in. He kisses me, his fingers digging into my lower spine, and I wrap my arms around him. After a moment he pulls away, one hand on my back, and opens the passenger door in that loose-limbed, graceful way he has. He offers me his hand and helps me in, and he doesn't look over his shoulder at the bonfire even once.

· · · ★ ★ ★ ★ ★ · · ·

LEVI RESTS his hand on my leg for most of the drive, except when he has to shift gears. Every time he puts it back, he moves it a little higher, makes me a little bit crazier.

"Pull over," I finally whisper as we barrel down a long, lonely stretch of the Appalachian Parkway.

"We're almost there," he says. "Ten more minutes."

"Could be now," I say as his thumb strokes my leg, callouses whispering over denim.

"Could be," he agrees, glancing over at me with that half-smile he has. "But it's not."

"Levi, are you turning me down?" I tease.

"You know full well I haven't got that kind of willpower," he says, taking his hand from my leg, downshifting around a sharp turn, putting it back a centimeter higher. "All I've got is patience, and I don't even have too much of that."

I put my hand over his, slide it higher, still feeling reckless, like I could burn it all down tonight.

"Seems like you've got plenty," I say.

"Because I want to take you home instead of pushing you against the side of my truck in a public picnic area?" he asks. "Not that I think I wouldn't enjoy that."

I swallow hard, pulsing with heat at the suggestion, and we keep driving.

Five minutes later, we pull into Levi's driveway, and he stops, so suddenly that I'm pressed against my seatbelt, jolted from thinking about Levi bending me over the tailgate of his truck.

Before I know it he's grabbed me, pulled me to the middle of the cab, claimed my mouth with his. His hand finds its way between my legs and even through the layers of fabric, he knows where my clit is, runs his fingers over it as I jolt.

Then he lets me go and he's driving again, bumping down his long driveway. Even in the dark I can see his erection straining against his pants.

I unbuckle, scoot toward him.

"That's hardly safe," he murmurs, even as he slows.

I put an arm around his shoulders, slide my other hand over his thigh.

"Then be careful," I say, and press my lips against his neck, cup his cock with my other hand. There's a low rumble from his chest and I pull open the first button on his shirt, the second, tug the neck toward his shoulder and bite the newly-revealed skin there.

Suddenly, the car rocks to a stop. He reaches over me, pushes at the gearshift, kicks the parking brake into place and then the moment that everything is dark and quiet, he presses his lips to mine again.

I throw my leg over him, straddle his lap. I press myself against his thick erection as he pushes his car door open, undoing the last button on his shirt, sliding my hand around his muscled torso.

I feel awful but it doesn't stop me from wanting him here, now. If anything, it makes it worse, like scratching this itch can obliterate my guilty conscience for a few minutes, like slaking this thirst can make all this go away.

After a moment he takes me by the hips, lifts me off

him, and then I'm on the ground and off-balance but Levi's there, his arm in my hand while I right myself, the heavy truck door shutting.

"I already told you, not in the truck," he says, that smile in his voice. "I didn't bring you all the way here just to fuck in there. C'mon."

With that *c'mon* he crouches, then lifts me before I know what's going on and then I'm upside-down, over his shoulder. I yelp and push myself up, hands on his lower back, but Levi doesn't react. Calmly, he strides up his porch steps, opens his front door.

"Hey, girl," he tells Hedwig.

Then, to me: "It's better if you stop wiggling. I'd hate to drop you."

Levi hangs his keys on a hook as if he doesn't have a care in the world, then crosses the living room, goes up the stairs. I give up wiggling and shut my eyes.

Through the bedroom door. It shuts, and then he pushes me off his shoulder and onto his bed and I bounce once, already sitting up, kicking off my shoes as he shrugs his shirt from his shoulders.

"Take your clothes off," he orders me, his hands already on the fly of his pants. The bulge below the zipper is so big that the waistband is gapping away from his skin, and as I watch, Levi slowly, mindlessly slides his fingers along the outline of his cock.

I whisk my shirt off, unhook my bra, throw it somewhere without looking. Levi's hand is still on his clothed cock and he's watching me like I'm the first and last thing he'll ever see.

I lie back on the bed, slide my jeans and panties down over my hips, all at once, kick them until they're off my feet and Levi finally, *finally* unzips himself and frees his cock, one hand still wrapped around the base.

Then he's on top of me, mouth pressed against mine, and it's every bit as wild and savage as the kisses behind the bar only this time we're both unclothed in his bed. He kisses me harder, presses my head against the mattress. He palms one breast, brushes his fingers over my nipples, then pinches it almost as hard as I can take, and I moan into his mouth.

"That," he says, my lower lip between his teeth.

"What?" I whisper.

"That's why I wanted you here and not the side of the road," he says. "I want you loud, June."

He shifts position, pushes my knees apart, kneels over me. My breathing is ragged but I look up at him, put one knee over his shoulder.

"I want you shouting my name and begging me not to stop," he says, and presses his lips to the inside of my thigh, his other hand roaming my body: breasts, belly, hips, until his thumb finds my clit and strokes it slowly. "You know you do that, don't you? You forgot about the scratches on my back, after all."

"I didn't forget," I say, my back already arching under the force of pleasure, his cock bobbing long and thick and hard inches away from me. "I didn't realize."

He leans in, the back of my thigh now against his hard chest, his naked cock just barely brushing my entrance, his knees under my ass.

"Do you realize that we've fucked in every position I can think of, every possible configuration of two bodies, and every time still feels brand new?" he asks.

I put my hands on his legs, underneath me, arching my back toward him.

"Are you saying I make you nervous?" I ask, half-teasing, half delirious with want.

He kisses the inside of my thigh again, his eyes never leaving mine, dark and unreadable.

Suddenly, he grabs my leg, lifts it over my head, flips me onto my stomach and before I know it, he's on top of me again, pressing me into the mattress, his lips on my spine between my shoulder blades. I push myself up, my hips still against the mattress.

"Do you realize," he murmurs into my ears, shivers down my back, "That this has been the best month of my life?"

He kneels between my legs, pushing my knees apart and then his hand is in my hair again, wrapping it around his fingers, and this time he pulls and I follow.

It's not hard enough to hurt. Not quite, but it's hard enough that I feel it, that the rush and the sensation send pinpricks along my overheated skin. It's hard enough that it jolts me into a hyper-awareness I didn't know I possessed, hard enough that suddenly I can feel every individual thread of his sheets against my knees and elbows, that the moonlight feels cold against my skin.

"Mine too," I say, and I don't mean to say it but it's true. By rights I should be at least semi-miserable, but I haven't been. I've been *happy*.

Happy, and I still haven't told him.

His breath rasps in my ear for another moment. My eyes close, and I press my lips together. I'm up on my elbows and I dig my fingers into his plaid comforter, savoring this small speck of time.

The drawer of his nightstand scrapes open, and I hear the condom box rattle.

"I'm on the pill," I say, and the sounds stop. I breathe, eyes still closed. "I didn't say anything because I wanted to be careful—"

"Fuck careful," he says, his grip in my hair tightening the tiniest bit.

Almost. Almost. I can feel him shift his weight, steady himself, and then the tip of his cock is bare and hot against my clit and my hips move on their own.

"Please?" I say and it's a request, a supplication, a prayer.

He doesn't answer. Not with words, because that isn't the language he speaks, not really.

Levi answers me with his body, sliding deep into me with a single stroke. He says *yes* and *of course* and *at last* and he pulls my hair and he bites my shoulder and he doesn't speak a word but he says everything.

It's hard, deep, slow. Levi fucks me as thoroughly as he does anything, moves and pulls and pushes and adjusts the angle until I'm crying out with every stroke, still up on my elbows with his hand in my hair.

I can't really move, pinned down and held up, and I don't really want to. All I can do is feel, and feel, and *feel:* Levi's body against mine, in mine, the potent slow churn of guilt that just won't leave. His sheets below me and beyond that the bed he makes every morning, the house he built himself, the trees he protects, this place that's part of him, sunk into the fibers of his being.

I whisper his name, or maybe I whimper it. I can't tell, but I'm rewarded with teeth on my shoulder, a sharp bite, a harder fuck and somehow, everything snaps further into focus. The sheets, the creak of the bed, a bird outside, and Levi, oh God, Levi.

I'm splintering apart, cracking down the middle. I gasp his name and I gasp *please* and *oh fuck don't stop please don't stop* and I grab his wrist with one hand where it's anchored to the bed and he pulls my hair one iota harder and I'm trapped here, in the cage of his body, and I never want to be anywhere else.

I come hard, recklessly, like I'm going into freefall. I come and with it I give him everything that I have to give, body and soul and guilt all wrapped up together, and then Levi joins me, suddenly wrapping his arms around me and squeezing so tight I can barely breathe, my name whispered on his lips just before he sinks his teeth into my shoulder again, like he needs more of me than I have to give.

Slowly, we shudder to a stop. He lays on top of me and doesn't pull out, and I don't move in the perfect stillness of the wilderness night. I try to memorize every inch of this: the scratch of his beard against my neck, his hand clutching mine, the slight tickle of his chest hair on my back.

And I tell myself, there in the quiet, that I won't regret anything.

CHAPTER THIRTY

LEVI

I wake up early the next morning, while June's still asleep. That's not unusual. June's not a morning person, but I've never needed too much sleep and I've never liked to waste daylight.

Before I get up, I kiss her on the shoulder, right on a red mark that might be from my teeth. I didn't mean to leave a mark, but I don't think I mind that I did. She's left one, after all.

I pull on clothes, go downstairs, Hedwig trotting quietly after me, the click of her nails on the floor loud in the silence. I let her out, pour myself a glass of water, drink it down.

I stare out my kitchen window and consider last night. I wonder if that's what *catharsis* means, because now, in the morning light, I feel purged. Lighter. Clean.

I feel hollow and scraped-out, like someone's rent the flesh from my skin, inside and out, but I feel clean nonetheless.

Water boils. Hedwig investigates several trees. Something in the house — *my* house — creaks. I make oatmeal, slip on an ancient pair of sneakers, and sit on my back porch in the chilly autumn sunrise.

· · · · ★ ★ ★ ★ · · ·

THE SUN'S well up when the door behind me opens and June steps out, still bleary-eyed from sleep. She's wearing her own pants and a plain navy blue sweatshirt, mine, several sizes too big for her.

"Good morning," she says, and sits without looking at me.

"I didn't make coffee," I tell her. "I didn't know when you'd be up."

A few weeks ago I got a small French press to keep at my house, just for her. I don't drink coffee, but she seems to live on the stuff.

"Don't worry about it," she says, and then for no reason, "Thanks."

In the yard, Hedwig flops dramatically over onto her side, wriggles in the scant grass. I take a deep breath, steel myself, because I know what's about to happen.

"When's the interview?" I ask, one simple question.

June freezes. I don't have to look at her to know, because I can feel it from where I'm sitting.

There's silence. I wait.

"Tuesday," she finally says. "I'm flying out tomorrow morning."

Her voice has a hard, ugly edge to it, flat and brittle.

"To South Dakota?"

"Right," she says in a hush, and then, "Levi—"

"Were you going to tell me?" I ask, because I can't stop myself. "Or were you just going to disappear and maybe call me once you'd started your new job, if you felt like it?"

"I'm sorry," she says.

I say nothing. I stand. I still don't look at her, because I can't, and I walk to the porch railing and look out into the wilderness beyond my property. It feels like fissures are opening in my skin, the cold working its way in through them, into me.

"I meant to tell you," she says, whispering now.

"That doesn't matter," I tell her, matter-of-fact. "You didn't."

"I wanted to."

"No, you didn't," I say. "If you'd wanted to you would have."

I finally turn to her, leaning against the railing, arms crossed over my chest like I can protect myself from her.

I can't and I know it. I never could. I can only hope to mend myself later.

"I didn't want to hurt you," she says, her eyes filled with tears. She won't look at me. "It was wrong, and I know it, but I just couldn't bring myself to——"

"So you lied?" I ask. "That's better?"

Inside I'm bubbling, burning, smoldering. I want to shout at her, rage, but I don't.

"I didn't lie," she protests.

"You're leaving and you didn't tell me," I say, crossing my arms more tightly, holding it inside. "I didn't even rate that courtesy."

"You don't know that I'm leaving, this interview might not work out," she says.

"I don't know anything, June, you don't tell me things."

"One thing," she says, and now she's got one hand in her hair and one on her hip, pacing the porch. "I didn't tell you this one thing."

"The one thing is that you're leaving for South Dakota," I say, louder than I meant to. In the yard, Hedwig looks over, alarmed. "Don't tell me I don't know that, June, because I do. If you don't leave now, you're leaving soon, whether it's for Maine or South Dakota or Alaska."

"You've always known that," she says, like that makes a difference. "It's not a secret that I've been trying to get a job and it's not a secret that it could be anywhere."

"But this was a secret?" I ask, my volume still too loud.

I turn away, take a deep breath. I don't know what I want from her right now, but I'm not getting it and I don't think I will.

"I thought we told each other things," I say, still too loud, my back still turned. "I knew you weren't here forever, but I told you about the crows and I told you about my father and I thought this was something real, not just some fling."

"It was one thing," she says, sounding defeated.

I turn back around, swallowing hard. Her jaw is clenched and she's fighting tears, losing the battle.

"I thought I mattered to you," I tell her. "I thought I was more than a side note, more than a post-it note left on my fridge one morning—"

"I wouldn't leave you a note," she says, blue eyes flashing.

"I wouldn't even get that?"

"I was going to tell you!" she says, and now she's shouting. Hedwig stands, softly pads up to the porch, sits between us looking worried. "I just hadn't yet."

"I don't know whether to believe you," I say.

"Fuck off," she sighs, turns, paces for the end of the porch.

"What else haven't you told me?" I ask, my voice dangerously quiet. "Are you really always working on articles about dogs? Did you really break up with your ex a couple of months ago?"

I don't mean it, even as I say it, but I'm angry and it gets the better of me, leaking out into my words.

"Jesus Christ," she mutters, rubbing at her eyes with the heels of her hands. June takes a deep breath, turns back around. "What the *fuck*, Levi? I didn't tell you because I was afraid to hurt you, because it makes me feel shitty, and because, I don't know, it felt easier for a while to just lie about it. I'm sorry. I'm sorry. I don't know how to else to say it."

"You thought so little of me?" I ask, my words picking speed, velocity, getting away from me. "That I could be put off, discarded, tossed to the wayside until it was better for you?"

"That's not it," she whispers. Now she's crying hard, tears running down both cheeks, and she presses her lips together like she can get a hold of herself.

"How long have you known?" she asks suddenly.

"Yesterday," I say, my voice dead, listless. "Silas told me."

There's a beat of silence, and I can see her doing the math: reckless carnality behind the bar, the drive home, the furious, almost brutal way we coupled last night.

"Yesterday?" she repeats, her eyes hard.

"That's right."

"What the fuck, Levi?" she asks, softly. She hiccups. "I've got a hand-shaped bruise on one thigh and teeth marks in my shoulder."

"And I've got scratches all the way down my back, so at least we both got something out of this," I tell her.

"That was an accident," she says, and she's crying again, her jaw clenched like she's desperately trying to stop tears and it's not working.

"You're good at hurting me without thinking about it," I say.

287

"You're good at keeping me hidden because you're afraid of my brother," she snaps back, bloodshot eyes blazing. "Better not to tell anyone that we were together than risk pissing him off, right?"

"You think I'm *afraid* of Silas?" I ask, taking a step closer to her, my voice rising again despite my best efforts. "I'm not afraid of your brother, June. I'm not some douchebag who he can scare off or frighten into running away like the rest of your boyfriends."

"So what, you respect him too much to tell him you're fucking his sister?" she says, her voice brutal.

"You're leaving," I say, and my voice has that hard, cold edge again, the anger leaking through. "Forgive me if I didn't ruin a lifelong friendship over something I knew all along was temporary."

June closes her eyes. Two more tears leak out and she swallows hard, takes a deep, shuddering breath, and I hate myself for it.

I hate myself for making her cry. I hate myself for getting hurt like this, for letting myself get attached, for falling so hard for this girl who was never going to be mine.

"I never should have thrown pebbles at your window that night," I tell her, voice still hard.

Her eyes are still closed, and she just shakes her head once.

"I'm leaving," she says, and she pushes past me, through the back door. She grabs her purse off a side table and practically explodes onto the front porch, then stands there for a moment, her silhouette framed by the doorway.

"SHIT!" she screams, so loud that birds fly away and the profanity echoes through the forest, off the trees and the brittle leaves. "SHIIIIIIT!"

It's not until I get to the front porch that I realize the problem: I drove her here last night. I swallow my black heart and grab my keys, call Hedwig in, shut the front door.

"I'll take you home," I tell her, already striding for my truck.

"I don't want a ride from you," she says, pulling out her phone.

"I don't want to give you a ride, but it's the best option," I say, pulling open one heavy truck door.

There's no service out here, and half a second later she remembers that, shoves her phone back into her purse.

"Just get in the truck," I say, not kindly. "I promise not to talk to."

Wordlessly, she crosses in front of the truck, gets into the passenger side.

I keep my word and don't say a thing. I barely even look at her, and she spends the drive staring out the window.

When we get to her parents' house, she thanks me for the ride brittlely and then she's gone, the door slammed, escaping up the sidewalk to her parents' front door.

I watch her walk in. She doesn't look back, and despite that, despite myself, I memorize the way she looks when she goes.

I can't help it. I want something to hang onto.

· · · ★ ★ ★ ★ ★ · · ·

I DON'T GO BACK HOME. I don't want to. I want to find a void, a nothingness, and I want to lock myself in it with my misery and my anger and I want to never speak with another living human being again.

The time's come. June is moving on and she's leaving me behind, and even though I always knew this would happen that knowledge doesn't dull the blow even a little.

I'm hurt, and I hurt her back because that's what a wounded animal does. We lash out.

I drive around for a long time, aimlessly. I drive too fast around the corners, wanting that half-second rush that comes with danger, wanting to fuel the urge I have to destroy everything that's still good in my life.

Eventually, I find my way to the ranger station where my office is. It's closed and locked, a Sunday, but I go inside and find the file I'm looking for.

While I'm there, my phone rings. Caleb. I hit the *ignore* button.

A few minutes later, he calls again. Same result.

Then Eli.

Then Caleb.

Then Caleb again.

"Jesus," I mutter, then flip the phone open. "*What?*"

"Well hello, sunshine," he says. "Mom wanted me to ask you if you could bring some marshmallows over this afternoon—"

"I'm not coming," I say, still going through papers with my other hand, quickly scanning USGS locations.

I'd forgotten it was Sunday and they're expecting me at my mom's house.

"To dinner?" he says.

"Was I unclear?" I say, finally finding a pink second-carbon-copy that says *Hemlock Bottom*. That'll do. "No. I am not coming today. Are there any other questions or was that it?"

"What happened?" he says.

I stare at the pink form. I tap one finger against it, not answering Caleb's question.

"Nothing," I finally say.

"Levi—"

"I've gotta go repair a footbridge," I say. "I'll be back

sometime Tuesday. Maybe Wednesday. We'll see how bad it is."

"Hold on," he says, and then I can hear him say something to someone else, quick footsteps, the slam of a screen door. "You still there?"

"For now."

"Will you wait?"

"There's not much sunlight left," I say, looking out the window.

"It's eleven-thirty," he says, and now I can hear the crunch of gravel under his footsteps. "Please? An hour."

I close my eyes. I don't want to wait an hour. I want to escape now, get lost from people and humanity and their noise and their needs and their opinions *right now*, go where things are simpler and there's no one to break my heart.

I want to hike until I'm too exhausted to think. I want to hit things, throw things, fix a stupid bridge, force my brain to shut off.

"Levi," says Caleb, softly. "Sixty minutes. Come on."

"All right," I say. "If you're not at my house by then I'm leaving."

"Sure," he says, and we hang up.

I grab the pink sheet, study it more closely. Rotting planks, broken handrail. This was submitted almost two years ago, and it's a travesty, really, that the forest service doesn't have the resources to deal with this any more quickly.

Then I leave, lock the door behind me, get in my truck, head back to my house. Hedwig's at the door, tail wagging, tongue lolling, and for the first time all day, I smile.

"Hey, girl," I tell her. "You want to go for a hike?"

She does.

· · * * * ★ ★ * * · ·

Fifty-five minutes later, there's a knock on my door.

"Yeah," I call. It opens, and Caleb steps in, backlit by the sun, wearing a frame pack.

He's followed by our father, and there's one second where I swear I can feel my heart stop.

Except of course it's not our father, it's Eli. Eli who's now the same age that Dad was in my earliest memories of him, Eli who came back from ten years of being away looking like the spitting image of Dad.

"Hi," Caleb says. "We're coming with you. Don't argue. It's happening."

"Yep," agrees Eli. "You're apparently going on an incredibly important bridge-fixing mission and we're going to help you, because we're both very skilled at hiking and camping and fixing bridges."

He's being slightly sarcastic, and I nearly smile.

"Is that dad's frame pack?" I ask, eyeing the ancient-looking hiking backpack he's got on.

"Yeah," he says. "It was the only thing we could find last-minute. Fits, though."

"It does," I agree. "You two ready?"

"Nope," says Eli. "I'm raiding your pantry first, then we go."

I sigh, my annoyance and irritation spiking.

"We're losing daylight."

"Stop it," Eli says, his pack already off, halfway into one of my cabinets. "Caleb, entertain him for ten minutes, will you?"

I glare at my youngest brother, who shrugs.

"You like card tricks?" he asks.

* * * * * ★ ★ ★ * * * *

FIFTEEN MINUTES LATER, we're finally piled into Caleb's hatchback. Eli gives me the front seat without even arguing about it and shares the back with Hedwig, which must mean he's worried about me, and we make the drive to the Jagger Ranch Trail mostly in silence.

I spread the map on the roof of Caleb's car, explain where we're going. I distribute the bridge repair supplies over the three packs, though I go a little easy on Eli since I think the last time he went backpacking might have been as a teenager. Hedwig has her own backpack. I think she likes having the responsibility.

I focus on this: the map, the supplies, the changing colors, asking Eli if he's got a warm enough sleeping bag. I glance at the sun, wonder if it's too low in the sky. I double-check that I've got my first aid kit, because Eli's going to have blisters.

And I don't think about anything else.

CHAPTER THIRTY-ONE

JUNE

When I get home, I shower. I avoid my parents. I hole up in my room and I try to apply for some jobs — in Washington State and Idaho and even British Columbia, Canada, because yes I am willing to work in another country, fuck yes I am — and I try to read and finally I just try to find some good pictures of meerkats for my next HypeFeed assignment, but nothing works.

I can't concentrate. My mind feels like it's a hall of mirrors, like every thought I have is refracted back at me again and again increasingly distorted forms, only in one of the mirrors is Levi saying *I thought I mattered* and I can't get out, I can only run into myself again and again.

I decide I'm going for a drive. I need to get away from here, and away from people, and I absolutely, definitely, certainly don't want to go for a hike or anything like it so a drive it is. I grab my stuff, shout some excuse to my parents who are doing something or other to the mostly-dead garden in the back yard, and get into my car.

Only for Silas's SUV to pull in behind me.

"Stop ruining my life!" I shout at the rearview mirror,

all my windows safely closed so he can't actually hear me. "ARRGH."

I hit the steering wheel. It feels good.

I'm just getting a hold of myself when there's a knock on my window, and I plaster a smile on, greet my brother.

"You're in my way," I tell him.

"No, you want to go a stupid way," he says. "Are you still… uh, is everything okay?"

I know I look like hell, and it's very clearly making Silas uncertain and more than a little uncomfortable.

"Everything's fine," I say, grinning like a maniac. "I'm super good, I was just going to go…"

I trail off. I can't even think of a lie.

"Go," I repeat, shrugging.

"You're going to go go," he says suspiciously.

"I meant what I said," I tell him with all the false bravado I can muster.

"Are you sure everything is okay?" he says, leaning down, resting his elbows on my car window frame. "You don't look okay."

And… cue the waterworks. Why is it that someone saying you don't look okay instantly makes you not okay?

"It's nothing," I say, grabbing at the stash of fast food napkins I keep in my driver's side door, like a normal person.

"Uh huh," Silas says, sounding completely unconvinced.

Then he sighs.

"C'mere," he says, and leans in through my driver's side window.

He somehow gets his whole torso into my car, wraps his arms around my head, and holds me awkwardly against his chest for several long moments.

"You wanna talk about it?" he asks.

I sniffle. It's a disgusting sound that does nothing to dissuade my brother.

"I dunno," I say.

"Talk about it or we're staying like this forever," he says, giving my head an extra and particularly uncomfortable squeeze.

I sigh. I swallow hard, and even though my neck is at an angle I don't love I lean a little into Silas.

"Fine," I say. "Get in, loser."

"Should you be driving?" he asks, unwinding himself.

"You think I've never driven while crying before?"

"I don't know your life," he says.

"Just go move your car," I tell him, and he does. A minute later I'm idling on the street outside my parents' house, and he gets in, a wad of napkins in his hand.

"I grabbed these out of my glove box in case you needed them," he says, and I nearly laugh. I nearly say *yeah, because you're a normal person who keeps fast food napkins in their car*, but I don't. I've already been enough of an asshole to Levi this week, I don't also need to out him to Silas.

"Thanks," I say, grab one, and blow my nose.

"Let me text Clara and tell her I'm not coming," he says.

Right. That's why he was here, to pick me up for Loveless Sunday Dinner, an event that I one hundred percent absolutely for sure cannot handle right now.

"You text Clara?" I ask.

"Yeah, I'm an insider," he deadpans. "I've got her email address, too. You impressed?"

"Shut up," I say, and start driving.

I leave my parents' neighborhood, then leave Sprucevale and drive north, away from Levi's house, and I just drive without thinking.

"So," Silas says as we pass cows, cows, horses, and more cows. "What happened?"

I clear my throat and grip the wheel a little harder.

"I was seeing someone, and it ended because I'm probably moving to South Dakota," I say. Technically, it's the truth.

"I didn't know you were seeing anyone," Silas says, and from the corner of my eye, I can see the shift in his body language.

"Don't," I tell him.

"What?"

"Just don't, okay? With the patriarchal bullshit? Not now."

He looks out the window for a moment, then sighs.

"Fine," he says. "Did this someone you were seeing have a name?"

I hesitate, because I obviously can't tell him the truth.

"Logan," I say, the first L-name that comes to mind.

I'm just gonna wing this and hope it works.

"We met on Tinder," I lie. "He lives in… Oakton, so you probably don't know him."

Oakton's an hour away to the east, and I can't think of any earthly reason that Silas would ever go there.

"I don't think I do," he says slowly, like he's thinking through the names of every man he's ever met. "How long had you been seeing him?"

Breathe in, breathe out.

"A month or so," I say. "But you know, it was pretty casual. Why get too serious when I was leaving?"

That last word has a slight hysterical edge to it, and I make myself breathe.

"Is that why you've been so weird?" he asks, giving me a puzzled look.

"Yes," I say quickly. Probably too quickly.

"I'm sorry, Bug," he says, and for once, my brother is utterly sincere.

"Thanks," I say, and I'm crying again.

Silas hands me a napkin, and I drive, and I cry, and Silas is just there.

"I think I really liked him," I finally admit. "God, Silas, what if I'm really fucking up by doing this? What if L... *Logan* is, I don't know, the love of my life and I'll never find anyone else? What if after this I just become a dusty plains spinster with a whole bunch of buffalo or something?"

"Well, that would be very South Dakota of you," he says.

I let out a sigh that's half-sob.

"But that's not going to happen, Bug," he says. "You're smart and interesting and talented and pretty, I guess, and the men in South Dakota will be lining up to date you, and wow I hate that sentence."

"I'm gonna host an orgy," I threaten between sniffles.

"I'm being *nice* to you right now."

"Orgies are nice?"

"And also, Logan sucks for breaking up with you and not even trying to work things out," he says.

He doesn't have to say, *Logan is probably a douchebag like the rest of your boyfriends*, because I know he's thinking it. If only he knew.

I feel a little bad for not quite telling Silas the whole truth, but the truth is just too much right now.

"I can't even blame him," I say, miserably. "He's right. I mean, even if I don't get this job, it's not like I'm sticking around here, you know? There are zero journalism jobs, all the ones that exist are in the butthole of nowhere so I can't stay, and Logan's not going to leave. His family's here, his job's here, he's got a house here. Here meaning Oakton, obviously."

"Obviously."

I shoot Silas a quick look, but his face betrays nothing.

"I just wish it weren't happening," I say. "There have been so many shitty dudes, Silas."

"Very true."

I ignore this.

"Why'd the good one have to be here?" I ask, rhetorically. "Why couldn't he live in Bluff City or something?"

"I wish I could tell you, Bug. I really do."

I sigh.

"You want me to beat him up for you?"

"For fuck's sake, Silas."

"I'm just offering," he teases.

I nearly tell him that I know about Jake Echols, but then I'd have to explain how I know about Jake Echols and that road leads back to Levi, so I drop it.

"Want to go get burgers?" he asks after a spell. "My treat."

I've mostly stopped crying. My eyes feel like sandpaper, and my nose is completely stuffed up, but I think I can make it through the next hour.

"Sure," I say.

"Next left," Silas instructs.

CHAPTER THIRTY-TWO

LEVI

All afternoon, I barely say a word. We hike uphill and downhill, we cross creeks and streams, we navigate a brief boulder scramble. The ground feels good beneath my boots, the cool air on my skin, the sharp smells of southern autumn. This time of year it looks like it's nearly sunset for hours, slanted golden light cutting through the trees, whispering that winter is coming on faster than we'd like.

Caleb and Eli chat with each other, but I don't really listen. Blessedly, they don't talk to me. They don't ask me what's wrong, or what's happened, or why I've suddenly decided that a footbridge ten miles inside the forest needs fixing right this very moment. They don't volunteer any opinions about life or love or, God forbid, women.

We just walk through the woods, and that's all.

That night, we set up camp in a wide flat spot under a stand of eastern pine. Their needles crinkle underfoot, and Caleb makes dinner — peanut butter sandwiches and ramen — while Eli and I set up the tents.

When we're done and we've got the sleeping bags inside, Eli looks down at the whole setup skeptically.

"Everything all right?" I ask, following his gaze.

"I'm not sure humans were meant to live this way, that's all," he says. "You know, in nylon pods that go inside other nylon pods?"

"Didn't God create nylon on the fourth day, according to Genesis?" I say, and that gets a smile out of Eli.

"I didn't really pay attention in Vacation Bible School," he admits. "I'll take your word for it."

"Caleb sucker you into this mission?" I ask, the closest I've come to admitting what's happening.

"Hey, I volunteered," Eli says as we head over to where Caleb's distributing ramen into mugs.

"It's true," Caleb says. "He was very brave."

"I've been hiking before," Eli says. "I went hiking *for fun* last weekend with Violet. And I built a deck onto our house, so I'm fully qualified to be here."

"There's centipedes," Caleb says.

"Shut up."

"Big ones," Caleb goes on, slurping ramen from a mug. "Three inches long, tons of legs."

"A hundred, I imagine," Eli says dryly.

"And they like to snuggle," Caleb says, and now he's grinning. "They find warm places and really just get up on in there—"

"No one likes centipedes!" Eli finally says. "You don't have to harass me in particular about centipedes, because no one likes those leggy little motherfuckers. I'm not alone in that."

"But you do have a particular aversion," Caleb points out.

"Caleb, don't torment your brother with nature," I tell him.

"I was *ten*," Eli says. "It was in my shoe."

"You still screamed."

I just sigh.

"See? Now you've upset Levi," Eli says, but he's laughing. "Nice job, buttface."

"You helped, fartmunch," Caleb replies, grinning.

We don't have any sort of serious discussion that night.

CHAPTER THIRTY-THREE

JUNE

"Is that everything?" Silas asks, looking at my suitcase.

I also look at it. It's a regular-sized suitcase, big enough that I have to check it.

"Yes?" I say, wondering what else he thinks I need to take with me.

"Coat?"

It's five o'clock Monday morning. I'm tired. I've had a hell of a twenty-four hours, so I just point at the coat that I'm obviously wearing.

"Suit?"

"Yes, I have my suit, I'm going for a job interview," I say. "I also have an alternate outfit and two pairs of shoes. Do you want to discuss whether I should wear pantyhose to the interview or not? Because Mom did so I'm all warmed up for my side of the discussion."

"I'm just checking," he says. "ID? Passport?"

"South Dakota isn't another country, it's just the Midwest," I say, dragging my suitcase toward his SUV.

"You should probably go and check it out before you make that declaration," he says, opening the back liftgate of his car, then grabbing my suitcase and tossing it in before I can even think about doing so.

"Ha ha," I say. "Ha."

"I assume you want to stop by the Mountain Grind before we leave?" he asks, giving me another once-over.

"Please," I say, and then I take a deep breath and remind myself that he's taking the morning off work to do me a huge favor. "Thanks for the ride."

"You're welcome, Bug," he says, and we drive off.

· · · ⋆ ⋆ ★ ★ ★ ⋆ ⋆ · · ·

ONCE I GET a giant coffee into me, I'm a little more human, and Silas and I manage to chat pleasantly on the way to the Roanoke airport.

We do not chat about *Logan*, which is fine with me. I'm already kicking myself for telling Silas everything that I did in my moments of weakness, because even though he can be a real idiot, Silas isn't dumb.

I don't tell him I called Levi — sorry, 'Logan,' — last night, and he didn't pick up. After I tried his house phone, I tried his cell phone, and then I even tried his work phone in a moment of desperation, but he didn't pick up.

I don't even know what I was going to say because I don't know what I *can* say. Nothing, probably, because the damage is done and no amount of 'sorry' can fix it.

I gave up, because I know when I'm being ignored.

And I cried. Then I cried some more. Then I considered canceling the job interview and just going to Levi's house and telling him I'd canceled in the hopes that he'd, I don't know, take me back and I could become the perfect country house-girlfriend who cans and jams and quilts and eventually has a slew of kids and never writes another word in her life.

But I didn't cancel. I know what I'd think of myself a year from now if I did, what I'd think of myself in five years. I'd think I gave up on my ambition, that I settled, that I traded in what I really wanted from life for a man.

"Does South Dakota have any good cuisine?" Silas asks as we drive down Interstate 81.

"Probably," I say.

"I mean, are there any regional specialties," he says. "Like we've got apple hand pies, or Wisconsin has cheese, or Kansas City has barbecue."

"Buffalo burgers?" I say, pulling out my phone. "I'm pretty sure South Dakota still has bison."

"They're endangered," he admonishes. "Don't eat endangered animals."

"They farm them," I say, pulling up a Wikipedia page.

"You can farm buffalo?"

"You can farm anything if you try hard enough."

"There's no way that's true," Silas says. "You can't farm whales."

"Has anyone tried hard enough?"

Silas frowns.

"There are animals who won't breed in captivity," he says.

"Is that why you're not married?" I ask, still looking at the Wikipedia page on South Dakota.

"June," Silas says, as if he's scandalized. "That was *sexist*."

"I'm full of surprises," I deadpan.

"Just don't tell that one in your interview," he says. "I don't know, or do. If you think they'll be into it. Read the room, I guess."

"Give me more advice, please," I say.

"Fart *before* you go into the interview room," he says instantly. "Don't hold it in, because then you'll end up gassing everyone in there, and they'll *know* it was you, and you will not get hired at that job. You will *not*."

I stare wordlessly at my older brother.

"According to a friend," he says.

"Any *other* advice?" I ask.

· · · ✦ ★ ✦ ★ ★ ★ ✦ · · ·

THE SUN'S barely up when Silas drops me off at the airport with a hug, a hair-ruffle, and one final admonishment not to hold in farts. The sky is getting lighter, but somehow, it feels worse than the dark.

I don't like sunrises. I know that sounds strange to say, since they're supposed to be symbolic of the hope of a new day or whatever, but to me, they've always just meant that the sun is coming up and I still haven't finished my homework. That I've stayed up all night and now the time to hit this deadline is well and truly running out.

I stand there, in the check-in area of the Roanoke airport, and look through the huge plate-glass windows at the sunrise, and I think of the windows in Levi's bedroom. I don't want to, but there it is.

Maybe this was never going to work out, I think, already feeling the tears welling in my eyes for the 345,577th time since yesterday. *He was always ready to see the sunrise and I always wanted it to stay dark for a few more hours and maybe that's some kind of metaphor for how we are and why we can't be together.*

I stand there. I stare at the sun, fully aware that you're not supposed to do that. I try to put together some explanation involving darkness people and daylight people, and I try to tell myself it was fated that we wouldn't work out, but I'm tired and I'm wrecked and I can't make any of it work, even in my own head.

All I can really think is that I'm here, staring at the

sunrise, and he's somewhere watching the exact same sunrise and we are so, so far apart.

* * * * * ★ ★ ★ * * * * *

Getting from Sprucevale to Bluff City is a lesson in how far apart small towns truly are, even in modern America. I know I should think it's amazing that I can get there in less than twenty-four hours, but mostly, I just think it's exhausting.

First, the two-hour drive from Sprucevale to the Roanoke-Blackburg Regional Airport. Then, two hours of waiting for a quick flight to the Charlotte Airport.

I call Levi again from Charlotte, sitting in an uncomfortable chair and staring out the window at planes and trucks going back and forth across the tarmac. There's no answer, so I hang up without leaving a voicemail because I still don't know what I would say.

Hi, I'm still sorry but I'm also calling you from a different state because you were right that I was always going to leave, I was just ignoring that problem?

Hi, I'm sorry and it doesn't matter because I'm gone anyway?

Then there's a plane from Charlotte to Dallas, a panicked sprint through the terminal that only leads to even more waiting, another flight, and then at last — at last — a bumpy ride on a small plane to Salt Plains, South Dakota and a forty-five minute taxi ride to the Bluff City Motel 6.

I fall asleep hard and don't dream.

CHAPTER THIRTY-FOUR

LEVI

My near-silence ends up lasting almost twenty-four hours. It lasts until Monday afternoon, when we've hiked from our campsite down to the footbridge that needs mending.

The repairs are simple and quick, especially with the three of us, and once we're finished, Eli busts out a bag of candy corn and we sit on a flat gray boulder, sharing them.

"What are these made of?" Caleb asks, tossing a handful into his mouth.

"Heroin and MSG," I suggest, slowly eating another, savoring the texture as I smash it between my teeth.

"They *are* addictive," Caleb mutters. "But they're also kind of gross? But good."

"Sugar and wax," says Eli.

"Really?" asks Caleb.

"Yup," Eli confirms. "There's also dye and gelatin, but it's mostly sugar and wax."

I'm lying on my back, and I hold up one kernel in front of my face, inspecting it.

"That can't be healthy," I say. "Wax?"

"Levi, I have bad news," Eli deadpans. "Candy corn is not, in fact, a health food."

I eat it.

"The sugar is probably worse than the wax," Caleb muses.

"Neither one is good," says Eli.

I pop another one into my mouth, staring up at the leaves above us.

Finally, I'm starting to feel like something deep inside me is unwinding, like a small door is opening. I thought I wanted to be alone but now that they're here, I'm intensely glad that my brothers came along at the last second.

It's good to have them along. It's good to have people who are willing to hike ten miles and fix a bridge and sleep outdoors without ever once asking *why* they're doing this.

"June is moving to South Dakota," I say, still staring up at the sky, the half-bare branches moving across the blue-white expanse. "Probably."

"Oh, shit," Eli says.

"Probably?" Caleb says.

I eat another candy corn and really pay attention to it: the sickly-sweet taste, the way the outside crunches under my teeth, the slight grit against my tongue.

"She has a job interview there in a few days," I say, and my voice sounds detached from me, like I've rehearsed this, though I haven't. "She's already had a couple interviews with this paper, so the in-person thing is probably just a formality. It's a good job. An editor position. If she does well for a couple of years she could move on to a major paper."

I sound reasonable, rational, like I'm not cracking apart.

I eat another candy corn. I watch the sky.

"And you?" Eli finally asks.

"Me? I'm right here," I say. "Just right the fuck here."

"Are you all right?" Caleb asks, even though the three of us all know the answer to that question already.

I'm quiet for a long, long time, because I can't quite get a handle on words. Or, rather, I can't get a handle on the right ones; now that I've broken the silence my head is full of nothing but words, clanging together, charging into one another, blaring and shouting and vying for my attention.

"She didn't tell me," I finally say. "I found out from Silas. She didn't even tell me."

Slowly, piece by piece, I tell them everything: the phone interview, the week in-between, Silas telling me, me confronting her.

In words, it's short. It doesn't sound like much, the sentences themselves nothing like heartbreak: she's moving away and still hadn't told me. She has a great opportunity and said nothing to me, and I don't even know why.

"You could ask her to stay, you know," Eli says.

"She lied," I say, grabbing a whole handful of candy corn. "For a week. She lied."

"Well, she just didn't tell you something," he points out.

"That's still fucked up," Caleb offers.

"People fuck up," Eli shrugs.

"I can't ask her to stay," I go on. "I can't ask her to give up on her dreams to stick around nowheresville, Virginia, and just sit back and think about what she could have done with her life."

"It's not *that* bad," Eli mutters.

"She thinks nothing of me," I say, leaning my head back, closing my eyes, letting the brightness of the sky settle against my eyelids. "She didn't even hold me in high enough regard to tell me she was leaving."

"Are you sure?" Caleb asks.

"Quite," I say.

"I mean, are you sure that's why she didn't tell you?" he asks.

"Yes," I say.

Caleb reaches out, takes the last candy corn, eats it, stands and crumples the bag.

"We should get back to the campsite," he says. "I hate cooking in the dark out here."

"I could use a jacket," Eli says.

"Make sure you shake it for centipedes," Caleb says, and Eli cuffs him on the head.

"Quit it," I tell them, yet again.

· · · · ★ ★ ★ ★ · · · ·

AFTER DINNER we sit around and Eli and I pass the whiskey flask back and forth. Caleb declines. He doesn't drink much. I'm not sure I've ever seen him drink hard alcohol.

"Long-distance relationships exist," Eli says suddenly, unscrewing the cap.

"She didn't care enough to tell me," I point out again while he takes a bolt, hands it to me. I do the same. "I always knew she was going to leave, you know? But she didn't even tell me. I thought we told each other things."

"I'm not sure people are always straightforward," Caleb says from where he's half-lying against a fallen pine tree, his hands behind his head. "You can't always say that because X, Y must be true. Humans are irrational actors. They don't make sense."

I hand the flask back to Eli.

"Listen to him, he's a woman expert," Eli says, taking another drink.

Caleb flips him off from where he's lying.

"Did you know that Mandy Hargrove and Danica Nelson got into a fight over him once?" I ask Eli.

"Oh, God," mutters Caleb.

Eli uses his flask hand to point at our youngest brother.

"Him?" he asks.

"I heard about it from someone who was there," I say, because June's name has been in my mouth all day today and I don't want to say it again right now. "Danica interrupted a tutoring session, so Mandy slapped her."

Caleb just sighs.

"What kind of tutoring was this?" Eli asks. "And how am I just hearing about it?"

"We'd graduated already," I say.

"I'm a very good teacher," Caleb deadpans.

"Sure," says Eli. "Your cosine brings all the girls to the yard."

Caleb just *looks* at him.

"I don't remember high school math very well," Eli admits.

"I don't think June didn't tell you about the interview because she has no regard for you," Caleb says, getting back to the matter at hand.

"I agree that she regards you well," Eli says.

I say nothing, just let the whiskey whir through my brain, pleasant and warm.

"It's hard to tell people things that you know won't make them happy," he goes on. "And should she have pulled up her britches and been an adult about it? Yeah. But I don't think the fact that she didn't is because she thinks nothing of you."

"She definitely doesn't think nothing of you," Caleb offers.

"You've never even seen us together," I point out. "You didn't know about us until a few days ago. The two of you have no basis for any of these statements."

"She's been at Mom's every Sunday afternoon for like

three months," Caleb says. "I see you guys together all the time, Levi, why do you think everyone instantly guessed who you were sleeping with?"

"Yeah, you get all bubbly around her," Eli says, taking another drink of the whiskey, handing it back to me.

"I do not bubble," I tell them, drinking.

"You kinda bubble," says Caleb. "And she finds a lot of ways to hang out near you."

"It's totally cute," says Eli. "And like I was saying, long distance relationships exist."

"They don't work," I say. "Not indefinitely."

There's a long, long silence. I look up at the stars, mostly blocked by the pines above us, the moonlight dimly filtering through the forest.

For the first time since Saturday, I explore the possibility that they're presenting: that June's not unkind, she just did an unkind thing.

It's much easier to live with.

Finally, Caleb breaks the silence again.

"You could move to South Dakota," he says.

"Everything is here," I say. "My life is here, my job is here, my house is here. My family's here."

"True," Caleb allows.

"Not June," says Eli, as if I didn't know.

"Everything else," I say.

"It seems pretty simple," Caleb says. "Just imagine a scale, and on one side, put everything that's here. And on the other side, put June, and see which one weighs more."

I try very hard to imagine this scale, and I try very hard to stack the things on it that Caleb's suggesting.

It doesn't really work.

"Is weighing more good?" I ask.

"Okay, fuck the scale," Eli says. "Don't listen to his imagination exercises. It's just this: if you'd rather be with

June than be here, move to South Dakota. I mean, is she great enough to sell your sweet house and get a new job?"

"I doubt she's great enough to make up for your brothers," Caleb says. "You've got *great* brothers."

"I don't know," I say, and close my eyes so it feels like I'm up above, floating in the stars, weightless in the sky.

"You definitely have great brothers," Eli says.

"Not about that part."

I lie there, head back on a log, thinking. I think in circles until my brain feels like it's swirling, the stars rotating above, and then Caleb's in front of me, shaking my shoulder.

"C'mon," he says. "You two old men can't sleep like this, you'll complain the whole way back."

I don't argue with him. I just get into my sleeping bag, in the tent I'm sharing with Eli, and I let the forest sing me to sleep.

CHAPTER THIRTY-FIVE

LEVI

E li slings his pack off of his back, positions himself in front of a pine tree, and rubs himself on it.

Caleb and I look up from the map we were studying and just watch him for a long moment, but he just keeps scratching. And scratching.

"You all right?" Caleb finally asks.

"My back itches," Eli explains.

"A lot, apparently," I say, and Eli just sighs.

"I've slept on the ground for two nights in a row and I have yet to complain about it," he points out. "Let me scratch my back how I see fit."

"Fair," Caleb says, and I shrug.

We look back at the map. It's the same edition as the one that June and I made from the logging records, the one that we consulted when we were figuring out where trees were likely to get murdered. Just looking at it, knowing that, makes me feel heavy, splintered.

I miss her more today than I did last night and last night more than I did yesterday. I miss hiking with her. I miss talking to her under the stars. I miss the excited look she got in her eye when she had an idea, the way she dove into a project she loved.

"It's about half a mile," I say, pointing at a dotted line on the map. "It's just off the trail, no big deal."

"Fine with me," Caleb says. "Eli, you gonna live?"

"I'm doing spectacularly, thank you," Eli says, still scratching his back. "Let's go see if these trees are happy or not."

"Thanks," I say.

We're checking on a stand of hemlock that had an infestation problem about a year ago that I treated. I need to see how they're getting on, of course, but that's not really the reason I'm dragging my brothers along to look at trees.

I'm making them ascertain the happiness of trees because I still haven't decided.

Some people are heart people. They dive into whatever they're doing. They fall hard, they fall fast, they're never unsure because their hearts are true and pure, or something.

Eli, for example, is a heart person, as much as he'd probably deny it. I doubt he ever thought twice about being with Violet, no matter what.

Caleb? Head. Daniel? Head, though he'd deny it.

Seth is… if there's something that falls harder and faster and deeper than heart, he's that.

I'm a head person, unsurprisingly. I envy the heart. I envy knowing exactly what to do, having that internal tug that pulls you in the rightest, truest direction no matter what.

I wonder what it's like, to simply *know*, to not weigh pros and cons, to simply do and not think.

We find the hemlocks. They're happy and still pest-free. We head back to the main trail, then make our way back to the trailhead.

By the time we get to Caleb's car and unload our packs and ourselves into it, I'm two-thirds sure.

By the time he drops Hedwig and me off at my house, I'm three-fourths sure.

I shower. I unpack. I brush Hedwig, get last specks of dirt and tree out of her fur. I make myself a simple dinner, and watch Netflix on my laptop while I eat it.

The show ends. I shut the computer, look around my house. I consider the fireplace, Jedediah the bear skin rug, the staircase, the drywall that Silas helped hang, the flooring that Caleb helped lay down. I think about everything that's gone into my life here: my house, my job, my family, my wilderness.

I don't know that I'm sure. I don't know how people can ever be sure, how you can properly weigh two unlike things on a scale and figure out which one is better.

But I do, finally, understand that thinking has reached its limit. I understand that I could make lists of pros and cons forever and I wouldn't get to the bottom of this, I'd only get more enmeshed in a web of my own making.

So I stop thinking, and I open the laptop again.

Thirty minutes later, I shut it, go upstairs, pack a few things.

Then I call Caleb and ask if he can dog sit for a few days.

CHAPTER THIRTY-SIX

JUNE

I stand outside the low-slung brick building at one end of Main Street and think: *I should have listened to my mother.*

Behind me, my ride drives away, and I adjust my briefcase over my shoulder, clutching it a little tighter to my thigh as though the leather's going to give me much warmth. I pretty much only take the briefcase to job interviews — I got it from an aunt and uncle when I graduated college, and it's way too nice to actually use.

Anyway, I wish I were wearing pantyhose. That's a wish I don't think I've ever had before — if anything, I've wished the opposite during fancy dress events and piano recitals where my mother *insisted* that I wear pantyhose — but it's very windy and *very* cold and my coat isn't helping my bare legs.

But I still take a minute, because I need one. Between my bad weekend and yesterday's long day of flying across half the country just to get here, I feel discombobulated, all odds and ends, like I've been whisked out of the timeline and plopped back in just slightly too late.

The sky is gray. Bluff City is all wide streets, pickup

trucks, low buildings, straight roads, and it's flat, the flattest place I think I've ever been.

I take a deep, cold breath, and I go inside.

And almost right away, I relax because this is familiar. Right away, I realize that I know where I am and I know what I'm doing, because there's a small reception area, a big fake-wood desk with The Bluff City Herald-Trumpet's logo on the wall over it, a ficus tree in each corner. There's the ugly and out-of-style glass coffee table with several editions of today's paper on it, along with a copy of *People* magazine and two copies of something called *Central South Dakota!*, the cover of which has two young, attractive white people drinking red wine in front of a sunset and laughing about something, probably what a great time they're having in central South Dakota.

The only thing missing is a human at the desk. I consider walking on through, heading into the newsrooms and just seeing if I can find the people I'm supposed to be interviewing with, but that seems rude and also, I'm five minutes early, so there's no need.

I sit. I wait. I pick up *Central South Dakota!* since I already read this morning's edition of the Herald-Trumpet at Mabel's Diner. It's mostly advertising disguised as journalism for South Dakota's wine industry, which apparently exists.

Three minutes later, two women come out of the newsroom and walk slowly toward the receptionist's desk, heads together in a way that suggests *gossip* rather than *business discussion*.

"I know and I can't believe it," one woman is saying. They're both middle-aged with shoulder-length hair, one blonde, one brown. Neither woman's hair moves on its own. "She's going to get run up the flagpole for that disrespectful mouth one of these days."

Neither of them glances over at me, but I stand, gather my coat and my briefcase.

One woman — the blonde — holds up a finger in my direction, the universal *hold on a minute* gesture, without looking at me.

"Well, ever since she came back from school in Chicago she's been too big for her britches," the other woman says. "The other day she got upset with me for not taking her phone messages! I wanted to say, missy, I have been here for twenty-three years and if you think I'm going to start taking messages for you just because you went to college, you have got another think coming."

"Did she try to tell you it was your job?" the first woman asks, still holding up one finger.

I'm getting tired of this, so I walk in their direction.

"Yes!" hisses the second woman. "I told her that just because I took messages for her predecessor didn't mean I was going to do it for her, and just because Pierce was a lovely man didn't mean I thought the same of her."

"Hi, I'm here for a job interview," I say.

The woman holding out her finger turns and gives me an up-and-down look. I don't like it, but I say nothing for obvious reasons.

"Just a minute, sweetheart," she says, then turns to the first woman. "You've got to stand your ground on this," she says to the second woman. "Next thing you know you'll be picking up dry cleaning too and we don't get paid enough for *that*."

"I know it," the second woman says, then disappears back into the newsroom.

The blonde still doesn't look at me. She walks behind the desk, sits in the chair, wakes up the computer, types something.

"The interview is with Edmund Sanderson and Adrianne—"

"Yes, I know," she interrupts me.

Then she goes silent. She's still not looking at me, just clicking away at the computer. She could be playing solitaire for all I know.

I'm at a loss, so for a long moment I just stand there, staring at her, thinking about the summer during college when I worked part-time as a receptionist at an accounting firm, and how very, very fired I'd have been if I did my job this way.

Finally, she sighs.

"All right, you can go on back," she says.

I force a smile.

"I've never been here before, actually," I say, just as friendly as you please. "Could you tell me how to find—"

"Through that door and you can't miss it," she says.

"Thank you!" I say, even though we've still not made eye contact, because I'm pretty sure I won't be getting more out of her.

Before I push the door open, I close my eyes for a moment, try to shake her off. She's clearly having some kind of day, and I can't let one rude person throw me off my game.

Besides, I'm about to be in a newsroom again for the first time in months. This is where the magic happens: the relay of information, the fight to find the truth, the tireless efforts to keep the public informed, everything that the fourth estate is and why it matters.

I push the door open.

Someone is *screaming*.

That's not exactly true. He's shouting very loudly, but I'm surprised and shocked enough that I stop for a moment, nearly tripping over my own tasteful black pumps, my briefcase swinging hard into my leg.

"What the hell do you call this?" a gray-haired, sweater-vested white man with gray hair is shouting, holding up a few printed pages in one hand. "It's a city council race, for God's sake, cover it like it. You think you're Langston Hughes? You think you're Maya fucking Angelou?"

The whole office is open-plan — no cubicle walls, just low dividers that don't even come as high as the computer monitors. Beyond the shouting man, someone's playing Minesweeper, not even looking back at the commotion.

"You're not," the man says, flinging the papers on the floor very dramatically. "You're here and you'll cover this goddamn race like we tell you to cover it or you will be out of a job, am I understood?"

Sitting in a chair in front of him is a young man who can't be older than me, the first black person I've seen since coming to South Dakota. I don't hear his response, but apparently, it's good enough to get the other man out of his space because Sweater Vest walks away, muttering.

"Are you here for the interview?" a woman's voice asks, and I'm jolted out of my eavesdropping, though to be fair I literally couldn't help it.

"Yes," I say, standing up straight and trying to recover. "It's supposed to be with Edmund Sanderson and Adrianne Pickett?"

"Right," the woman says, and half-smiles. She's middle aged, her black hair streaked with white and in a no-nonsense bun, and she gives me a feeling, knowledgeable look. "Adrianne's office is right there. She's probably expecting you. Good luck."

"Thanks," I say, and follow where she's pointing: an open door to an office. It's got windows. It's relatively bright and cheery, and when I knock on the open door, the woman behind the desk stands and gives me a wide, heartfelt smile.

"You must be June. I'm so glad you could make it," she says, extending a hand. "I'm Adrianne, the Managing Editor. Edmund will be here in a few minutes. Please have a seat. Can I get you water, coffee, anything?"

"I'm fine, thanks," I say, incredibly relieved to have finally found a normal person.

"How was your trip?" she asks, sitting again.

I give her the polite highlights of a boring day. I compliment Bluff City. I mention that it's my first time in South Dakota, and she tells me that if I get a chance, I should visit Badlands National Park even though it's a little chilly this time of year.

It's nice, *normal* small talk, until finally she looks up as someone else comes through the door.

"Ah, Edmund," she says, still perfectly cordial. "This is June, our interviewee for Metro Editor."

The man in the sweater vest stands there. He gives me a thorough up-and-down look, and only once he's done looking does he extend his hand.

"Good to meet you," he says to me, then turns to Adrianne. "Why aren't we in my office?" he demands. "We should be in my office. Why the hell are we in here? What must she think?"

He gestures at me.

"I think my office is fine," Adrianne says, and sits behind the desk. "Now, June, I was going over your clips and I couldn't help but be impressed by…"

· · · · · ★ ★ ★ · · · ·

"Sure," Edmund says to Adrianne, slouching in the chair next to mine, arms folded over his chest. "Yeah, she seems fine."

Adrianne has her hands laced together on her desk, and she smiles at me apologetically.

"June," she says. "I'm so sorry, could you give us a moment?"

"Of course," I say, getting to my feet and gathering my bag. "No problem. Thank you. It was nice meeting you both."

They both watch me — Adrianne smiling, Edmund not — as I close the door to the office, then stand there, once more not exactly sure what's going on.

A few people glance over. The woman with the bun nods at me once. The black guy who was being shouted at has earbuds in and is steadily typing away. Whoever's playing minesweeper in the back corner has switched to an episode of *The Office*, right there, in the middle of the newsroom.

Maybe they're on lunch break, I think.

That was the weirdest job interview I've ever had, and I've been to plenty of job interviews. I've been to interviews where the people doing the hiring tried to test me. I've been to interviews where at least one person clearly wasn't paying the proceedings any attention. I once had a job interview where one of the interviewers insulted my shoes the moment I walked in, and then after they offered me the job, told me that he "just wanted to see how I handled it."

I kind of miss that guy right now, because there was something going on just now in that office and I still don't know what. Adrianne, the managing editor, was perfectly nice, professional, and lovely.

Edmund, the Editor-in-Chief, interrupted her every thirty seconds to disagree with something she said, or to tell her that he didn't think my clips were all that impressive, or to ask something utterly unrelated to the interview at all.

At one point, he just told Adrianne, "She'll have a lot of catching up to do, sophistication-wise."

None of it was directed toward me, though he kept glancing over at me, chewing on the end of his pen.

I'm starting to wonder if I should go to the bathroom, just so I'm not standing here awkwardly any longer, when the office door opens again, and Adrianne is standing there, still smiling like a normal person.

"Thanks for waiting," she says. "Come on back in."

I come in. I sit.

"Job is yours," Edmund says before Adrianne is even seated. "Forty-one a year, full benefits after three months, even get a parking spot with your name on it."

"We'd like to officially offer you the position," Adrianne says, ignoring Edmund. "We think you'd be a great fit for the Metro Editor position here, and we'd be delighted to have you on board."

"If you say yes now and start tomorrow," Edmund says.

Adrianne frowns and opens her mouth, but he holds up one hand.

"Thanks," he tells her dismissively, then finally looks at me. "You say yes now and you start tomorrow or we're done here," he says.

"Edmund," Adrianne says. "Give her—"

"Not really interested," he says. "What do you say, June?"

I'm well aware of what a red flag looks like. I'm aware of what a thousand red flags look like, for that matter.

But I've applied for well over a hundred jobs, and I'm tired. I'm tired of disappointment and I'm tired of feeling like I've got nothing to offer, and to be honest, I'm tired of applying to jobs. I want to be in a newsroom again, writing something that matters.

Two years, I tell myself. *Two years and move onto the Tribune, the Times, the Post...*

I don't let myself think of Levi, not even for a second.

"I'll need to go home next week to pack my things," I say. "And I'd like for the paper to subsidize some of the cost of staying in a motel until I've found a place to live, since I'm having to come here on such short notice."

"We can work something out," Adrianne says, but Edmund's already standing.

"Make it happen," he tells her, and without another word, he's through the door.

I look at Adrianne, feeling left in the dust.

"We'll figure out the timing," she says, smiling. "Welcome to the Herald-Trumpet."

CHAPTER THIRTY-SEVEN

JUNE

"Yeah, they went ahead and introduced me around the office," I say to the window in my motel room. "The people seem really great, you know, *midwestern nice* is a thing."

"It's amazing that they wanted you to start so soon," my dad says.

"You must have really impressed them," my mom adds.

They're on different lines in their house, something which has already caused some confusion during this call. Between the two of them, not with me.

"I hope so," I say, still gazing out at the Motel 6 parking lot.

"I know you did," my mom says.

We keep talking, and I pace the room as we do. I'm already out of my suit and into my jeans, walking back and forth in front of two double beds, sticking my head into the bathroom, turning on the light, turning it back off, walking the same path back to the window.

I'm antsy. I'm restless. I'm anything but sure that this

job is a good idea, not least because of the knot that took up residence in my stomach the moment I said *yes*.

But it sure seems like the only idea. I haven't got a better one, and what's the worst that could happen? I get fired and have to live with my parents?

Finally, after another fifteen minutes of this, my parents say more nice things about me and then get off the phone. I sigh, flop onto one scratchy comforter, then immediately get off and yank it from the bed, because I've seen those shows where they blacklight motel rooms.

Then I flop again, turn on the TV, grab my phone, and try to figure out how to get Chinese food delivered because I really think I deserve General Tso's chicken right now.

I'm still trying to figure it out and starting to realize that Bluff City might not have a single Chinese restaurant, when my phone sings again. Silas.

"June Flynn, employed person," I answer.

"Congrats, I just heard from Mom and Dad," he says. "You excited?"

"Yeah," I say. "The job is a big step up from where I was before, and it pays way better than I was expecting and the whole paper seems great. Like, really great."

He pauses for a moment. It's probably just the phone.

"Really great?" he asks.

"Yup," I confirm, lying back and flipping through muted channels. "My boss seems like he's a really, you know, interesting guy, and I met some of coworkers today and they're all... cool. I start tomorrow!"

There's another pause and it's definitely not the phone.

"Is something up?" he finally asks.

"What? No," I say. "What would be up?"

"I don't know, you just sound weird," he says.

"I'm great."

"You keep using that word," he says. "Are you sure everything's cool?"

I stop flipping and, for a moment, just stare at an infomercial for a stretchy garden hose.

"Yeah," I say, but my voice betrays me and I do *not* sound like everything is cool.

"You just had this rough breakup," he says. "Of this secret relationship with *Logan* that no one knew you were in, and now you're sounding weird and starting a brand-new job tomorrow and you can't tell me that something isn't up, June."

I pause. And pause. Finally, I take a deep breath.

"The job seems like it might have some challenges," I tell him. "I'm not sure that all my coworkers get along, and my boss seems like he might be a little intense, but I can handle it."

"I see," he says.

The pause this time is very long, and I note some impressive qualities of the stretchy garden hose.

"June, you're better than a job that sucks," Silas finally says, his voice quiet, sincere. "I know that you've had a really hard couple of months, and I know you were really down after losing your last job and that assface dumped you, but you're better than a shitty job."

I close my eyes, take a deep breath, and fight tears yet again.

"I don't have other options," I remind him. "I've applied for a hundred and five jobs, Silas, this is the one that's available."

"It's not your fault that newspapers are dying, that's because of... uh, the internet, I think," he says. "If you want to come home and spend a while just figuring out what it is you want to do, that's okay. No one thinks less of you. No one here is pinning your worth on whether you're employed or not, and you shouldn't be either."

I swallow an enormous lump in my throat.

"Who is this?" I demand.

"Huh?"

"You're being nice, and my brother Silas once held me down and farted *into my mouth*, so you're obviously an imposter," I say.

"I never did that."

"Yes, you did."

He's laughing, because he knows he did it.

"You must have me confused with another brother," he says.

"I'm pretty positive I've only got the one."

"Then I guess you're just confused," he says, then clears his throat. "Bug, if you're happy, I'm happy, and if this is really your dream then Godspeed. But you wouldn't be worthless if you turned down a bad situation."

I pull myself to sitting on the bed, and an attractive woman on TV makes an astonished face at the stretchiness of this garden hose.

"Thanks, Silas," I say. "I'll be fine."

We talk a little longer, then hang up. I watch a reality TV show about people who live in Florida, drink too much vodka, and are obsessed with whether or not other people are 'respecting' them.

I never do find a Chinese restaurant, so I end up at the diner next door again.

CHAPTER THIRTY-EIGHT

LEVI

Four forty-five in the morning may as well be midnight. It's still dark, still deadly quiet. In mid-October, in the mountains, the mist winds through the air like it's a living being. Even in town it floats, sits, thinks, parts in front of you as you walk through it like it's allowing you to pass.

It allows me to pass. It's cold. It's dark. The moon is gone, and there's not a single sound as I cross the street and climb the steps to Silas's townhouse and knock on the door before I can let thinking get in my way.

Then I step back and wait. I know full well that I'm waking him up and that finally coming clean at this hour makes me an asshole, but I'm also confident that in about three minutes the time won't be the thing he's angry about.

I shift my feet, rub my hands together. My breath fogs in front of me, and I quietly hope that Silas is simply slow getting out of bed, that I haven't triggered something. I know what a loud knock can sound like.

Finally, I hear footsteps inside, rushing down the stairs. I stand up straight. I steel myself.

The door opens.

"Levi? What happened?" Silas says, wearing nothing but flannel pajama pants and a robe, his hair wild and his eyes wide.

"Nothing's happened," I say. "I have a confession."

Silas stares at me, a long, hard, penetrating stare, like he's trying to decide whether I'm real or not, so I go on.

"Silas, I've been——"

He punches me right in the face. I stumble backward, the railing on his steps catching me as I cup both hands to my nose, gasping in pain.

"Jesus!" I shout, the word garbled, warmth already dripping over my lips. "What the *fuck*?"

"You know what the fuck," he says, stepping out onto his steps after me, clenching and unclenching his hand. "What the fuck is for making June——"

I punch him back. It's not a very good punch, but it glances off his mouth and he stumbles backward, toward his doorframe.

"Fuck!" he shouts, hand over his mouth, blood already dripping down. I must have cut his lip on teeth. "You don't get to hit me, you're the bastard who's been fucking my sister."

"You hit me first, you asshole," I say, one hand still over my face, ready to duck another punch at a moment's notice. "You don't even know what I was going to say!"

Silas stands up straighter for a moment and something ugly and dangerous flashes in his eyes. I'm backed up against the railing of his front steps, and though I'm still not afraid of him, there's a moment where I wonder if I should be.

"Silas," I start.

"Why does everyone think I'm some sort of idiot?" he asks, bringing his hand away from his mouth. "Did you seriously think I'd never know? Did you think that *my best friend* could bang *my sister* and I'd never cotton on?"

He turns, slams the palm of his hand into the door-frame, leaving a small but dark smear of blood.

A light goes on in the townhouse next door. We both see it, and Silas gives it and then me a long, wary look. I just squeeze my eyes shut against the pain searing through my face and hope that my nose isn't broken.

I really don't want to fly with a broken nose.

"I didn't think that," I say.

"You made her cry," he says, swiping at his mouth with the back of his hand.

I take a deep breath, carefully prod at my nose.

"I know," I say. "I'm sorry."

The porch light goes on next door.

"Shit," Silas mutters. "Think you can come inside without punching me again?"

"As long as you can," I say.

"I'm standing outside at five in the morning and bleeding onto my fucking robe. Come inside, you jackass," he says, turns, and swoops into his townhouse. The bathrobe swirls dramatically.

I follow. If he's luring me into his house so he can beat the shit out of me, so be it. I know how any real fight between us would go; he spent years in the Marines and the last time I got into a scuffle I was fourteen and it was against my younger brother.

"The fuck is wrong with eight in the morning?" he demands, stalking into his kitchen. "Paper towels are on the counter, don't bleed on my floor."

I grab a paper towel, press it under my nose, then grab another one and hold it out to him. He takes it, presses it to his lip, looks at it, puts it back.

"I'm flying out of Roanoke at nine," I say as he yanks

the freezer open.

He just turns and looks at me. He looks at me for a long, long time, like he's never seen me before and is taking my measure.

"Don't you dare fuck with her," he finally says, his voice low, flat. "I swear to God, Levi, if you toy with June, if you go beg for her back and then dump her again and then show up underneath her window with a ring and a proposal or some bullshit like that, I will kill you."

I tilt my head back, against his cabinets, eyes shut.

"Silas," I finally say. "When the hell have I ever toyed with anyone?"

"This better not be a first," he says, and I hear him rummaging through his freezer. After a moment, I open my eyes again.

"It's not," I tell him, simply.

"Here," he says, shoving a bag of frozen hash browns at my chest.

"Thanks," I say, and hold it to my face, closing my eyes again.

It helps.

"I'm looking at apartments," I tell him. "I have two tours set up for tomorrow and one for Friday morning."

This announcement is met with silence, and after several seconds, I move the hash browns and open my eyes.

"In Bluff City?" he says, leaning against the counter opposite me, the words blurred by the frozen peas held to his mouth.

"Yes," I say.

"After you dumped her because she was leaving?" he says. "I mean, because *Logan* dumped her because she was leaving?"

"I assume I'm Logan?"

"It's not a very good pseudonym."

"It's slightly more complicated than that," I say.

"I'm listening," he says.

I try to give Silas the brief rundown: June didn't tell me, my feelings got hurt, her feelings got hurt, staying together seemed impossible until my brothers talked sense into me.

But he asks questions, and I end up telling him the whole story from the beginning, or at least the highlights. I skip some parts.

When I finish, he's quiet a long moment.

"I knew it," he finally says, and tosses the peas onto the counter next to him. "You remember that time at the Mountain Grind when you two were talking about a wireless router?"

"She was annoyed that my house didn't have Wi-Fi," I explain.

"I've never seen you look at anyone like that," he says. "I should have known then. God, it was obvious."

"Probably," I agree. "Everyone knows wireless routers are definitely a couples thing."

He's silent another moment.

Then: "What have you told her?"

I take the hash browns off my face before I get frostbite. "About you?"

"Yeah."

"Nothing."

"She can't know," Silas says, crossing his arms over himself, his robe still open and slightly bloodstained, his voice low and urgent. "Not about the dreams, not about the episodes, not about what we had to do or what we saw or — or any of that, Levi, I swear. She can't."

"I haven't told her anything," I say softly.

"She's my baby sister," he says, and now there's a desperate edge to his voice.

"I have no intention of discussing your business with

June," I say. "That's yours. It's got nothing to do with me. Nor, for the record, do I have any intention of discussing June's business with you."

Silas frowns.

"What *business* does June have?" he asks.

I just raise one eyebrow and say nothing. He narrows his eyes.

"Point taken," he finally mutters.

We're both silent for a long time, standing in his dark kitchen, nursing the wounds we gave each other.

"You could tell her," I say. "I know you don't think you could, but you could. It might help."

"I don't know," he says.

"She's not a kid."

Silas just gives me a dangerous look.

"You know what I mean," I tell him.

"I do," he says, and then, "She took the job."

I just nod. I knew June would take the job. Everything I know about June told me she'd take the job.

"Good," I say, and toss the hash browns on the counter. "It sounds like a good job. I know she wanted it."

Silas pokes at his lip, then gives me a funny look.

"Yeah, she did," he says, half to himself.

"I gotta go."

"I haven't given you permission yet," Silas says.

"Don't need your permission to leave," I point out.

"To date my sister," he says. "Levi, you do *not* have my permission to date June."

"I didn't come here to get your permission," I tell him. "I came here because I thought you should finally know."

With that, I walk out of his kitchen and for his front door uncertain how I've left things between us. My nose hurts, and I cut my hand on his teeth when I punched him back, but I can't say I think that makes things bad.

"That was a test," he calls after me. "You passed."

"Of course I did," I call back, and I leave Silas's house and walk back into the dark gray of early morning.

· · ✦ ★ ★ ★ ★ ✦ · · ·

AIRPORT SECURITY DOESN'T LOVE it when you've got an obviously-recent black eye and a swollen nose, but I manage to smile and tell the security officer that I've got a new puppy who just got a little too excited when I told her goodbye this morning, and after being wanded and patted down, they let me through.

I sit in the Roanoke airport and stare out the window. I wonder if June stared out this window, two days ago. I wonder whether she'll even take me back after what I said to her. Deep down, I wonder if it's possible that I've been reading this whole thing wrong all along, that I've been falling in love while she was just having a good time.

I wonder if I'm flying to South Dakota — three flights, two connections, a rental car — just to have my heart broken again.

I could have called first. It probably would have been the prudent thing to do, the rational thing. Call her and talk to her instead of showing up halfway across the country, apologize and discuss and tell her that I'm willing to move there, I just want to be with her.

It really lacks something, though. I don't consider myself someone with a flair for the dramatic, but even I know that going to her is the right move and if she turns me down, she turns me down and it's really over. Anyone can *say* they'll move to a new state.

I'm pretty sure you only make the offer in person if you're truly and psychotically in love.

CHAPTER THIRTY-NINE

JUNE

BLUFF CITY, S.D. — At the end of yet another lengthy harangue disguised as a campaign speech, City Council hopeful Patty Gold finally sat with a faraway look on her face, as if she might begin to cry at any moment. Her hands sat limply in her lap, and her face wore the lines of bad politics, shattered promises, and lies told so often that even she had begun to think they were true.

"What the fuck?" I whisper to myself.

The article — which is supposed to be about a Town Hall meeting in which several people running for City Council answered the public's questions — goes on the same way, full of light misogyny and very purple prose.

I get through two paragraphs before I stand up and make my way over to Ned Tucker, the author of this... *thing.*

"Ned," I say, standing behind him. I can see his

computer monitor perfectly. He is, at least, working in a Word document, not playing Solitaire.

"One second," he says, and finishes typing something, then turns, relaxing in his chair as he looks at me. "What can I do you for?"

Ned is one of those middle-aged men who thinks he's rakish and isn't. He needs a shave and a haircut, he needs to not take his shoes off in the office, and he needs to not act like the two of us are buddies since I'm now in charge of his work.

"I have some concerns about this article you wrote about the City Council race," I say, holding it up.

"Do you, now?" he asks, both eyebrows rising comically.

He's making fun of me. I'm not an idiot.

I *am* going to ignore it, though.

"Yes," I say. "For starters, you use some extremely sexist language in the lede. I'm sure you know that the verb *harangue* has a lot of negative connotations and is almost exclusively used about women?"

"Huh," he says, as if I'm a dog that's done a mildly interesting trick.

"Yes, it's true," I say, and manage to sound only slightly sarcastic. "In addition, do you realize that this is supposed to be a three-hundred-word summary about last night's Town Hall meeting, not a discussion of the various candidates attractiveness levels, don't you?"

He gives me that smile that I'm sure he thinks is charming, reaches out, and takes the papers I'm holding.

"Sorry about that, boss," he says. "I'll work your edits in before I leave."

"Thanks," I say, and head back for my desk, where I sit, hands on my keyboard, and stare at my empty desktop.

It's a small mercy — maybe the only one I've gotten

today — that my desk is the last one before a blank, windowless wall, and my monitor faces it. It's still in view of anyone who walks past, of course, but not of anyone and everyone in the newsroom at any given time.

I sit there, and I remind myself that the first day on any job is fraught, and difficult, and filled with problems that feel insurmountable. It's hard to get used to a new workplace culture, new coworkers, a new way of doing things.

Was that fight where Natasha called John a stupid son of a bitch and he called her a haggard old lesbian just a new way of doing things? I think. *That's two days in a row you've seen people shouting in here, and it's only your first day at work.*

That is, admittedly, not great, but maybe I'm starting at a rough time for the Herald-Trumpet. Of course, there was also Mike, a reporter who informed me that he "doesn't do" meetings when I asked him to attend ours; Edmund shouting on the phone in his office on two separate occasions; Nancy, the Lifestyle editor who literally turned her back on me when I introduced myself and offered a handshake; and now Ned, who I'm fairly certain is trolling me.

I'm not going to let it get to me. I'm going to do my job well and not involve myself in any of the toxic drama that clearly goes on here, and it will still be worth it.

I wonder what Levi's doing right now.

The thought's almost physically painful, a dull stab to my sternum, so I instantly pull up the project management software the paper uses to track stories, and set about trying to learn it.

I'm finally getting the hang of it an hour later, when Ned drops by my desk again.

"Sent you back that article," he says. "Really thought you made some interesting points, so I took all the edits worth taking. Have a good one!"

"Thank you," I say, but he's already walking back to

his own desk, where he grabs his coat without missing a beat, puts it on while walking and heads through the door.

It's 4:15.

Is he coming back?

He just went out to smoke or something, right?

I open the file he's sent me.

It's exactly the same. Apparently, all the edits worth taking were zero, and I'm now totally sure that Ned just left work for the day.

I close my eyes and count to ten, taking slow, deep breaths.

When I open them, Natasha — who is, judging by the pictures on her desk, a lesbian, but who is not haggard — is leaning over the short partition between our walls.

"When Peter was still here, he just rewrote everything that Ned turned in," she says confidentially. "Adrianne's been doing it lately. You having a good first day?"

. . . . ★ ★ ★ . . . .

I TRY to walk back to the Motel 6 from the Herald-Trumpet. It's only seven o'clock when I leave, and even though it's been dark for a while, a small town in the early evening can't be that dangerous and I really, really need the walk.

I rewrote Ned's awful article. I briefly discussed my concerns with Edmund, who brushed them off and told me that Ned was a "great guy" who "took some getting used to." I finalized tomorrow's Metro section, re-edited everything three times, and went over every single mark the proofreader made.

It's good. It's as good as I can make it, at least, and that's what I tell myself as I walk down the utterly empty

Main Street between buildings so vacated they seem like they've never had people in them, even once.

I can make it. Quitting is for losers. I won't let them get to me. I can be stronger than this, more determined. I can rise above an awful workplace and make something good of this time in my life.

We'd be eating dinner right now. Hedwig would be there and he'd be telling me about the day's good forest gossip and I'd be talking about whatever Wikipedia research hole I went down that day, or maybe making him look at videos of cats riding Roombas because I'm basically positive Levi's never seen a video of a cat riding a Roomba—

And there it is, I'm crying again. It's freezing and this town is empty and I'm crying while trying desperately not to because I'm a little afraid that my tears will freeze to my face. At least today I'm wearing pants.

Then, suddenly, I realize I'm at the end of Main Street, where it turns into a two-lane road with no sidewalk and no shoulder that stretches off into the dark, under the freeway and toward the two motels on the other side.

I fight the urge to scream — *I just wanted to take a walk on this stupid day is that so much to ask?!* — then pull out my phone and request a rideshare.

The app tells me it'll be here in twenty-five minutes.

· · * * ★ ★ ★ ★ * * · ·

FIFTEEN MINUTES LATER, I'm still standing there when a white hatchback suddenly slams on its brakes right in front of me, then speeds up only to slow down a hundred feet away at the nearest open parking spot along Main Street.

I pretend not to notice it, but of course I notice it. I'm a woman alone on a nearly-empty street at night. I notice *everything*.

I notice when a man gets out of the car, backlit by the

streetlamps, and starts walking toward me. I notice that he seems completely locked in on me and doesn't turn his head even once to look into the dark store windows or at the cars driving along down Main Street.

I'm about to get murdered, I think to myself, staring dead ahead at nothing, determined not to look at him. If I look at him, I might look scared, and I can't afford that.

This has been such a stupid day, of course I'm about to get murdered.

I decide that, if he gets too close, the best course of action is to start shouting at him, and if he doesn't leave, the next thing to do is run into the street. If I run into the street, someone will almost definitely notice me.

He keeps walking. He gets closer. I realize that I probably should have run at least ten seconds ago, because now my heart is pounding and my palms are sweaty and my feet are freezing and I'm keenly aware of every single noise within a one-mile radius.

And then finally he's too close, and I really wish my ride would hurry up but Kelly in the blue Civic is still not here, so I take a deep breath and I turn to face him and I shout, "FUCK O—"

I stop mid-*off*, my mouth still open, because now that he's finally close enough for me to see and I'm finally actually looking at him I'm off-balance in a way that's more metaphysical then physical, like reality's just flopped on its side.

"...Levi?" I finish in a whisper.

CHAPTER FORTY

LEVI

"I can fuck off if you'd like," I offer.

I thought about what to say the whole way here: the flight from Roanoke to Philadelphia, Philly to Chicago, Chicago to Sioux Falls, and then the drive from Sioux Falls to Bluff City. I thought about it all that time and I came up with a thousand possibilities.

I can fuck off if you'd like wasn't one of them, but June has always surprised me.

"I'd rather talk, though," I say, and she shakes her head slightly, like she's dazed. "I didn't mean to scare you. Actually, I assumed you'd recognize me."

That snaps her out of whatever reverie she's in and now June closes her eyes, gives her head one more quick shake, opens them.

Smiling. She's smiling.

June is smiling at me and in this moment, right now, the whole trip becomes worth it.

"You're super backlit," she says, nodding at the streetlamp, one hand pressed to her chest. "And I had no reason at all to think you'd be in South Dakota."

344

I glance over my shoulder at the streetlight, my hands shoved into the pockets of my coat, then back at her.

"Fair enough," I say. "To be honest I thought you'd be harder to—"

June reaches out and touches my cheek with her fingertips, brow furrowing, the tip of her nose pink and her lips red with cold, her eyes slightly glassy and a little too bright. I stop talking.

Then she pulls her hand back, takes off a glove, touches the swollen bridge of my nose and my left cheekbone with the cold pads of her fingers. The frown deepens.

"Levi," she says, and then she takes me by the elbow and turns me so I'm facing the streetlight that had backlit me before, and she touches my face again and I close my eyes.

"You told Silas," she says.

It's not a question.

"I did," I say. "I stopped by his house at five this morning to tell him that we've been seeing each other and also that I'm moving to South Dakota."

She stops again, her fingers on my face, and now I take her hand, fold her cold fingers in mine, press her knuckles to my lips.

June looks at me like I'm an alien, then looks around, like she's expecting to see something.

"Here?" she says.

"Here," I tell her. "I'm touring a place on East Sweetwater Road tomorrow morning, and then one on West—"

"You can't move here," she says.

I squeeze her hand harder.

"Why?" I ask.

June looks away, the cords in her neck standing out. The wind picks up again, blows her dark hair in front of her face, so I tuck it behind her ear.

"You have a job," she says, still looking away. "And you have a house, and you have your brothers and your mom and your niece, and Silas, and Hedwig, and... everything is in Sprucevale, you can't just leave it."

She looks back at me, and I raise my eyebrows, can't help but smile.

It's contagious and she gives me a look that's half smile, half question mark.

"What?" she says.

"You know what I'm about to say."

"That you can move wherever you want?"

"That not everything is in Sprucevale," I tell her.

My heart thuds in my chest and I slide my fingers into the spaces between her knuckles, like if I can fit my body to hers just right, I'll know what to say.

But I don't. I've never known what to say. Knowing what to do has always been easy for me, but words fail me more often than not, and none of the thousand things I practiced while I was in transit are coming to mind right now.

I wing it.

"It wound up being a question of numbers," I start. "I imagined all those things that you mentioned, and I put them on a scale and weighed them, and then on the other side—"

What the hell am I talking about?

I look into her eyes for a long moment, take a deep breath.

"I wanted to be with you more than I wanted anything else," I say. "That's all."

"I'm sorry," she says. "I should have told you about the interview sooner. I should have told you when I found out, you were right there, but I didn't. And then I didn't tell you the next day and also the next day, and then suddenly I had this secret and I had to tell you about the interview and also admit that I hadn't told you yet, and... I don't know. I fucked up, Levi. I'm sorry."

I open my hand against hers, and she slides her fingers between mine, cold as icicles.

"I understand," I tell her.

"There was a part of me that felt like if I just didn't tell you it wouldn't be real," she goes on. "And I wanted the job, but I also wanted to stay with you. And I didn't want to pick, so I avoided it and it all exploded in my face."

I kiss her fingers slowly, thoughtfully, one by one.

"Are we fixed?" she whispers.

"I think so," I say. "So long as you'll let me share in your problems."

"If you'll let me share in yours," she says, her eyes on my face again, on the spot where I can feel my blood pulse through my swollen nose and black eye. "I wish you'd let me tell Silas."

"It seemed like the wrong time to keep a secret," I say.

"He wouldn't have punched me," she points out. "And your pretty face wouldn't be all fucked up right now."

I slide my other arm around her waist, pull her closer.

"Are you saying I'm not pretty?" I ask.

"I'm saying I wish you'd gotten that looked at instead of getting on a billion flights."

"You're looking at it," I point out.

"I mean by a medical professional," she says, half-rolling her eyes. "Obviously."

Her other hand is still gloved, against my chest, and I swear I can feel her warmth even through the layers of shirt and sweater and coat that I'm wearing.

"He didn't give me his permission," I tell her.

"For what?"

"To date you."

347

June raises an eyebrow.

"Did you ask for it?" she asks, incredulous, and I grin even though it hurts a little.

"Of course not," I say, and I finally lean down and kiss June.

She kisses me back gingerly, tenderly, her gloved hand on my face. Her lips are cold but soft, careful, tentative.

"He didn't punch me in the mouth," I tell her without letting my lips leave hers.

June just laughs and kisses me harder. She presses herself against me, layers between us, and even though we're fully in public on a sidewalk, cars driving past, I open her mouth with mine, sink my fingers into her hair, deepen the kiss.

Just then, a car honks, loud and long and insistent and finally after a few seconds, June pulls away.

The passenger window of a blue Honda Civic rolls down and a woman leans over.

"Hey!" she shouts. "Are you Jane?"

She looks at her phone.

"Sorry. June?"

"Oh, shit," June says aloud, mostly to me, then clears her throat. "Sorry, I actually found another ride, I should have cancelled but I got distracted—"

The woman rolls her eyes so dramatically I think she might hurt herself, and her tires squeal as she pulls off, not even waiting for June to finish her sentence.

"That's not Midwest Nice, is it?" I ask.

"I hope not," she says, then looks back at me. "Sorry, I forgot that I requested a ride share like twenty minutes ago. I guess that was Kelly."

"I love you," I tell her.

June looks at me, eyes bright, cheeks red, and she starts smiling.

Then she starts laughing.

"What?" I ask, looking around. "I think this freezing, deserted sidewalk is *very* romantic—"

"I love you too," she says.

"It wasn't a hard decision," I tell her, the words suddenly tumbling out of me, like Kelly in her Honda Civic is what jarred them loose. "Not once I got some space. I went camping for a couple of nights—"

"Oh," she says.

"—To clear my head, and it turned out it was simple because I love you, and I love you more than the things that could lay claim to me elsewhere, and I think I've loved you ever since that morning after the thunderstorm when I opened the office door and you'd already been researching the puzzle of the tree murders for hours."

I close my eyes, kiss her on the forehead.

"It took me a long time to realize it, but that was it. I knew right then I'd never met anyone quite like you," I say.

June looks down, like she's slightly embarrassed, then looks back up at me.

"I was six and you were nine," she says quickly. "Silas put my stuffed elephant on top of the fridge, and you climbed onto the kitchen counter and rescued her for me. I still can't believe you never knew."

I kiss her again.

"I know now," I say.

"Good," she says. "I've still got a huge, wild crush on you, Levi."

"How wild?" I ask, and June just laughs.

"Are you hungry?" she says.

· · · · ★ ★ ★ ★ · · · ·

"So," I ask, as the waitress is walking away with our menus. "Who's Logan?"

June laughs. We're in a booth somewhere in the middle of Mabel's House of Breakfast, a diner that I'm sure has looked exactly the same since 1975.

There are four small carafes of syrup on the table next to the salt and pepper, and June lifts one, peering inside.

"Why, are you jealous?" she asks.

"I might be," I tease.

"Silas could tell I was upset when he came over Sunday, so I had to tell him something," she explains. "This is probably strawberry, right?"

"Could be raspberry," I say.

"How'd he take it?"

I don't answer her right away, just give her a long look.

"Well, besides that," she says.

"Besides the fact that he punched me in the face for being with you, it went well," I tell her, also grabbing a syrup carafe. "If it helps, I punched him back."

June's examining a second syrup bottle, and she looks up in surprise.

"You did?"

"Of course I did," I say and hold up my right hand, cuts across the knuckles. "I'm no fighter, but I have four brothers. I've thrown punches before."

"Good," she says. "Is that why he didn't give you permission to date me?"

"I didn't even ask why he denied permission," I say, crossing my arms on the table and leaning forward. "I just told him I didn't want it."

"How mad was he then?"

"You should consider giving your brother a little more credit," I tell her.

"Why, for not forcing you to run away from town and join the Army?" she says.

I snort.

"Not that he could," she amends herself.

"It could be interesting to see him try," I muse aloud.

"Disagree," June says.

"He claimed that not giving me permission was a test," I tell her. "At the very least, he knows you."

"Does that mean you're still friends?" she asks. "I'd think that the whole punching situation would mean you're not, but I can't say I've ever understood your relationship."

The waitress comes back, puts eggs and bacon in front of June, a stack of pancakes in front of me.

Suddenly, I'm starving, and these pancakes look like the greatest food ever conceived in the history of cuisine.

"Could you bring four small saucers, please?" I ask the waitress.

She gives me a big, wide smile.

"Of course, hon," she says, depositing a handful of jams on the table. "I'll be right back."

June watches her go with her eyes slightly narrowed, one eyebrow slightly lifted.

I frown, look over my shoulder at the waitress, in case she had a third arm or something that I hadn't noticed.

"You really don't know, do you?" June asks.

I cut a dry triangle of stacked pancake and put it in my mouth as quickly and yet politely as I can, then just shake my head.

"She's flirting with you," June says. "I mean, sort of. Not hard. She wasn't hitting on you or anything, but she definitely thinks you're cute despite your face situation and you're gonna be getting those saucers *very* — mhm, yup, there she is."

"There you go, hon," the waitress says. "How's everything?"

We tell her it's great. She smiles some more, exchanges another pleasantry, and she's gone. I carefully pour a few tablespoons of each of the four syrups onto the saucers, and June watches me, clearly entertained.

"If I mix them, I won't be able to tell which one is the best," I tell her. "I can't just haphazardly slop them onto my pancakes and expect to come to any sort of reasonable conclusion."

"Of course not," June agrees.

I cut another triangle and dip it into the syrup all the way on the right while she watches me, still trying not to laugh.

"I think that one's blueberry," I say, chewing.

"It's definitely not a color found in nature."

June reaches out with the back of her spoon, dips it in, licks it off.

And even though it's bad blueberry syrup in a diner booth, I'm mesmerized. I stop eating and watch her a little too closely, feel my chest constrict a little too much.

"You know, if you really cared about scientific results, you'd do a double-blind test," she teases me. "Here. I'll blindfold you, swap these around, and then you pick which one you like best and you won't be led astray by this sort of... purple-brown shade."

I eat more pancake, consider her for a long moment.

"What do you say?" she asks.

"I say if you want to blindfold me and then do stuff with syrup, I'm game," I tell her.

The pink in her cheeks deepens and her eyes sparkle.

"I'm trying to discuss serious scientific experimentation," she laughs.

"We can experiment," I offer.

She stabs a forkful of scrambled eggs, then dips them in one of my syrups before eating them.

"Now you've ruined my laboratory conditions," I tell her.

"Where are you staying tonight?" she asks, tilting her head to one side.

I take my time with the next pancake triangle: stab, dip, chew, consider how best to answer the question.

"Your bed," I finally say.

"Good," June answers.

CHAPTER FORTY-ONE

JUNE

L evi stomps the floor of the car as he parks, then curses under his breath.

"I hate driving an automatic," he says, turning the keys off, undoing his seatbelt. "I can never get the hang of it. Feels like I'm driving nothing at all."

He says the last word with his lips against mine, already twisting out of the driver's seat to kiss me, one arm braced against his headrest and the other curling through my hair.

I kiss him back, opening my mouth under his and pressing in. I fumble for a moment and then I finally undo my own seatbelt, let it snap back into place and push myself up on the passenger seat.

My knee hits the gearshift and I make a noise, but then Levi makes it back at me and I squirm again, find the front of his coat with my hand, grab it.

I wonder, for a moment, how many times I've made out with Levi in a vehicle, how many times I've been breathless and wanting in the passenger seat, how many times I've accidentally kicked a gearshift and fogged up windows.

I wonder how many more times we're going to do this.

I hope it's a lot. I hope we can never keep ours hands off each other quite long enough to get inside. I hope we always want each other so much that it's hard to wait.

"I just don't like this tin can," he says, then kisses me again. "I feel like I'm driving a Hot Wheels down the interstate."

His hand moves down my side, finds its way under my clothes, onto my hip.

"And it's way too small," he says. "That's the good thing about my truck. You could put a mattress in the back."

I catch his lip between my teeth and Levi grunts, a low, rumbling sound laced with need.

"You've never once put a mattress in the back of your truck," I tease, my voice coming out rougher than I meant.

Levi just laughs, then reaches past me, unlatches my door and pushes it open.

"Come on," he says. "Take me to bed already."

The mid-October chill of the Motel 6 parking lot feels like it's already winter, and for a moment, I remember where I am, what my day was before Levi showed up, and then I banish those thoughts completely because I have twelve more hours before I have to go back there and I'll be damned if I'm going to spend them thinking about the Herald-Trumpet.

"That's all you brought?" I ask, as Levi lifts a duffel and laptop bag out of the trunk, then slams it shut, slings them over his shoulders, and walks toward me.

"This whole endeavor was poorly planned out and poorly executed," he says. "I decided on this late last night, left my house at four in the morning, got into a fistfight at five, and still made my nine o'clock flight."

I can't help but look at his face again, the bridge of his nose purpled, deep shadows spreading to under his left eye.

"I still wish you'd let me—"

Levi stops me with his mouth on mine, the kiss fierce, insistent, quick.

"I didn't," he says, one hand holding his duffel bag, the other under my chin. "I'm the one who's beholden to him, not you. Telling him was my task, so I did it. I'd do it again. Simple as that."

"I know, bu—"

He puts one finger over my lips, and a shiver runs through my whole body that has nothing to do with the cold.

"Stop talking about your brother and take. Me. To. *Bed*," he says, his face inches from mine, his eyes the color of dark copper, sparking and blazing.

I kiss him again, his finger sliding from my lips, and then I pull back, find my motel room key in my pocket, pull him along until we're at the right door.

I unlock the door, go inside. His bags hit the floor and then his coat, and his lips are on mine again before I've got my own jacket unzipped.

Four hands take it off, and it falls to the floor and I'm already on my tiptoes, hands around Levi's neck, one in his hair. Without missing a beat, he reaches back, pulls the knot out and it falls messily to his shoulders.

I put my hands in, let it sift through my fingers. He pushes me back five steps, six, and then my butt hits the dresser with the TV on the other end and I can hear the thing shake. Levi pays it no mind, just grabs me, lifts me onto the dresser so our faces are nearly even.

Then he pulls back, his hands on my thighs, his forehead against mine. He's already hard as a rock, his length pressing against me.

I hook one finger under the top button of his flannel shirt and undo it, his skin warm below it as his breathing hitches, evens out again.

356

"I'm about to be very honest with you," he says.

"I don't usually get a warning," I tell him, opening another button.

"I need you," he says, his voice dropping. "I feel like I'm faded and frayed around the edges, and what I want more than anything in the world is to be inside you hitting that spot that makes your eyes roll."

I flush despite myself, pull at his buttons as his fingers curl under the waistband of my black work pants and he smiles.

"Are you blushing?" he murmurs, teasing.

"No," I lie, pushing his shirt off his shoulders.

"What if I tell you that this is going to be fast and hard because I don't just need you now, I needed you five minutes ago in the parking lot and ten minutes ago in the car?"

"Not blushing," I say, pulling his belt from its loops as he unbuttons my blouse, his big hands surprisingly nimble.

"What if I tell you how tempted I was to pull into an empty parking lot and beg you to ride me in the driver's seat?" he asks.

I pull my shirt off. My bra follows a second later and then his hands are on my breasts and his lips are on mine again as he pinches my nipples, rolls them between his fingers and I moan into his mouth.

"Not blushing," I gasp, even though I'm very definitely blushing.

I unbutton his pants and then he grabs my wrist, guides my hand to his cock, rolls his hips so he presses against me.

"There's a mirror right behind you," he says, his voice so low it's at the bottom of the ocean.

I close my fist around his cock, stroke it. I listen to his breath hitch in his throat.

"And you want to watch us while we have our hard, fast, messy fuck?" I ask.

"How'd you know?" he says, his words turning to a growl as I squeeze, stroke him again from root to tip.

"I must be psychic."

"Guess what I'm thinking."

Stroke. Groan.

"You're not sure why I'm still wearing pants."

His hand leaves mine and in a moment my pants are unbuttoned, undone, his hand inside and under my panties, fingers exploring my wetness and I buck my hips, make a noise low in my throat.

"Not quite," he rumbles. "I'm thinking that I brought condoms, but I'd rather go bare again."

He slides two fingers around my clit, pinching it between them, a bolt of pleasure rocketing through my body.

"Yes," I whisper.

We kiss again, fiercely, my teeth against his lip it's so hard, and then he suddenly pulls back, strides away.

"Take those off," he says over his shoulder.

I do.

The lights go off and suddenly it's very, very dark. Levi's pants hit the floor somewhere by the table and then at the end of the dresser, a lamp goes on and then he's back and he takes my head in both hands.

"Ta-da, mood lighting," he says, and kisses me hard, leaning me backward against the dresser, his cock thick and insistent and hot against my belly.

"*Now* it's romantic," I murmur, and I swear Levi smiles into the kiss.

"I love you in ways I didn't know were possible," he says, his lips still half on mine. "I wake up thinking about you and I go to sleep thinking about you and whenever I see you, I feel like spring. How's that for romance?"

He kisses me harder, leaves me speechless, then pulls away and turns me around all at once, wrapping one arm around my torso, right between my breasts, holding me tight to him.

His erection bumps against me and I bite my lip, stand on my toes, brace myself on the dresser. In the mirror, Levi's eyes lock on mine as his thick head slides along me, pressing against my clit, steadily moving lower.

"I love you desperately," he whispers in my ear. "Never doubt that."

Then the thick head of his cock nudges between my slick folds and Levi sinks himself into me with a single stroke. Everything goes fuzzy and I hear myself make a noise that's half moan and half groan and all loud as hell.

"Holy fuck, June," he rasps. His voice is rough, ragged, like he's just climbed a mountain.

"More," I whisper but he's already pulling out, a hand on my hip and a hand on my shoulder, pushing back in as I rock back against him, on my tiptoes.

He gives me more. He gives me more, faster and harder and he growls in my ear. I brace myself against the mirror as he drives himself hard and deep, as he adjusts his angle ever so slightly until soon I'm moaning with every stroke.

Levi does things to my body I didn't know were possible, draws reactions from me I've never felt before. He makes me want and want, and when he touches me it's electric, lightning striking every time.

He puts one arm around my chest, pinches one nipple between two fingers.

"I never get to see your face when I take you from behind," he says, his voice a rasp against my ear. "I love it when you're wild and out of control and about to come, you know."

I try to answer him, but he thrusts again and he hits that spot so perfectly and I'm on edge, about to dive over, and the only word I can manage is, "Please."

"Always," he says, and he does it again.

I come. The last thing I see is my own eyes closing and I feel the coldness of the mirror underneath my hand, and then I'm shouting his name and pushing back against him and gasping, my mind in a million pieces.

Finally, my head is on my forearm, resting against the mirror as I gasp. He traces a finger down my spine and he moves inside me and I shudder as he rubs against my sensitive spots and it's only then that I realize he's still hard and then he does it again and my body responds in goosebumps and a deep thrill that craves *more*.

I turn, pulling him out, put my hands around his head, kiss him hard. Before he can kiss me back, I push him toward the bed, three steps and then he's lying on it and I'm already on top of him, straddling him as I kiss him deeply and his fingers dig into my hips.

Then I lean back, fit us together again.

This time he's the one who groans as I sink my weight onto him, the one whose hands tighten on me as I move. I go slow at first, savoring every inch, letting Levi lose control. I like the feel of his skin against mine and I like the way he sighs explosively when I hilt him, the way he palms a breast and slides his calloused hand over a nipple.

But I can't go slow for long, despite myself. Soon enough I find the angle and the spot and the rhythm, and then I can't help it. I spread my hands on his chest and I want more and fast and *now* and God, it shouldn't feel this good, *nothing* should feel this good, and then somehow he's got his thumb on my clit and I'm riding him hard and fast and I come again, my whole body rattling and shaking.

This time he doesn't stop. This time I'm still coming as Levi rolls me over onto my back and I wrap my legs around him and he buries his face in my neck and I swear I'm still coming as he drives himself into me deep and hard and then he comes too, groaning and shuddering.

We lie there for a long time, Levi's head on my chest, my arms around his shoulders. This still feels unreal, like a hallucination or a long realistic dream. Maybe I got hit by a bus. Maybe I'm in a coma.

I'm tired, drained, exhausted, but I fight sleep. Partly because I haven't brushed my teeth, but mostly because once I go to sleep, then I'll have to wake up and say goodbye to Levi for the day and go to the Herald-Trumpet and slog through another day.

It will get better, I tell myself. *The first day at a job is always hard.*

It has to get better, because Levi's moving here to be with you and if it doesn't get better, you've cost him all that for nothing.

That thought makes me hold my breath for a moment, as if someone's tied a rope around my lungs and then dropped a weight from it.

I realize, all at once, that this is what love is. It's the happy moments and the laughing together and making out at stoplights and the looking forward to seeing them every single day, but it's also the simple, astonishing fact that now I have to take him into account.

Suddenly what I do matters to another person, and somehow, I was unprepared for this. Levi knew. He looked at the situation, refused to ask something of me that I didn't want to give, and got on a plane to South Dakota.

"What is it?" he asks, looking up at me.

I just shake my head.

"It's something. You're not there," he says, slowly pulling himself off of me, pushing the pillows back, leaning against them. He's still stark naked and doesn't make a single motion toward modesty, utterly comfortable in his own skin.

"Just thinking about work tomorrow," I say. "Today was a little rough, so I'm just thinking about ways to make it… not that."

I'm already lying, or at least, not quite telling the truth. The weight around my lungs threatens to strangle me.

"Ah," he says, and drapes an arm around my shoulders. "Anything I can help with?"

"None of my coworkers are trees," I say.

"I work with humans," he says. "Frequently, even."

"Not these humans," I say, mostly to myself.

Levi leans over, kisses me on the top of the head, and it sends an ugly black prickle of guilt down my spine.

"Show me the apartment you're looking at tomorrow," I say.

· · * * * ★ ★ ★ * * · ·

IT's 3:26 a.m. when I wake up. I don't know why I wake up, but I do, all at once like I've just come up for air from the depths. I roll onto my other side and try to fall back asleep, but I know right away that it's pointless.

Still, I stay there for a while, on the cheap motel sheets in the double bed that's really too small for us to share, but neither of us wanted to sleep separately. Levi sleeps on his stomach, one arm over his head, and for a long time I watch his back rise and fall, rise and fall, rise and fall.

It's nearly four when I get out of bed, find our clothes in a pile on the floor, locate a shirt, pull it on. It's his, plaid and long-sleeved, and I get a fresh pair of underwear from my suitcase and then I go to the table and chairs set up by the window and I sit.

Briefly, I wonder if I should have put a towel down, but it's too late. I know I could go into the bathroom and turn the light on and read on the toilet, but I don't want to read. I want to sit here in the dark, staring at the light leaking in through the cracks in the curtains, and think.

It doesn't take me long to decide.

CHAPTER FORTY-TWO

LEVI

I know there are people in the world who can sleep in after an exhausting day or a late night. I know because I long to be one of them. What must it be like, to sleep until ten in the morning? Eleven?

Noon?

The last time I slept past seven in the morning I had the flu and a fever of 103.2. Before that, I'd stayed up for seventy-two hours straight finishing a project in graduate school after my group project partner revealed that she'd done absolutely nothing in the two months since we'd received the assignment.

When I open my eyes, the clock says 5:10. That's 6:10 Eastern Time, so it's actually not too bad. I slept in by ten whole minutes.

I stretch, roll over, and realize that June's not next to me. I have one sickening moment where my heart plummets — *I dreamed this, she changed her mind* — and then I see her.

She's sitting at the table, in the dark, almost motionless.

"June?" I whisper.

"Hey," she whispers back.

I pull myself to sitting. She turned the heat to *jungle* last night, so it's warm in here, making everything feel a little stranger, more dreamlike.

"What's wrong?"

"I couldn't sleep," she says, and she sounds further away than the six feet between us should allow.

I stand, move through the unnatural warmth, grab some boxers, sit down opposite her.

"Tell me," I say.

She's wearing the shirt I had on yesterday, the sleeves six inches too long on her, the shoulders too wide. It's unbuttoned and in the light coming through the window, sneaking around the blackout shades, I can see her pale skin, the slight curve of a breast and I think, unbidden, of her on my porch that day after the thunderstorm, pointing at her chest, asking who Joe was.

"I'm giving up," she says quietly. She doesn't look at me, her fingers knotted together on the table in front of her.

I reach over and take her hand and she finally looks at me, her eyes light in the dark.

"I'm not taking the job and I'm gonna stop looking," she says.

I rub my thumb over her knuckles silently, because she doesn't seem finished yet.

"And I have no idea what to do," she says, her voice quieter, a whisper. "I've been doing this since I graduated from college, and even before then I wrote for my college paper and I was the editor, and before that in high school, and for as long as I can remember I loved *Murphy Brown* and *All the King's Men* and *His Girl Friday* and I always wanted to be there, writing headlines and getting the scoop and *telling the truth* and it's just not…"

She trails off, looks down at her hands.

"It's not that," she says. "I can't go back to the Herald-Trumpet. When I went in for an interview the first thing I saw was my boss *screaming* at a reporter about writing too fancy. Screaming. Right in his face."

My spine stiffens.

"I can't do that to myself," she says, like she's just realizing it for the first time. "I don't think my dream is my dream anymore. I think my dream left while I wasn't looking, and now that I'm finally paying attention again, it's gone and I don't have anything to put in its place."

She swallows hard, takes a deep breath.

"You don't have to know," I tell her.

"I don't even want a different journalism job," she says, and finally she looks up again, tears brimming in her eyes. "There was a time when I was young and cocky and idealistic and I thought that even being a cub reporter in Elko, Nevada, or Sitka, Alaska or one of these middle-of-nowhere places could change the world but I don't think that anymore. I wish I did. But I don't and in its place there's... nothing."

I hold her hands and she holds mine back, fingers squeezing, interlaced.

"Can I tell you about a motivational poster?" I finally ask.

"Yes?" June says. I've obviously baffled her.

"In the central Forest Service office up in Harrisonburg, there's this woman who's the volunteer coordinator. Tammy. That part's not important. But Tammy really, really has a thing for motivational posters, you know, the kind with a majestic view and then big words underneath?"

"Uh huh," June says.

"Well, one of them says 'When God shuts a door, He opens a window,'" I tell her. "And honestly, I'm not really sure about it as an inspirational saying, because doors and windows aren't the same at all. One's designed for ingress and egress, the other is really just for letting light and air in—"

"Is that also on the poster?" she asks, laughing even though the tears have spilled onto her cheeks.

"No," I admit. "That's just my opinion on the thing."

"I see."

"What I'm saying badly is that life is rarely a windowless room with a bolted door," I tell her. "And, I don't know, maybe the windows are wallpapered over and you'll have to search to find them, but they're there. Or maybe it's another door. Maybe it's a bigger door. Or maybe it's a—"

"You're slaughtering this poor metaphor," June says gently.

"I meant what I said about sharing your problems," I say. "Let me do this with you."

She smiles, looks down. A tear drops and she quickly wipes it away, takes a deep breath.

"Can you?" she says, half-laughing.

"I can try," I tell her. "I did once spend a weekend removing wallpaper—"

"That metaphor died already."

"How about this," I say. "You call the paper and quit. I call this apartment and cancel the tour. We fly home. You…"

Suddenly my mouth goes dry and my heart skips a beat because I didn't mean to have this particular talk at five-twenty in the morning while June was having a life crisis, but here we go.

"…move in with me, officially, and then we figure out together where you're going next."

She looks down at our hands for a moment, then back up at me.

"Okay," she says.

And then she smiles. It's all I need, all I really wanted: *okay* and a smile and suddenly I'm floating.

I'm finally realizing that what fills my heart up and makes it overflow to bursting might not be what I'd anticipated. Not that I'd ever given a great deal of thought to the possible romantic moments in my life, but some part of me had always assumed that they would involve rings and flowers, grand gestures, maybe the Eiffel Tower.

But that's not it, is it?

It's research scattered on the floor, a bright-eyed girl who excitedly tells me about long-dead brigands named Phineas and Obadiah. It's microfiche and a wireless router. It's sharing your solitude with someone and realizing that she makes it better.

It's the early-morning agreement in a cheap motel room that you're going to leave together, go home together, tackle life together.

"We should figure out flights to get home," she says, disengaging our hands, lightly playing her fingertips over my knuckles. "I canceled mine when I agreed to start right away."

"Mine were one way," I tell her.

June gives me an incredulous look, and I laugh.

"Because I didn't know what to expect, not because I thought I'd never go back," I say.

"I should call the paper," she says, already listing off what's to be done. "Tell them they can go fuck themselves, pack…"

I stand, her hand still in mine.

"C'mere," I say, and pull her up.

"I love you," she says, the quiet of the early morning sinking into her words.

"I love you too," I say.

"I'm glad you came," she tells me as I press my lips to her forehead.

"Me too," I say.

CHAPTER FORTY-THREE

JUNE

"Golf tournament," Levi says, his voice rumbling through me.

"You can't guess that anymore," I tell him, my head resting against his shoulder. "You're banned. Blacklisted. Whatever."

"But I think this one really is," he says, nodding lazily toward the man wearing khakis and hauling ass along the terminal while dragging two small roller bags behind him.

"Why?" I challenge. "There is nothing about that man that says *I am going to a golf tournament*, and you've guessed that about the last six people just because you think it's funny."

Levi's quiet for a moment. Somewhere far away, there's an announcement for what sounds like Blitheroy Mazendorf to please hurry to their gate.

"I've forgotten any other places where people might go," he finally admits.

We're both slouched at an empty gate in the Charlotte International Airport. We've been here for two hours, and we've got two more to go before hopping a short flight to Roanoke and then taking a two-hour drive home.

"The only place or event you can remember is *golf tournament?*" I ask without moving. "Weddings. Bar mitzvahs. Vacations. Conferences."

"Golfing vacation?" he asks.

"You don't even like golf," I mutter, just as his phone rings.

That gets my attention. Levi doesn't exactly get a lot of calls, so I watch him as he flips his phone open — *flips*, my God, if we're going to live together I have to do something about that — and answers.

"Loveless," he says, then listens. He clears his throat. "Yes, I think — uh, I really am feeling much better today. I'm on the mend. My fever is considerably reduced to... ninety-eight? or so. I expect I'll be back tomorrow."

I just cover my face, like it can block out how bad he is at lying.

"You did?" he says and shoots me a look. "Uh huh. Uh huh."

A pause.

"A chainsaw?"

I sit up straight, suddenly not tired any more. Levi's just listening intently, staring at me, his face dead serious.

"Thank you for calling me," he says at last. "I'll see you tomorrow."

His phone shuts with a snap, and he turns to me.

"One of the rangers covering the area with a lot of likely victims caught a man and a woman hiking out of the forest cross-country," he says. "With a chainsaw."

I gasp, my hand flying to my mouth.

"Is it them?" I hiss.

"There's a very good chance."

"Did they confess?"

Levi just shakes his head.

"Are they being held?" I ask. "Can we question them when we get back, or is it gonna be too late?"

"I'm not sure what kind of authority you think National Forest rangers have," Levi says.

"They can arrest people," I say, now sitting on the edge of this uncomfortable chair. "I looked into this. On federal lands, they have the authority to make arrests and hold suspects."

"Sure, in theory," Levi allows, rubbing his face with one hand. "But in reality, I don't know a single ranger who's ever made an actual arrest. I don't even know how. That's not really why we go into forestry."

I slump back into the chair and sigh.

"Jenna did give them a citation for sawing on public lands without the proper certification," he says. "Do the names Marjorie and Donald Thompson mean anything to you?"

I stare at the airport ceiling, something tickling my brain.

"Yes," I say slowly.

Levi waits. I stare at the ceiling and do my best to remember how I know that name, because I'm positive I know it from somewhere. Marjorie Thompson.

Who the fuck is Marjorie Thompson?

Come on. Come on.

It's been a long day, even though it's not even eight at night yet. I woke up too early, sat in the dark, cried, quit my job, and decided to move back home and live with my boyfriend before it was even six in the morning, and I am *not* a morning person.

Then there was spending a horrifying amount of money on plane tickets, the drive to Sioux Falls, a flight, an airport, another flight, and now I'm sitting here feeling like my eyes are covered in sandpaper and my sinuses are half-desert, half-sludge.

"It's not a big deal," Levi says. "We work with the state police on stuff like this, we can——"

"The historical society," I say, the words coming to my mouth before they even pass through my brain.

I sit up. I stare at Levi.

"You stole her pen because she was a jerk to me," I say. "*She's* the tree murderer?"

"We don't know that," Levi says. "We just know that she and someone who I assume is her husband were in a highly-patrolled area with an unauthorized chainsaw."

Now I'm pacing back and forth in the airport, in front of Levi.

"It makes sense," I say. "She knew the story. She had all the same documents that we did. God, she even knows how to use microfiche! There's a reader *in the historical society!*"

"I sure hope that knowing how to use microfiche isn't a crime," Levi deadpans.

I ignore this.

"We've gotta go get the data from those cameras," I say, still pacing. "I hope she cut down one of those trees."

Still seated, and now tossing his phone up and down in one hand, Levi just raises his eyebrows.

"You know what I mean," I tell him. "If there was another tree crime, I hope it was to one of the trees that we can get solid evidence from. When can we head out? Tomorrow morning? I've got a memory card reader some-where, though I might have to get a separate dongle to connect it to my phone…"

"June," Levi says, and stands. He takes my shoulders in his hands.

"I'm getting ahead of myself?" I say.

"A little," he says, that half-smile I love on his face. "Let's get home first, okay?"

I lean into him, and he wraps his arms around me. A woman walks by, dragging a suitcase and talking loudly on her phone about how many appetizer trays they've got somewhere.

"Wedding," Levi says.

"Could be a golf tournament," I answer.

"Do you know any other airport waiting games?" he asks.

· · * * ★ ★ ★ * * · ·

I FALL asleep on the final flight, my head on Levi's shoulder again while he borrows my phone and watches a documentary about sea turtles.

As we drive home on Interstate 81, I watch the trees flick by and try to stay awake. Even the gas station coffee I got isn't doing much, though it seems to be working for Levi, who occasionally borrows my cup for a sip and then inevitably grimaces at the taste.

"It's bad coffee," I allow, tucking one foot under me in the wide expanse of his truck's cab.

"All coffee is bad coffee," he says. "It tastes like acidic dirt."

I take another sip and consider this.

"Sure, but it's really addictive, so it tastes like *good* acidic dirt," I say.

"You're going to put a coffee maker in my kitchen, aren't you?" he asks, that smile in his voice as he drives.

"I am," I confirm. "And not just the French press that's already there. I'm gonna get the biggest coffee maker I can find and take up all your counter space."

Levi just sighs dramatically, and I laugh.

"I've thought of lots of ways to re-decorate your house," I lie. "First is the huge TV I'm going to put over your fireplace. Then I'm going to get about fifty of those tiny, skinny tables that don't really do anything but that everyone seems to have in their houses, and I'm going to put them everywhere. And a rug. I'm going to get the loudest rug I can find."

"On one condition," he says. "Jedediah stays."

I put one hand to my chest as if wounded.

"I would *never* do anything to Jedediah," I say.

"Good," Levi says, and reaches for my coffee cup again.

· · · ★ ★ ★ ★ ★ · · ·

I DON'T SPEND that night with him. Instead, he drops me off at my parents' house and kisses me goodbye, because I really do owe them a detailed, in-person explanation.

They're still up when I get home, and the three of us sit in the living room and I talk for thirty minutes straight, telling them everything that's happened since I lost my job and my boyfriend and moved back home a few months ago.

To their credit, they just listen. To their further credit, they don't seem at all surprised — my mom already knew about Levi, sort of, but she didn't know the whole story.

When I finish, it's early morning and I've been awake for nearly twenty-four hours. Both my parents give me big hugs and tell me exactly what I need to hear: that I'm doing the right thing, that I'll figure my life out, that quitting a single very bad job isn't going to somehow doom my future.

They also tell me that they like Levi and have always liked Levi. The words 'nice young man' come out of my mother's mouth more than once.

Finally, they go to bed and I hop into the shower, because I need to wash airports and airplanes and Bluff City and the Herald-Trumpet off myself, and also because I drank a ton of coffee late at night, so I'm wired and jittery.

And I need the quiet space to think, because telling my parents was the easy part. They're not exactly permissive parents, and they especially weren't when I was growing up, but as an adult they've been content to let me take the reins of my own life.

But I still haven't talked to Silas.

CHAPTER FORTY-FOUR

JUNE

Behind me, the door of Eggs Over Belgium chimes delicately, and I turn.

It's a group of women I don't recognize, not him. He's now seven minutes late, which isn't like my brother and I'm starting to wonder if he's changed his mind and gone off the rails, or... something.

I don't even know what *or something* would look like. I don't think it's happening. But I also know that my brother hasn't always been reasonable where I'm concerned, though based on his offer to take me to brunch at the fancy new spot downtown, I think he might feel bad about that.

The door chimes again. This time I make myself sip my coffee, eyes ahead, calmly waiting for my stupid older brother to hurry and get here.

"Sorry," his voice says, behind me, and *now* I turn. "They're fixing the sewer at the other end of town so there was a detour by the river, and it took forever."

"I didn't run into traffic," I tell him as he sits, shedding his jacket.

He's got a cut on his lip, a dark, scabbed-over line, the

flesh under it just barely swollen still. Silas sees me looking and touches it with his hand.

"Yeah," he says. "I guess he told you?"

"His black eye told me," I say, and Silas at least has the grace to look embarrassed. "Really?"

"He showed up at my house at five o'clock in the morning to tell me that he'd been lying about banging my little sister for the past month," Silas says defensively.

Two women at the next table glance over.

"So you *punched* him?"

"June—"

"Your best friend came up to you and said, *hey, I'm in a consensual relationship with your adult sister*, and your response was to haul off and sock him in the face?" I say, lowering my voice to a hiss.

This is not going as planned. Today is Saturday, and I took yesterday to sleep in, gather my wits after the week I just had, and plan some talking points for this brunch with Silas. The talking points included things like *have a reasonable discussion about toxic masculinity* and *assure him that you don't want to interfere in their friendship*.

Turns out I'm madder than I thought.

"He lied to me," Silas says.

I lean back and cross my arms.

"I'm trying to protect you, Bug," he says. "I know you think I'm old-fashioned but you're my little sister, and I can't help but—"

"Spare me," I say.

The other table looks at us again, and I continue to ignore them.

"I thought he'd hurt you," Silas says. "The day before that you cried in your car and told me that some guy named *Logan* had broken your heart, and yes, I put it together, I'm not a moron."

"Not a reason for violence," I tell him.

"So I'm supposed to just stand by and let you get hurt?" he asks, leaning back, one ankle crossed over his knee.

"Yes," I tell him.

"I can't."

"Would you have given two shits if I were your brother and some girl came to your door?"

"I wouldn't punch a girl," he says.

"You shouldn't punch anyone."

"You didn't mind me scaring off Brett when he came to your window," he says, arms crossed over his chest.

I lean my elbows on the table and pinch the bridge of my nose, because I really wish I hadn't called Silas to deal with that. I should have called the police, or just waited for him to leave, or anything but asking my over-protective brother with caveman tendencies to come interfere.

"I shouldn't have asked you," I tell him. "Listen, that was a mistake, okay?"

"What? Why?"

"Because in your mind that validated every action you've ever taken against a romantic interest of mine," I say. "The one time I really needed your help I *asked* for it. I didn't ask you to punch my boyfriend or to be a jerk to everyone I've ever dated or to make Jake Echols *join the damn Army*."

Silas says nothing.

"Levi told me the real reason you crashed the truck into the creek," I sigh.

"What else has he told you about me?"

I stare at Silas for a moment, searching my memory vaults.

"That you're thinking about getting a dog? I don't know, Silas, we don't discuss you that much."

"Hi! Y'all ready to order?" asks the waitress, who just

materialized out of nowhere by our table. The perkiness of her tone tells me that she's definitely aware that she interrupted a fight.

"You go first," Silas says, glowering.

I smile at the waitress. I smile too much.

"I'll have the stuffed Belgian waffles, please," I say, and she nods.

Silas clears his throat, skimming the menu.

"I'll take the eggs Benedict," he finally says. "Thanks."

"I'll be right back with more coffee!" the waitress says brightly, then leaves.

I look at Silas. He looks back at me. We both look away, and for several minutes, neither of us says anything. The waitress comes and goes with the coffee, and we both thank her politely.

At last, I carefully rearrange my silverware next to my plate, sigh, and break the silence.

"You fancy now?" I ask.

Silas just narrows his eyes.

"Eggs Benedict," I say.

"They're good," he says. "And God knows I can't make them myself."

"Fancypants Flynn over here," I say.

"Yeah, I'm fancy," he says, and a smile creeps onto his face. "You want to know how fancy?"

"Tell me."

He leans forward, like he's about to tell me something in confidence.

"I bought the name-brand orange juice," he says.

"No," I gasp.

"Don't tell Mom and Dad," he says. "You know what else? Thousand thread count sheets. And enormous, fluffy towels. I'm living like a king, Junebug."

"I had no idea your tastes were so sophisticated," I tease.

"Yeah, I'm at the cutting edge of shit," he says, smiling.

Then he looks away for a moment, at the wall of Eggs Over Belgium, but he's obviously not looking there. He's looking somewhere else, far away, and for a long, my normally-talkative brother is dead quiet.

"I bought the sheets because I thought it might help me sleep," he suddenly says, his voice quiet, with none of the cocky swagger it had a moment ago. "And I bought the towels because I also bought a bunch of nice bath stuff, because I had this idea that I could take more baths, that it might help me relax sometimes when I can't sleep."

"Does it help?" I ask.

"I can't tell," he says. He takes his coffee mug and holds it between his palms, looks into it. "The therapy helps. The meds help. Having close, stable relationships helps."

Silas has never said the words *post-traumatic stress disorder* aloud in my hearing, but I'm not stupid. He did three service tours. No one comes back from that unscathed.

"He's never breathed a word to me," I tell him. "He wouldn't. You know Levi. He's *Levi*."

Silas nods, still staring into his coffee.

"It's weird," he says. "It's gonna take me a little while."

"I get it," I tell him.

"But I'm also glad you stopped dating douchebags," he says, finally looking up at me. "Levi's…"

Silas trails off.

"He's a good dude," he finally says. "A really good dude. And I probably shouldn't have punched him in the face."

"Probably?"

"It was five in the morning," Silas says, lifting his coffee to his lips. "No. When he *left* it was five in the morning and

381

we spent a while in the kitchen with frozen food on our faces, so it was even earlier than that when he showed up."

I sigh and give him *that* look.

"You may not understand getting mad about someone dating your sister, but I *know* you understand getting mad about someone knocking on your door before the sun is even up," he says.

"So you're going to apologize?" I ask, ignoring the fact that he's right and most of my violent fantasies have come about as a result of being awoken before the sun.

He just looks at me, sipping his coffee.

"Silas," I insist, and he laughs.

"I'll apologize. I'm just giving you a hard time, Bug."

The waitress comes back, puts our plates in front of us. We thank her, then examine our brunches.

"Want to trade?" Silas asks, looking over at mine.

"No."

"Want to share?"

"*No*," I tell him.

He reaches his fork toward my plate.

"Just a—"

I smack his hand, but he gets a piece of waffle anyway.

"You are such a pain in the ass," I tell him.

"You gonna eat all that?" he asks.

CHAPTER FORTY-FIVE

LEVI

On the ground in front of me, something moves in a brief flash of shiny black and then it's gone, twisting under the cover of the leaves. I hold out one arm to block June.

"Are we there?" she asks, looking up and around, confused. "This isn't it. Is this it?"

"No," I say lightly, watching the snake reappear, mosey around a mostly rotted log, and vanish into the forest. "Just hang on a sec."

"Okay?" June says, holding onto the straps of her backpack and glancing around a little nervously. "Is there something I should be worried about, or…?"

"Nope," I say. I give my slithery friend one more moment to disappear fully, then put my arm down. "All clear."

June steps forward, looks around suspiciously, and then we start hiking again.

"There's not a mountain lion staring us down or something, is there?" she asks, glancing around at the trees.

"If I'd seen a mountain lion, I promise I wouldn't be

calmly walking on," I tell her. "Those are some bad news kitties."

"Bad News Kitties is the name of my all-girl punk band," June says, still looking around, though she's looking up into the trees, not at the ground. "Bear? Was it a bear?"

"No," I tell her, glancing over, trying not to smile. "Could you please accept that I saved you from a horrible, gruesome fate and stop asking?"

"How gruesome?" she asks.

"I'm trying to keep you blissfully unaware," I tell her.

"I just want to know how much to appreciate your self-less gesture," she teases. "Are we talking mauling, or being eaten, or—"

She gasps.

Trying to keep information from June has always been and will always be pointless.

"It was a snake, wasn't it?"

I don't answer, just glance over at her again, but the jig is up.

"It was definitely a snake," she says to my silence, our feet still crunching over the deep leaf cover on the forest floor. "Ugh. Thank you."

Then she shudders.

"You're welcome for my remarkable act of heroism," I deadpan.

"They move wrong," she says as we keep walking. It's the same thing she always says about snakes. "It's unnatural. They're just a tube, they shouldn't be able to get around—"

"And they're too shiny, swallow prey whole, and have poison teeth?" I finish for her.

"They don't *all* have poison teeth," she says, mimicking my role in this conversation.

"It was just a black snake," I tell her, as if that'll help.

"They don't have poison teeth, and since you're not a small forest rodent, you don't interest them much."

June just wrinkles her nose, and we keep going. I don't mind snakes, but ever since the first time she told me she doesn't like them, I've been unable to help but see her side of the argument.

They *do* move wrong. It's a little unsettling.

We hike another quarter mile, around some rocks, over a small stream that's nearly covered over with fallen leaves, and then we're there.

I look up, not sure what I'm hoping for.

There's a tree missing. The big oak is gone, and I clench my jaw because I know what I'm going to find: a tree almost as old as this country sawed to pieces, in chunks.

Jail is too good for them, I think.

"It's gone, right?" June asks, and she sounds excited. "Didn't there used to be another tree? A bigger one?"

"Yes," I say, my tone clipped.

"Now we just hope the camera worked," she says, and grabs my arm by the elbow.

The site's exactly like I knew it would be: massive tree, freshly cut, in pieces. Looks like it was done by a chainsaw.

"Okay," June says from twenty feet away. "It looks like it's in good shape, though I think something might have chewed on this one corner? But I assume these things are built for being chewed on."

I sling my pack to the ground, reach into the correct pocket, and pull out blue nitrile gloves and the evidence collection bags given to me by the state police.

It's now been almost five days since Marjorie and Donald were caught with a chainsaw. The Forest Service is a slow-moving bureaucracy and trying to work with another agency like the state police instantly halves the speed.

I spoke with State Police detectives and a Forest Service investigator. They spoke with each other. They spoke with a lumber expert, who spoke with a tree trafficking expert, who spoke with a conservationist, all of whom tried to determine the value of the destroyed trees.

Eventually, I asked if I could at least go gather evidence. That's when I got the evidence bags since I am, technically, an officer of the law.

June holds out one hand, and I give her a pair before snapping some on myself. She crouches, looks up at the camera, then gingerly unscrews something and lifts the dark green, very heavy duty camera off its mounting pole.

I cross my arms over my chest and wait while she opens the casing, fiddles with something, shakes it, and then pulls a small, flat rectangle out.

"Evidence bag?" she asks.

I hold it open, and she carefully deposits the camera, still holding the memory card. I seal it.

"Okay," she says, and pulls some electronics from an outside pocket of her pack. "Moment of truth."

She slides the card into the card reader, then connects it to another cord that she connects to her phone. Faintly, something whirs to life, and for a few minutes, June watches her setup intently.

Then she sighs a sigh of relief.

"It worked," she says, and unplugs the card reader, removes the memory card. I offer another evidence bag and she puts it in. "Now we just have to find them."

We stand huddled together, and I watch over her shoulder as she scrolls through pictures of the forest. The camera trap is motion-triggered, so the pictures are usually of animals — mostly squirrels — doing something. There are some deer. There's a bear. Two bears. A hawk, some rabbits.

Then, suddenly, there's a pant leg. June holds her breath and taps that picture, flips to the next one, then the next one.

It's exactly what I expected. Two people, midday. They have a chainsaw. There are several pictures of them standing, discussing, gesturing at each other.

Then they take the tree down. The man is the one wielding the chainsaw, but just from the way they're standing, the way the woman is pointing, I can tell who's in charge.

"Gotcha," June whispers, then pauses on a picture, zooms in with two fingers.

It's her, the woman who runs the historical society, who was a total jerk to June and me when we visited. She's standing there in all these pictures, sour-faced, utterly disrespectful of this tree, of the forest, of nature and of the earth—

"I'm so glad you stole her pen," June says. "Good. Fuck her. You hear that? Fuck *you*, Marjorie."

I kiss June on the top of the head.

"We did it," I tell her. "The long nightmare is over."

She shuts her phone off, leans back into me.

"There's one more tree to check on," she says. "I assume the Forest Service wants both its cameras back, right?"

"We could pretend it got mauled by a bear," I suggest.

"Oh, come on, Levi," June laughs. "A little hiking never killed anyone."

· · · · · ★ ★ ★ ★ · · · ·

THE SUN IS STARTING to fade as we get to the other tree we camera-trapped, and thankfully, this one's still there. I heave a quick sigh of relief when I see it ahead of us, stretching mightily for the heavens.

June collects the camera, and we put this one in an evidence bag too, just in case, though I'm sure the most interesting thing on it will be a bear. *Maybe* a mountain lion, but I swear those cats have some sort of sixth sense even about cameras, given how well they manage to avoid them.

We set up camp there, below the massive tree. I cook while June sets up my backpacking tent, fills it with our sleeping bags, and then we eat in the light of a tiny lantern.

"I brought a treat," June says as we finish, and reaches into her pack.

"Is it my whiskey?" I ask. "If so, I also brought that treat."

"Nope," she says. "My treat is perfectly legal *and* won't lead to the dissolution of society."

She tosses me a packet of hot chocolate.

"I don't think my whiskey's *that* good," I deadpan. "Or that bad, honestly."

"Keep trying," she says, filling the pot with water again and lighting the camp stove.

We drink hot chocolate and she leans against me in the cold night. I think about the last time I made hot chocolate on a camp stove, about June in the thunderstorm, about her hunting me down on my mother's front porch and striking a deal with me.

"Do you like nature now?" I ask, remembering what she told me that first evening.

She's silent a moment.

"I think I do," she says, sounding slightly surprised. "I totally forgot that I was trying to do that."

Another pause. She sips her hot chocolate.

"Am I different?" she asks.

I look over at her.

"When I moved back, I decided to reinvent myself," she says, her voice sounding like it's in a confessional. "It sounds kind of stupid to say out loud, but I was just so tired of myself, and tired of being someone whose life wasn't working out, and I felt something had to change so I figured it may as well be me."

Then she laughs.

"And for some reason, item number one on that list was *become someone who likes nature*, and I never got a whole lot further than that, but that was the idea. Anyway, I guess I'm different because I'm about to sleep on the dirt and I'm perfectly fine with it."

"For the record, I liked you both ways," I tell her. "I'd like you even if you never stepped foot in a forest."

"No, you wouldn't," she teases. "Levi Loveless, I cannot imagine you tolerating someone who's afraid of getting dirty."

I just raise an eyebrow at her.

"You know what I mean," she says.

"You do have that thing about snakes," I point out.

"*Levi*," she says, insistently. "They. Move. *Wrong*."

I'm quiet for a long moment.

"Fine," I admit. "They do move wrong. That's how much I love you. I've somewhat reconsidered my opinion on a perfectly harmless critter."

June just laughs.

"Victory!" she says and hits my steel mug with hers. "I know it's like eight o'clock, but can we go to bed? I'm freezing."

"I thought you were an outdoorswoman now."

"Yeah, but I'm a cold outdoorswoman," June says, and she stands, offers me her hand. "Come on."

I take her hand and let her pull me off the ground, and then I grab her by the waist, pull her in.

"Better?" I ask as she snuggles in.

"Better," she says. "Love you."

"Love you too," I say.

· · * * ★ ★ ★ ★ * · ·

We're about to leave our campsite and go home the next morning when June turns, looks at the tree, and stops.

And stares. Eyes narrowed, chewing on one lip, the thinking face I've come to recognize.

"Tree thoughts?" I ask.

"Sort of," she says, and then walks away from me, back toward the two-hundred-odd-year-old-tree that we saved. "Look. Is that anything?"

I follow in her footsteps, gaze up at where she's pointing: a small, dark hole in the tree, maybe twelve feet up.

"It's a hollow," I say. "Is a hollow anything?"

"Probably not," she says, still considering. "But the story does say that Phineas hid his treasure in the hollow of an oak tree, somewhere around here."

"You think he got this far after leaving that saloon?" I ask, also gazing up at the tree.

I take a step closer, trying to see in, but it's impossible from this angle.

"No," June says. "I don't think he made it much of anywhere before dying of exposure, and I definitely don't think he left a cache of coins anywhere."

I lower my gaze from the hollow in the tree to her.

"But despite all that, you want me to give you a boost?" I say.

"Please?" June says, grinning at me. "We're here. There's no reason not to look."

390

"If it's treasure, I want half," I bargain.

"What? It's not even your idea. Forty percent," she says, laughing.

"You need me to get up there."

"I didn't know it was going to be a negotiation," she says, narrowing her eyes in mock suspicion. "Fine. Forty-five percent, final offer."

"You drive a hard bargain for your own boyfriend," I tease, and she laughs.

"Take it or leave it, Loveless," she says, walking to the tree. "Come on."

"Fine," I say, and follow her.

I crouch in front of the trunk and, very carefully, she climbs onto my shoulders.

"You okay?" she asks. "Tell me if I'm hurting you."

"You're fine," I say. "Hold onto the tree."

"Keep your back straight!" she says. "Lift with your legs."

"Thank you," I say, standing with perfect form, just as I was going to before she told me to. "Anything?"

"Crap," she mutters. "Could you be maybe a foot taller?"

"I'm trying."

She shifts her weight very, very slightly, and I hold onto her ankles.

"I could just reach in there—"

"Please don't do that," I tell the bark in front of my face.

"I don't think there's anything in there."

"I'd prefer you not find out blindly."

She sighs.

"Could be snakes," I say, even though it's extraordinarily unlikely to be snakes.

There's a pause above my head.

"That was low," she says.

"When something strange doesn't bite your hand and your hand therefore doesn't turn gangrenous and fall off during our hike back home, you can thank me," I tell her.

"Oh!" she says, and then wobbles slightly. I hold onto her ankles tighter, then look up, just in time to see a quick, bright flash in the hollow, followed by a few more.

Then there's a too-long silence.

"Do you need to get down?"

"There's something in there," she says.

"Something alive?"

She pauses again, and I look up to see June, gazing at her phone.

"I think it's a box," she says, finally, sounding confused. "Hold on."

There's more silence, more flashes. Then, after a few more minutes, she reaches in and pulls something out.

"Okay," she says.

Getting her off my shoulders is harder than getting her up there was, but we manage it and then she's standing in front of me, leaves and bark on the fleece she's wearing.

There's a box in her hand. It's not big, slightly smaller than her hand, metal worked in some sort of curlicue design. Brass, maybe.

And it looks old. Very, very old.

June's holding her hands out flat, the box perched on top like she's waiting for it to take flight.

"Will it open?" I finally ask.

She runs a finger around the edge, finds two hinges on the back, looks at them. Then she pushes up on the opposite side with her thumbs and after a moment, it opens.

"Oh, my God," June whispers. "Holy shit."

There are only two things inside: a worn, dented man's

wedding ring and a bundle of papers, tied tightly with a leather cord.

June picks up the ring, turns it around in her fingers. It's silent out except for the background noises that are always there in the forest: the wind in the trees, faraway chirping.

She puts the ring back, gently picks up the bundle of papers.

"Looks like letters," I say.

"I'm not brave enough to untie them," she says, her voice low. "I'm afraid they'll just disintegrate."

I agree. She puts the letters back carefully, closes the box. I take it from her, turn it around in my hands, careful to touch only the corners, the edges, as if I can do damage to it that two hundred years in a tree didn't.

"That could be from anywhere," June says, still watching it in my hands. "We could be looking at a historical object from 1997."

"Could be," I agree. "Do you think that?"

"I think we should get someone more qualified to look at it," she says.

I take it over to my pack, pull out the shirt I wore yesterday, wrap the box carefully in that and then place it, carefully, in my sleeping bag, hoist the whole thing onto my shoulders.

"Ready to go home?" I ask June.

"Yeah, let's go," she says, lifting her own pack. I help her settle it onto her back, and before she leaves, she glances back at the oak tree one more time.

"I guess that excuse to spend time with you is over," she says, a smile in her voice.

"Now you'll just have to settle for seeing me every morning."

June laughs.

"Where's the mystery?" she teases. "The danger, the intrigue?"

I give her a quick kiss on the lips, her warmth flooding me despite the cold air.

"I'll start wearing a cape," I say, and her laugh echoes through the forest.

EPILOGUE

JUNE

Six Months Later

I crouch in front of the fridge, trying to see past a shelf full of green, leafy things as the door hits me in the back.

"Where's the other thing of seven-layer dip?" I ask over my shoulder.

"I already put it out," Levi answers from the sink, where he's refilling a pitcher of water. "Apparently your dad dosed the first one with hot sauce, so we needed an alternative."

I sigh, resting my head against the cold shelf in the fridge.

"She's keeping an eye on the new one, right?" I ask.

"I asked her to."

"Thanks," I say, and stand.

One second later, Caleb's head pops around the corner and into the kitchen, and he looks from Levi to me and back.

"Oh good, you're both in one place," he says. "Cool. Stay there."

"Hold on."

"No!"

Levi and I speak simultaneously, and we're rewarded with Caleb briefly reappearing.

"Silas and I got you a housewarming present," he says. "Just stay here for a sec, okay?"

Then he's gone again. We look at each other.

"Oh," I say.

"Huh," Levi agrees.

It is, technically, a housewarming party, even though I moved in several months ago with very little fanfare.

"That was nice," I say, still a little uncertain about this whole situation because I didn't know Silas was getting us anything, and I'm not exactly sure why I can't leave the kitchen.

We share a glance.

"It's nice, right?" I ask.

Levi leans back against the counter, folds his arms in front of himself.

"We should probably assume it's nice until proven otherwise," he says. "He's come a long way."

He means Silas, of course. Caleb wasn't the one with the problem.

And he's right. Silas, while clearly having some weird hang-ups that I don't entirely understand, has mostly been cool. We've been having him over for dinner about once a week, and I know that he and Levi still hang out without me.

Every once in a while, I do still have to give him a quick talk, but overall, he's been good.

It's an adjustment, but I think everything is going to work out just fine.

"Okay," says Charlie's voice, followed by a loud *slap* on the island that separates the kitchen from the living room. "I don't like this ending."

She points at the copy of *The Atlantic* that she just smacked onto the counter.

"Everybody's a critic," I tease.

"A suspended sentence?" she asks, pointing at the magazine. "They did all those tree crimes and got a two-thousand-dollar fine and suspended sentences?"

"They pleaded guilty," I shrug. "And it turns out that cutting down trees isn't that bad of a crime."

"It's because they're considered property crimes against the federal government," Levi says next to me. "The original draft of her story went into that more, but they cut it because they thought it wasn't *sexy*."

I put one hand on his arm.

"It's not," I tell him.

"I thought you made it very sexy," he says, raising one eyebrow and half-smiling.

"Thank you," I laugh. "But in a story about brigands and hidden treasure, *How do we properly value a tree?* isn't really the part that grabs one's attention."

Levi sighs. When my editors cut the part about the fascinating economics of national forests, he was more put out about it than I was. I mean, I understand that it's not the most interesting part and there are space restrictions in a magazine.

He, on the other hand, grumbled about it for days. I think he might have been more offended that something I wrote got cut so much, even though I tried to explain that this is just how it works, and I wasn't upset in the least.

The Atlantic still published a story I wrote. They can do whatever they want, they're *The Atlantic*.

"They've at least got records, right?" Charlie asks,

spreading cheese on a cracker and popping it into her mouth. "Tell me now they can't get jobs in the government or carry firearms and all that. Or vote. I don't want them voting."

I'm about to answer when Caleb's head pops around the corner again, and this time he's grinning. He is grinning *too much* and I don't think I like it, because I've learned that Caleb smiling too much can be trouble.

"You can come out now," he says. "Follow me, please."

Levi and I exchange another look, then follow his youngest brother through the living room and out the front door, his hand steadily on my lower back.

When we get to the front porch, I see Silas look at the hand.

Then he looks back at *something* that's six feet tall by four feet wide and currently covered by an old sheet, and when I follow his gaze, I panic a little bit.

"Silas," I say, my tone a warning, but my older brother just smiles bigger. Behind me, Levi sighs.

"All right," he says.

"Shall we unveil it?" Caleb asks Silas.

Together, they grip the sheet, count down, and pull it off.

It's a chainsaw carving of two bears, and it leaves Levi and me speechless.

The bears are upright and smiling. The taller one is holding a fishing rod and the shorter one is holding a fish, and in front of them is a sign that says WELCOME TO OUR DEN!

"Wow," Levi finally manages to say.

"You shouldn't have," I deadpan.

"I think it matches Jedediah perfectly," Caleb says. "And it really captures a certain *je ne sais quoi* about Levi, don't you think?"

"And the craftsmanship is masterful," Silas says, also regarding the carving. "I think this piece welcomes yet threatens at the same time, revealing the duality of the hospitality experience in America."

I can't stop staring at it, mouth open, because I can't quite comprehend that this thing is on my porch.

It's so... big. And wooden. And friendly.

And *tacky*. Lord, is it tacky.

"You love it, right?" Caleb asks, glancing over at us. "We had this specially commissioned for you two, and we were a little bit worried that it wouldn't be ready by the party, but luckily Silas knows the sculptor and he was able to do us a favor."

This is *custom-made*?

For *us*?

"Okay, you're going to give them an aneurysm," Silas finally says to Caleb, and Caleb just laughs. "I saw it outside an antique store for fifty bucks."

"Oh, thank God," I sigh immediately.

"That was unkind," Levi says.

"I thought you'd had some sort of break with reality," I tell Silas. "The duality of the hospitality experience? Get the fuck out of here."

"You're welcome."

"Thank you," Levi says, very, very politely.

"Yes. That," I agree, still looking at the statue.

"But you're also taking it away, right?" Levi asks.

That gets a laugh.

"It's still a gift," Silas says, crossing the porch and heading for the front door. "I can't take back a gift. It's rude."

With that, he and Caleb go back inside and leave us standing on the porch together.

"I think she kinda looks like you," Levi says. "You know, she's got your eyes. And your fish."

"I can't tell if this is Silas still being slightly angry or Silas trying to tell us that he's no longer slightly angry," I say, and Levi just sighs.

"It's a mystery," he says. "Would you like another drink? I'd like another drink."

· · · ★ ★ ★ ★ ★ · · ·

THE PARTY STRAGGLERS are finally gone by ten, and at ten-fifteen I'm lying on the couch, the coffee table next to me strewn with empty glasses, plates, and copies of *The Atlantic* with my story in them.

Yes, I have a bunch of copies and display them prominently in my own home. If not here, where?

In the end, faced with the photographic evidence, Marjorie and her husband Donald pleaded guilty to their forest crimes and got reduced sentences, which turned out to be fines and no jail time.

That part wasn't satisfying. The satisfying part was donating the box we found to Haverwood College, a smallish school about an hour away, where they've got a conservation lab that specializes in local early Americana. The Sprucevale Historical Society will never, ever house it, so help me God.

The box itself turned out to be a jewelry box that probably originated somewhere near Baltimore and was likely stolen from a woman on the Wilderness Trail. The ring is more of a mystery, but it seems to be a wedding ring.

The letters were the real prize, though. They were water-damaged and two hundred years old, but with the magic of science, they've deciphered a few and it turns out that Phineas Harte was secretly married to a former prostitute named Pearl. The letters are hers to him.

None of it's really valuable, unless, of course, you run the Sprucevale Historical Society and would love to get your hands on something like that.

"Leave cleanup for tomorrow," I call into the kitchen, where I can hear Levi clanking things around.

"Then we'll have to do it tomorrow," he points out.

"Yes, that's the point," I say, still lying on the couch. "Tomorrow isn't now. Now is now."

He says nothing, and I sigh, then heave myself off the couch. Everything tilts a little bit because I had one whiskey too many, and I stand still until the world rights itself.

"Come on," I say, walking into the kitchen past Hedwig, who's politely waiting for us to take our eyes off a cheese plate.

"If we leave this for tomorrow, you just won't want to do it then," he points out, stacking plates next to the sink.

I wrap my arms around him from behind, lean one cheek against his back.

"That sounds like a problem for future June," I say.

He's warm. Very warm. And very solid, and all sexy and muscly and stuff and also he's *washing dishes* and I'm drunkish and oops, I think I'm getting wet.

Levi shuts the water off, dries his hands, then turns around in my arms.

"You're not going to let me clean up, are you?" he asks, his voice low, sonorous.

"Nope."

"Can I put the cheese away before Hedwig eats it?" he asks.

I sigh dramatically.

"*Fine*," I say, and he kisses me on top of the head, then grabs the cheese and puts it into the fridge.

I grab his butt while he's bent over, and in one swift move he turns and then traps me against the counter.

"How about I seduce you instead of doing the dishes?" I ask.

He's holding onto the counter on either side of my hips, looking at me like he's amused.

"Go on, I'm listening," he says.

I grab his belt loops, tug him in.

"Well," I say, still drunk-ish. "First, we make out some in the kitchen while I get you out of your clothes, and then we go upstairs and I dazzle you with an array of erotic delights. Or I dazzle you on the couch. Or I just dazzle you right—"

I don't get to finish listing the places where I could dazzle him, because he kisses me instead, his lips slow and warm against mine, his hands sliding through my hair, his hips pinning mine to the counter.

"I'm dazzled," he says, his voice so low and quiet it's barely audible.

"That was easy," I whisper.

"Well, I'm easy when it comes to you."

I put one hand on his chest, his heart beating under my palm. We kiss again, and then he pulls away, his thumb still on my cheekbone, and he looks at me.

Just looks. I've almost gotten used to this, but not quite: the way he looks at me like I'm a map of hidden places, like he finds something new every time he searches.

"Thank you for making me have this party," he says.

"You're welcome," I say, surprised.

"It can be easy to give into hermitude," he says. "I think you're good for me, June."

"Even though now you own an atrocious bear statue?"

He smiles, glances down at my lips.

"Can I tell you a secret?"

402

"Anything."

"I kind of like the bear statue."

"Levi," I whisper in mock-horror.

"It's growing on me," he admits. "I didn't like it at first, but it's sure something."

I sigh, both hands on his chest. I'm not thinking about the bear statue. I'm thinking about what I'm going to do to Levi once I get him naked.

"Can it at least go on the back porch?" I ask. "That can't be the first thing people see when they visit us."

"All right," he concedes. "Can I tell you another secret?"

"It is also home decor related?"

"I have a wild crush on you, June," he says, putting his forehead to mine, and I laugh.

"Do you?"

"Yes."

"Good, because I've got a wild crush on you," I say. "And I've got no intention of stopping."

"Promise?"

"Promise."

We kiss. I've always liked kissing Levi and I think I always will, because he kisses the way he does everything: thoroughly, properly, and in his own time.

He kisses me, and then I do exactly what I promised: I get him naked and take him upstairs and seduce the hell out of him, and afterward we lie curled together in his bed and say nothing.

My story in *The Atlantic* didn't say anything about this part. Levi is in it, of course, but the story is about old trees and forest crimes and early American brigands, not about how I fell in love with the man who introduced me to all this.

That part of it doesn't belong in some article, written

down for the world. I don't think I could ever do it justice. That story belongs here, in the quiet spaces where we're together, where our hearts beat in harmony and I can feel our lives intertwining into weeks, months, years.

"You dazzle me," I say quietly, not even sure that Levi's awake.

He says nothing, just gently kisses the top of my head, and I listen to his silence like I've learned to do.

In it, he says everything.

THE END

ABOUT ROXIE

Roxie is a romance author by day, and also a romance author by night. She lives in Los Angeles with one husband, two cats, far too many books, and a truly alarming pile of used notebooks that she refuses to throw away.

www.roxienoir.com
roxie@roxienoir.com